SHE WHO WAS

Life on the other side of retirement is never dull for R.K.J. Adams. With childhood dreams of becoming an author, she dipped her feet into the world of writing, successfully publishing her first novel in July 2022. Later came an anthology of poetry for adults, followed by several children's books. In 2024, she published a second anthology of poems. When not dancing with words on the computer screen, there is always a camera to hand. She adores capturing the beauty of Sutherland, the county she now classes as home, where she lives with her long-suffering husband and their four rescue dogs.

For more information, visit https://rkjadams.com

R.K.J. Adams

For Adults

Wasn't Me, Miss!
Birth, Death & The Bits In Between
Searching For Light
She Who Was

For Children

What shall I be?
Who's That Snoring?
It's not fair!

SHE WHO WAS

R.K.J. ADAMS

First published by Rowham Morrex Publishing
in the United Kingdom in 2025

Copyright © R.K.J. Adams 2025

The moral right of R.K.J. Adams to be identified as
the author of this work has been asserted in accordance
with the Copyright, Designs, and Patents Act 1988.

All rights reserved. No part of this book may be reproduced or used in any manner whatsoever, including information storage and retrieval systems, or transmitted or circulated in any form or by any means, electronic, mechanical, photocopying, recording, or otherwise, without the express written permission of the copyright owner, except in the case of brief quotations embodied in critical reviews and certain other non-commercial use permitted by copyright law. For permission requests, contact the author/publisher at the email address below.

Email rkjadams@gmail.com

Every effort has been made to trace copyright holders and to obtain their permission for the use of copyright material. The publisher apologises for any errors or omissions and would be grateful for any corrections that should be incorporated in future editions of this book.

This is a work of fiction. Names, characters, places, and incidents are either the product of the author's imagination or are used fictitiously. Any resemblance to actual persons, living or dead, events, or locales is entirely coincidental.

Illustrations © The Anonymous Illustrator

Cover designed using Canva

Printed and bound in the United Kingdom

A CIP catalogue record of this book is available from the British Library

ISBN (Paperback UK) 9781739322915

DEDICATION

To my original green-eyed lassie,
thank you for everything.
The sacrifices you made long ago
will never be forgotten

ACKNOWLEDGEMENTS

As always, my thanks and love go to my long-suffering husband who puts up with endless moments of, "Can you just listen to this?" Without you, I am nothing.

My grateful thanks go to The Anonymous Illustrator and for creating the illustrations for this novel. From the briefest of ideas, some beautiful images have been created to depict the Norse goddesses Hel, Snotra, and Iduna. Thanks also to T. Roe for her ideas.

Thank you to everyone who has supported me in this crazy author journey I'm on. Without you, my motivation would be lost. Special thanks to Alison, Anne, Debra, Sue, and Victoria. Those involved in Write That Book, especially "The Dynamics," continue to be brilliant, and inspirational.

Finally, if I had only one wish, I would say thank you also to my oldest sister-in-law, Anita, for believing in me. I tried to get this story written for you to read before your passing, but sadly it was not to be. Thank you for your support. I miss you so very much.

HEL
Goddess of Death

PROLOGUE

Fire races through my veins. A wild, uncontrollable inferno consuming a forest of flesh in the heat of summer. I ripped my skin to relieve the intensity of the blaze, but now, my limbs are lifeless. The flames rage unchallenged, engulfing me in misery. My head roasts. Only the slightest movements from my naked torso suggest any attempt to escape from lava rushing through my body. The instinct to rise from the bed is still strong, but the unseen volcano inside my ivory shell remains active whilst I lie paralysed, partially covered by a lilac duvet cover bought less than a month ago. Pretty bedding for the greatest day of my life, without envisaging its use in my deathbed scene.

Hel[1] has me in her sights. She has teased me with death for so long that I am tired of her tricks. When I studied Norse mythology, she was the goddess that puzzled me most. Supposedly she takes the sick or those who are old. I am neither. If she judges my soul, I don't want to be cast into the dark as she was. To exist in a shadow-like world petrifies me. For too long that has been my life, surviving in the bleakest of places without joy or light. If I die, let me pass to sunshine and happiness. Yet, it is the burning of my skin that troubles me.

Maybe it's sparks from the fires of Muspell [2] that burn within me: the pyre of secrets, half-truths, and lies that have finally combusted, bursting into flames, sending me to eternal damnation.

I often contemplated my end, wondering how it would eventually come. The average life expectancy for a female in the United Kingdom is eighty-three years plus a couple of months. Thirty-one is too young to die. Living a long life has never been an option because of who I am and who I was. Since becoming the hunted, my life was inevitably going to be much shorter than most.

In my younger days, dreams and aspirations spurred me to do well and to make something of myself. Losing control of my life, I was nothing more than a powerless, discarded puppet. Now the once-ambitious marionette lies dying, my strings severed, never to move again. Is this a terrible dream from which I can wake?

Night terrors frequented me, never vanishing. Occasionally there would be respite for an evening or two, but they always return, more vivid and real. Demons tormented me, knocking on the doors and windows until I hid under the bed covers for hour upon hour, silently screaming for them to stop. Sweat saturated my nightwear, and when my dreams were unbearable, I wet myself, too scared to go to the bathroom. Shadows played tricks, voices whispered my name through the letterbox.

The level-headed woman I once was is lost in the mirror. Now, my reflection shows a fool overwhelmed with a deluge of irrational thoughts. Involuntary searches of cupboards and wardrobes were routine whenever I returned home. What followed was reassurance and belief that no one was hiding in wait. When out running, I swung around, fearful of approaching vehicles. These actions were ludicrous. No one could find me here, miles away from anywhere, with harmless old crofters for neighbours. Naive hope lingered too long; the nightmares never faded away into the mists of time.

The problem was that the faces of my persecutors were unrecognisable. In fairy tales, grey, ravenous creatures tormented the Three Little Pigs or disguised themselves as Grandma to trick Red Riding Hood. Wolves died out in the wilds long ago, but in the world in which I lived, they still exist, howling on the hillside and stalking their prey: some in plain sight, some in disguise. Their messages, carried by the wind, whisper,

"Revenge will taste sweet."

In my dreams, they appeared in human form, full of secrets and lies. The irony is that those two aspects of this armour shielded me... until my guard came down, and wolves came running.

Almost three years of loneliness destroyed me, seeping into my soul, crippling me with anxiety and dread. The emotional baggage I hauled around far outweighed the small suitcase with which I arrived. With Death knocking on my door, its presence shaped me forever, destroying any semblance of normality. I still grieve the loss of myself and my old life. Starting again has not been easy. Here in this place, I finally discovered a sense of belonging and a happy future. Fate and destiny teased me, lulling me into thinking I was safe. Of course, I have never been safe.

Coordination and strength disappear. I can no longer stand. My muscles, which days ago ran ten miles, lie spent as Hel encircles me. Concentrate, concentrate! Don't fall asleep! Wake up before it is too late! Submission envelops my body. There is no escape. Hope vanished long ago.

An old movie reel plays in my mind, flooding thoughts with forgotten images. With an outstretched hand, Mum pulls me up from a red plaid picnic blanket on the grass. Her face is full of sunshine as she smiles. For the briefest of moments, her hands cover my eyes. When light returns, Dad stands before me holding a cake. Ten candles flicker in the breeze before I take a huge breath to blow them out with one attempt. My parents grin and clap at their only child reaching double figures. My father, my hero and strength, will save me. Dad, help me!

A small Jack Russell bounds towards my knees for a treat. The softness of his black velvet ears comforts me. The ball I hurl through the air disappears into the distance and he runs away. Compelled to call him, his name is lost forever. Come back! Come back! I must remember but my mind is playing tricks.

A bell rings. There is a playground full of colour and happiness. Laughter fills the air as children race and chase each other. Suddenly joy vanishes, noises fade, and in my despair, I realise that I shall never be a mother. Sunshine disappears, replaced by foreboding skies, grey and bleak, endlessly stretching from earth to heaven.

Fear grabs me as I try to launch a scream. There is no one in earshot, even if I could cry out for help. Vocal cords no longer work in tandem with the air from my lungs. They are corrupted. Motionless and dry, my lips remain still, unable to shape sounds. A once gently spoken tongue lies redundant, all words lost.

Carved in white marble with black lettering, a gravestone stands in front of me; my mother's name is veiled by tears, a grief too raw to explore. Blood, shared for the first nine months of my existence, oozes from a finger where a rose thorn pierces my skin, mingling with the single red stem I place on her grave. Is this where the nightmare ends? It certainly began at this moment in my past.

Void of life and hope, silence presses into my flesh until the pain is all-consuming. No one hears. No one will come. Faces from my past smile at me. Their mouths move, but I can't hear their voices. Before I can remember their identities, their images vanish. Pictures flash quickly now, mere glimpses rather than recollections of who I was. Row upon row of people dressed in black, onlookers watching and clapping. Tears drip from the corners of my eyes as the inferno in my mind gathers strength.

This illusive merry-go-round, spinning through time, revolves faster and faster. Any attempt to get off it is futile, It races away, and the projector spins out of control, spewing out the film of my life. One corner of the screen turns brown, filling the air with smoke as it begins to distort and disintegrate. Finally bursting into flames, the images from long ago are gone.

My breathing slows. The gasps for air have stopped. Tired of fighting, my eyes close. Tiny murmurs float into the ether from my body for the last time. Not audible; they only make sense inside the fraction of my mind that remains alive. I am... I am... My name no longer matters.

There are flashes of colour, first vivid, then pale, until all is black. As darkness entombs me, I hear fading words that make no sense, as my brain loses the capacity to comprehend what is spoken: one confident voice, the other more hesitant, asking question after question.

'Is she dead?'

'Not quite. It won't be long now.'

'Hearing is the last sense remaining as you die. Do you think she can hear?'

'She passed that point a while back. Anyway, what does it matter? She's not going to survive. We'll get her off this bed to dump her body.

'Are we taking her now?'

'Patience! All in good time.'

An odour wafts in the air, one I should recognise if I still possessed my sense of smell. A potent cocktail of sickly sweetness mingles with an intense bitterness. Normally, I would frown when recognising it, but my freckles remain motionless. Death has arrived, clinging to my skin and my long red hair, defiantly insisting my final few breaths taste rank. My existence on the planet slips away. One gentle sigh, and I am gone.

Confidence smirks. Hesitance shakes. As my brain switches off, with a last glorious act of defiance, my body jerks. My beautiful green eyes open for one final time, staring at the guilty.

††††††

There is light, a piercing light, too bright and intense to comprehend. I scream, but there is a deafening silence. Trying to pull myself together, I rub my eyes for the nightmare to be over. My vision clears, but what I see in front of me makes no sense. Why am I weightless, hovering over a scene below, looking down on a body? The vividness of this dream is too sharp, too painful to bear. A body lies on a familiar lilac duvet. I try to rub my eyes, then I realise. Fuck! I'm finally dead.

For a moment, Hesitance gently strokes my hair whilst Confidence laughs hysterically, screaming something I don't understand, then barks orders at the submissive.

'Mors dulcis! Get on with it, you fool!'

As if following some stage directions from a crummy play, the manoeuvring of my body begins. The awful truth smothers me as I witness the grabbing and pawing over my flesh, the struggling and panicking to clean up the crime. The scramble to erase my existence commences with all traces of the person I had become obliterated, leaving only the shell I left behind. I look away, not wanting to see what happens next. There is no point.

The light is mesmerising, exquisite even. I want to bathe in its beauty, to rid myself of the evil that has taken place. Instead, in these first moments of death, I'm urged to distance myself from the cottage that was home for the last two years, and from the surrounding land and water. The space between myself and anything recognisable increases until only the light is all-consuming, compelling me towards it.

As I journey closer, to what I consider must be infinity or a heaven if there is such a thing, flashes of colour whizz past, iridescent globules of vividness. Most dodge around me, but some pass through me, bringing an all-encompassing brightness and comfort.

Without warning, my passage stops. The absence of whatever force has been propelling me forward causes confusion. There is no longer enchanting light, only a cold, bleak darkness. Perhaps twinkling stars will appear, but none are visible. Blackness moves through me.

Not choosing Christianity has brought me to darkness. I should have learnt to pray. I should have fought harder to find belief. When I first arrived, I dabbled with attending services at the local church, but the prying eyes and lack of acceptance drove me away from the doors of God.

Instead, peace was found in other, ancient faiths. The attraction to the old ways, those belonging to the Celts and the Vikings, was appealing and made sense as the myths and legends surrounding them matched the landscape where I lived.

Hoping for the appearance of a deity to explain my new state of being, I sense a shadow ahead and peer towards it, hoping for answers. This must be Hel or some such figure; they must be ready to judge me.

Instead, in the gloominess, a man is wearing a t-shirt and jeans, bloodstained from gaping wounds in his chest. He moves past, not even raising his eyes to acknowledge me.

Another dark shadow comes into view. This time there is a woman dressed in black rags. Her face seems to be covered in patches of dirt, but when I look more closely at her thin, grey face, I realise the marks are bruises and that she is sporting two black eyes. A scarf of abuse with purple fingertip marks encircles her neck. Her wrists are raw from gashes made by her own fingernails in numerous attempts to harm herself, scratching away at her skin to find a modicum of comfort. Her lost hope overwhelms me as my eyes divert to her arms, which tightly clutch a blanket to her chest. The folds of the cloth move, revealing a baby's head. I open my mouth to scream, but no sound leaves my lips. In fact, the deafening silence hurts my ears.

A third shadow moves closer, a girl younger than myself. She ignores me just like the others. Ruby red blood is splattered across her cheeks; her blonde, shoulder-length hair is stained from a wound on the side of her head.

Am I invisible? Only after several seconds do I understand. All these people have signs of a violent end. Could this be where the hopeless souls of the murdered linger? This place is neither heaven nor hell; it is a void for justice that may never come. I am not being judged. I am in limbus.[4]

Faces appear, first one or two, then hundreds and thousands, until I realise darkness smothers all of us, fleeting shadows of the people we once were, blocking the light. This is not my destiny; evil will not succeed. My soul is pure; I did no wrong. Being murdered brought me to this place. To pass to the infinite light, I'll traverse the deepest, blackest parts of this emptiness to escape, dropping a trail of breadcrumbs for the hunters who seek my justice. For now, my restless soul hurtles towards the last rays of flickering sunlight. Stars begin to twinkle in the night sky, welcoming my mortal body as it's placed in Loch Spiorad. The gentle breeze causes ripples on the surface of the water, leaves rustling for my wake. No one can hurt me now. Evil will be avenged. I will make it so.

CHAPTER 1
Tuesday, 23rd September, 1:00 a.m.

Four hours of sitting in a rowing boat, waiting for a tug on his line, made Jimmy Mackay stiff. Rolling his shoulders in controlled circular movements relieved some of the tension and tightness in his neck. The cold could not be blamed for his pain. His khaki corduroy trousers, tucked neatly inside a pair of green waders, were perfect for a night of fishing. There was no need for the several layers of tops and a faded brown waxed jacket he normally wore to keep out the cool night air. The weather was dry for once, and the water was calm. September nights did not get any better than this in the Highlands. It was lack of action, hunched in the same position, that made his old bones ache.

Even though a new moon brought darkness, Nature's torch lit the way. Raising his brown eyes to the sky, the presence of the Plough offered comfort in showing the direction north. A shimmering hue, rippling on the surface of the water, caught his attention. In spectacular beauty, there it was: the pale shafts of light known to many as the

Northern Lights. Luminescent curtains twinkled and glistened as they danced on the horizon.

The Aurora Borealis were awe-inspiring, making him feel so small and insignificant in the universe. Whilst not so vivid to the naked eye, as photographers would suggest, the pale green arc sparkled and twirled, occasionally emitting flares of red. Solar particles mixed with nitrogen and oxygen at the edge of the Earth's atmosphere in a wondrous petri dish that Mother Nature created. It offered a glorious display across the night sky, the first light show of the season for Jimmy, occupying him as he waited for a fish to bite.

He knew the loch well, and on an evening such as this, he did not need a torch to find his way around. Apart from the aurora and the starry sky, the blackness of night surrounded him, but his eyes adjusted to the dark. Through occasional breaks in the bushes and trees on the eastern edge of the loch, he would often spot vehicles heading north or south, but no headlights were visible for hours. He was miles away from any other human but was not alone. Hundreds of deer would be roaming the hills, owls were out hunting, and there were plenty of trout beneath his rowing boat if only he could find them. Lack of contact with other humans never bothered Jimmy; he enjoyed the solitude, especially when the aurora and the fish were his companions.

Towards the west, the hills in the foreground sloped gradually until their tops became overshadowed by the shape of Ben Meagaidh, one of the mountains in the area that dominated the landscape. In the darkness, it was easy imagining all the enchanting stories he heard as a wee bairn about giants creating mountains from lumps in their bed linen. He smiled as he remembered what his grandmother told him each winter when he saw the first signs of snow on the tips of the mountains.

'The giants are plumping up their pillows, Jimmy, ready for winter. That will be the white feathers landing on top of the blankets.'

He could recall her stories but struggled to remember her voice; the memory of her soft Sutherland accent had long faded. He attempted to keep her tales alive by retelling them to his children and his grandchildren, but sadly none of them were as keen to listen to fairy stories as when he was a bairn. They were all too old and too engrossed with their mobile phones or computers for stories of giants.

There was no snow yet. It would be a couple more months before the giants plumped up their pillows. The heat of the summer had faded, and the nights were distinctly cooler than his previous fishing expedition. For some reason, he shuddered. His layers of clothing were perhaps more useful than he had thought. In early October, night frosts would soon appear, covering trees and bushes with magic sprinkles and lacing cobwebs with white glitter.

Jimmy shivered again, finding reassurance in snuggling into his jacket, the one his wife hinted had seen better days. His fisherman's gloves kept his fingers and thumbs warm. His waders were cold, but he was thankful for the clothing nearer to his skin and the woolly socks his wife knitted, which kept his toes toasty.

Years before, he laughed when his father wore a deerstalker to keep his ears snug on an August night when they fished this loch. Now, he too wore such apparel, covering his silvery hair with faded brown and green tweed. His sandy sideburns, moustache, and beard, once wild and wispy like a seventies rock star, were gone. When he looked in the mirror of late, he saw a wrinkled, old man with neatly trimmed pewter and silver bristles. After reaching seventy, there was a strangely familiar carbon copy of the last two male generations of Mackay staring back at him.

The fisherman nodded to himself as he smiled at the family memories which flashed through his thoughts more frequently with the passing years. Their presence was near, and he drew comfort in that thought. Fishing was in his blood. Jimmy's father fished, and his grandfather before him. All his forebears for generation upon generation, born on Sutherland ground, fished Loch Spiorad.

The angling season was coming to an end. Although this evening had proved fruitless, earlier fishing expeditions in the year were more successful. Even though he had caught little so far, Jimmy considered himself fortunate to have these hours of solitude and a wife who allowed his indulgence for his freshwater fishing passion, which often took him away from home at night during the season. His mouth watered at the thought of cooked trout.

Lifting his face to the stars, he inhaled the night air, wishing he could smell grilled fish. A rumbling stomach brought him back to reality. It was well past midnight, time for a sandwich. He reached for his rucksack, fumbling about until his hand landed on a parcel wrapped in tinfoil. He knew instinctively what his nighttime snack would be. He grinned as he unwrapped the silver package to reveal his meal. Several half rounds of seeded bread were piled on top of each other, with slices of cheese, and a generous dollop of caramelised onion chutney oozing out at the edges of each sandwich. There was never too little, never too much, just how he liked it. His wife, of forty-six years, knew him well. Carefully taking hold of one so as not to spill any contents, he took a first bite and sighed. The joy such a feast could bring at this hour of the morning always surprised him.

A cup of coffee would keep him awake. There was still time to net an eel or two. He would stick it out for a few more hours before heading home just as everyone else was waking. He loved these calm nights, alone with the stars, the fish, and, of course, his cheese sandwiches.

††††††

Hours later, Jimmy accepted defeat. Even the lovingly prepared bait, the final crumbs from his snack, hadn't brought any miracles. Having caught hardly anything, he conceded that the fish had triumphed again, but the solitude was enjoyable. The idea of forty winks or more when he got home appealed greatly. He began the short journey to dry land. Now that sunrise was beckoning, the dawn chorus replaced the sound of several owls hunting.

He winced as he began to slowly manoeuvre the boat towards the shoreline and a gap he could make out in the trees, where he knew his car was parked. His arms were stiff from lack of movement, and the now chilly night air made rowing uncomfortable.

Jimmy cursed the arthritis his doctor recently diagnosed. He would soon be out of the boat, and the pain in his shoulders and arms would lessen. The sound of oars breaking through the surface of the loch reassured him. Ripples widened as the synchronised movements became more regular. Taking a couple of deep breaths, he pushed away thoughts that he was getting too old to manage the short row back.

'Get a grip, laddie! Keep going.'

He could hear his father's voice once more. Words spoken on this loch when Jimmy was a bairn. Given the responsibility of rowing the little boat back to shore, he'd struggled with the effort required for a seven-year-old, but Da encouraged him.

'I hear you, Da! Just getting a bit old in the tooth... What the hell...?'

From nowhere, an agonising pain shot through his hands, up his arms, and seared through every muscle in his body. The boat rocked violently, hurling Jimmy one way, then the other. Both oars flew out of his reach. Frantically, he grasped to gain control, his knuckles whitening as he gripped the two wooden paddles harder for fear of losing them again. Heart pounding, he attempted to regain his balance. Overwhelmed by the occurrence, he cursed.

'Christ Almighty! Damn it! Keep the heid!'

Trying not to panic, his heart screaming to be released from his rib cage, he took three deep breaths before attempting to investigate the cause of the problem. Perhaps an oar was tangled in reeds nearer to the bank. He avoided them hours earlier when rowing out to the middle of the loch. Tired and not concentrating properly, he swore at his stupidity. Attempting to move forward, he tried to raise both oars out of the water. Although the right paddle moved freely in its rowlock, the left was a dead weight, too heavy to lift. With his remaining strength failing to make it budge, Mackay was stuck.

Experience told him to calm himself, but he was desperate to be free of the entrapment. He began to tug frantically at the oar, pushing and pulling and willing it to release itself. With an enormous splash, the boat rocked fiercely once more. Full of adrenaline, he pushed against the obstacle with one final piece of strength. The oar flew into the air. Fighting to keep his balance, he steadied himself, then sank to the floor of the tiny vessel. Ripples of water, forming larger and larger concentric circles, extended further away from the boat. For a moment, silence fell, and then, prompted by the movements of the oars, a gurgling sound hit the air as something rose to the surface.

Grabbing the torch, Jimmy switched on the full beam. The dark waters beneath him unveiled a vision that set his heart racing even more. He jumped back in shock, the force rocking the boat for a third time. Uncontrollable shivers racked his body.

Just inches beneath where he sat in his wee boat in the middle of Loch Spiorad, a lassie was staring back at him with lifeless green eyes. It was a ghost of a face, pale and peaceful in a watery grave. A beautiful, naked loch goddess with auburn hair drifting gently with the movement of the water, casting a spell on anyone who saw her. Jimmy gasped, not only at the dead body but also at the beauty of this young woman. His cheeks reddened, not from the cool night air, but from the embarrassment of seeing only the second woman in his life naked.

His chest exploded into panic with his heart pounding so loudly that his ears ached with the gushing noise. Struggling to seeing, the light from the torch flickered for a moment or two. There was no doubt about what lay next to his boat. The largest catch of his life, without a rod or bait, left Jimmy shaking from head to toe.

Immediately, the fisherman felt for his mobile phone. His wife always insisted he take it just in case. This was a *"Just in case"* moment. Thankfully, when he touched the screen, he saw several bars for getting a signal. With trembling fingers, he managed to press 999 and waited for a voice to reassure him that help would come soon. It felt like an eternity whilst Jimmy sat in his wee boat, trying not to look at the body lying near him. A retired oil rig worker, he had seen many tough things in his life, but never a dead body, apart from his father years before.

Religion never featured in Jimmy's life, although his grandparents and parents were churchgoers. Sunday services and prayers never appealed to him. The strictness he remembered of the Sabbath and the need for formal clothing for church visits brought no comfort. He was shocked; his thought of prayer came within seconds of seeing the body.

At first, no words spoken made any sense as fear took hold. The Lord's Prayer, forgotten since leaving school many years before, evaded him. He shivered, desperate to find relief, and began whispering a makeshift prayer, struggling to find phrases. With eyes tightly closed, Jimmy begged he would not have to look at the corpse again. Its face etched an image in his mind that he would remember for eternity.

'Dear God ... if there is one... ma heid's mince. Ah didnae ken how to do this. I've ignored you for seventy-six years. I need you now. Please, God, help me.'

Tears fell as words gushed out. He remembered the obligatory "Amen" and found himself frantically drawing the sign of the cross on his chest. How long would he have to sit on this remote loch, ten miles from home, with a dead woman floating next to his boat? Hours, it would be hours.

The silence was mortifying. Jimmy thought he would die if help did not arrive soon. His mind raced, desperate to grasp at anything possible to calm his nerves: the sky, the loch, the fish, but nothing brought him comfort. The loch goddess discarded his attempts to erase her image. He fought on. Memories of him fishing the loch with his father and grandfather battled against the goddess, protecting him from her spells and enchantment. They were both strong crofting men who were known in the community as dependable in any crisis. Men who helped when cars got stuck in snowdrifts, who helped if a calf or lamb was proving troublesome to be born on a neighbouring croft. Men who carried coffins to the graveside in Loch Dubhglas. He must pull himself together. He was a Mackay. He was surely not scared of being within inches of a dead woman.

'You auld, great eejit! Pull yourself together, man! At least I'm nay like the poor sod in a watery grave. What a lassie. God rest her soul.'

Slowly and carefully, the fisherman used his expertise to manoeuvre the boat away from the find. Stiffness was replaced with relief as he rowed further from the loch goddess. A torrent of fear swept through him as he stepped into the shallow waters of the shoreline. With one last piece of strength, he pulled the rowing boat a yard or two from the water's edge.

Weak and emotional, he sank to his knees. Tears spilt from his eyes. When he replayed the events over and over in his mind hours later, he wasn't sure why he cried but it was the only way he could cope. For a few minutes he stayed in that position, once more praying for help and for the lassie's soul, until the pain from his knees forced him to rise. A few yards away from his boat and the shoreline, he paced backwards and forwards on the road for more than an hour. Finally, he could hear vehicles in the distance.

'You're safe now, lassie. The police are almost here. You'll be oot ah herm's way soon.'

The urge to comfort him overwhelms me, but I am unable. It's in this moment the realisation I am dead confronts me. There will never be another human hug or conversation. No touch of skin on skin or a kiss of love and affection. There can be no intimacy or smile one gives a lover

when in a crowded place; both are often lost in a sea of people. No polite handshake to welcome a stranger, and Jimmy is a stranger. I never met him, but he has seen my naked, dead body. I cannot blush or be embarrassed.

All I can do is create a gentle ripple on the loch's surface to distract him from my corpse. The shock of seeing my Earthly shell, lying in the water, cannot be undone. I am glad it is this man, with a kind soul, who has found me. My presence makes him shiver as a fleeting coolness touches his cheeks. I whisper on the breeze but he can't hear me.

'I am here. You aren't alone. I promise that finding me will be rewarded.'

I will weave magic, creating a web to entangle those who did me wrong. But first, I will bring harmony to those who need it most. For nothing is without coincidence. In the space in which I now exist, there is no time, yet everything is destined in order: my death, being found, and what will happen next. The fisherman's life will change forever because he has found my earthly remnants.

CHAPTER 2
Day 1 : Tuesday, 23rd September, 7:00 a.m.

The key was in the ignition of his blue BMW when the work mobile rang. He groaned. Could they not leave him alone at this unearthly hour, especially in the morning after enduring another black-tie charity event? He had no hangover. Only a couple of drams had passed his lips, and those were before nine o'clock. His love affair with drink was long over, but he still enjoyed a whisky every now and again. He had left as soon as it was polite to do so and was in his bed by half past ten. Booze nor lack of sleep was the cause of his exhaustion. That was brought on by the pleasantries expected at such occasions. Deliberately ignoring the phone until it rang five times, he already knew what an early call meant.

'Hello, Detective Inspector David Chisholm at your disposal. What time do you call this? You're in the office early!'

His mood lightened as a sarcastic female voice responded.

'I've got nothing better to do, and besides, dead bodies wait for no one! We have a female corpse in Loch Spiorad in Sutherland, found by a fisherman. Local police think it's suspicious and have triggered the MIT's response but it's likely to be a false call. Who knows? Everyone's travelling up as I speak, divers and forensics.'

Hair stood up on the back of his neck as his face paled. Goosebumps raced across his body. An enormous iron weight pressed deep into his chest.

No air! Suffocating. Breathe man, breathe.

Forcing his lungs to fill with oxygen, he pushed his feet deep onto the car floor as he inhaled. The world spun faster and faster, out of control. The Glaswegian voice at the other end of the call knew nothing of Chisholm's discomfort and continued as he struggled to take control of himself.

Loosen the tie! Open the window! Now breathe!

'The chief says to get there pronto. You'll be acting as the SIO. The location's coming through now to you . I'll see you there. Just to warn you, apparently this place is in the back of beyond!'

Calm! Stay calm! This can't be happening!

'Boss, did you hear what I said? It's remote. Shall I bring Euan along?'

Think! Get the brain into action!

His head pounded and, out of nowhere, fierce tremors wracked his body, which he was powerless to control. Deep within his brain, a muscle memory was triggered, enabling him to bark instructions at her.

Breathe!

'No! Leave him at H.Q. Cordon the place off, and we'll need an incident tent. Proceed as if it's a suspicious death, just in case. More than likely it's one of these bloody stupid wild swimming idiots, wasting everyone's time.'

The line went dead. There was an edge to Chisholm that morning, which unnerved her. The cheeriness from his initial greeting had disappeared, and there was no *"please"* or *"thank you."* As for leaving the newest, keenest detective, Euan Sinclair, in the office, it felt wrong. The lad's enthusiasm was always infectious, and he would have been good company on the drive up north. She didn't argue with her superior. Perhaps, when Chisholm was in a better mood, she would tease him. Something told her it was best not to comment upon the sharpness of his orders until she'd had the chance to find out what was wrong.

It wasn't the thought of a dead body that caused his stomach to lurch nor the sixty-mile journey from Inverness to the middle of nowhere. Loch Spiorad. The name crashed like waves on a stormy ocean into his thoughts, pounding his flesh until the maelstrom reached his bones. There was no escape from its power, battering and shredding his head into tiny pieces of seashells, memories so lucid that the pain and agony became unbearable. It was a location so excruciating to recall, yet somewhere that meant so much. He didn't want to make the journey north, not to Sutherland, and definitely not there, of all places.

Adrenaline bolted through his body, racing through tissue, muscles, and organs, galloping into a frenzy in his brain. Fight or flight? His immediate reaction was to call in sick, but he knew that was not an option. The case was already assigned to him. It was the thought of revisiting the past, something he had shunned for years.

It was probably a false alarm. No one ended up dead in Loch Spiorad. There was nothing there but a few trout, eels, and trillions of midges. It would not be a murder, even if there were a body. Some foolish tourist skinny-dipping ended up dying from a heart attack due to the freezing water or getting caught in reeds. The local police were probably overdramatising the whole thing.

Various scenarios played in his head. There must be a way out. Could he take urgent leave and book a holiday abroad? Helen would cope. As an experienced detective, there was no need for him to visit. He'd work from photographs and forensic reports. Nothing serious ever happened in such a remote area to warrant a police officer of his rank in the Major Investigation Team in those parts... until now.

Making a conscious effort to calm his breathing, he began to rationalise his thinking. His professional reputation was of a man who could deal with any situation. Everyone at headquarters would notice if he remained in Inverness. Questions would be asked by his superiors, not to mention the small band of detectives he worked with. Could he manage to be the SIO with just a single visit to the scene? Surely, he could make a single trip to the place he had grown up. His throat tightened. The place was forever a noose around his neck.

Think. Think.

As if to soothe himself, he ran his fingertips in circles on his temples. Trying to concoct a plan whilst panicking brought no conclusion, other than there was no way to avoid the case. He'd managed to put off any connection with the place for the best part of thirty years.

He breathed heavily, pushing air deeper and deeper into his lungs for as long as he could bear until his chest begged for release. Only after repeating these actions several times could he stop shaking.

The stormy waters calmed. Perhaps it would be a good idea to lay ghosts to rest, cathartic even. He gripped the steering wheel. Maybe breakfast would take away the tight knot that took hold in his stomach. He doubted anything would help.

Being a man who liked routine, he stopped at his usual café to grab a sausage sandwich and a coffee to take out. Breakfasting at Moira's was convenient but unhealthy. He knew that he needed to break the habit and start to look after himself more carefully, but he was in a rut, and he was drawn to the café for some inexplicable reason, like a bad habit. He even contemplated getting a packet of crisps and some chocolate. He sensed he would not get much time to eat for a while.

'Hello, Sir. Is it your usual?'

Moira, the café owner, instantly recognised him, although she didn't know his name. He was a regular, nicknamed *"Mr. Serious"* in her mind. He bought breakfast from her most mornings with little change in his orders.

Invariably, it was an egg and bacon or egg and sausage sandwich with brown sauce to go. He was forever in a hurry and always on his own. He never sat on one of her white wooden chairs or leaned his elbows on one of her beech-coloured tables.

She found him intriguing, but he never seemed like a man for small talk, even though he had bought breakfast from her for the past three years. His appearance was always immaculate when he entered her establishment each weekday morning. Unbeknownst to her, he would have visited on Saturday and Sunday too had the café been open because of the convenience. She recognised an air about him that commanded authority, so she guessed he was one of her *"professional"* types.

His uniform these days was his grey suit, a gleaming white shirt, always crisply ironed, and black brogues. He looked different from many of her other clientele. His fingernails were well-manicured, and his hands were clean. The same body spray, a pleasant, clean odour, made him stand out from some of the people who frequented the café later each day. His immaculate manners were memorable. There were always impolite customers, but this man was one of her favourite gentlemen. She tried to surmise his age. Late forties or early fifties was her guess. This morning, she noted his hair and face seemed grey, as if he had aged overnight.

'I'll have a sausage sandwich to take out. No egg and a strong coffee with milk please. No sugar.'

'Of course. Anything else for you?'

Moira always asked, although she guessed her customer's response would be negative. However, today's reply jolted her into thinking something was amiss.

'I'll take some cheese and onion crisps and a KitKat.'

She wondered what could have prompted his change of order. Dismissing it from her mind, as she would never know, little did she realise he was about to face the toughest of days with no time to eat. Instead, she told him the total to pay and waited for him to thank her as she gave him his change. She smiled as she always did at this point in their daily interaction, but he didn't smile back. He always thanked her politely; occasionally he smiled, but today all he gave was a frown and a brief nod.

She turned away to cut the white bloomer into slices, disappointed and shocked at his abrupt manner; her eyes remained fixed on the sausages sizzling away in the frying pan while pondering the man's emotions. On days when he seemed more tense and preoccupied, he usually ordered no egg. The lack of a thank-you was a first.

The need for pleasantries was a million miles away from the darkest of emotions he was experiencing. He grunted his thanks after she handed over the food and drink without making eye contact.

As he left the café, having stuffed the crisp packet and chocolate in his jacket pockets, he strolled back to the car, clutching a brown paper bag in one hand and a disposable cup of warm coffee in the other. He sat eating the sandwich, staring into the distance without focus.

He took a sip of his coffee, but one thing only occupied his mind. Not the body floating in Loch Spiorad but the return to an area long buried in the depths of his mind.

†††††

Hovering just below the permitted speed limit, he made good time. The traffic moving north was not too heavy. It was one of those journeys when the miles slipped by without noticing, and suddenly he realised he needed to head inland from the coast.

Thoughts of the area he was to visit distracted him from the police procedures needing mental preparation. He tried to focus. Preserving the scene, ensuring nothing was touched, observing, and making an initial assessment of the case were his priorities. He struggled to concentrate on anything but driving. The feeling of foreboding engulfed him. His fingers clenched the steering wheel, and his shoulders tightened, making the journey uncomfortable. The churning in his stomach was no longer from lack of food. The breakfast now joined the angst buried deep within that had festered there for years. Each mile nearer made him dread his destination. He paid no heed to a number of small villages he passed. When he reached the sign for Loch Dubhglas, he breathed deeply, fervently wishing he was back in his office in Inverness.

It was a clear, sunny day, and not a midge in sight. The village had sprung to life several hours before, with workers driving to their employment, mainly to the east or south. The older youths had already boarded the school bus and were bound for the high school twenty miles away. On mornings such as this, the familiar sight of younger children dawdling as they made their way to the primary school took him back to a distant time. They laughed and played along the footpath adjacent to the loch, several of them devouring bags of crisps or chocolate for breakfast. A couple of parents struggled with pushchairs, whilst another grappled with a pram. One child stopped, lifted his foot onto the low barrier that separated the path from the water's edge a few yards away, and tied his shoelace. Two lads raced to the school, perhaps to meet their friends for a game of football before the school bell rang, like David did years before.

There were no banners adorning the streets and no trumpets proclaiming his return. The place felt eerily familiar. Life had carried on without him. The knot in his stomach tightened, but an unexpected emotion took him by surprise. Relief crept through his soul as he watched the villagers going about their daily business and it created an unfamiliar sense of warmth for the place, as if he had never been away. A tiny droplet of water dripped from the gigantic piece of ice that had encased his heart for thirty years.

Driving past the last few houses at the far side of the village, he continued north until the normal two-way road narrowed to a single lane with just enough width for one vehicle to travel at a time. Every few yards, on one side or the other, the grass verge was replaced by a wider space designated for drivers to pull in to allow oncoming, or overtaking vehicles to pass. Each of these places were announced by a white diamond sign with black lettering declared *'Passing Place.'* To the untrained, tourist eye, these places looked like lay-bys which frustrated locals who frequently needed to travel this A road.

Loch Dubhglas sparkled in the sunlight on his left. Reflections of the purple heather hills shimmered on the water. In the distance, in the middle of the loch, an oddly shaped tree originating from a seed blown on the breeze years before had grown on a rock. Its battered shape showed the direction of countless winds blowing from west to east. Life clinging to a stony outcrop, surrounded by water.

Beyond the loch, he could see the majestic outline of Ben More Assynt. He drove on, passing a house or two dotted along the road. In this part of the country, deer outnumbered people a thousandfold. This land was wilderness and always had been. Only sheep or the occasional herd of Highland cattle gave any clue that some of the land was farmed. There were signs that deforestation had been underway for some time on stretches along the way. Large patches of land lay ravaged by logging machinery. Pine forests were stripped bare of timber, leaving a landscape rutted with tree roots, bracken, and debris from fallen branches and twigs.

A further ten miles through similar surroundings, and D.I. David Chisholm instantly recognised his destination. There was no turning back as he spotted hordes of police cars parked on verges as far as the eye could see. Tape was placed across a small path between two sections of trees, signifying a prohibited area, and a tent was hastily being erected. Everyone dressed in white suits, with their heads covered by hoods and their shoes and hands covered to ensure that the scene remained preserved.

The familiar face of a pathologist caught his eye as he drove past a man putting on his disposable outerwear. Managing to find a place to park, David stopped and turned off the ignition. Determined to get on with the job as quickly as possible, he got out of the car without stretching his back or limbs after the journey and went immediately to the boot to rummage for the essential tools needed: a disposable white boiler suit with a hood, gloves, and shoe covers. He would not corrupt any evidence, even if he was keen to leave the area as soon as possible.

The lead forensic officer walked towards him.

'Good morning. A good drive up north?'

Chisholm stared at the scene ahead and brusquely got straight to the business in hand.

'What have we got?'

'A white female. Found by a fisherman early this morning. His oar tangled in reeds, and the body came to the surface whilst he tried to free himself. Local police arrived at the scene first and established a need for backup. Police divers located the body and brought it ashore a few minutes ago. It's been placed in an incident tent. Tim Shore, the pathologist, is carrying out his initial examination as we speak. The area is contained and sealed. You might want to speak to the fisherman, but I warn you, he is very shaken.'

He gestured towards a lonely figure slumped on a rotting tree stump a few metres away. Noting the sickly pallor of the fisherman's face and his inability to control his trembling, Chisholm gathered the man was in severe shock. The body finder stared at the ground, not able to look back in the direction of the loch. The detective headed straight to him.

'Get this man a blanket,' he barked.

Jimmy barely looked up, dazed by the nightmare in which he found himself trapped.

'Good morning. I'm Detective Inspector Chisholm, the senior investigating officer. Can I ask your name? I gather you found something in the water. Please tell me what you know so we can get you home soon.'

The authority of Chisholm's voice calmed the man. Other officers tried to soothe his distress when they arrived on site two and a half hours before but were unsuccessful. Over and over the images flashed through his mind: losing control, the rocking of the boat, the woman in the water, her eyes staring up at him. He could not recall how he freed himself from his entrapment and managed to row back at near Olympic speed, hauling his boat out of the water in his vain attempt to disassociate himself from what he had just witnessed.

He stared at the detective, trying to process what the officer said. For a second or two, he sat in silence, not knowing where to start. The first utterances made little sense; his speech was jagged and broken.

'Sir. I'm Jimmy, Jimmy Mackay from Dubhglas.'

Attempting to regain his composure, he swallowed hard. Solitary words came first, followed by pauses, and then whole sentences exploded as he tried to offer information on what he recalled.

'I... I... have been... coming to erm... Loch Spiorad... since I was a bairn. I ken the water well, but I havnae seen anything like this. I cannae get the image of that wee lassie out o' ma heid.'

Jimmy trembled in disbelief as the woman's face and green eyes unwittingly flashed through his mind. A police officer placed a foil survival blanket around his shoulders and quietly moved away, trying to avoid disturbing the conversation.

'I'd been here all night from just before nine o'clock. I love the peace of the place. I caught a couple of eels and a trout.' He indicated to the boot of his car, a short distance away, and then continued,

'I was rowing back to the shore when an oar caught what I thought were reeds, about a hundred yards out.

I pulled at the oar, but it wouldnae move, so I gie it laldy[6] until there was an almighty gurgle, and something rose to the surface. I grabbed a torch and looked back into the water; a face was staring up at me. It was a lassie with green eyes.'

Tears trickled down his ashen cheeks. Chisholm felt sorry for the man, but he needed as much information as possible from him as a key witness. He listened intently to the fisherman's story, noting every detail.

'I am sorry to ask this. I realise such an image won't be pleasant. Did you notice anything else?'

'Sir, I noticed she wasn't wearing a stitch. It's awfie cold for a lassie to be like that, with no dignity.'

'Did you recognise her?'

Jimmy slowly shook his head. To stop himself from breaking down completely, he focused only on a small, grey stone that lay on the ground.

'Did you see anyone else during the night you spent out here? Did any vehicles pass by?'

'No one passed the loch last night after I rowed out at about nine o'clock. It was very quiet. Sir, can I ask you something?'

The detective nodded.

'If I can answer, I will. I've just arrived from Inverness, so I'm still getting up to speed with the events of the night.'

Trembling from head to foot, Jimmy continued staring at the ground. There was no eye contact with the police officer for fear of what the answer to his question might be.

'Do...Do... Do you think she might have been alive when I found her and that I killed her by pushing down on my oar? Did I kill her?

'I very much doubt that, Jimmy. From what you have told me, it sounds like the woman was already dead. You found her and saved her from a watery grave.'

Jimmy exhaled loudly. His shoulders relaxed, and he started to sob. Chisholm felt in his jacket pocket for the packet of tissues he religiously carried. Instinct told him this man was telling the truth. There was nothing else he needed from Jimmy at that moment. Another officer could take his statement in the comfort of his home. The fisherman was clearly in no fit state to drive himself the few miles to the nearest village where he lived. Chisholm handed him a tissue and said he would organise transport for Jimmy and his vehicle as soon as he was ready to leave. He sensed it would be the last time Mackay would fish Loch Spiorad. His last catch had probably put paid to any thoughts of returning in the near future. He thanked the man for his help and was about to walk away when Jimmy lifted his eyes to meet the detective's gaze.

'Do I know you, sir? There was a family who crofted up at Kinness, just a few miles from here. Their name was Chisholm. You have the look of old Donnie and his son Donald. The same-shaped nose and blue eyes.'

Oxygen! I need oxygen!

The detective struggled to breathe as panic rose. Within minutes of his arrival, his past lay bare, open to the elements. No one in the force knew his background, and he wanted it to stay that way. He tried to be vague when anyone questioned his origins, but this man had instantly uncovered an ancient, festering wound. His cheeks flushed as a torrent of anger swept through him, highlighting the reason for his reluctance to return. It stirred memories he wanted, and needed, to forget. Guilt, pain, and exhaustion from thinking about Loch Dubhglas led him to conclude it was best to forget everything from the past. Why did a body have to be found here in this godforsaken place?

Hearing names last mentioned more than three decades before, David's mind went blank, and he couldn't think straight. The words twisted and lingered in the air. Someone remembered his grandparents, and parents; the family he'd pushed to the back of his mind to relieve the heartache and painful memories. He wanted to scream for the noise to stop. Instead, words spurted from unwilling lips as he unleashed the truth.

'Donnie was my grandfather. Do you remember him?'

Stupid! Stupid! Why that question?

Had he lost all sense? Why would his brain not engage? The agony escalated as Mackay continued the conversation.

'Aye! Chisholm was a great man. He would help anyone. Are you Donald's bairn, David? How are you, laddie? I went to school with Donald and your mother too. I knew the whole family. What a tragedy!'

Pursing his lips, the detective did not want to enter further into conversation with Jimmy about his father or grandfather, and certainly not his mother. He nodded and turned to walk away, using the organisation of Jimmy's transport as an abrupt excuse to curtail the conversation. Suppressing the great urge to scream, he instantly regretted his reaction and rudeness towards the fisherman but could not bring himself to turn back. With each step, the word that summarised everything echoed in his head.

Tragedy!
Is that what people remember here?
No, not a tragedy!
A complete bloody disaster!

He didn't need a stranger, a witness, or even a potential suspect to rake over his childhood. The past was the past. He couldn't change history, in fact he wanted to bury it.

Coming to this place was a mistake. He would go off sick, feign some kind of serious illness that he couldn't possibly work with for a week. That would solve everything.

David did not see the fisherman raising his hand to his heart as a signal that no more would be said. Silently, Mackay dabbed his eyes with the crumpled tissue. It was years since he last saw David, a quiet, studious teenager. He longed for a conversation with the man, but now was not the time. Neither he nor Chisholm were in the mood to venture back to the past.

The officer assigned to drive Jimmy home thought that the fisherman's tears overflowed because of the body in Loch Spiorad. She attempted some bits of small talk to lighten what had been an eventful, traumatic morning for him. He tried to engage in conversation, but his mind was lost in remembering Kinness, a place he'd never quite forgotten. He fell silent, so eventually, the officer left him to his thoughts.

When his wife opened the door, relieved Jimmy was home, she saw his pale, broken face, smeared with traces of recent tears. Taken aback, she could only recall once before seeing her husband in this state. It was the time when he was mourning the loss of Donald, his best friend.

Chisholm was a seasoned detective, witnessing many dead bodies over thirty years on the job. He was planning in his head when he would feign illness, but first there was a job everyone would expect of him if he was to carry out his duties as SIO. His brain welcomed the distraction, even if it meant seeing a dead woman's body.

The reaction he suffered on encountering his first corpse, as a police constable, was never repeated. His initial response, back then, was to throw up over a hedge, spewing his breakfast into the bramble bushes. Chisholm remained calm and steady in the years since, never losing his empathy for the dead human before him. It was too late to save each person from death, but he followed a routine with every corpse he came across in the hope they would give up their secrets for him to fulfil his promise to them. He bore a pang of guilt even now that he had failed two bodies in all the years of being a detective. As he approached the hastily erected police tent, he began mentally preparing for the sight he dreaded so much.

An officer, besuited in her white disposable apparel, opened the tent's flap as Chisholm neared the entrance. She smiled, but he barely gave her a nod, his eyes fixed on the body lying on a white, plastic sheet. A photographer was capturing images of the woman. Another officer placed bags over the woman's hands to preserve any evidence held in her fingers and nails.

David scanned the image, programmed to do so by his police training. Naked female, probably in her twenties, with no marks on her neck. Long, dark ginger hair flattered her petite face. Scratches on her forearms and shins, were raw in several places.

The other two officers moved away from the body as he bent down to take a closer look at the woman, seeing the same stark image as Jimmy the fisherman had hours before: fading green eyes, melancholy, lost, and committed to their fate. As he did with all dead bodies he saw in his line of work, he had only one thought when he first saw a corpse and muttered words that no one else could hear.

'So, here you are. I'll do my best to get you home to your loved ones, whoever you are.'

He stood up and paused for a second. How could he let this woman down now that his promise was made? At that moment he knew there would be no turning back, even for personal reasons. Avoiding a case was not his style. He would push the past to the darkest recesses of his mind once more. The *"tragedy"* would not define him. There was a job to do, and he would carry it out to the best of his ability, no matter who she was or where she had been found. He began a second scan of the body just as the pathologist returned to the tent.

'Ah, admiring the catch of the day? She looks incredibly athletic for a dead person!'

Having met Chisholm before, in similar circumstances, Tim Shore knew that the detective despised him for his sense of humour, so he antagonised him further. Ignoring the sarcasm, Chisholm pressed on; he wanted answers.

'Any ideas yet? Do we have a murder, rather than a naturist out swimming and having a heart attack?'

'There are few visible marks or bruising, apart from some interesting scratches to her arms and legs, recent by the look of them. The cause of death is inconclusive until I get her back to the mortuary. What I can tell you is that this woman has not been in the water long.'

He began to explain the effects of rigor mortis, water, and body temperatures, but Chisholm held up his hand, signalling him to stop. He wasn't in any mood to cope with the fine details of the woman's death. All he wanted were the headlines.

'Sorry, I forgot this stuff makes you queasy! I won't go into blowfly larvae at this time of the morning then. Hope you are not planning rice for lunch.'

Ignoring the remark, Chisholm's brain overflowed with questions. However, he knew from experience that on day one of an inquiry, the forensic team and the pathologist had a job to do, and he did not envy them the task.

As he left the tent, Chisholm glanced back towards the body and sighed heavily. Currently, there were no clues to the woman's identity other than what was on her skin and hair. Within her body, there would lie other clues but it was yet to be explored.

He was glad to be outside. The air was fresh, and he took a deep breath to clear his lungs. Casting an eye over the landscape, he had to admit that Loch Spiorad was in such an idyllic setting. On days such as this, during the first weeks of autumn, the purple-heather mountains, with rolling hills dancing at their feet, rose to touch the clouds. Burns crisscrossed the land, creating waterfalls as slopes sharply fell away. Deciduous trees, at the edge of the loch, began to change their coats from greens to reds, oranges, yellows, and browns. Native fir trees, like a large emerald blanket, covered the land beyond the loch on all sides. The scent of pine hung heavily in the air, cones and needles covering ancient forest floors.

Sunshine caused the loch to sparkle, with watery droplets resembling diamonds. People surrounded Chisholm at the scene, but if he blocked out all human voices, he could hear the gushing of a waterfall less than a mile from where he stood.

There was a familiarity with the scenery, although it had been years since he last stood in this place. Loch Spiorad was a second home to him during the long summer holidays of his childhood and youth. A smaller freshwater loch than the neighbouring Loch Dubhglas, it was a short distance away from the foot of Ben Meagaidh. Voices interrupted his memories. First, a young officer tried to pronounce the mountain's name. Then, he detected a voice that brought instant relief.

'It's pronounced *"Meggy,"* numpty! It means boggy. Are you sure you were born in the Highlands?'

Detective Sergeant Helen Daniels had finally arrived.

†††††

Chisholm was reluctant to work with Helen when he first encountered her. He felt her cheerful nature would grate on his nerves, but something about the officer created energy and a spark of life even in the middle of a murder inquiry. She strolled over, giving him a broad smile. Her hazel eyes twinkled as she teased him.

'Before you start complaining, my car broke down. Well, that might be a little porky. I was driving on vapours and didn't want to run out of fuel completely. So, I ruined my trainers walking along overgrown grass verges to the nearest garage. I got a lift back to the car from a very charming mechanic, and here I am!'

Here she was, the yin to his yang, complete opposites, but somehow, they worked well together, *"Mr. Serious"* and *"Little Miss Sunshine."* When they weren't dressed in disposable forensic gear, he wore a suit, collar, and tie; she dressed casually in blue jeans, a t-shirt, and a short blue leather jacket that ended at her slim waist. His soft Sutherland accent sounded like a beautiful, calming melody when he spoke. Her Glaswegian tones were lively and more dramatic, especially in a crisis. Greying locks, wrinkles, and sharp, craggy features made Chisholm feel his age, two years after celebrating his fiftieth birthday.

A radiance shone from her small, rather bonnie, tanned face, often framed by long, curly, black hair, when not tied back in a ponytail. Although she was of slender build and average height for a women, she often reminded him of a character from one of the myths his grandmother loved to share when he was a bairn.

Scáthach[7], a female Celtic warrior, charged into battle, just as Helen had a few days previously. She caught sight of a druggie running into the Eastgate Shopping Centre after he failed to appear at court in Inverness.

Racing up the escalator, a few steps behind the man, Helen grabbed him just as he was about to step onto the tiled floor of the main shopping area. The onlookers cheered as she handcuffed him while trying to caution him through gasps of breathlessness.

Their age gap meant Helen could have been David's daughter, had he been a father. It made their relationship professional, as she respected his seniority. When she put herself in dangerous situations, he felt a paternal concern. Her bravery was sometimes foolish, and Chisholm told her so when they debriefed after an incident on the Kessock Bridge two months before. Attempting to talk down some random woman from jumping into the Beauly Firth, more than a hundred feet below, Helen climbed over a safety barrier, placing herself at risk. Often, she joked that she wanted a better view of *"Caley Thistle,"* the football stadium on the southern shore of the bridge.

They rarely socialised but Helen had felt a duty to organise a surprise for his fiftieth when she'd teased him about plans to celebrate the occasion. He'd played down the whole age thing and tried to wriggle out of her plans for a drink after work but she'd stuck to her guns and insisted. David was taken aback that the pub was packed. What she hadn't mentioned was the fact she'd bribed colleagues with a first round of drinks for free.

One thing they had in common was that neither said much about their home lives. The D.I. had not spoken about his marriage failing three years before. Sharing the same philosophy, Helen kept her love life private, although Chisholm noticed she wore a silver ring on her wedding finger, which she habitually touched on the rare occasions when she spoke of home. After listening to a conversation with an inquisitive new colleague when she moved up to Inverness from Glasgow, he gathered she was a dog owner but mentioned no partner. Her next of kin was her mother. She jokingly informed him of this following an incident when they'd come close to real danger the previous year.

'This had better not be a wild goose chase after my adventures. What's the craic?'

She sensed immediately that *"craic"* was perhaps the wrong word. Chisholm's sour face never altered. His mood was even more severe than usual, and her recount of the misadventures with the car fell on stony ground. He replied brusquely.

'White female. No signs of bruising. The woman has no clothing. Fit, athletic-looking build.'

'How long has she been in the water?'

Chisholm shook his head.

'No idea.'

There was little point in having a conversation with the senior detective when he was in this mood. He could be grouchy, but she would usually raise a smile with a bad joke or a funny story. Today, for some reason only known to him, he was grumpy, offering minimum effort to continue any conversation she tried to have with him. He'd appeared fine, even slightly jovial, on Friday when she last saw him, and was animated in discussions about how he could avoid the big charity event in Inverness. Maybe he was tired after a long evening of being civil to the people who splashed their cash. Perhaps he had drunk too much. He was not a great drinker, but maybe the event depressed him enough to drive him to one too many whiskies.

Instead of pursuing any more conversation, she pulled up the hood on her disposable boiler suit, making sure not to expose any hair, and entered the tent. Helen knew what to expect. Although she had the kind of personality that lit up a room, she always knew to be respectful in the presence of a dead body. It was the first thing that Chisholm liked about her. She loved to joke, but he knew that her lightheartedness was sometimes more about a lack of confidence than being the team joker.

She stood, taking in the sight of the woman's body lying on the plastic matting. She was as fit as Chisholm described, but he failed to mention that the woman was young and pretty. No more than thirty, she guessed. The green eyes surprised Helen. Although this was a lifeless body before her, and she'd seen a number of corpses since joining the force, the stare, together with the beauty and age of the woman unsettled her. Only around five or six years younger than herself, she surmised. There was an empathy for the lifeless shell of this random stranger which she didn't normally experience.

The corpse's alabaster breasts seemed a perfect size for her body. The skin was flawless apart from one or two small red marks that looked like midge bites and a series of minor scarlet wounds on her arms and shins. Scratches by the look of them. A well-toned physique suggested this woman had looked after herself, perhaps even being a member of a gym. Her long auburn locks enhanced her beauty as they cascaded down her body towards her waist. Someone must be missing such a stunning woman.

Helen stepped outside the tent and, like her boss a few minutes before, took some deep breaths to ground herself. When she regained her composure, questions flooded her thoughts. Loch Spiorad wasn't an area she knew well. Most of her work centred around the city of Inverness, although, in her spare time, she climbed Ben Meagaidh and several others in the area in her attempt to notch up a tally of *"bagging"* Munros.

She shuddered. It was the perfect place to dump a body. Remote. The loch was a beautiful setting. Several of the Munros she climbed were visible in the distance. Soft carpets of heather and peat bogs covered the lower hills in the foreground. The single-track road lay a few metres away but nothing else. There was less traffic at this time of year than at the height of the tourist season.

Yet, the body was found in this isolated spot. By the look of it and the lack of decomposition, the loch quickly relinquished its newest secret. Surely the lass had not been in the water for more than a few hours. No bloating with gases like some corpses she witnessed. It could have been a wild swimming session gone wrong, but it smelt like murder.

Loud cries distracted the detective from her thoughts. She swung round in the direction of the voices. Moving quickly towards the shoreline, her superior beat her by a fraction to reach the place where they both could see the police divers, a natural slipway jutting out into the loch from where Jimmy Mackay pushed his rowing boat into the water hours earlier.

Having quickly recovered the body, a team of divers was looking for anything else of interest. Both detectives peered towards the police dinghy, curious to establish what other precious treasure was found. They hauled a light-coloured bundle out of the water and into the hands of an officer in the boat. An incredulous voice came over the walkie-talkie.

'Boss... It appears to be a wedding dress!'

Weaving skilfully through the reeds, the dinghy moved towards the shore. A diver placed the garment in a large evidence bag before passing it to Chisholm. The detective examined the contents through the plastic pouch, turning it over several times for any signs of marks or labels. Folds of cloth caught the sunlight, revealing the delicate ivory colour of the fabric. A dress containing future plans and dreams.

David spoke first, softer than before.

'Is it a wedding dress? Someone must be missing her if she was married.'

He handed the bag to Helen, who studied the package, turning it over for any further clues. Not bulky or too heavy. No frills, layers, or elaborate petticoats. It would be surprising even if it was a fishtail style, as the package seemed too small. She guessed from the thickness of the bag that the dress was perhaps a simple A-line, elegant with slender straps. No labels were visible, nor intricate lace detail or pearl beading. Like the corpse, the dress looked practically flawless with few blemishes. Helen began to hypothesise as she handed the bag to him.

'She may have been married for a few years, and the marriage turned sour. You know statistically if she was murdered, it is likely her partner or someone related to her. Perhaps, the husband dumped her and her wedding dress in the loch. A bit extreme but it could save a costly divorce.'

Try as he might, Chisholm could not stop his cheeks from reddening at the word "divorce." He brushed away the comment by posing another question.

'What if it *was* her wedding day? The dress looks new, or is that my imagination?'

Helen nodded. She agreed. The modest package would be tested for any evidence, and photographs taken, so it was pointless to speculate about the design. No signs of murder, and having observed the body, there were still doubts in her mind if there was any foul play. Probably an accidental death by drowning. Yet the wedding dress puzzled her.

Voices from the loch broke her thoughts. There was another discovery from one of the divers. It was brought onto land and handed to David, once again, in an evidence bag. The gap between his eyebrows narrowed. He held out the find to Helen.

'What does this indicate to you?'

The sergeant glimpsed a wreath of fresh flowers made from pink roses, white jasmine, and silvery green eucalyptus leaves, intertwined with ivy. She gasped. The circle of blooms was exquisite and caught her off guard for a moment. Both officers felt the poignancy of the find.

'These flowers were recently cut, which leads me to think this lady was about to get married or was just married. It's a headdress, not a wreath, I think.'

'My conclusion, too. Something is wrong here. I want you to go back to H.Q. and organise an incident room to be set up in Loch Dubhglas. It's a priority to get a local base up and running so we can start to establish a presence in the village. Get Euan to track down all marriages and pending nuptials in the area. Remember to tell him to check churches and registry offices.'

'Aye. Euan will also need to check registered celebrants for the area. Not everyone is religious. A wedding can take place anywhere.'

'Sorry for earlier. Just tired from the early start.'

Helen briefly acknowledged the apology and smiled but said nothing. She turned away and hurried past the incident tent and along the path back to her car parked on the verge, not stopping to speak to anyone or offer any wisecracks.

Wiping away tears from her cheeks, she wasn't sure why she began to cry. It certainly was not Chisholm's mood or snappiness. The floral headdress upset her. Perhaps it was because she was planning a similar flowery crown for her own nuptials, three months away. Turning the key in the ignition, the engine roared into action. She blinked away tears and tried to concentrate on the job at hand, wanting more than ever to establish the identity of the bride.

The woman was beautiful; her bridal gown and ring of flowers would have looked sensational as her crowning glory. Daniels hoped that the wedding took place, that the woman celebrated her love for someone. She sighed. But there was no evidence of a ring to signify a marriage. The corpse showed no signs of jewellery or indentation marks on her fingers to indicate the wearing of rings. With her enquiring mind, Helen contemplated whether the woman had committed suicide. It would explain a body being in the remote loch without the addition of the most exquisite dress she'd probably ever owned? She was totally naked, her wedding dress cast adrift on the loch along with her floral headdress; everything abandoned for some reason.

†††††

These two detectives are good people, but they have secrets. I know all about secrets, my own and the ones they bury within their souls. Not shocking secrets like mine but things they prefer to keep from the world. Each has festering scars where life's joys trickle out, day after day, leaving them lost and empty.

When there are secrets, no one wins, for everyone tells lies to cover their tracks in case those tiny morsels of truth spill out from mouths that have been silent for so long. Even a glance in the wrong direction or the briefest of body movements can give the game away. So, they are polite, professional, and always on guard. I see their tiredness, the weariness of holding their secrets within them. Privacy is what each yearns. Within their destinies, because of my death, they will suffer anguish as their secret worlds open like a can of worms for public consumption.

Like everyone else at Loch Spiorad, they are too busy to notice me, for I am a small bird taking flight high above their heads. One of my tiny, white feathers drifts gently to the ground. I land on a nearby branch, tweeting my sweet song for all to hear.

'My truth will be known; your secrets also before too long. Events will unfold, and the spilling out of secrets is inevitable.'

In human form, I was a private person. Secrets ruled my life, wicked little secrets that smothered every ounce of air from my lungs, ripping out my soul. It is liberating to no longer care. To be naked and vulnerable means nothing now. I am free of mortal chains, but seeing my body lying in an incident tent sparks a flame.

I ignore the contents of the first evidence bag because looking at what lies within it fuels my fire. A loneliness too unbearable to endure. Lies were my downfall, my own and those of others.

For some reason, it is not the dress that brings the greatest emotional response but the contents of the second evidence bag. When I see the circle of flowers, picked by my hands three days ago, my rage burns on the heads of those who sit in a boat on the loch or stand at the shoreline. They feel warmth, unaware of flames roaring, furious at the senseless death I endured. Sweat pours from the faces of those who wear disposable suits. They will search until they uncover every facet of my life and my death. My soul is pure. All I seek, and all I've ever sought, is justice. Then I see the woman crying. She has empathy. She understands.

CHAPTER 3
Day 2 : Wednesday, 24th September

The next morning, Tim Shore was in his "office" down in the bowels of the mortuary building to examine the body pulled from the waters of Loch Spiorad. He prepared himself, putting on his green surgical tunic, trousers, wellies, and disposable cap to cover his greying hair. Scrubbing his hands thoroughly, the soapy bubbles and warm water soothed his skin as he sang the theme tune to *Goldfinger*.

He and his technician set to work immediately. Jarvis pulled the corpse, in its black body bag, from the refrigeration unit onto the trolley and wheeled it into position under the lighting, ready for Tim. With expert hands, he and the pathologist transferred the body to the mortuary table.

Both felt comfortable in their familiar surroundings, sharing the space only with dead bodies and each other most of the time. Today, however, they would have two visitors: Shona MacPherson, who attended autopsies for sudden or suspicious deaths, and acted as a forensic anthropologist to assist with identification, and David Chisholm. On these days, when the mortuary was bursting at the seams with the living, Tim needed to be on his very best behaviour. Neither MacPherson nor Chisholm showed any sense of the dark humour he and Jarvis shared.

Shona arrived first, confident in her surroundings. Nothing fazed her. The most gruesome of sights still gave her a thirst for the job even after thirty-odd years. Her dark hair, peppered with silvery wisps, was obscured from view by the surgical hat she wore, making her stunning blue eyes sparkle like sapphires. With a razor-sharp mind, she was ready to draw any conclusions she could from her first observations of the body.

Still unsettled from having to visit Loch Dubhglas, Chisholm wished the formalities were over and the dead woman was off his case load. Never keen to witness a post-mortem, he took his time to reach the mortuary, half hoping to miss the proceedings. Mostly, in these situations, he would glance away from the body laid out in front of him and concentrate on the speckled patterns of the non-slip flooring, willing everything to be over. On these days, he would not visit Moira's café or any other establishment for breakfast, skipping a meal—just in case.

As Tim got to work, the only sound in the room was his voice as he spoke into a microphone, detailing every single millimetre of the woman's body. Each minute aspect of his observations was shared.

'Examination of a corpse found in Loch Spiorad. I note the unidentified white female was found naked. She is of slim build, nourished, with green eyes and long red hair.

There are no signs of blunt force trauma. Jarvis, can you help with her height and weight, please?'

The assistant stepped forward to support the pathologist. After finding the necessary measurements, he spoke,

'Fifty-five kilograms and height is one hundred and sixty-seven centimetres.'

Tim recorded his findings as Jarvis began to photograph the body.

'I would put her age initially between twenty-five and thirty years old. At this point, identification will be handed over to Shona MacPherson who will work through dental records and any other means available. Clothing found in the loch might prove useful. We have yet to establish if this wedding dress, located near her body, was worn by the woman. It's at the lab for analysis.'

Shona wanted to help and eager for the pathologist to draw some conclusions so that her work in identifying the woman could begin. There were few clues to who the woman was, making it a case she would relish.

'I'll try to get those results hurried along for you.'

Tim nodded as he stared at the body, willing it to offer him information. His eyes fell on the victim's neck, slender, pale, and flawless. Like the rest of her corpse, it looked unmarked. No bruising from finger marks or any sign of a ligature was visible. There was nothing to support a theory of strangulation. He cleared his throat before continuing.

'I conclude from a visual inspection of the whole body that there is little bruising ante-mortem. One thing to note straight away is that the body looks in good shape. Few signs of putrefaction in the incident tent yesterday suggest this woman was not in the water long before her body was recovered. Chisholm, I'm talking about bloating when...'

David grimaced and held up his hands in an attempt to stop Shore from expanding on his description of bacteria and expelled gases. The pathologist smirked at the detective's discomfort. Examining the woman's hair, he extracted samples of reed entangled within it.

'Her hair is red in colour, and in length, it's halfway between her shoulders and waist. It appears to be naturally curly.'

Shona interjected.

'Ringlets would be a more accurate description. Women would die for that hair!'

Tim raised his eyes for the briefest of moments, amused at the comment, then continued. He noted no discernible features on the face apart from some pale freckles across her nose and cheeks. There were still no marks to help with this woman's identity or cause of death.

'Her pectoralis majors to the left and right are well developed, as are her triceps, showing this was a woman who regularly worked out. Her muscles are toned, and she appears to have been physically fit.'

He paused for a moment, casting his gaze across the woman's body, then turned towards his assistant to prompt him into action.

'Photographs, please, Jarvis.'

When he examined her hands, he took off the evidence bags placed on them at Loch Spiorad, carefully inspecting each digit before taking samples from under her fingernails.

'Samples taken. No indication of rings being worn. Unlike all other characteristics of this person, the nails are ragged and bitten. There are what look like pieces of skin under a couple of longer ones.'

The only other blemishes on her body were a couple of recent insect bites around one wrist and what looked like scratches on her forearms and shins. By their position, they looked jagged, and raw in places.

'I note scratches on the forearms that may have been self-inflicted, as the direction of them supports that theory, but swabs will be taken just in case another party was involved. Several are larger and have pierced epidermis to greater depths. Photos, please. I'll measure all the marks at this point. Smaller surface scratches are also on both shins. Two are deeper wounds, both on the right shin. There are two midge bites around her left wrist made recently by the look of them.'

As he moved further down the body, he noted that the woman's pubic hair was trimmed and tidy. There were no obvious signs of sexual activity, but he would swab the area and inner thighs.

After turning the body over, with help from Jarvis, Tim investigated the corpse once more. When he came to the woman's legs, he located a birthmark on the back of the left calf, a couple of centimetres below the crook of her knee. It wasn't half as large as a penny but it had a similar copper colour. Forgetting his audience, he uttered a cry of delight.

'Bingo! Finally, a clue, albeit rather small. Take another photo, please, Jarvis.'

MacPherson and Chisholm stepped forward in unison, both eager to see Tim's discovery. Sensing the detective's desire to observe the find, the pathologist voiced his thoughts more sarcastically than he should have.

'Blimey! You're keen! Give me a chance. I've only just begun. For your information, it's a birthmark.'

Chisholm, a man of few words, was exasperated.

'A birthmark! Come on, Shore, I want more than this. What's the cause of death? I need to know as soon as possible so I can get this woman off my caseload. Is this accidental or murder?'

Tim was not to be hurried into any conclusions by the forthright question. He knew, as usual, that little banter would pass between him and the policeman; there never was. Other detectives were much warmer in their approach to him, but not Chisholm.

Shore shrugged his shoulders and sighed heavily. He felt weary of the usual questions officers asked, and he knew not to bamboozle them with medical terms. Often, he witnessed their pallor change as nausea took hold of them, and they tried not to puke. Annoyingly, their eyes glazed over if he gave tours of a corpse in-depth. He delighted in using terms of anatomical correctness, which he adored.

If brutally honest, he also loved showing off. Too long in the tooth to play games, Tim was known for his sarcastic comments. All detectives wanted was the answer to one question, and Chisholm was no different. He offered the usual kind of speech to impatient officers.

'From my initial inspection, indications are that this lady was in the water no longer than ten to twelve hours before the discovery of the body. I'll confirm whether she drowned when I examine the lungs. There is no evidence of murder, as there are no obvious strangulation marks, stab wounds, or anything to suggest a suspicious death but I'm about to find out a lot more by delving inside. Cause of death will be apparent when I see the organs.'

Chisholm gave no response. His stomach lurched, and as his skin paled, he tried desperately not to retch. A battle going on between his head and the contents of his last meal broke out. Professional to the last, David slowed his breathing in an attempt to gain control of himself. Sensing the detective's predicament, Shore knew not to waste his breath with immature jokes. David Chisholm was a cold character, colder than some of the dead bodies he examined. So, he got to the point quickly.

'There's only blood and gore now to witness. Leave whilst the last smidgen of colour is left on your face.'

Chisholm did not need any further invitations to escape. As he turned to exit the mortuary, Tim winked at Shona and smiled. Her stoic expression cracked as she stifled a giggle. Once the officer left the room, she whispered,

'Stop teasing the poor man! You're incorrigible. I'm leaving too. Keep me updated if you find anything.'

Tim began the internal examination of the woman in front of him on the mortuary slab with renewed vigour. Next would come the fascinating part for the pathologist, the dissection of organs, swabs from every orifice, along with blood and skin samples galore.

✝✝✝✝✝

A busy morning continued. The process of cleaning the mortuary table for another corpse began. With the observers gone, the mood lightened considerably. Turning to Jarvis, Tim gave him the best instruction of the day.

'I feel like a few bars of the Eurythmics. Can you do the honours, please?'

Jarvis, his obliging assistant, nodded. Having supported Shore for the past fifteen years, every day was varied and exciting while working with the jovial pathologist. When people asked him about his job, he never shared any of the gory details that they wanted to hear. Instead, he talked endlessly about the skills of his colleague, the respect Shore possessed for all the dead people who lay on his mortuary table, and the brilliance of the doctor's mind.

They both got stuck into a second post-mortem to the tune of *'Sweet Dreams'* after Jarvis pressed play. He knew he was in for an hour or more of sore ears as Annie Lennox belted out her beautiful lyrics to Tim's accompaniment and, in between times, recorded notes for necessary reports. The only way Javis had learnt to cope with the dead was to join in with vigour!

✝✝✝✝✝

Several hours later, after completing the procedure for the third corpse of the day with specimens taken and labelled, all body parts examined, and Jarvis suitably entertained with music and jokes, Tim took off his scrubs and moved to an office upstairs.

He sank back in a black leather computer chair. Frustrated by the castors falling off the standard NHS plastic seating, which finally collapsed after years of service to his posterior, he'd treated himself to a seat of luxury. These days he needed comfort as he worked at his desk after hours down in the mortuary, bending over dead bodies. Usually, his brain flicked from one idea to another as he pinged off emails to various associates. Today was different. Something was distracting him. For the first time in living memory, Tim Shore sat still, elbows on his desk, his hands cupped to support his chin. All he could think about was the woman in Loch Spiorad.

Her death was a conundrum, and he was fascinated. A near-perfect specimen with a catastrophic death. Toxicology would prove useful in this case, as physically all he knew was that the female had not drowned because her lungs showed no sign of water present prior to death, nor was she strangled, shot, or stabbed.

There were no signs of a cardiac arrest. He knew her heart better than she had. It stopped beating, but there was no disease. There were signs of contraction of the respiratory tract at the time of death. Why was there a build-up in her lungs of such fluid and massive bleeding in the stomach and intestines? The woman's liver, kidneys, and spleen all failed. Her heart ceased because all other organs collapsed.

She was not a smoker, with little body fat, and he surmised her cholesterol levels would be low. There were no injection or junkie puncture marks on her skin. Her nose showed no signs of snorting coke. The stomach held few contents. It appeared from signs in her throat and on her teeth that she vomited, but death was not caused by choking. Analysis of samples was awaited.

A pathologist for more than thirty years, Tim had never seen anything like this before. Total organ failure in such a young, seemingly healthy woman was unusual. What caused this woman's body to shut down so dramatically? A symphony of conjectures began to play over and over in his head. Puzzles and mysteries captivated him. He pursued one train of thought from something read in a medical journal years before. The idea was absurd and could not be possible, not here in the Highlands, and especially not in Loch Spiorad of all places! Banging his palm on the table, exasperated at his hypothesis, he swore.

'For fuck's sake, man, let the science lead.'

With the computer switched on, his thoughts were already racing into top gear. He typed in words he believed inconceivable for a corpse in his mortuary. Avidly reading all he could, he then googled a case from almost fifty years before. He had been a teenager at the time, but his thirst for the macabre, even as a youngster, meant the headlines had caught his attention back in 1978.

After twenty minutes of research, Tim was convinced he was on the right path with a theory that sounded bizarre. He sat pondering the enormity of what he was going to investigate. He needed the final part of the puzzle, something missing from his examination of the body. When he picked up the phone to request Shona MacPherson's presence once more, he was certain there was a treasure to find in the corpse from the loch.

He raced down the two flights of stairs, oblivious to the people he passed. Normally he would smile and start up a conversation with these colleagues, but he blanked them; his mind was set on the prize ahead.

Jarvis was surprised to see his boss return so soon. His eyes grew wider, and his blink rate increased rapidly as Tim uttered the incredible theory to be worked upon. Although he knew the doctor well after all these years, this was by far the strangest of ideas he had ever heard. For the briefest of moments, he contemplated if his boss was intoxicated, but the urgency and garbled messages that passed Tim's lips told Jarvis this was not the case.

As he donned his mortuary wellingtons, Shore stared at the clothing he wore. Might he be wrong? Yes. Might he seem a fool for dragging Shona back? Possibly. What if his hypothesis was correct? The responsibility of his work weighed heavily on his mind, and for once he did not whistle, hum, or sing a tune. He remained silent as he carefully washed his hands and arms, ensuring his skin was thoroughly cleaned.

As she reached the door to the mortuary, Shona realised she was out of breath. The call from Tim, half an hour before, had caught her off guard. Nervous anticipation etched on her face, she silently prepared herself, changing her clothing and scrubbing her arms and hands, wondering what lay ahead. As she emerged from her changing area, she hesitated for a brief moment before she entered the examination room.

All three scientists stood wearing hazmat suits. Shona and Jarvis had listened to garbled explanations from Tim, but, until now, his theory made little sense. Here they were, both paralysed with the reality of his proposal, yet anxious to support their colleague.

'I promise you this isn't a wild goose chase. Well, I don't think so. If it is, I apologise now, and drinks will be on me, whether or not I'm right.'

'Let's calm down before we proceed. Go over the idea again, Tim, and how you have reached the conclusion to investigate further.'

Shona needed the information replayed to her at a slower pace. She couldn't quite find her usual professional composure. Her mind was overflowing with the news that gushed from Tim's mouth across a phone line. She and Jarvis stood listening, this time taking in the theory he suggested about the woman from Loch Spiorad. It was a mad idea but utterly brilliant, if true.

There was no longer any hesitation from his colleagues. All three moved quickly, pulling the woman's corpse onto the immaculate slab swilled down by Jarvis less than an hour before. Tim studied the corpse as he began to speak into his microphone, determined to record every detail that he could log. Never before had it been so important to be so accurate, even with the most complex of corpses he'd scrutinised.

'A re-examination of the body found in Loch Spiorad due to a lack of conclusion and some new conjecture over the cause of death of the unidentified female.'

He looked at the woman's skin. Butterflies floated around in his stomach, a mixture of excitement and nerves at what he might discover. Suddenly, everything felt real. He leaned over her and, in a hushed voice, addressed her directly.

'Let's find this little surprise you didn't share with me last time. Where is your secret hiding?'

In the only way he knew, he began to feel each millimetre of the woman's skin and to observe it under magnification. His gloved hands moved slowly across her scalp in circular movements to ensure he missed nothing. No treasure was revealed. His fingers moved further and further down the woman's body. The room was silent apart from the odd sentence Tim uttered as he continued to explore the woman's skin.

Perhaps he was wrong. The pathologist began to doubt his theory as he moved lower and lower down the woman's body until all that was left to minutely examine were her legs. He would feel foolish if his theory proved to be wild and stupid. This body did not want to give up its secret. Tim's fingertips moved towards the woman's thigh, but as he went up and down her skin towards her knee, he stopped.

'It's pointless. I'm sorry. This was a mad idea!'

Just as he was about to ask Jarvis to help him turn the corpse over onto its back, the luminosity of her skin seemed to change as the light caught a glimmer of something initially dismissed. Two tiny red dots on the woman's left wrist, ignored as midge bites, lay unexamined. Leaning forward to gaze at the marks once more, he requested Jarvis place a head torch and loupe magnifying glasses on his head.

'Jarvis, can you also get me a pair of tweezers? I see something tiny sticking out from one of the bites. Perhaps it's the proboscis of the creature that bit her.'

His eyes moved to the area to extract the tiny shard. It looked like a fragment of metal under the magnifying glass. He felt a small swelling as he pressed deeper into the wrist. Tim began cutting through the flesh until death's secret revealed itself. Jarvis took photographs as both scientists peered at the little treasure. Shona smiled and turned towards Tim as he carefully lifted a tiny speck of silver from the body. They all held their breath as Tim transferred the precious find to a sample tube. Concentrating intently on Shore's hand as he sealed the lid, Shona was euphoric and could no longer keep her inner monologue to herself.

'Got you, you little bastard!'

Elated at his find, Tim burst out into a spontaneous roar of laughter. Shoulders shaking at the unexpected response from the woman, he smirked.

'A little bastard indeed!'

There is no sunshine today in Inverness, nor thunder, lightning, or tempestuous storms. People living and working in the city pass the time of day, politely calling it dreich[8]. It's the usual weather in the northern Highlands at this time of year. Nothing out of the ordinary for the start of autumn. Except this is an extraordinary day yet no one has known until now.

The city folk brace themselves for a deluge as they glance to the sky. Grey clouds are full of gloom and despondency. Some people take comfort that they thought to wear raincoats that morning to work, whilst others wish they had listened to the weather forecast and dread the run to the car at the end of the day so as not to be soaked.

Then it begins. Tiny droplets fall on windscreens and minute beads on jackets and bags, leaving a wetness on skin and hair. Gently at first, then gushing and flooding, water teems from the sky. Raindrops tap furiously on the windows of the mortuary, dripping down the glass to form puddles on the ground outside. At this moment, as the pathologist's dream of a sensational find becomes a reality, my tears are endless. The knowledge of how I died fills me with despair. In this parallel existence, there is only hopelessness.

CHAPTER 4
Day 3 : Thursday, 25th September

Tossing and turning, Tim Shore barely slept. Each millimetre of the woman's skin played over and over in his mind all night. The anticipation of his theory being correct swirled in his stomach, making him restless and impatient for answers. His wife glanced at the illuminated alarm display on the bedside table and groaned.

'What the hell's the matter? It's not even two o'clock yet. For pity's sake, whatever it is can wait until morning. The dead may slumber forever, but I need my beauty sleep!'

Without giving Tim the chance to explain, she rolled over and emitted a loud snore. To escape the noise, and so as not to disturb her even further with his movements, he tiptoed downstairs to his office. There was only one thing on his mind: to check his work emails in case the results were complete. Despite examining his inbox several times, there were no new messages.

He slumped down in a fireside chair and wrapped himself in a blue and cream woollen blanket normally draped over the top of the chair for effect rather than for use.

His eyelids closed, and his head jolted several times before he dropped off to sleep at half past four, dozing and waking until a ping woke him, announcing a message at quarter to six.

MacPherson had kept her promise. Some of the toxicology results were returned, although there were still more tests to perform and process. Tim, often was disappointed by the assurances of other colleagues, so he'd also telephoned someone in the lab he personally knew. The pathologist's bribes of a meal, if samples were tested as quickly as possible, were not particularly tempting. However, when Shore warned him what he expected to find, his friend and other colleagues were hooked on the bait. A code red for an unusual sample or two caused quite a stir down at the laboratory in Glasgow. The need to wear hazmat suits meant the scientists were working through the night, excited to discover if the pathologist was correct in his theory.

Tiredness made the letters unclear and muddled as Tim rubbed his eyes. The brightness of the screen dazzled in the darkness. He re-read the email several times before managing to process the words. Glancing at the clock on the wall, it was a waste of time to attempt further sleep. Although he expected the news, the reality of the findings from the woman examined less than twenty-four hours before made him need to take stock of the situation. It was still early; he decided to take a shower. Droplets of water ran onto his face and trickled down his body. He grinned... a hunch paid off.

The smell of bacon cooking wafted up the stairs, waking his wife. When Tim worked on an important case, disturbed sleep was a part of the household, but a cooked breakfast on a workday was unknown. She covered herself in her white towelling robe and went downstairs. As she reached the kitchen door, she could hear her husband singing along to *The Greatest Showman* title track, and was curious to discover what had put her husband in such a good mood.

'It sounds like you're jolly. What's with the cooking on a Thursday morning?'

Without waiting for an answer, she walked to the sink and turned on the tap to swill out a glass she'd taken to bed the night before. He rushed behind her, wrapped his arms around her waist, and kissed the back of her head.

'I can't explain too much at this stage but let's just say something I've uncovered is going to make headlines around the world when the news is released. Better still, I'm about to make that miserable detective David Chisholm's day and that feels good! So, me making breakfast is to say sorry for waking you in the night, and to put more hairs on my chest!'

She swung around to find her husband with a broad grin across his face, and they both laughed at the thought of more chest hair on what she'd often teased was his *"Hairy Coo."*

When he arrived at work, full of breakfast and good cheer, Tim sat at his desk, willing the hands on the wall clock to advance to eight when it would be a civilised time to make a call. At one second past the hour, he picked up the telephone, itching to have the conversation with the dour detective. Usually, he would avoid speaking to Chisholm but, for once, he was raring to impart the news.

It rang four times before he heard the curt male voice on the other end of the line.

'Good morning, Chisholm. It's Tim Shore here. You need to meet me immediately. I am staggered by what I have found. A few of the results are already back from the lab. You might want a stiff drink after hearing what I've got to say… and I'm buying. Our body has just given up an incredible murder weapon!'

†††††

Chisholm was silent as he strode into the pathology building. Troubled at keeping up with his pace, Helen jogged to stay close as he began to climb the stairs to Shore's office. There was no explanation for the speed at which he walked, nor did he mention his discussion with Tim. From the tone Chisholm used to bellow across the office to her to follow him, she knew it was something of the utmost importance. Her boss never did anything at speed. He was cautious and steady in all cases.

'What on earth is going on, Boss? The suspense is killing me. No pun intended!'

The senior detective remained quiet. Although she knew he was not into gossip nor was a great raconteur, she'd managed, over the past couple of years, to thaw his personality somewhat and he often laughed at her jokes. He'd even been known to tease her on a couple of occasions. Despite him having a reserved, taciturn nature, this morning she found his silence more unnerving than usual.

It was only when they reached Tim Shore's office that Chisholm leaned towards her. There was a firmness in his voice as he whispered,

'This is a time to listen.'

He entered the office after the briefest of knocks, without waiting for an answer. Tim sat at his desk, ready for the interrogation he knew would follow from the man who never smiled. MacPherson sat with her back to the door, turning sharply to see the entrance of the police officers. She quietly smiled to herself at the sight of Chisholm and Daniels standing in a corner, squashed together like a tin of sardines.

Shore began by explaining he and Shona had re-examined the body because of a hypothesis Tim held about the cause of the woman's death. Helen listened, following her boss's instructions and nodding at appropriate moments. She remained silent, as did her mentor. She sensed that this was no time to joke or pull the one-liners she often offered. The two scientists spoke. Knowing something important was being explained, she took out her notebook, ready to write notes.

'I'll cut to the chase. I felt something was wrong when I carried out the first postmortem. The woman suffered multiple organ failures, highly unusual for someone in perfect health. Then there were signs of irritation on her skin from the self-inflicted scratching, which was confirmed when the results came back. She bit her nails, as was noted when you were present yesterday. What was found under the small amount of nails she had were tiny particles from her own skin and no one else's.

Something did not sit right. There were no signs she used recreational drugs, so I began to consider poisonous substances and became convinced death was caused by something toxic, but it wasn't swallowed or inhaled.

So, I re-examined her skin. Originally, I considered the two minor, red puncture marks on the left wrist to be midge bites, as they were of a similar appearance. Something in my head, call it instinct, made me examine the site thoroughly. After this second examination, a tiny fragment of metal was located and extracted from one of the wounds. It's what I'd hoped to find, piercing the skin, less than two millimetres into her flesh.

There was a case I remembered reading about at medical school. It was the stuff of spies, so stuck in my mind. In London, back in 1978, a guy who called Georgi Markov was killed. His death made headline news across the world. This woman died in a similar way. I can tell you that it's the cleverest and most bizarre murder I have ever come across!'

'Georgi Markov? Never heard of him! How can a fragment of metal kill someone?'

Chisholm glared at Helen to convey the need to remain silent. He looked at Tim, eyes widening at the realisation of what the pathologist was saying. His body stiffened; he knew the name and the implications of Shore's findings.

'The guy on Waterloo Bridge; the one shot by an umbrella tip? It was the stuff of spies!'

'Yes. I waited for the results to come back from the lab to prove there was something rather evil in that fragment of metal. Even though I hypothesised it, the truth is shocking!'

A sharp intake of breath from Helen made the two men and Shona stare at her. She giggled. It was involuntary, a sign of nervousness and embarrassment. Forgetting to remain silent, she shook her head.

'So, a woman found dead in Loch Spiorad, in the middle of nowhere in the northern Highlands, is poisoned by a bit of metal like in a *James Bond* movie. You cannae be for real!'

For once, Chisholm let the comments go without the look he usually gave Helen if she said something inappropriate. Everything sounded absurd, but he knew by Tim's expression and Shona's that the pair were deadly serious.

'In addition, the woman can be linked to the bridal dress. DNA match, luckily not lost in the water as it has only been in the loch for a few hours. Zolpidem, a kind of sleeping tablet, was also in her system, not enough to kill her but definitely enough to knock her out for a few hours.'

Gasps of disbelief echoed around the room. This was an unbelievable set of results. A tiny speckle of metal caused the woman to suffer a catastrophic death and endure total organ failure. David stared at the pathologist. The gravity of the situation made bubbles explode in his stomach as Tim summed up his findings.

'My conclusion, from the samples and the location of the splinter, is that the woman's skin was pierced by something metallic. She would have felt a tiny prick and maybe thought a midge had bitten her twice. In that second, two microscopic particles of metal were injected, containing ninety percent platinum and ten percent iridium. That's a special alloy that hardens platinum. Its uses are varied and can withstand high temperatures in the manufacture of things like pen tips and compression bearings. The poisonous substance will have crept into her veins with no way to escape.

Despite being a healthy, young woman, she suffered multi-organ failure within a few hours of being injected. She would have felt unwell; she would feel her skin was burning, hence the scratching; she would have been sick and then would have been in and out of consciousness until she died. The most remarkable death I have ever seen.'

'So let me get this straight. You are saying that she died from platinum and iridium poisoning being injected into her wrist?'

Shona MacPherson answered.

'Chisholm, the tip of the metal was laced with something deadly. The victim was poisoned with a concoction of chemicals. If it's similar to the components of A-234, it is likely to be untraceable, but the metal fragment found within her wrist lead us to this theory. We were lucky to find the fraction of one of the casings, as they often dissolve. Our thoughts are that she was most definitely targeted. She was, in fact, executed!'

Both Helen and David gasped. Tim began to laugh.

'Your expressions are priceless. Wish I had a camera!'

'Executed?'

Chisholm shook his head, incredulous at the word Shona blurted out. Her tone was emphatic, assured, and confident. Her face told him everything; the euphoric smile in locating the metal was the find of hers and Tim's careers. He needed more information to clear his head and the millions of questions racing through his mind.

'How the hell was she executed? What makes you think the woman was targeted? Could it be a random attack? '

He pondered for a few seconds, finding it hard to take everything in that he was being told. Somewhere in his mind, an alarm reverberated, bringing a sudden fear. Before Tim or Shona responded, he couldn't stop himself from blurted out his concern.

'If so, that would cause mass panic!'

'Those questions are ones you need to find answers as detectives, I'm afraid. Whoever the woman was, I think it is safe to say she was targeted. No way was this a random attack, with such a substance for a murder weapon. It was stealthy, committed, and calculated. It's imperative we find her identity, as this might unlock clues to why she was killed.'

For Helen, unaware of Georgi Markov, it felt bizarre and inconceivable. She hoped that Shore would smile and shout out, *"April Fool!"* but this was late September, and she was struggling to find a way to comprehend the news. Normally she would be firing questions at this point, but having already broken her silence, she sank her teeth into her top lip in an attempt to stay quiet. The room was stuffy and cramped. She needed air.

Her eyes focused on the silver bracelet she found herself playing with, wrapped around her wrist. She never normally wore jewellery on duty but had forgotten to remove it before work that morning. Without thinking, she blurted out an idea.

'That's how it could have been injected... a bracelet or maybe a bangle!'

Three pairs of eyes stared at her. David's mouth dropped open as Tim and Shona congratulated her on the idea. The theory fit perfectly. The mood lightened for a few moments as they concluded she might be correct in her assumption. It needed further investigation but was a highly plausible theory. When the excitement died down, Shona returned to the formalities, quickly regaining her composure.

'The procurator fiscal has been informed. Goodness knows where this will lead!'

Tension rippled through the group as Shona continued, sharing her knowledge. The after-effects of the discussion ricocheted off the walls.

'Chemical and biological weapons such as ricin are highly toxic, and until recently, many were difficult to trace. When it enters the system, it attacks human cells, preventing them from creating proteins. Eventually, without proteins produced, the cells die, and the organs fail. How quickly death occurred will be a matter of conjecture, but I believe the poison acted quickly in this woman, no more than twenty-four hours after she was injected. It is, without question, murder. We'll hopefully get more results as to the exact chemicals when toxicology is finalised.'

Tim listened intensely, then interjected.

'Whoever carried this out never planned for the body to be discovered. For this woman, the fisherman coming across her corpse was pure luck, at the right time and the right place. If she hadn't been found, she would likely have lain rotting at the bottom of the loch. Over time, with the waters polluted, the fish would die or even mutate. Who knows what happens to this stuff; it's a lethal and highly dangerous cocktail of chemicals. However, the good news is that she was found within hours of being placed in her watery grave, so there will be no effects on Loch Spiorad's creatures.

These are our conclusions to date, barring more results we're awaiting. Anyone in close contact with the corpse will need blood tests in case of contamination. And, of course, I'll need to inform the powers that be, which will set off a chain of events, and there will be officials poking around from goodness knows where.'

Silence fell as all four adults contemplated the information shared. For the scientists, this was a defining moment in their careers, a case of significance to talk about on the circuit of luncheon and dinner speeches when they retired.

David stared at the grey linoleum beneath his shoes. He was lost for words. The more he tried to digest the information, the more it whirled around in his head. Searching for a deadly bracelet would be like looking for a needle in a haystack. Where should they start? He was a detective people looked to when there was a storm, a steady, calm hand at the helm. For once he had no answers. His mind was blank except for the fact it was inevitable he needed to return to Sutherland, something he dreaded more than being in the mortuary.

†††††

In Inverness, a chilliness creeps into the bones of everyone who feels autumn's presence. They all agree that fires need to be lit or central heating put on for the first time since spring, as the city is cold and dank. People are comforted in the thought that the heat this evening will keep them warm. I no longer feel or need heat, but I seek light wherever I can. It is the only way I can find hope. I want to scream, but no one can hear me. I sense the wolves are roaming the hills of Sutherland once more. No one can truly be safe from them if they want something so badly. They hunt until satisfied they have their prey. Caught when least expecting in a trap, they will snare whoever gets in their way to ensure they remain unexposed.

CHAPTER 5
Day 4 : Friday, 26th September

Chisholm sat at his desk. His memories of 1978 were limited; it was the year he started primary school. When he searched the period online, he found it was the time of John Travolta and Olivia Newton-John in *Grease*. He also discovered the oil tanker *Amoco Cadiz* ran aground, the world's first test tube baby was born, and bizarrely, the end of the original production of the iconic Volkswagen Beetle.

He smiled. Of the few photographs he possessed from when he was small, there were only fleeting recollections of being so young. Occasionally he imagined a red Beetle car and a blonde-haired woman wearing sunglasses, smiling as she drove along. Often, however, he was inclined to wonder if the memories were false, as there were many days when he struggled to visualise anything of his early childhood. At five years old at the time of Georgi Markov's death, David knew nothing of the wider world. There was, however, a stark realisation for him that year. When he started school, he found out from various "*News time*" sessions within the class, he was the only child without a father. When he remembered that part of his history, the smile disappeared.

Markov was a Bulgarian chemical engineer and teacher in his earlier life. Becoming more and more repulsed by the ruling regime of his homeland, he began to question and criticise their actions through his writing. He fled to Italy nine years before his death, hoping one day to return to his native country. In 1971, having his passport extension refused, he decided to stay in the West, relocating to London and gained political asylum. Working for the BBC World Service, he found the freedom to continue to highlight the truths behind the government in Bulgaria.

On a seemingly normal morning, whilst waiting at a bus stop on Waterloo Bridge, Markov's hand flew to his right thigh as a fleeting pain shot through it. Glancing behind, he saw a man lower an umbrella, hiding his face so that Georgi could not see him. The brolly and the gentleman disappeared into a taxi within seconds, forever lost. Markov continued to the office and told a colleague about the incident. The journalist feared he had been poisoned. Within hours, the small, raised mark, caused by whatever was injected into him, led to a fever and a hospital admission. Four days later, Markov died at the age of forty-nine.

No trace of ricin or metal pellets was found in his leg, but a tissue sample taken from the site of his injury confirmed a minute nugget of platinum and iridium. Scientists from Porton Down examining the sample discovered two microscopic cavities drilled into the pellet. A sugar-like substance, coated over the holes, acted as bungs to suspend the ricin. Once inside the journalist, his body temperature acted as a catalyst for the fusion of the substance, turning it from a solid to a liquid. As it flowed into his bloodstream, the poison within the pellet seeped into every vein, every nerve, and every cell to silence him forever. From Tim Shore's recent explanation, the woman in Loch Spiorad experienced a similar occurrence, proved by the entry marks left on her wrist.

Conspiracy theories abounded. Headline after headline sensationalised Georgi Markov's death: *"Killed by an Umbrella," "The Bridge of Spies," "Tip of Death."* Suspicions of who carried out the assassination centred on the KGB, which was linked to the regime and the Bulgarian Secret Service. His death remained unsolved, shrouded in mystery for decades.

David recalled the case mentioned at a Prevent anti-terrorism conference in Edinburgh a few years before. It fascinated him, and the finer details were filed in his brain. It was well documented there were rises in hate crimes that targeted specific groups within communities. Since the poisonings in Salisbury[9] and Amesbury in 2018, every police officer needed to remain vigilant no matter where they worked. Terrorism, spies, and assassinations were usually incidents occurring in busy cities like London. Ricin attacks were relatively rare across the world, but David knew that making assumptions because of remote locations was idiotic. Perhaps the woman was a foreign national, hunted for being opposed to a distant regime.

As he scanned the information available, similarities surfaced between the modus operandi of the two deaths.

Could Tim Shore be wrong? There might be a first time for everything. No one put out contract killings on lassies this far north. Then he remembered tales from some of the older police officers when he first started in the force. Stories of them being involved in Operation Klondyke to catch criminals in the Wester Ross area who were smuggling vast amounts of cocaine into the country. Anything was possible if Ullapool had once been a den of iniquity!

Archived news from the date of the murder and later reports filled his screen. The more he read, the more he felt he was venturing down the wrong rabbit hole. Questions jumped out at him, his brain running amok as he considered what to do next. Why this woman? Was she the real target of the chemicals, or had she just been in the wrong place, at the wrong time? Was there any chance of catching a killer?

Those responsible for Markov's death were never caught, nor were they ever likely to be. Almost certainly by orders from the highest levels of government in Bulgaria or possibly from their U.S.S.R. associates, the dissident was assassinated. Justice had never been served.

An email alert pinged. The lab results had arrived in his inbox. He stared at the screen. They made sober reading. After studying the final lines of the report, the detective leaned back in his chair and closed his eyes. As if to soothe himself, his fingertips traced repeated circles from his hairline to his eyebrows and back again. Sighing heavily, he took a few more minutes to digest the words.

Images of Markov remained in his head. Spies, Russia, Bulgaria. It was all too far-fetched for a death in a remote loch in Sutherland. The words in the report shocked him. The effects of chemical poisoning didn't make easy reading but couldn't be unwritten. Shore was correct; David had never really doubted him. The woman had definitely been murdered.

Chisholm did not want to admit defeat before even beginning the investigation. Science had moved on in those intervening years since Markov's death. Policing also changed, along with far more links to international databases on terrorism and assassinations. Being killed in this manner sounded implausible for a beautiful green-eyed woman found in Loch Spiorad, but it was now a fact. Frustrated at the slowness of his brain, and his inability to process all the information, his voice broke the silence in the empty room.

'Who the hell can get their hands on chemicals like this? And why that damn loch of all places?'

His stomach tensed. The return to Sutherland was something he could no longer avoid.

✝✝✝✝✝

The detective's next task would be to inform the chief inspector, something he dreaded. Whilst there was no objection to following rules and enjoying the boundaries that they brought, his boss devoured them and spat them out to her officers at every possible opportunity. A career police officer, swiftly rising through the ranks, she forgot what it was like to visit a bloody murder scene, to witness a junkie dead from their vomit in an alleyway, or to see relatives of the dead engulfed in grief. All Alison McLeod wanted was improved crime figures, a fast detection rate, and making sure no warring drug peddlers crossed her county lines.

Chisholm recalled no personal conversation with his superior. Even he knew that it was good for morale to go for a drink occasionally. Although David wasn't particularly keen on the habit of alcohol to celebrate the successful conclusion to a case, he indulged more for team spirit than anything he drank.

McLeod mixed in very different circles. She dined with influential people in trendy restaurants, willingly choosing from the extortionately expensive menus in her quest to rise to the top echelons of the police force. She never socialised with *"the plebs"* beneath her rank out of hours. When she attended police conferences, she became the life and soul of any group with whom she socialised, but never displayed this trait at work. David knew nothing about her. It was her loss of vision, for what it was really like to be a police officer, that he despised.

Her sleek, dark brown bob always remained immaculate. Nothing betrayed her nor gave any information about her background, cards that she held close to her chest. Her nails were beautifully manicured, and her makeup was as perfect. She certainly did not look her age, which worked in her favour. Her forty-two-year-old eyes were set on a move to the Central Belt or even further afield, and nothing would halt progression towards the end goal she held of becoming the Chief Constable. Her eagerness to gain promotion was unchallenged.

David began to press the familiar keys of the telephone, dreading the voice that would answer. On the third ring, he heard her Perthshire accent, the only thing she could not entirely mask.

After making him the senior investigating officer on the case, she had sent him to Loch Spiorad expecting an accidental death. Murder was unheard of in the area. On the rare occasion that police needed to investigate a death in those parts, it was always a suicide or a car crash.

'You say a white female, late twenties, early thirties? Any other description?'

'Yes, Ma'am. Long, flowing auburn hair and green eyes. Slim build. The reason I'm informing you is because the pathologist has been very specific about the cause of death.'

'And?'

David heard McLeod's breathing change as he gave his initial briefing to her. A gasp, then followed by deeper inhalations as he gave an outline of what Tim Shore suspected and toxicology reports confirmed. There were no interruptions or questions. As he shared all that he knew, he considered whether the sound of her breathing was anxiety. Then he realised. It could be excitement at the prospect of a case of such magnitude. This could be her break into the speaking circuit. She listened. The sound of her breathing lessened as she regained her composure. When Chisholm completed his briefing, she spoke.

'The protocol for incidents of this kind will commence immediately. Such a murder triggers national security even if the body was located in such a remote location. A meeting at the highest levels will be called to brief appropriate advisors. I propose a police presence in Loch Dubhglas until initial facts are established by the Northern Constabulary. The situation will be monitored. Keep me abreast of any information. I want any autopsy and test results copied to me.'

He sensed further tension in her voice as she stated the gravity of the situation.

'Set up an inquiry team to find out what you can in the area, with the aim being to establish the identity of the victim. The modus operandi should not be shared with the public, nor the fact that the woman has been murdered at this point in the investigation. Use the *"unexplained death"* routine, even with other officers, until such time I give you the nod to release more facts. Naturally, personnel involved in recovering the body will need testing for potential poisoning, but try to contain conjecture to a minimum. I'll contact the appropriate team leaders.

Search for the suggested murder weapon, although this might be a needle in a haystack. It's unlikely that a murder of this kind was carried out by a local unless they have connections abroad. You will remain the SIO on the ground until higher officials take over the case.'

Her curt voice irritated him more than normal. Throwing caution to the wind, he snapped.

'*Higher officials...* What is meant by that?'

'If it is deemed a matter for national security, then it may be the National Crime Agency or even MI5 officers who take over the investigation. For cases like this, there is close cooperation between the police and N.C.A. You will be notified when you are relieved from your role. I'm sure you understand, Chisholm, that deaths of this kind are beyond the realms of normal police officers like you.'

The words sounded harsh to a man with so many experiences of investigating serious crimes. No cases were easy especially when someone had been killed. His curriculum vitae held a long list of enquiries into murder, embezzlement, drugs, and even terrorism. The Highlands were no longer the idyllic place everyone imagined.

He found the chief inspector patronising, yet she loved every scrap of praise in the press when Chisholm solved a crime. She enjoyed the news interviews on verdict days when justice was served to one criminal or another from David's caseload. Most of all, her figures would look good in her reports to politicians.

He didn't bother to comment on her words. It was futile, and for once, having heard that chemicals were involved as the murder weapon, he knew there would be interest from much further afield than Inverness.

'Brief me twice daily. Proceed with caution.'

Chisholm finished the call as quickly as he could. He mulled over the conversation and McLeod's instructions. He was particularly perturbed by her warning of *"higher officials."* No mention of *"if."* The phrase used was *"when,"* meaning there was limited time until the case was taken from him.

The conversation with the chief was enlightening for several reasons. A heavy-handed explosion of N.C.A. or MI5 into the small village of Loch Dubhglas would panic the inhabitants. Police rarely had a presence in the area. Usually, an officer might visit to investigate the theft from oil tanks or to check gun licenses. Every year there were many visitors to the area at the height of the holiday season, but the busy period was almost over, and lots of strangers would be suspicious, triggering unwanted attention and social media posts.

He slumped back in his chair. At least Helen would be working with him. She already knew of the chemical aspect to the case. She was a light-hearted detective but discreet when needed. He must solve this murder before it was taken out of his hands. Time was ticking. To find the woman's identity was crucial; where and why she died would unfold.

He began to consider a few days up north. The panic experienced when he'd first heard the name Loch Spiorad was strangely lessening. What had persisted was a knotted feeling in his stomach. Whilst coming to terms with the initial shock of revisiting the past, a deep pain remained. Like a knife cutting into his flesh, he felt exposed by the agony of its sharp blade. A sudden drop in the room's temperature made him shiver. It was time to confront his demons at long last.

†††††

Returning home to his flat, he folded and carefully packed a few clothes and a wash kit into a small case after booking himself into a Bed & Breakfast a few hundred yards from the incident room. It would mean he would avoid the hundred-mile round trip each day to Loch Dubhglas. If he was to find information in the area and identify the woman, he needed to be in the vicinity. He also acknowledged, begrudgingly, that he was not averse to spending time in Loch Dubhglas after all these years.

Other officers with families needed to return home each evening as they had lives outside of work, he conceded. He remembered a normal life, full of decorating the house he and his wife, Jane, shared, going on holidays abroad, and going to concerts in Inverness, Aberdeen, and Glasgow. A shared love of Andrea Bocelli led to adventures across the length and breadth of the United Kingdom and Europe to see him perform. For some reason, David still liked to listen to Bocelli's music whilst he drove. It brought him comfort, especially in times of stress, such as now.

Initial differences between him and Jane were ignored and washed over in the early years of their relationship. As tides turned, their habits grated on each other's nerves until the soft, sandy beach where they walked as lovers became stony and harsh.

He was immaculate and tidy; she was a hoarder. Long work hours finally drove the couple apart; he with his policing and she as a nurse. For years they joked about being *"ships in the night,"* but Jane sailed into someone else's arms, leaving David to rot away in a dry dock.

After being a divorcee for the past three years, Chisholm treated his clothes, like all other aspects of his life, in neat, orderly piles. Ironed shirts hung, categorised by colour, and suits in varying shades of grey, together with two black suits for funerals and court appearances.

Pants arranged in the top drawer of his Ikea dresser. Black socks, always paired, lay in the second. If the truth were known, he preferred not to argue over a plate left unwashed or magazines and books strewn on the living room floor.

Grabbing more items from both drawers, the detective placed them into the case: several tops, a couple of jumpers, one pair of jeans, three more shirts and another suit in a garment bag. A second pair of black brogues in a canvas bag and a small pouch containing shoe polish and a shoe brush. Wheeling the suitcase out to the car, he carefully positioned it in boot, before reaching inside the rear passenger door to locate the hook for hanging his suit bag. Now prepared for a few days away up north, he double-checked that all windows were locked and set the intruder alarm. His final routine was to shut the apartment front door, triple-checking everything was secured before getting into his car.

Over the Kessock Bridge, up the A9 towards Sutherland, Andrea Bocelli drowned out the noise of other vehicles on the road. Chisholm, as with many other aspects of his life, maintained certain routines and rituals as he drove: checking his mirrors every few seconds, keeping the distance between his car and any vehicles ahead, maintaining the speed to gain optimum efficiency from his engine and fuel, the volume no louder than fifteen, and signalling at a certain point when he was a quarter of a mile from the junction.

Everything was precise and ordered in David's life apart from jarring anomalies that now taxed his brain at all times: the unsolved murders of two victims and their assailants, ten years apart. He hated unanswered puzzles. Tormented by these deaths, nightmares always returned when new murder cases emerged. Being a perfectionist meant an intense dislike for untidy endings. Guilt and failure bore heavily on him.

Exactly a quarter of a mile from the junction for the shortcut towards Loch Dubhglas, he began to signal to turn left off the A9 and onto the final part of his journey. The road, full of sharp bends, dipped down to cross several bridges over burns before rising higher and higher until it reached a viewpoint.

David pulled into a lay-by, planning to take in the vista for a couple of seconds. Instead, he put on the handbrake, turned off the engine, and got out of the car. The golden hour was rapidly approaching. In this light, he could see the distant summit of Ben Meagaidh if he squinted. A couple of villages on the shores of the Kyle of Sutherland were nearer, some of the rooftops glistening in the late sunshine. The water, a few hundred feet below, was calm. Breathing the pure air into his lungs and soul for a few seconds, he took in the beauty of the view.

As he drove off, he descended the hill. Navigating several sharper bends, the car began to dip down further to a road junction. A familiar, beautifully preserved AA box at the bottom of the hill stood at a small pull-in, signalling the turn. Indicating left, he now followed the shoreline of the Kyle, catching glimpses of the sunset, twinkling as beams of light on the water a few feet away.

He skirted past three more villages before the road began to rise again for a few miles. Five or six plumes of smoke from chimney pots poked holes into the fading light in Loch Dubhglas. Chisholm felt a coolness now as he approached the village. Thankfully, a padded jacket lay on the back seat. He remembered how autumn felt here and how he hated this place.

†††††

He was shown into the bedroom where he would be sleeping for the next couple of nights by the owner of the Bed & Breakfast. David didn't listen to the man as he attempted to engage the detective in conversation. He was not the slightest bit interested to know about the owner moving to Loch Dubhglas a few weeks before or the story surrounding how he ended up there by chance. The new guest was not one for polite talk by the short answers given on his arrival.

'You are lucky to have a room. A couple of folks from down south booked into the other two rooms this afternoon. Breakfast is served from seven to nine. Would you like a full Scottish?'

Chisholm nodded.

'Yes, please, at seven.'

'Not a problem. You'll be up early on holiday to get out and about then?'

'Thanks. That will be all.'

David ushered the man out of the room as soon as he could. He was not keen to share his business, and besides, with his nature and training, he would never trust anyone or give anything away. The owner abandoned the conversation and any attempt to extract information from the rather abrupt new guest.

The only other vehicle in the village car park apart from his BMW was an old green Land Rover. The village was quiet. He collected his bag from his boot and knew he would probably have to brave his host before he got any peace. No one was about as he gingerly stepped into the hallway and crept upstairs, ready for an attack from *"Mr. Friendly"* at any time.

After arranging all his belongings, the detective decided to go for a walk to clear his head. Donning his jacket, he left the Bed & Breakfast without any encounter and headed down the high street to the edge of the loch, which ran the length of the village. Feeling in his pocket for his wallet, he made a deliberate choice to turn right at the bottom of the road and strode to a place he hoped still existed and was still frying. The KitKat bought at Moira's several days before lay in his pocket, unopened but rather flattened and unappealing. As he neared his destination, he began to feel more optimistic about his mission. The smell of fish and chips wafted from the fryer and hung in the air as he reached the chippy.

'You're just in time! We close in five minutes. What will it be?'

'A fish supper, please, with salt and vinegar.'

Once his meal was ready, David spotted a picnic table and benches a few yards from the takeaway, and, ignoring the coolness of the air, he settled down to his meal, feeling like a king. For once, he felt ravenous, devouring each morsel of the delicious haddock flakes.

He could not help but think of the fish Granda caught in the loch in front of him and the meals they shared. Now he'd returned to Loch Dubhglas, it was inevitable the memories would fill his mind. He could no longer avoid them, but tomorrow he would concentrate on the body found in Loch Spiorad.

Back in his room, he was surprised at the comfort he found in sleeping in Sutherland once more. Drifting off to sleep he thought of the laughter, warm summers, and a blissful childhood. For once, his dreams were peaceful.

He sees a shiny, silver salmon leaping upstream, crashing onto the rocks, as it fights its way against the gushing river. Spray from a waterfall catches the light from the golden sunset. Multiple rainbows, created in the water droplets, fall a few feet into a pool below. The creature's scales glimmer and glisten. Magnificent and strong, no one can harm it, he hopes. The salmon gleams, light capturing its essence. Without warning, it metamorphoses into a mermaid with long red hair.

Shaking his head, he gasps at the sight, never having seen before something so magical or wondrous. She balances on a large rock in front of him, with only her fin dangling in the water. She is perfect, with translucent skin, pale and flawless, from her waist upwards. Her small, exquisite breasts are covered by locks of auburn hair that tumble down from her beautiful face to touch the top of her pearlescent scales. Her peridot eyes transfix him as she looks around, comfortable in her environment.

Suddenly she sees him, but she does not flinch nor jump into the water. Instead, she beckons him to approach, enticing him with a smile from her delicate pink lips. He wants to walk towards her, careless of any consequences of entering her world. He makes a move but then stops. In the woods nearby, a snapped twig alerts him that he is not alone. He turns and chooses to take cover behind a huge oak.

A wolf comes into view, surveying the site, its jaws dripping with blood from a kill it has made. Particles of flesh from its latest victim are caught in the gaps between his gums and incisors. He anticipates another feast.

The mermaid! What will happen to the mermaid? Will this creature kill her? He calls to her to escape into the water, but as he stares at the rock on which she sits, it is no longer occupied by his enchantress. He looks to the water, needing to catch a glimpse of her, to know she is safe. Scanning the pool and the waterfall, at first he sees nothing.

Suddenly, a salmon rises from the water, twisting in the air. He holds his breath. Will she make the jump upstream? So many fail as they attempt their journeys, crashing onto the rocks, trying and trying, smashing their bodies for one last effort to return to the place they were hatched. But she is special. He witnesses her strength as she masters a leap towards her life's purpose. She lands with a magnificent splash on the top of the waterfall, away from the drop.

There is joy in seeing her amongst rippling shimmers, alive and vibrant. In an instant, she slips away towards a quieter part of the river. He turns to the wolf, ready to face it, but it too has vanished.

Mine was a pure soul as a mortal; no evil act occurred by my hands. I have discovered something extraordinary since being trapped in this in-between space that is neither heaven nor hell. At my judgement day, as humans call it, when I died, I gained privileges that some do not earn in their earthly skins. My discovery is that I have the ability to touch humans, no longer by soft, gentle hands but by creating a whiff of a breeze or by warming a brow with the sun's rays. I can make stars twinkle and change people's moods with my magical dancing aurora. If human destiny was afforded to me, I would take revenge on those who did me harm, but I hold no power over life or death.

Water is my dominion this evening as I reach into his dreams and speak with him. He turns over and snores into his pillow, but he has seen me and felt my presence.

CHAPTER 6
Day 5 : Saturday, 27th September

The next morning, as he descended the stairs from his bedroom, he overheard voices spilling from the breakfast area. The two other guests stopped talking as he entered: a woman and a man, both in their forties. Forcing himself to sit at the only other table available a few metres away, he immediately picked up the menu card to avoid their gaze. He was aware their eyes followed him to his seat, and, by the stupid grins on their faces, they hoped to exchange pleasantries with the other guest. Instead, he scowled and ignored them, pretending not to notice. With the menu read several times, he grabbed a newspaper from a rack on the wall next to him, and disregarded the pair, praying they would leave him in peace to read.

He assumed they were a couple, but when they ordered their breakfasts separately, he noticed no affection between them or banter like he and Jane used to share. Not being a good judge of relationships, he was almost certainly wrong. They were probably a married couple of twenty years or more. They resembled the epitome of boredom, with nothing remarkable about either of them. Both had short, mousey hair with no strong facial features. Their clothes suited them well, as they too were mousey brown, blending into the décor of the featureless beige room in which they sat.

If I close my eyes, they might disappear without a trace into the wallpaper and furniture.

Unfortunately for David, the man wasn't put off by the detective's grim face. He leaned over and, with the poshest of English accents, began his questions, like a wasp irritating his victim before an attack.

'Are you up on holiday?'

None of your...!

'Business.'

'What line are you in?'

Go away, you annoying little man!

David flicked the paper over to another page, ignoring the wasp.

'Do you fish? I hear the salmon are fabulous up here.'

'No.'

'Have you come far?'

For the love of God!

'Inverness.'

Without waiting to see if David would ask why he and his companion were staying there, the wasp offered his own explanation. David barely listened.

'We're on holiday, colleagues, both professors from London. The geology in the region is outstanding! Have you ever been to Knockan Crag?'

He turned to his companion and gushed at the delights of the geopark, a geologist's heaven.

'I can't wait for you to see the evidence of the Moine Thrust[10] for yourself.'

The one-sided conversation was halted whilst the Bed & Breakfast owner asked David which hot drink he would prefer. The man shuffled back into his kitchen.

No headlines caught his attention. His mind was still full of a weird dream that he was desperate to recall. Flashes of images surfaced, but there were no explanations for anything he remembered. Nothing made sense. Eating so late must have affected his imagination.

Flicking through the paper, he spotted a photograph of the recent charity ball. Thankfully, he wasn't in the image, but some of the local dignitaries were there, smiling and posing with those who all made significant donations.

Good cause, but more money than sense! When I retire, there'll be none of this nonsense.

The female wasp attacked without warning.

'I say, the weather's holding up well, isn't it?'

Will they ever get the bloody message?

'It's glorious for the end of September. Do you know the area well?'

Lowering his newspaper, even he could not ignore the pesky beasties now. Chisholm nodded. A female wasp was about to launch into more small talk when breakfast arrived. It silenced the woman as she stared at her plate and that of her colleague.

When he caught sight of his food being brought to his table, David's mouth watered even though the sausage looked overcooked and the toast was burnt. It certainly wasn't up to Moira's standards, but there was something about Loch Dubhglas that made him feel hungry. He considered if he was seeking comfort through feeding his stomach. All he had done since arriving last night was eat. Places he dreaded visiting, places that invoked memories, seemed less frightening after he devoured a Lorne sausage, two rashers of smoky bacon, two fresh eggs, mushrooms, baked beans, and a potato scone. The pièce de résistance was a large helping of Cockburn's haggis, a prize winner from Dingwall, which was delicious and luckily not burnt. He contemplated asking Moira if she could serve this in her café.

With the two professors occupied with their own breakfasts, David mulled over the woman's death as he ate. He concluded the chief was correct in one aspect of the case. No one surely in the village or surrounding area would have access to chemicals or be capable of carrying out such an attack. The locals were honest, hard-working folk with no military capability. Crofters did the odd dodgy deal over a sheep, but they were not assassins.

When he stood up to leave, the couple was engrossed in conversation, so he sidled off unnoticed, relieved to be away from his inquisitors. He decided to take a stroll before heading to the incident room. A walk would ease his waistline and give him headspace to prepare for the day ahead.

††††††

David had forgotten the beauty of the village on a day like this. A chill lingered in the late September air, but there were no frosts yet. Summer was disappearing quickly, leaving Autumn to display her multicoloured coat. He walked along the high street a short distance from the Bed & Breakfast. When he was a bairn, thriving shops festooned both sides of the road.

Now the old bank building lay empty, a cobbler's premises was converted to a holiday home, and the grocery shop sold its last loaf years before. The shabby awning that once proudly advertised Macdonald & Son lay ragged over the faded front door. Businesses were long gone.

He continued down the road, passing what once had been the butchers. His memories were sharp. Back in time, sparkling white tiled walls contrasted starkly with red and pink pieces of meat on display, and various carcasses, such as rabbits, hung in the window. Now, instead of links of sausage, pork chops, and venison, stood a bronzed metal statue of a stag. It gazed indignantly back at voyeurs, amongst a collection of brightly coloured bric-a-brac associated with holiday gifts. Postcards with snowy mountain views, together with an array of tartan scarves, revolved on racks outside.

Down at the end of the road, an ironmonger remained. Established before David was born, it survived against competition from DIY stores over fifty miles away. Seemingly it wasn't changed. A roll of anaglypta wallpaper in the window display could well have dated back to the last time he passed the shop three decades before, given the look of the faded pattern and colour. A feeling that the best years of Loch Dubhglas were gone overwhelmed him. Like one of Jane's houseplants, he'd neglected to water since she left, the village had shrivelled and died long ago.

At the bottom of the high street was a junction. Left took travellers south or west, and right took them north or east. Instead of following either, David turned around and strolled back along the road, crossing over to look in the tweed shop window. Woollen threads of every imaginable colour were displayed in scarves, handbags, waistcoats, ties, and jackets. The woven materials reminded him of his grandfather, who wore tweed breeches when helping with shooting parties on the local estate. He turned away from the shop display and headed towards the car park outside the village hall.

Casting an eye towards the Victorian school building opposite, he remembered Loch Dubhglas Primary School. The sight of the old building brought back memories of being a pupil and his mother's illness. It resulted in him being enrolled at the school for two years, whilst his grandparents took over his care. Apart from a new sign and a few modern bits of play equipment on the playground in front of the building, nothing had changed. The old school bell had not been rung for decades. It remained intact in a tiny tower, high above the roof of the main block, somehow surviving the annual storms that battered Loch Dubhglas.

His heart was heavy with family memories as he entered the village hall. The ceilidhs that his grandmother loved, how she adored the dancing. The fiddlers on the old wooden stage tapped their feet to the jigs and the reels as their elbows proudly glided across the strings of the violins, backwards and forwards in a frantic rhythm. His grandfather dressed in his finest kilt, anxiously messing with his collar and tie but wanting to please his wife by attending.

A young lad named Davey watched all the men adjust their attire in the same way until the drink was flowing and no one cared. Everyone joined in. There were always sore feet the next morning but hearts full to the brim with happiness. The hint of a smile crossed his lips as he remembered.

The same pine panelling covered the walls. The smell of furniture polish still lingered in the air. Normally, the place was used for badminton or parent and toddler sessions, but today it was empty apart from a small team of uniformed and plain-clothed officers who were congregating. Incident and interview rooms were set up in the building. The smile vanished. He was there with a job to do.

At his request, Helen had organised the use of the hall for a couple of weeks whilst enquiries into the identification of the woman took place. The investigation would eventually move back to Inverness, but for now, David and the team would focus on the area around Loch Spiorad and try to establish the victim's identity.

Loch Dubhglas was the largest settlement in the area, and it made sense to work from there. A plan of action was relayed to the gathered group of officers. Acting as SIO, David would record all aspects of the inquiry as usual and any decisions made about how the investigation would proceed.

It was the standard practice for an incident of this magnitude. However, as the team was short-staffed because of annual holidays and given the remoteness of the location, David would do some investigating himself and would remain in the vicinity of Loch Dubhglas for a few days to direct the detective work. He emphasised, as instructed, that conclusions were yet to be drawn about the woman's death, but murder remained a possibility.

The first line of inquiry would be to identify the lady in the loch and to inform her relatives. From there, other leads would emerge as to why she was in the area. Was she a local or on holiday, and with whom was she in contact? David showed no hint of emotion as he outlined the task ahead and what he hoped to achieve while there was an incident room.

He said nothing about growing up in the area; no one needed to know that information. It served little purpose and detracted from the task at hand. In a few days, the investigations would move back to Inverness, and he, for one, would be cheering.

†††††

Posters were hastily being printed to place in the small handful of shops that remained in Loch Dubhglas and on lamp posts spread across the village. Door-to-door enquiries would begin to gain any information the villagers might know about the woman. The key to solving this murder would be to find out who she was. Although the death was kept as low-key, local press officials were champing at the bit to get interviews, and Scotland Tonight sent up a film crew.

The priority was to give a first briefing to the team that assembled from both Inverness and the nearest police station in Tain.

A steady stream of locals and visitors came throughout the morning. None offered much information of consequence. Most were purely nosy. The tourists saw it as another local attraction. Even the geologists paid a visit, clearly out of their depth with death. After all, they specialised in solid matter within rocks and the living organisms, like lichen, that grew on them. No one stayed longer than a few minutes to stare at so much activity in one place, bemused at the occurrence. None recognised a description of a young woman with auburn hair and green eyes. One visitor summed up what others wanted to say.

'She cannae be local. Everyone knows everyone here. You cannae fart without someone knowing in the village.'

Others tried to over-help.

'It might be a lassie staying in one of the holiday cottages, over Ullapool way.'

When asked for more details, they shrugged their shoulders. No one was specific, but the police officers dutifully noted down everything, in case it brought a lead.

†††††

The camera crew arrived and started to set up for the interview. Chisholm hated this aspect of his job and tried to avoid it whenever he could. The chief inspector enjoyed being on camera, and David often played to this fact, suggesting she should appeal for information as she was good at capturing interest.

On this occasion, the chief was busy on another couple of cases and could not be persuaded to drive a round trip of over a hundred miles for an interview that would last a few minutes. He could see her point but still would have appreciated her appearance on television rather than his. Checking his tie for a second time before leaving the toilet, he had a moment or two to stare at the haggard face looking back at him. Brushing off a speck of dust from the left shoulder of his jacket, he walked towards the door. With one last inspection of his flies, he was ready for the interrogation and questions.

The television crew resembled a comedy duo. A man, balancing a video camera in one hand and a sound boom around a metre long in the other, stood testing his equipment. Clutching a small, compact mirror, a female reporter hurriedly applied red lipstick. They wanted the backdrop for the interview to be in front of Loch Dubhglas, at the bottom of the high street, a spot where David had stood the evening before in his quest for his fish and chips.

His pace slowed as he reached the spot, ready for the interview to begin. He acknowledged his arrival with a nod and stood ready for them to begin recording.

'Rory, am I okay in this position? There aren't shadows on my face, are there?'

The cameraman, intently peering into his viewfinder, sound boom at the ready, told her she was fine to begin and that he was ready to record. The reporter's face instantly changed and she went into her serious interview mode.

'So, Detective Inspector Chisholm, could you give us some information about the incident at Loch Spiorad?'

David cleared his throat before launching into his speech, churning out only the details that he could share.

'I can confirm that the body of a young woman in her mid-twenties to early thirties was found on Tuesday morning in Loch Spiorad. As yet, she remains unidentified. She had long auburn hair and green eyes with no other distinguishing features.'

'Can you tell us the cause of death?'

'Tests will establish how the lady died. Initially we are appealing for anyone who might recognise this lady to come forward so we can identify her.'

'Do you have any leads yet as to how and why she was found in such a remote place?'

'As soon as we establish the identity of this lady, this will help us to find what happened to her. It is too early to speculate on her death until we know who she is and how she came to be in the area. Our enquiries are ongoing, and we appeal to anyone with information, no matter how small, to contact us at the incident room set up in Loch Dubhglas Village Hall or by telephoning the number that you see on the screen.'

The journalist leaned forward and smiled at the camera, thanking the detective and finishing the recording. The cameraman began to pack away the video camera and sound boom, ready to move on to the next location at Loch Spiorad. She was hungry for more information.

'Off the record, it's odd, a body turning up here, right?'

Chisholm had spoken to the reporter before. He was giving no clues or secrets to her. He was too long in the job to make rookie mistakes like talking to the press, except when it was beneficial for a case. It was the same question whirling around in his mind since seeing the body in the incident tent several days before.

'We hope to know more soon.'

The detective strolled away, pondering his lies. Loch Spiorad was the sort of place to lose a body forever. The killer did not count on Jimmy Mackay discovering the woman so soon. From the results back from the lab and Tim Shore's observations, the body had only been in the water for a few hours. Such an elaborate and deliberate execution, but foiled by a pensioner! Perhaps that indicated the woman had been dumped in a hurry.

As he retraced his steps towards the hall, his eyes could no longer avoid looking towards the church, rising steeply away from the lochside, a short distance from where David stood being interviewed a few minutes before.

On a promontory, overlooking the whole village, the building held many memories of the welcoming of newborns and the farewells to both young and older inhabitants of Loch Dubhglas. In the churchyard, David knew he would find the family grave where his father, grandfather, and grandmother lay buried. He bit deep into his lip as he visualised his mother lying in a lonely grave in Inverness. One of her last requests before she died was that she did not return to the village of her birth. A hard decision for her, but one she made to ensure

David did not feel obliged to visit her resting place in a village that brought so much pain to her and her son. The location of her grave would not matter once she was dead, she concluded.

His mother never envisaged that the boy might become a detective and that an unexplained death would bring his return to a place he'd avoided for thirty years.

The wish to visit the grave took a different course than the one he had expected. For too long, he held no desire to go anywhere near, but now, as if pulled by a magnetic force towards the centre of the solar system, he knew it was inevitable that he would step into the graveyard during his stay in the village. First, there was a murder inquiry to continue until the case was taken out of his hands. Time was still ticking.

†††††

Back inside the incident room, villagers continued to drop in to do their public duty, even though they knew nothing. Few people brought any useful information, but the motions of taking statements were gone through.

An elderly couple entered the room expecting the tables and chairs to be laid out for a pensioner's lunch, which was normally held once per week. News that police were commandeering the village hall had not reached the pair who stood in shock at the doorway.

Chisholm watched the couple. Their bemused faces, incredulous at the sight of police and no roast lunch, took a toll on both. Feeling lightheaded, the old man grabbed at the nearest chair to stop himself from tumbling onto the wooden floor. Frantic for her inhaler, the lady felt her pockets for the lost object. Panic-stricken, she couldn't find it and also held the back of a chair, attempting to maintain her balance.

In a hall full of people, the couple were invisible to everyone else. Chisholm moved quickly across the room. With assistance from the detective, they both sat down. The tightening of the woman's chest eased a little when the missing puffer was located in an inner pocket of her jacket. Both pensioners settled, apologetic to be causing a fuss.

Suddenly, he spotted a familiar face enter the hall. The detective wondered what the visitor, the man who had called his family a *"tragedy,"* wanted.

For now, his mind returned to the conversation with the pensioners. The old lady's breathing took time to recover. Slowly, deep, steadier breathing replaced the frantic gasps. He did not expect they would have any information but he began going through the motions of scribbling some notes about a potential sighting of a lady fitting the description.

'We only came in for the lunch, but I'm sure I saw a wifey fitting the description out Dubhness way. My husband's cousin is a crofter up there. A few weeks back in the summer, we went to collect some hens he was selling.

To get to his farm, we passed a cottage he rents out to people long term. He told us he had a tenant at the place for almost two years. I saw the woman sitting in the garden, long auburn hair tied in a ponytail.'

David's ears pricked.

'Did you notice anything else about the lady?'

'Aye, she was a pretty lass. I remember that. As we drove by, she got up from her garden chair and hurried back indoors. She wasn't in the garden when we returned home.'

Trying to show no inkling of emotion, he nodded.

'Thank you, Mrs. Mackenzie. I'll let one of the constables take your details and that of your relative, the crofter, so we can check this lady out. That was useful information. I'm so glad you both feel a little better now.'

The detective signalled to a young officer standing nearby to complete the information. He stood up, shook hands with the elderly lady and her husband, then left them. He made his way to Jimmy Mackay, who'd entered the hall.

'Lad, you're the picture of your da today. I'm glad you are here. I remembered something I didnae mention when the young policewoman took my statement and I think it's kind of important.'

David ushered the fisherman to a table in a quiet corner of the room and beckoned for him to sit down.

'Okay, Mr. Mackay, what have you remembered?'

'No need for formalities. It's Jimmy to my family and friends, and to everyone who knows me. Your father was my best friend. I ken your mother too. We were all bairns together.

The colour drained from David's face, and in the artificial hall lighting, he looked grey. The news that the man staring at him was his father's best friend shocked him.

His heart was shattered into a thousand pieces to speak to someone who remembered him after all that time.

'I'll get to the point. I said in my statement that no vehicle passed by Loch Spiorad when I was out on the water. Nothing passed either north or south. But when I approached the place where I always park, a van was there, so I drove a few yards further on. I'm awfie sorry that I forgot to mention this earlier. I think it was the shock.'

'Not a problem, Jimmy. You experienced something few people ever do: finding a body. What happened to the van after you parked?'

'It flew past me as I pulled off the road. The van went north, a few metres to a larger passing place, made a three-point turn, and headed south towards Loch Dubhglas.'

'Did you catch the make of the van, by any chance?'

'Aye, it was an old red transit. The start of the registration plate was memorable, OH02. You get to know vehicles and who drives them in Loch Dubhglas. I'm sure I've seen it knocking about the village before, but ma heid's mince at the moment.'

'The next question is…?'

Jimmy interrupted Chisholm in his urgency to spurt everything out.

'I didnae see the driver. I'm annoyed with myself as I turned down my full beam as I drove past. Sorry.'

'No worry, Jimmy. You have remembered something that may be very useful. Thank you.'

David was about to stand up, to end the conversation, when Jimmy leaned forward and placed his hand on the detective's arm. Normally, Chisholm would have flinched and sat back to avoid such human contact, especially from a witness. He stayed in position, not moving, unusually comforted by the stranger who seemed to know so much about him.

'This must be odd, coming back after all this time. I always wondered how you were doing. Such a tragedy, laddie. This has brought back so many memories, meeting you up at Loch Spiorad.'

David felt compelled to comment. To brush off an old family friend for a second time would be rude. Besides, he still held a curiosity about the father he never knew. Everyone spoke well of him when David was growing up. When he was a teenager, he resented everyone comparing him to his dad. The rebellious nature he once possessed made him fight against being lost in the shadows of a dead hero, examined in detail to find similarities rather than to find his way and to be his own person.

'It's been too long, Jimmy. Nothing called me back to the place. I briefly returned when my grandmother died, but my mother was still recovering from her illness, and everything was too much for her. We left soon after the funeral. She made the decision never to return, even in death.'

'Aye, lad. I understand. I understand. If you want to talk while you are up this way, take my number.'

Saturday passed quickly. David spent hours in the incident room, going over plans and strategies. He wanted to be ready to begin the week with firm decisions taken as to how to proceed with the investigation.

He tried not to let the ghosts of the past invade his head, but slowly and quietly they returned each time he took a break from his paperwork to stretch his legs in the village. So, he decided to confront the past head-on. After finishing for the day, he returned to the Bed & Breakfast, changed, and slipped out without being noticed.

Any warmth left in the day was disappearing quickly, and the light was fading. His pace quickened as he drew closer to his destination. The short walk uphill was only five minutes from the high street. As he reached the gate of the churchyard, he momentarily turned to look back down on the village. From here, he could see lights being switched on in various houses and cottages, the smoke from fires lit in people's homes, and the dusk triggering streetlights to welcome the dark. The loch below was still. He could just make out the shapes of the mountains in the distance to the west and north.

Lifting the latch on the lychgate, he entered into the churchyard and followed a path to the left. Although it had been years since he made the one journey to the site of the family grave, he remembered where to go.

He turned on his phone torch and bent down. Despite the stone being discoloured and the grave needing some care and attention, when light poured onto the headstone, he could clearly make out the wording.

David wasn't a man to cry, but when he knelt down and began to read the inscription, his eyes brimmed, and he wept. Recollection of his grandparents' funerals were burnt into his memory. Seeing the words and reading the names, so matter-of-factly carved into the Caithness stone, sent his head spinning into a thousand pieces. He read the first epitaph.

IN LOVING MEMORY
DONALD DAVID CHISHOLM
TAKEN TRAGICALLY ON 16TH APRIL 1973
AGED 24
LOVING SON TO DONALD & ELSPETH,
HUSBAND TO CAITLIN & FATHER TO DAVID
REST IN PEACE, BONNY LAD.

Then below, the two people who had been his *"parents"* and his haven during his formative years. Each name cut deeper into his soul. Wiping away the tears, the guilt of not paying homage to three of the most important people in his life for so long was too much to bear. Staying a while, he whispered messages to each one, things he regretted not saying before, until the light from his mobile began to fade.

DONALD DONNIE CHISHOLM
DIED 22ND SEPTEMBER 1988
AGED 75
LOVING HUSBAND TO ELSPETH,
FATHER TO THE LATE DONALD,
& GRANDFATHER TO DAVID
A TRULY GENTLE MAN

EILSPETH CHISHOLM, NÉE SUTHERLAND
DIED 8TH DECEMBER 1991
AGED 72
BELOVED WIFE TO THE LATE DONNIE,
MOTHER TO THE LATE DONALD,
& GRANDMOTHER TO DAVID

He needed to make amends, to honour and cherish their memories, and promised each of them that he would return regularly. It was time to deal with the past. The selfishness, especially to his grandmother, leaving her to manage the croft alone once his grandfather had died, was unforgivable. Crofting was the last job he'd ever wanted, given how his father had died. He rebelled, ignoring the guilt in not visiting his wonderful grandmother. In his fifteen-year-old head, a life in Inverness seemed far more appealing. Besides which, he'd been a carer to his vulnerable, unstable mother who had needed him more.

When he tried to fall asleep, he tossed and turned, disturbed by thoughts of his return to Sutherland, and what it meant to him.

✝✝✝✝✝

A man and woman appear in his dreams, both elderly with greying hair. A boy walks toward them, and instinctively, they open their arms to greet him. Their faces are familiar, yet he can't remember their names. A younger lady, half their age, also approaches. She hesitates, unsure of his reaction in seeing her.

He looks away, trying to ignore her presence. All three adults call his name as they set about searching a deserted croft looking for him. The boy hides in plain sight, leaning against an old stone wall, but he ignores their cries.

In the shadow of the barn, a tall, dark figure stands observing the scene. The boy tries to go closer without being spotted to see who the stranger is, but he struggles to get a good vantage point without being spotted by those searching for him. Each time they move closer, he runs to find a better hiding place, but the figure he seeks is always obscured from view.

When the detective awakes, he will be tired and distressed by the nightmare. He holds a determination to make his peace with them and bring change to his life.

I want to cry out, to let everyone know my name, but I can no longer make a human sound. Instead, autumn-coloured leaves rustle in the streets of Loch Dubhglas, shaken from trees. A gate rattles. A ginger cat meows and runs under a lilac bush to hide. Gossips run riot, and the curtains twitch as people fear there is a killer in their midst. Invisible and silent, no one sees or hears my sobs.

CHAPTER 7
Day 6 : Sunday, 28th September

Chisholm avoided the geologists by staying in his room on Sunday morning until he heard the front door close. He was relieved when he spied the pair walking towards the car park, maps in hand and rucksacks on their backs ready for a day out in the field.

Deciding against the full Scottish breakfast, he opted for porridge and fruit instead. The warm, creamy oats trickled down his throat. He had forgotten how delicious and comforting the milky concoction could be.

The Bed & Breakfast owner's attempt to engage him in small talk fell on deaf ears. He gave nothing away of his intentions for the day despite the man being inquisitive. Besides, he hadn't fully made up his mind how he would spend the next few hours.

If time allowed, David took a rest on the Sabbath, not for religious reasons but purely to clear his head. Sometimes he liked to ride along one of the cycle routes around Inverness, but as he was away from home and had no bicycle, he took a road trip to the north coast. It had been years since he was last up that way.

Twists and turns along the narrow single-track road held surprises around every corner. Initially, the route followed a riverbank upstream, gently meeting smaller burns along the way. Some were no more than ruts in the bogs, while others were faster flowing and varying in width and depth.

In the distance, as far as the eye could see, lay a series of mountains that surrounded the road, cosseting him on all sides into the bosom of northern Sutherland. The sun shone across the land, forcing him to reach into the glove compartment for his sunglasses.

In the middle ground between the mountains and the road, peat bogs stretched far into the distance like a khaki brown cloth spread across the earth, rising and falling, seeming to have no beginning and no end. Like many who passed that way, his presence was insignificant in such an enormous landscape.

The road rose higher, and he lost sight of the river as he came towards a forest of tall, stately pines. For now, all views to the hills and mountains were blocked, with row upon row of the evergreens hiding any vista. Visitors often felt as if they were moving through a living cathedral of darkness and reverence. There were signs of fallen trunks within the forest, ready like dominoes to knock others down as their shallow roots upended, outgrowing their holy altar. For now, it was Nature's sanctuary for a range of creatures who lived within it.

Eventually, the forest line petered out, and he found himself high on a ridge. From this vantage point he could look down to the bottom of the strath[11]. He stopped in a passing place to stare at the view. As he wound down the window to take in some air, he could hear the roar of angry water, gushing and crashing down over rocks on the opposite side of the ridge, and dropping into the river below.

The few surviving trees on the opposite side of the strath, unable to escape the winds that raced through the valley, were misshapen into bizarre forms that stretched their branches like tentacles across the sky in one unifying direction. Apart from the waterfall and the trees, there was nothing but murky peat bogs and a lone yellow-legged buzzard that circled, ready to swoop at any moment towards its prey. David had forgotten the harsh beauty of this place.

Setting off again, he was determined to keep an eye on the weather. When leaving Loch Dubhglas, it had been sunny and warm. Now, oppressive grey clouds brought a chill to the air. His sunglasses lay redundant on the passenger seat, but he continued to live in hope that the sun would battle through as the coast drew nearer.

Few people lived between Dubhglas and the sea in this remote area. Just one dilapidated cottage sprang into view during the last fifteen miles of his journey. The only other signs of humans existence were occasional tyre tracks on the various estates he passed, made by ghillies managing rich men's acres. Keeping the deer herds healthy and well stocked was their job, together with entertaining hunting guests by preparing their guns for shooting parties out on the hills.

These wildlands were merely the playgrounds of the super-rich, for the pleasure of making business deals and securing contracts to keep them in the lives to which they were accustomed.

No estate mansions were on view from the road. Only signs saying, *"Private Road. Keep Out!"* gave a hint of population in the wilderness beyond. He'd read an article a few years back stating that there were now only a handful of British landowners in the north of Scotland and a tiny percentage of those were Scottish. Much of this area was owned by billionaires from foreign shores who rarely visited, let alone resided here.

When he came across the first hamlet, an hour away from Loch Dubhglas, he heaved a sigh of relief, for once, to be back amongst people. His euphoria did not last long, for there was just a hotel with an empty car park, three or four estate houses, a red phone box, and an old school building that looked as if it had been left to rot, given the weeds in the playground and the sign that hung by one rusty old nail that swung in the breeze, even on a calm day like today.

He continued his journey across various burns, spotting a couple more buzzards and a kite before he saw the landscape changed dramatically around the next bend in the road. He arrived on the north coast, the meeting place of the Atlantic and the North Sea. As a broad strip of golden sands came into view, the sun reappeared. The task of finding somewhere to park proved easy.

A few yards away, a sign *"To the Beach"* directed him down a grassy slope to the sandy shoreline. For some reason, he had the urge to take off his socks and trainers and feel the grains of sand and the cool water between his toes. He strolled along the beach with nothing in his head but the contentment of the pilgrimage he'd made. When he glanced up at the houses that lined the hill above the water, he felt the place was more beautiful than he remembered. A good memory from childhood of a holiday filled with sandcastles, picnics, and laughter. The coastline was stunning, and on such a day, when the sky was blue, the sea azure, and fluffy white clouds floated on the breeze, there was no better place to be.

On the drive back, he thought about how much he enjoyed the remoteness of the journey and the beauty around each corner. For a few short hours, murder was the last thing on his mind; the knots in his stomach were forgotten. He had driven past Loch Spiorad on his travels north and did not glance at the place where the body was found. Now he chose to pull off the road to stretch his legs. The incident tent and police vehicles were gone. The only signs of anything occurring here were the police tape still wrapped around tree trunks to mark a prohibited area and an incident board near the road asking for witnesses to come forward.

He retraced familiar steps to the shoreline and looked towards the reed bed where Jimmy came across the woman. His training taught him to question everything. The more he stared at the water, the more he became convinced there was a reason for the body being dumped in Loch Spiorad . Maybe it was close to where she lived.

He was about to turn his back on the loch and return along the path, through the trees, to the car when he paused. Maybe the clue was in the name, Spiorad[12]. How did a targeted death, in such bizarre circumstances, link to the loch? Surely, this murder was not sacrificial. He shuddered. This place was haunting.

Something stirred more family memories. He closed his eyes and images raced through his head: his grandfather, his grandmother, and his mother and everything they did to make his younger life as good as it was. With a deep sigh, he hoped one day his father would also appear. When he opened his eyes once more, the late September light danced, creating glistening shimmers on the water. He took off his jacket and, let the warmth of the sun bring him comfort and the serenity of the loch feed his soul.

Back in the car, David wondered if he should take a detour before returning to the Bed & Breakfast but he continued on instead, deciding to keep this day special. He wanted nothing to spoil his revived love with his home county. It was time to move on, but he was tired, and the final journey of repentance could wait a few more hours. Everything harked back to Kinness: his childhood, his mother's illness, the divorce, being D.I. Chisholm—all of it drained him. His heart needed to return from the cold.

The herd of red deer race across the ridge, pausing only if two lookouts are spooked by an unfamiliar sound or smell. When the burn comes into view, they graze a while and take in the cool water that they have been seeking.

Still the lookouts do not rest, nor do the hinds, who pay attention to their spring-born fawns, wary of the dangers they all face. One older female cocks her right ear, fearing something ahead. She sniffs the air, sensing the season will come soon for her kind to be hunted. She understands danger, having watched her own mother dying when she was young. Protecting her baby for as long as she can is her only priority. His season will come one day too.

A lookout senses all is not well. He stirs, moving quickly behind some bushes, and the herd follows. Something is wrong, and he needs to get them to higher ground once more.

The detective is calmer. He needs a clear head and to keep his emotions in check if he is to find me. The wolves are circling, and like the deer, he must remain vigilant at all times. There are dangers everywhere when you least expect them.

CHAPTER 8
Day 7 : Monday, 29th September

The Monday morning meeting with Helen proved difficult. Kicking thoughts around provided some suggestions as to who might have access to chemicals capable of killing. As they were currently silenced from making announcements, even to colleagues, the struggle with keeping quiet whilst investigating lines of inquiry made the task nigh on impossible.

'Do you think McLeod is setting us up to fail? I thought she liked high rates of detection for her statistics.'

'I've no idea, Helen. This case won't be solved by a dead body alone. We don't even know the woman's identity, and we are almost a week on from when Mackay found her.'

He hesitated, deep in thought, as the door to the room opened. Their jaws dropped as they heard the unmistakable click of stilettos. A figure entered unannounced. Helen's words were barely audible, as she whispered under her breath,

'Speak of the devil!'

There in front of them, in a navy jacket and figure-hugging cream dress, stood Alison McLeod, carrying a navy briefcase, part of her accessories for the day. Perfectly made up and her hair immaculate, she looked remarkably fresh for a woman whose long drive north was a first for her. Rising to his feet to acknowledge her seniority, David held out his hand to greet his boss in case Helen had been overheard. The chief gave no hint as to whether she had heard the remark.

'There is no need to stand, Chisholm. I've come to bring information that you may lack.

Tests have shown that the nerve agent was most likely manufactured abroad. There is reason to believe it is old stock from the former Soviet Union. Analysis of the lethal cocktail released into the woman's body is similar to that used in the case back in 1978 and on several other occasions. However, there is not an exact match to any data held in the UK. It is being labelled as A4-7.

There has already been a sweep of all video footage from airports and ferry terminals around the country. Current thoughts are that an assassin or supplier of the toxic substance will be long gone. Unfortunately, there is a low success rate for both capturing and bringing to justice assailants for this type of murder, but we can try to piece the parts of a jigsaw puzzle together to make sense of what has happened.

As we speak, agencies are investigating all potential links she might have to any organisations, but so far, she is unknown. It is important you understand the people you are potentially dealing with and the gravity of the situation. For now, all of this will remain quiet but keep an open mind.

We have permission to release more information to the public about how the victim was murdered, so brief all your officers before any press release goes out. Do not mention the possibility of a bracelet being the weapon at this stage, as this is pure conjecture. I have a press conference booked for tomorrow, and I want you there. Take a look at this information I've been given to pass on to you.'

Placing her briefcase onto the table, she pulled out a thin, blue document wallet. No clues lay on the cover as to what was contained within it. Chisholm lifted the flap and took out four pieces of paper he found along with three photographs. Casting his eye down a list of names, he spotted several he recognised. On the other sheets were more details of three individuals, a woman and two men. He tried to scan the information, but McLeod spoke, breaking his concentration.

'Look at these documents. You will see a list of people of interest; some of whom are oligarchs. Historically, the countries they have allegiances with are linked to similar assassinations. From intelligence, three in particular carry strong political persuasion because of the money they each donate. It's likely they help to fund attacks on countries such as Ukraine. You won't need to investigate them, but listen out for their names. There's probably nothing linking them to our victim, but it's useful to keep them in mind.

The two men have connections with organised crime across Europe, such as drugs and people trafficking. They're also linked to money laundering carried out behind what appears to be legitimate businesses. The woman originates from Eastern Europe but has now taken American citizenship. There's strong indication she's helping to fund the Project 2025 initiative. It's ironic as she has not led the typical clean living, right-wing, fundamental Christian lifestyle until recently. Despite being friendly with *Uncle Sam*, she has strong links with areas that were once part of the U.S.S.R.'

They read the list and studied the images, memorising what they could. Helen shivered. The thought of such money and power was frightening. In Glasgow, her old stomping ground, she dealt with some hardened criminals and knew only too well some of the things people were capable of doing to other humans. David picked up one of the images.

'Hasn't that guy just bought a football club in France for £300 million?'

McLeod nodded.

'Yes, Dima Chenko is a billionaire with investments in many countries, including the United Kingdom. His roots are firmly in Russia, and his brothers are both reported to be top agents in the Federal Security Services of the Russian Federation, previously known as the KGB. Officially they are all businessmen. A few years back, one of their henchmen was imprisoned for drug running in Dunfermline. Of course, there were no official links to Chenko or his brothers.'

Helen lifted another of the photographs to take a careful look at the second image. The man's face was familiar, but she could not place him.

'Why do I know this man?'

'Roberto Marino, the most famous on the list, made his name as a television cook. On the surface, he is a master of business and a major shareholder in some of the largest companies in the world, an Italian billionaire who has a private life he keeps away from prying eyes. It's claimed he is married to a top mafioso's daughter. Nothing sticks to him or his in-laws, but Interpol has them in their sights for all sorts. This man has connections in many countries through his cookery shows and books. One of his latest cookery books was entitled "*A Trip Through the Scottish Highlands.*"

As if in unison, Chisholm and Daniels pursed their lips, in disapproval at the title. When David picked up the final photograph of this modern-day triumvirate, both detectives recognised the woman instantly as a supermodel adorning every magazine and newspaper across the globe. Helen gasped.

'Natasha Boskova isn't an oligarch, is she? She has too much cocaine up her nose for that! That's what the headlines say. The chemicals she's involved with are for her own recreation.'

'That's what is clever about this woman. She recently reinvented herself, supporting the authoritarian, Christian nationalist plan. She has the money and has been politically motivated, using funds to drive agendas through. Currently, the story goes that she is clean after leaving rehab and finding

God, hence her different stance. Her associates are powerful people in the U.S. She's been in the U.K. promoting a new global social media platform to rival Facebook, TikTok, X, and Instagram.'

With so much information swirling in his head, David needed clarification.

'So why do you think that any of these three may be involved in our case? It's a bit far off the beaten track for the likes of these people.'

'MI5 believes all three have the money. Forget how rural most of the Highlands are. Drugs are everywhere, seeping into the tiniest of veins, spreading misery across cities, villages, and hamlets. Maybe the victim is a woman who crossed one of them or an associate. It's highly unlikely they carried out the murder themselves but take heed. These are all dangerous people who will stop at nothing to make a fast buck by fair means or foul. They are as slippery as those eels in Loch Spiorad.'

Silence descended briefly as David and Helen stared at each other, too perplexed to speak. Alison McLeod glared at each of them before making her final speech.

'Don't think because we are in the middle of Sutherland, something like this can't happen. It's on our doorstep. Chisholm, you were in the same room as the two men and the woman at the charity event the weekend before last. It's quite the coincidence that all three were in the Highlands around the time an extraordinary murder was committed. There's no such thing as coincidence when an assassination takes place.

It's planned and calculated, especially when the killing has all the hallmarks of the former U.S.S.R. involvement.

'But wouldn't they have the sense to be a million miles away from a death they funded or sanctioned?'

Helen's question provoked a reaction from McLeod.

'Hiding in plain sight is often how these people operate. Alibis from a crowd of police officers and local dignitaries.'

David remained silent, his brain working overtime. The realisation of being in a room with such people depressed him. He tasted the bitterness of corruption on his lips.

McLeod closed her briefcase.

'It's imperative you find out who the woman was. Go back to basics. Our aim must be to find this woman's identity. Why would a woman in a remote area of the Highlands be targeted? What did she know? Who would want to kill her? These are the issues we should deal with. Only by concentrating on these matters do we stand any chance of finding out the truth behind her death.'

As she walked towards the door, she turned to focus on Helen.

'By the way, Daniels, I'm not the devil! I'm your boss.'

She left the room as dramatically as she entered. The sound of her expensive heels clicking on the wooden floor faded after a few moments. Like the wicked stepmother in a pantomime, she disappeared in a puff of smoke, created by her fancy Mercedes being revved to cause attention. She had certainly left an impression.

A gasp exploded from Helen's mouth. She shook her head in disbelief, her cheeks burning with the humiliation of being overheard.

'You saw these people in Inverness at that black-tie event you didn't want to attend? Weren't all the senior officers commanded to go? What the hell is this case about?'

The information floated around like froth in his head: huge gaps of space, the rest covered with bubbles fizzing, then bursting. He sat quietly and didn't speak to try to make sense of the enormity of the task they faced. They had just taken a hundred paces into a minefield, and each tiny step felt like it could cause an explosion at any moment.

He leaned back in his chair and considered the evening in question. Most of the time he'd avoided conversation and taken himself away from the main room into the bar area. In the dimly lit corner, he'd enjoyed a couple of malt whiskies without interruption. Occasionally, someone would nod to him, but for the most part, he had been an observer, left to himself. The main room had been filled with circular tables, all decorated with various floral arrangements, mainly themed with thistles, heather, and white blooms to complement the pale lilac table runners. Place names, written on white cards with gold ink, indicated where to sit.

David was grateful that his card was on a table towards the back of the room. There he sat with seven other police officers of similar rank from across the north of Scotland. Most people he knew by sight from courses he had attended in other regions; a couple were less familiar. He spoke when spoken to, had a lengthy one-sided conversation with an older man who talked about his impending retirement, and listened to a woman he knew from Aberdeen who mainly moaned about how much her feet ached in high heels.

His seat offered a good vantage point for the whole room. As his colleagues droned on about feet and retirement plans, he cast his eyes left and right. The three people McLeod mentioned were there. The woman had caught everyone's attention by wearing an outrageous black satin gown that gave the impression, when she walked, of sitting on a black cloud. Her feet were invisible in the chaos of what lay above her toes and beyond. He remembered the good-looking, suntanned guy who made the woman with aching feet swoon slightly as she paused the conversation about her plantar fasciitis for a brief moment when the guest entered the room.

'Roberto Marino! 'What a dish!'

Chisholm had not replied to her nonsense. From memory, he did not recall seeing Dima Chenko.

'We are being played; three billionaires were wined and dined by the Highlands' top business people, and senior police officers present. You and I are chess pieces in a far more dangerous game than we imagined.'

He leaned forward, and looking at his colleague, he was direct and precise with his serious words.

'We stick to our jobs. Investigate, as we always do in every case we ever work, and plan lines of inquiry to assist until someone knocks our chess pieces from the board. Most importantly, we cover our backs!'

With McLeod gone, Helen and David immersed themselves in the more familiar world of murder investigation. Involvement by the Mafia, old-school Soviet, and oligarch theories would be left to others more knowledgeable in those affairs. The main hall was full of police officers, noting down information from the public.

When the room went quiet, David gathered all the officers together and informed them of the developments. It was a murder case, and the method of killing suggested an assassination. When he mentioned the phrase *"chemical agent,"* eyebrows shot up around the room and the gasps were audible, along with several expletives. The atmosphere altered dramatically. The electricity and tension in the room was palpable.

'Can you find out if the staff at that garage, where you got petrol, served anyone driving a red transit van with a distinctive number plate? Maybe they had CCTV.'

Helen laughed at the prospect of security cameras.

'Boss, it's pretty run down. That was clear when I ran out of petrol. I'd say there's not much chance of anything fancy. Is it okay to go now?'

Chisholm nodded, understanding Helen's need to clear her head after McLeod's visit.

††††

The garage, a couple of miles from the village and the last petrol station for more than eighty miles north, was like stepping back in time. Rusting petrol and diesel pumps stood in the forecourt. A large metal shed housed a several cars, both on ramps, while two other vehicles awaited inspection to the side of the faded blue double doors. A mechanic sat on a wooden stool by his workbench, tucking into his lunch. Hearing footsteps, his head turned towards Helen as she approached. Instantly he recognised her as the woman who needed petrol a few days before and stood up.

When he acted as her hero and sorted her fuel problem, it was his shoulder-length, dark brown hair and rugged features that she'd noticed. Now, with a professional eye, she scanned him more closely: white male, thirties, with an Inverness accent, medium build, about five feet ten, unshaven, with a couple of days' stubble.

'Have you run out of fuel again?'

Daniels smiled at his joke and laughed as she remembered the first time she met the man.

'Don't remind me! Thanks once again for helping in my hour of need. I wonder if you can do me a favour. It's not fuel I want this time.'

'I'll try!'

When she showed him her I.D. card, his shoulders tensed. The cheeky grin dissolved instantly to be replaced by a scowl, which told her she was less welcome than a few seconds before. She was used to reactions like this when anyone realised her job. It was embedded into people's minds, even those who were law abiding citizens. The badge made folk feel on edge, and often uncomfortable. Interestingly, the guilty always played everything cool initially but always became defensive under pressure.

'I promise I'm not investigating anything else apart from the body of a woman found in unexplained circumstances a few nights ago up at Loch Spiorad. I'm looking at a few leads we have regarding the lady's identity and how she got to the loch. You don't by any chance have CCTV here, do you?'

'No!'

Ignoring the sharp response, she continued.

'I wonder if you can recall any red transit vans calling in for fuel last week.'

'No!'

'So, no red vans at all?'

'Look, why don't you just come out with what you want? You know I own a red transit van.'

Helen was taken aback at his sudden aggressive tone. The mechanic was defensive and certainly wasn't keen on speaking to the police. His guarded attitude made her wary of him, and uneasy. With such a change in his manner, she knew he would be hiding something. To calm him down, she lowered her voice, but was determined to get to the bottom of his defensiveness.

'I had no idea about your red van. Can I take a look at it, please?'

'Don't think I have a choice, do I?

He jumped from the stool and, leading her towards a set of double doors at the back of the shed, he slid open one of them to reveal a yard not visible to the public. In front of her, a battered old red van was parked. "Fuck U" was written in the grime on the back doors. Ignoring the filth of the vehicle, she moved her hand across the rear registration plate, checking its details. There was no OH02. She noticed the screws on it were shiny and much cleaner than the rest of the vehicle but said nothing. Not wanting to provoke him further, she didn't react but continued with her questions.

'Thanks. Did you see any other red transits last week?'

Alec Sullivan did not flinch. He turned away and returned to his lunch without answering. As she drove back to the incident room, she wondered why he didn't want a visit from the police.

The reaction to her being a detective fascinated her. Some gave her patronising glances and sarcastic comments. Worse still, when arresting someone in a pub or bar in Glasgow for a fight or for smashing up the premises, the predictable sound of grunting and oinking annoyed her intensely. There was no point in attempting to silence drunks. It would make things worse.

'You don't look like a copper.'

'What's a nice wee lassie like you mixed up with the polis?

She often wondered what a police officer should look like. As a detective, she didn't wear a uniform. Would the public take her more seriously if she had handcuffs at the ready on her belt or if she carried a truncheon or taser? Some people overshared their stories with her, insisting on telling every detail like she was a best friend. Others snubbed her for police misdemeanours in the national press. For some, they wanted to hide illegal goods or to act cool when she knew their involvement in a crime. The mechanic, who days before had acted as her hero, was concealing something.

A search through DVLA brought no red nor any other colour transit van with a partial registration OH02. False plates were the only conclusion that could be drawn, unless Jimmy Mackay had made a mistake.

David planned to visit the garage himself at some point over the next few days, perhaps even pulling in the man in for questioning, but he needed more evidence. More likely than not, the guy was ripping people off with car repairs, using cheap parts instead of branded goods.

†††††

After a phone call from Shona McPherson informing him there were no dental records in any database to match the victim, Chisholm decided to follow up on the elderly couple's information of a woman renting a place in Dubhness, making the decision to go himself.

Back on the single-track road north, houses became sparser. Keeping the loch which gave the village its name, on the left, he travelled to the point where a bridge marked its end. The road crossed one of the rivers that fed the loch. A couple of miles further on, he passed several tracks leading to various crofts lying out of sight over the hills. At the fourth such turning on the right, David spotted a signpost and signalled.

Dubhness had only two properties and, as such, was not even classed as a hamlet. The place was remote and seemed further away from the main village than the eight miles indicated on a signpost at the bottom of the lane. The road rose sharply uphill. He drove through a huge plantation of oak, hazel and rowan trees, a route carved into the forest floor years before.

The management and regeneration of the land was continuous. Some of these majestic giants fell naturally towards the ground; their enormous roots lifted from the earth and lay exposed to the elements. Harvesting the trees that remained standing was a necessity for the road to continue to be safe for use and to bring profit for the estate owner. When they reached maturity, the green lords of the woods were ripped from the land and taken for building or furniture. Scraps were used for pulp to make paper. Replanting of fir trees began once the ground recovered. Today, as David drove through the forest, both sides of the road were thick with greenery. Surrounded by the sanctuary of trees, he felt the presence and comfort they brought to the land.

On a sunny September day with blue skies and white fluffy clouds, the drive, as pleasant as it was, brought memories flooding back of times he travelled along the road to school in an old Land Rover his Granda drove. Through sun, rain, and snow, he went to school if the vehicle could get through. On wild, windy days, the heater would keep him warm as he snuggled into the grey duffle coat Grannie insisted he wore. When the midges covered every inch of the windscreen in summer, he would slap himself in an attempt to ward them away as they bit through his clothes and hair.

Shuddering at the thought of the wee beasties, who thankfully were disappearing to their autumn slumber, he was surprised at the overwhelming sense of contentment he felt. In Inverness, he would be rushing to and from headquarters, demanding information from Helen or another officer on the team. Time slowed in Loch Dubhglas.

Seeing the sign for the Kinness turning, he ignored it and continued north. He drove on until he reached the crest of the hill. From here there was a perfect view for several miles to the north and south. Down below, the waters of Loch Spiorad could be seen in the distance. He'd seen the view on countless occasions, but after all this time, its beauty made him gasp.

The track continued past a neat, white cottage. A few yards on, the ground plateaued, and the road abruptly ended. Beyond, lay a ramshackle croft house and a courtyard festooned with old, rusting agricultural machinery, abandoned and rotting where they were left. The place had seen better days. An elderly crofter was walking from the house to a nearby barn. Suspicious of visitors, he turned and walked towards Chisholm.

Seeing a turning point after the tarmac ended, David drove onto the rough ground and manoeuvred his car until it was turned to go back down the hill. He parked so as not to block the track and got out. His hand went instinctively to his jacket buttons to fasten them, something he always did when he got out of his car. The crofter looked for an explanation from the visitor. Maybe he was a tourist, but he seemed too well-dressed for someone on holiday.

'Hello, sir. I'm Detective Inspector David Chisholm. I'm investigating the unexplained death of a lady in Loch Spiorad a few nights ago.'

The man wasn't used to many visitors, and certainly not policemen. The creases in his weather-beaten forehead narrowed. Not sure how to react, he frowned. His shyness often made people think he was ignorant. His voice was barely audible at first.

'Aye. A friend told me something happened.'

His head tilted gently to the right, and he nodded, signifying the direction of the loch a few miles away.

'Can I have your name, please?'

'Glen Mackenzie, sir.'

He took off his faded brown cap with his left hand, revealing a balding head with a few wisps of silvery hair. Spontaneously, he wiped his right palm on his old tweed jacket before offering it to the inspector.

'Excuse my manners. How can I help ye?'

David smiled and shook his hand. The hand-wiping and firm grip reminded him of the way his grandfather would greet his fellow crofters.

'We have opened an incident room in Loch Dubhglas village hall so that we can establish the lady's identity. A couple of villagers mentioned to us that they were up here to buy some hens from you a few weeks back and that a woman was renting one of your nearby properties. Is that correct?'

'Aye, a quiet young lassie. She lives at Dubhness Cottage, the one you passed, just down the lane.'

With a bony finger, he pointed back down the track.

'Can you tell me her name and anything about her?'

'Aye. Anna is her name. An English lassie. She lives alone. Keeps herself to herself. A bit of a loner, a writer by all accounts, runs up and down the hills and sometimes as far as Loch Spiorad and even further. I've seen her out with her camera a lot. Been here for about twenty months or more.'

'Have you seen her in the last few days?'

'Nay. I normally see her eating her breakfast on the patio in the summer, but I havenae seen her lately. The air is a bit nippy, so I guess she's staying indoors.'

'Do you recall when you last saw her?'

'My memory is nae what it used to be, sorry. Probably about a week ago.'

'Can you give me a description of Anna? What's her surname? Anything you can think of that may be useful.'

'The lassie's name is Anna Green. It suits her as her eyes are like emeralds. A scrap of a girl, in her twenties I think, with long red hair.'

There was a shyness and hesitancy as he uttered his last words. A lifelong bachelor, who rarely looked at a girl, never mind asked one out to a dance in his younger days, he lowered his voice before continuing,

'A pretty lass.'

As David devoured all the information, the hairs on his arms and neck stood to attention. The descriptions struck a familiar chord. He did not want to alarm the crofter; this might be a wild goose chase. The woman living at the property was probably safe and well, but instinct told him differently.

'I'm going to see if Anna's at home. If you can stay here whilst I check, I would be grateful.'

He returned to his car. Grabbing a pair of shoe covers and gloves from the boot, he set off the short distance down the track to the property. As he moved towards the tarmac road, his legs felt like lead as he wondered if he was about to enter a potential crime scene.

Set back from the road slightly, a whitewashed building stood on about a quarter of an acre of land. David stopped a few yards before Dubhness Cottage to take in the location. Only the old croft house lay beyond. Each property was isolated and away from prying eyes. Behind the house were hills. To the front, the main road and the loch lay below, and beyond, the hills unfolded as far as the eye could see, towards Ben Meagaidh.

The cottage was typical of the kind built in the area over a hundred years before, with a slate roof and walls made from local stone, and at some point in its history, was extended and pebble-dashed. The single-storey building stood snugly in its plot, nestled by pine trees on three sides, forming a natural screening from the world. The original front door had been blocked up and moved to the right side of the building. A brick porch helped to stop the winter winds that cut through the land at will.

To the right, a few yards away from the porch and past the shingle driveway, lay a neatly lawned area recently mowed. Flower beds around the edges of the grass were full of rose bushes, still displaying pink and red blooms, even in late September. The scent of honeysuckle and jasmine still hung in the air.

To the front of the cottage was a patio area, half hidden from the road by bushes. Circular in shape, it was made from coloured concrete slabs, the sort seen in garden centres. The centre of the circle looked bare, void of seating or a table, yet marks on the ground suggested something had been there. Pots of various colours and sizes were placed around the edge, filled with flowers and plants. Most petals had died off after their summer show. The largest plastic pot contained a eucalyptus tree, around four feet in height.

He instinctively put on his blue gloves and shoe covers, opened the five-bar gate, and carefully placed the blue rope back onto the post that acted as a latch. The shingle crunched beneath his feet as he stepped into the driveway. As he looked through the half-glazed door, he noted the porch was more like a mudroom. The wooden shoe rack was empty. No jackets or coats hung on the hooks on the honey-stained pine panelling near the inner front door. The tiled floor looked fresh and clean. He knocked on the outer porch door, but when there was no response, he opened it and stepped gingerly onto the tiles. The smell of bleach rushed to the back of his throat and caught his breath.

He knocked on the brown wooden inner door, but no one came. Returning to the shingle driveway, he continued forward to a pebble-dash garage a few yards from the cottage. The white metal door was not fully closed, and he began to push it up to see if a vehicle was present. A knot twisted in his stomach when he found nothing inside. He once again gagged at the smell of bleach. It was spotless, the cleanest garage ever seen. He returned swiftly along the track to the crofter, who obediently stood waiting for him.

'There seems to be no sign of the lady. Can you tell me what vehicle she drives?'

'It's one of those foreign things, a red Toyota Yaris.'

'It's not in the garage. Perhaps she has taken a trip down south or gone on holiday.'

'Nay, the lassie rarely goes oot. I'm used to being on my own and it's isolated up here, but apparently, she likes the quiet to write. Perhaps she's out walking or running. Check for her boots, and jacket in the porch.'

'The porch is empty, and there is nothing in the garage. Both are spotlessly clean.'

Shaking his head, a puzzled expression brought a frown to the crofter's face. He knew the garage had been full of cardboard. The lassie recently received some parcels, and she was going to take the empty boxes to the rubbish dump in Loch Dubhglas. They spoke about it a few weeks before when he popped around to sort out a problem with a bathroom tap.

Normally the lady was quiet, but on this occasion she seemed happy, blethering[13] away about a forthcoming celebration. She didn't explain her excitement, but the enormous grin and laughter made him think it might be her birthday or perhaps she was expecting people to stay.

'Does she have many visitors?'

Glen shook his head.

'Nay many. At night, I've heard a car coming up the hill occasionally. Especially in the last few months. I think it might have been a boyfriend, as she hinted someone might move in with her for a while.'

'Did you see anyone there?'

Glen shook his head.

'There was someone there last weekend, I think. Didnae see who it was, because they went into the house as I drove the tractor down the lane. She's a good tenant. The rent's paid on time; I don't interfere in her business. She is such a nice lassie. You being a police officer, I'm sure she won't mind if you check out the place if you're worried. I have a spare key.'

Chisholm put on an overall and placed his hood over his hair. If he walked into a crime scene, he might jeopardise a future prosecution. He got more gloves and shoe covers from the car and made his way back to the porch. Stepping into it once more, he carefully placed the key in the lock and turned it until he heard a click. The door was opened, and he called out, but no reply came.

The air, full of bleach, once more caught his breath. He turned left in the hallway and continued until he came to the kitchen, the door left ajar. Without stepping inside, he cast an eye around the room. The faded curtains were open. There was nothing on the work surfaces: no kettle, microwave, or anything he would expect to see in a kitchen. Suspicious at the lack of equipment, he stepped into the room and opened several cupboards. There was nothing, only the overwhelming smell of bleach. Each of the cupboards were bare, as were the fridge and freezer.

Leaving the kitchen, he moved into a room with a fireplace. There were some drab, cheerless, beige curtains, a few bits of old wooden furniture: a table and four chairs and a small brown settee. Faded marks on the wooden floor suggested a rug had been positioned there but had been removed fairly recently.

The bedroom was the same: old blue curtains, a fairly plain wooden bed frame with a mattress, an ancient wardrobe in keeping with the nineteen-thirties headboard, and a bedside table in the same dark wood style. The strong smell of the bleach lingered in the air, but there was no evidence anyone had lived there. The place was empty and scrubbed clean.

He locked the door and walked towards three rubbish bins. All reeked of bleach but were empty. A sense of uneasiness grew in his stomach. A hunch told him this was a crime scene. Something wasn't right and felt odd. He returned to his vehicle and took off his disposable clothing before speaking to the crofter.

'She's not at home. The house is empty, all but furniture and curtains, and recently cleaned. Do you think she would have left without telling you?'

Colour drained from the old man's face. He shook. His hunched frame began to give way as his legs collapsed from beneath him. To save himself, he grabbed David's arm and clung on to it for a few seconds. When he had regained his balance, he loosened his grip on the detective. Steadily and slowly, they made their way to the farmhouse. When they reached the door, the crofter led the way into the kitchen and sat down on an old wooden chair at the table.

An ancient black Aga warmed the room. David filled the kettle from a Belfast sink and placed it on the warm plate. It was only when he sat down on a seat opposite the crofter that he caught sight of a black and white collie curled up in a dog bed at the side of the stove. His ears pricked slightly as the men began to talk but soon settled back into his slumber. The image of the room struck a familiar chord with the police officer, but he said nothing, trying to listen to the crofter.

'She wouldnae up and leave without giving notice or saying cheerio. A lovely lass from my experience of talking to her. We pass the time of day when I see her in the lane. She likes running and is always out and about, walking the hills with her camera or out in the garden. Please tell me, she's nae the woman in the loch, is she?'

Shrugging his shoulders, the detective found it hard to offer any words of comfort to the crofter. Not wanting to frighten the old man, or to jump to any conclusions without proof, he lowered his voice as he explained what would happen next.

'I've requested a team come to check the cottage out, to be on the safe side. In the meantime, please do not enter the building. Perhaps Anna has gone away for a few days, or taken off without notice, but I think we should investigate the disappearance further. Was she up to date with the rent?'

'Aye, always paid on time, in cash. When she arrived, she paid a deposit and the first month's rent.'

'Tell me how the tenancy came about. Did you advertise the property was for rent? Did she telephone you for a viewing?'

'Nay. The property was advertised by my nephew on Gumtree and Facebook. They're all beyond me, so I left him to put it on the internet. Initially, it was her uncle who telephoned and made an inquiry about renting the cottage long-term. He said he was looking for a furnished place for his niece to stay as she was relocating to the Highlands. She was a writer and wanted a quiet retreat. I made it clear: Dubhness is very remote, has no internet, and might not be to some people's taste, but he seemed satisfied.'

'Do you have any contact details for the uncle?'

Glen shook his head.

'No, I never spoke to him again, nor did he visit as far as I know.'

With every word, the knot in David's stomach tightened. As he mulled over the information about the woman, Glen threw a grenade into his thoughts.

'You say your name's Chisholm. There's a croft near here at Kinness where a family of that name used to stay. There were generations of the Chisholm clan up there, but the place was sold back in the early nineties. Are you related to them by any chance?'

The detective inhaled deeply, trying to calm himself. Not wishing to snap at the elderly man, he tried to be polite. Later, when pondering the conversation, David wasn't sure why he responded in the way that he did. Almost certainly David's father and grandfather knew the man. Perhaps it was easier to talk to a stranger. Perhaps it was because Glen reminded him of Granda. His history spilt out: fewer complications, less emotion, and perhaps less sympathy.

'I was born a mile or so from here at Kinness. I am Donnie Chisholm's grandson.'

The old man gasped.

'Of course! I knew your family! I was about ten years older than your father, Donald. I remember his death. It shocked the whole community; a lad taken far too young whilst working on the land, and you, a wee bairn a few weeks old, weren't you?'

'Three months old when he died.'

''Twas a tragic accident. A momentary lapse of concentration as he drove up the track to the croft house, a path he'd driven hundreds of times. As he went too close to the edge and lost control, the tractor's centre of gravity shifted, forcing the vehicle over the slope. There was talk that he had fallen asleep at the wheel, through sheer exhaustion.'

Whether it came from the warm Aga or the iron panic crushing his chest, he didn't know. Sweat oozed from his forehead, David's cheeks reddened, and his throat dried. Packed deep inside his heart, he knew the story, but hearing the truth laid bare, he couldn't breathe. He was the lead detective in a murder inquiry that would hit international news, and all he could do was sit with a stranger, eyes brimming with tears.

'It was lambing time, and with you, a new bairn, Donald had no sleep. There, there, lad. Don't take it to heart. It must be hard, an old man like me, raking it all up for ye. Fate dealt a cruel hand, a terrible accident, pure and simple.'

It was hard to listen to the facts of his father's death. Logic told him a twelve-week-old baby could not be blamed for a parent's lack of sleep, yet guilt engulfed any rational thought.

Only faded photographs offered him glimpses of a smiling man who died at the age of twenty-four, sitting on the tractor that later brought about his demise. Another showed him with his arm around a young, pregnant, nineteen-year-old girl; their flared trousers, shirts with long, pointed collars, and tank tops could only belong to the early years of 1970s. Whenever David studied the images, he wondered what the lad with shoulder-length, dark hair and sideburns would have looked like had he lived.

He hurriedly tried to wipe away each tear that fell, but another rushed in to take its place. A stranger was performing unexpected surgery on his troubled heart. The release of tension felt immense.

'Apologies, Glen, it's been difficult to return to the area. This isn't very professional of me. I need to go, but I'll be returning with a team to examine if the cottage next door has been the scene of a crime. I think it's rather odd your tenant has disappeared without saying anything to you. It sounds out of character for the lady, from what you've told me about her. Again, please do not enter the property or even step onto the driveway. A forensic team will be here, probably tomorrow, but for now, a police constable will be guarding the cottage.'

Deep furrows on the crofter's brow showed only a small fraction of the anxiety rushing through the old man's body. His bones ached with weariness. Born in the house he had lived in at Dubhness for eighty-six years, he expected to die there. Trouble lay at his doorstep, and he felt several feet closer to his grave than ever before. The only comfort he found was that David, the grandson and son of his old neighbours the Chisholm family, would be looking for answers.

Normally, in late September, Dubhness was peaceful. As David drove down the track, he couldn't help thinking about his ancestors and Glen Mackenzie's too. Why did the area suddenly feel like home, yet he hated it so much?

†††††

Returning to the hall in Loch Dubhglas, David called the team of officers to a briefing to ascertain how things were progressing. The team of fifteen men and women, some in uniform, gathered in front of the stage where David positioned himself.

'Okay everyone. Listen up. We have a potential lead to identify the body. Following a witness statement taken from a couple who described seeing a woman of similar description to our victim, I paid a visit to a croft at Dubhness, a few miles out from the village. For those who don't know the area, it's uphill and overlooks Loch Spiorad. The officers assigned door-to-door duties haven't made it up that far yet. I met an old crofter. He confirmed a lass has been renting a cottage from him. The tenant is a lady called Anna Green. Her description gives me cause to believe we may have found the victim.'

The officers glanced at each other, and a murmur of anticipation broke the silence. This could be the breakthrough they all needed, and a chance to clear the case. The inconvenience of working away from Inverness each day was taking a toll on everyone's nerves.

'Unbeknownst to Mr. Mackenzie, the crofter, the rental cottage has been stripped of all belongings. All that's left are a few bits of furniture. It's like the woman never existed. There is also a pungent smell of bleach. The SOCO team will be arriving to join us as I speak.'

A young detective put up his hand. The newest member of the team, Detective Constable Euan Sinclair, was full of questions. David nodded to him.

'Boss, when you say stripped, you mean everything?'

'Let's say whoever cleaned the place has done an excellent job. It's too perfect. The bleach odour hits the back of the throat. It's that intense a smell.'

Euan let his imagination run away with him.

'Boss, do you think the crofter has killed her and cleaned up his work?'

'He's a guy in his late eighties and not very strong on his legs. Appearances can be deceptive, as we all know, but I would be very surprised if Glen Mackenzie was an assassin.

For now, we can't completely rule him out, and we'll bring him in for a formal witness statement. It's highly unlikely he had anything to do with the woman's death, and I'm not currently treating him as a suspect.

Bring me up to speed with your enquiries about local weddings. Have any nuptials been cancelled? Are any women reported missing in the area?'

Assigned to find information about registry offices and churches, and keen to impress the senior officer, Euan cleared his throat, smartened his tie, fastened his jacket button, and prepared to launch into his findings.

'Boss, five weddings took place in the county in September. All brides are accounted for, and their identifications are verified. I have seen and spoken to three of them who live fairly locally. The fourth went off to Paris, and the fifth is on honeymoon in Barbados. I have spoken to both on video calls.

No weddings took place at the church in Loch Dubhglas. I spoke to the local Church of Scotland minister who serves three churches in the area. He nor any colleagues from Caithness and Easter Ross know of any recent ceremonies. The Catholic priest in Tain also confirms he hasn't married anyone recently, and I'm reaching out to other faith leaders, just in case: the imam at the mosque in Inverness, and the leaders of the Church of the Latter-day Saints in Invergordon, Elgin, and Inverness too. The nearest synagogue is in Aberdeen, but I will contact the rabbi. I'm still to check the Kingdom Hall that local Jehovah's Witnesses use near the Dornoch Bridge.

As for celebrants, there are loads of them who might perform a blessing of some kind. It's popular for couples to hire someone to come to stage an event such as *"jumping the broom."* Searching for people who carry out these services is taking time. Also, no joy from local florists who could have made the headdress.'

David held back a smile. He remembered the days of enthusiasm and an eagerness to solve cases. Not wanting to deter the young officer, he nodded his approval.

'Thanks, Euan for a comprehensive update. Keep me posted on leads should you find any. Helen, can you enlighten the team on your visit to the local garage, please?'

Daniels told everyone about the mechanic and that she suspected the man was hiding something.

'We should pay another visit to this guy to find out what he's hiding. Probably dodgy deals or MOT scams, but he's worth pursuing, seeing as he is the only person in the area with a red transit van.'

The working day was drawing to a close. The energy levels disappeared as the room emptied until there were just two officers left. Helen turned to David. Now they could speak frankly, with their guards down.

'Do you really think that Anna Green from Dubhness Cottage is the victim?'

Without hesitation, Chisholm nodded. There was no consideration in his mind that the missing woman could be anyone other than Anna.

'Helen, the descriptions of the woman in the loch and Anna are so similar: young, long red hair, pretty. She must be dead. My question is why the hell would she be assassinated and her body dumped in there? Who was this woman? Who would deserve such a death?'

'Nothing makes sense!'

Standing up, he stretched his arms, and in an attempt to ease the tension in his shoulders, he rolled his head from side to side and backward and forward. He tried not to show how tired he was but Helen could see dark circles appearing around his eyes, and there seemed more fine lines on his forehead than she'd ever noticed before. She knew it would be a long night ahead for him.

'You need a coffee to keep you awake. Get something to eat. Anna Green might turn up as the perfect tenant who scrubbed the house but never gave notice of her intention to leave.'

The edge of David's lip quivered as he winked.

'Ever the optimist, Helen. And the Loch Ness Monster has flown over to Loch Spiorad and dumped a body! Now go on your way. I'll grab a sandwich, then wait for the team to arrive. It could be hours yet.'

✝✝✝✝✝

The forensic team arrived at Dubhness as darkness fell. They emerged from a minibus, cases at the ready. From being a group of individuals dressed in a range of clothing and shoes, each with their own identity, a few minutes later they were a posse. All sense of individuality was lost amongst white disposable boiler suits, shoe coverings, hoods, and masks. They walked into the driveway, now lit up with temporary lighting, for a showdown to capture all the clues they could find to match the victim to the property. Each person was briefed as to what their role would be and the routines they would follow. All knew the training and the importance of not corrupting evidence.

David sat in his car watching the proceedings, occasionally winding down his window to speak to someone or to grab some of the fresh air that his lungs craved. Before it was too late, he knocked on Glen's door to make him aware of the team's presence. He sat for a while with the crofter, and they drank tea, chatting about the Kinness croft.

Stars were still in the sky when the lights were dimmed and the team left. Signs of anyone living at the cottage were bagged and tagged. Scrubbed door handles and flooring meant few secrets were untangled. It was as if no one ever lived there. Whoever stripped the house bare did a good job of obliterating any signs of life in the property, but bleach did not cover everything. A partial fingerprint was found on a bathroom cabinet, and although the shower was clean, hairs were found in the waste trap. Any DNA matches to the victim would be known as soon as it was possible.

†††††

There is no point in expecting the police and scientists to work harder or faster. Being impatient will not bring conclusions. They do not realise this is merely one layer of an onion peeled back of my life. At times, I questioned who I was. Perhaps one day the detective will be able to fill in the missing blanks. Investigating the core of my existence is both simple yet agonisingly complex. She who was will make an extensive list. For now, as I am slowly, so painfully slowly, revealed, I scatter the tiniest of dandelion seeds, hoping that some may find places to settle in good soil, bringing answers to those who seek them. The seeds lost on the winds that blow through Sutherland, no one will ever know.

These men and women who work to find the truth are tired and must sleep. I won't walk through their dreams tonight. Both the policeman and his colleagues seek peace in their lives, but first they search for mine.

CHAPTER 9
Day 8 : Tuesday, 30th September

Dawn was breaking when David crept into bed. Progress was being made. He sensed Anna Green was found, but just like her death, the cleansing of her home was ruthless and performed with military precision. Someone very clearly wanted her identity to remain hidden.

Barely closing his eyes for a couple of hours, David showered and dressed, ready for a morning in Inverness. The chief inspector was holding a press conference, and the world was about to erupt at the news of a toxic chemical attack in Loch Dubhglas. Not stopping for breakfast, he drove down the A9 and headed for his favourite café.

Moira was surprised to see *Mr. Serious*. He was much later than usual and in a good mood. When he said he was eating in, the announcement took her breath. The rudeness he'd displayed a few days before was forgiven as she cooked his meal. He devoured a full Scottish breakfast and washed it down with two cups of coffee.

He beamed at the Cockburn haggis on his plate. As he paid, he made small talk about the weather and that rain was expected on this, the last day in September. Something was different.

The press conference went as expected. Alison McLeod took the lead, which pleased him. He said very little, except what was necessary. A frenzy of camera flashes lit up the room when certain words and phrases were used: *"chemical substance," "woman assassinated,"* and *"potential terrorist links to a murder."*

A torrential downpour of questions followed. Was it an act of terrorism? If it was chemical warfare, were the Russians involved? Was the attack carried out by Islamic extremists? Were there links to drug trafficking? When would the police have an identification for the woman? The last camera stopped recording twenty minutes later when the police officers refused to give any more details. McLeod wouldn't admit they had little more information themselves. Chisholm's prediction for the weather was correct, and he sensed more storms ahead.

††††

A growling noise, emanating from his stomach, broke the silence. He had not eaten since breakfast at Moira's. It had been a long day, mainly spent in Inverness where he briefed his chief with details about Anna Green. After completing paperwork, he made it back to Loch Dubhglas before dusk. He decided not to repeat the fish supper experience, delicious as it was. Needing some exercise and to fill his lungs once again with the

Sutherland air, he headed for the village shop. His meal would be simple but much needed. Grabbing a baguette, slices of cheese, a ready-made salad, and a bottle of orange juice, he went to the till to pay.

'Turned out a cooler day, didn't it?'

The last thing David needed was small talk, but he indulged the shop assistant. There was no one else about, and the woman seemed in no rush to scan the items. The name *"Janice"* was on a name badge, pinned to her top. Dark roots were peeping through her short blonde hair. A raspy voice, along with nicotine-stained fingertips, suggested the woman smoked. Her pale, gaunt face and tiny frame made her seem older than her forty-two years.

'Not too bad.'

'You're the officer in charge of the investigation at Loch Spiorad, aren't you? I saw you on the television.'

He managed to force a smile.

'Yes, that's me. Could I have a bottle of Balblair, please?'

Janice stretched up to reach a grey box of twelve-year-old mature whisky, but David stopped her.

'No, I'll take the eighteen-year-old instead. It's for a special occasion.'

As she returned to the counter, she coughed into her elbow. Although it was tough for everyone in the Covid pandemic having to wear masks, he wished at that exact moment to be wearing one once more.

'Am I right that the body found was a woman in her twenties with long auburn hair?'

David nodded.

'If you have any information about a potential sighting, you need to...'

She interrupted, bursting with information she wanted him to hear.

'I've kept meaning to come over to the hall to tell the police, but I've been on shifts and haven't gotten around to it. There's a lassie like that who comes in here. She shops and occasionally posts letters and parcels late at night. Our shop has a post office counter that's open until ten. She always turns up just before closing when it's quiet.'

'That is very interesting. You don't happen to know her name, do you?'

The shop assistant leaned on the counter for a second or two, breathing heavily before answering.

'No, she hardly ever speaks. She's a shy young lass, but I know her mail is always sent to the same place in Birmingham. I noticed because of the name.'

David's eyes widened at this information.

'She always sends everything to an address in Bournville, to be exact. Dark Lane was always going to stick in my mind!'

The detective's head leaned gently to the right, puzzled for a moment. Undeterred, Janice grabbed a bar of chocolate, wrapped in a rich red colour, emblazoned with gold wording, and held it up, as if showing a most prized trophy.

'You know, like the dark chocolate bar, Bournville?'

Finally, the penny dropped.

Chisholm nodded.

'And I remember the surname on the letters.'

Now the shopkeeper held his full attention. He inhaled loudly. This was a breakthrough. It had to be.

'Go on.'

Again, she coughed into her elbow, then cursed.

'This damn cough. It'll be the end of me! Rose. The name was Rose. Can't you see the irony?'

This time, to make herself crystal clear, she grabbed the abandoned Bournville bar yet again and stretched to the top shelf behind her for a box of Roses chocolates.

'Look...Cadbury's! They are both made in Birmingham!'

'When was the last time you saw her?'

'That's easy. It was a week last Monday morning. Her car was in the car park before the shop opened, and she was the first customer in as I turned the key in the door. She looked terrible and could hardly stand up. Such a pale colour, I felt sorry for her. When I commented it was an unusual time for her to visit the shop, she told me she was suffering from an upset tummy. She posted a package.'

'Did she send it to the same address?'

'I never noticed. It probably was. It's so easy to remember: 322 Dark Lane, Bournville, Birmingham.'

'Do you have any CCTV?'

The shop assistant shook her head.

'Don't be daft; this is Loch Dubhglas, not some big city. Nothing ever happens here usually!'

'Do you think you could give a statement to one of the officers tomorrow at some point? It would be good to formally record this information. Give as much detail as you can remember.'

She'd been animated in her chatter until this point, but now her eyes didn't meet his gaze. For a moment, she didn't respond. Then, with the briefest of nods, she began scanning the items. Sensing Janice didn't like the idea of formality, he made no further comment, paid for his food and thanked her for her time.

He returned to his car and sat replaying the conversation over and over in his head. It seemed the victim had potential links to the Midlands. Where did a woman called Rose fit in? Perhaps she killed the woman in the loch. He needed results from the lab if anything was to make sense and confirmation that Anna Green was the green-eyed loch goddess.

†††††

Stretching across to his glove compartment, he searched for a scrap of paper containing a telephone number. Trembling, he pressed the digits on his mobile and waited for the sound of ringing. A familiar voice answered.

'Hello, Jimmy Mackay speaking.'

'Jimmy, it's David Chisholm. Would you like to come for a ride up to the old croft at Kinness? Sorry if I'm disturbing your evening. Perhaps tomorrow instead?'

There was the briefest of pauses before Jimmy spoke.

'Nay, lad. I've waited for your call for more than thirty years. Come and fetch me. I'll be ready.'

The engine roared into action. Jimmy gave him the instructions to find his house, just on the outskirts of the village. As he pulled up, the door opened, and out came the fisherman towards him. Once inside the car, David felt he needed to unburden himself immediately.

'I owe you an apology, Jimmy. I'm so sorry for being standoffish but I've been pre-occupied with work. There hasn't been the opportunity to catch up with you before this evening.'

He paused for a moment, then softly added,

'It's been a massive thing for me to return to Loch Dubhglas after all this time.'

Home was Sutherland and always had been. Only now was David ready to acknowledge and accept the grief before he could move on. Fate, in the form of a murder victim in Loch Spiorad, found by Jimmy, brought him back to a place he avoided because of his past. Although they were, in effect, strangers, words gushed from his mouths, each understanding the significance.

'Losing Dad so young took me on a different path to the future he and Mum planned: the son of a crofter, belonging to the Chisholm clan. The consequences of tiredness and an accidental death at such a young age led to more tragedy for our family.

As you know, we moved away to Inverness a few months after his death. Mum tried her best to recover, but she never got over what happened at Kinness and attempted suicide several times. She spent time in *The Craigs*[14] when I was still at primary school. The bonds made with my grandparents during that time became strong. Returning from Inverness to live with them while my mother recovered from a breakdown brought comfort and stability to me. Summer holidays were always spent here throughout my childhood and teenage years, but Mum only ever dropped me off and picked me up. She never stayed at the croft.

I idolised Granda. Probably the seeds of wanting to be a police officer came from him, as he taught me honesty, a sense of right and wrong, and to always help others. He was my hero, whilst my Grannie acted like a comfort blanket to me. She hugged me, kept me warm and safe, tucked me into bed at night, and fed me divine homemade bread that still makes my mouth water at the thought of it.

Granda died of a heart attack when I was fifteen. We'd returned to Inverness, and Mum was stable for a while. With my grandfather gone, I sought the hustle and bustle of Inverness and the anonymity of city life.

I couldn't bear the thought of Kinness; it was my hatred of the place and determination not to return that made me abandon my grandmother. She died several years later; her loneliness haunts me. I could have helped her, gone back, and taken on the croft. Instead, I chose my usual survival tactic of digging a big hole in the sand in which to stick my stubborn and often complex head. She's long gone now, but the guilt weighs heavily in my heart. The world truly ended when she was gone. There were no more hugs or comfort blankets.

The board placed at the end of the lane for the sale of the croft is the last thing I can remember. The animals were sold, along with all the farming machinery.

Mum grew more and more distant. Kinness had been her home after her parents died. With all the grief of losing them so young and then my father dying, it was a lot for a lass of barely twenty to manage. After the best part of twenty years to perfect her skills at taking her own life, she finally achieved her ambition to die. Ironically, the cause had not been suicide but a stroke that was swift and unexpected.

It was the final tipping point to a world of emptiness. I coped by losing myself in the police force and shutting out all signs of emotional attachment to anyone or anything. My marriage failed because of my lack of emotion.'

Jimmy listened. He wiped away tears as David talked of the good times and the bad. It was sad the lad had no memories of Donald. He knew most of the history of the family, but to hear the story from the son's point of view was upsetting.

For a while, neither man spoke. David headed towards Dubhness, then turned off for Kinness. The two men approached the familiar entrance to the croft at the end of a narrow lane. The first stars appeared in the twilight. In a turning circle, in front of the gates, David manoeuvred the car until it pointed back down the hill.

From here, in the distance, they could see Loch Dubhglas to the south and Loch Spiorad to the north. He parked on a grass verge a few metres from the wooden sign, 'Sealladh[15],' similar to the one passed each day on his way to and from primary school. Painted white with black lettering, the name stood out far more than he remembered from his childhood.

He glanced in his rearview mirror, looking back at the scene behind him. Several lights twinkled from the old croft house. A dark-haired woman in her early thirties stood at the door, calling three young children in for bed. At first, they ignored her, but when she called again, they ran across the yard in wellingtons, pushing and shoving each other as they finally obeyed their mother. One slightly taller than the next. Had the light not faded, he would have witnessed two boys tanned by their love for the outdoors, together with a girl, smaller than her brothers, with long dark hair like a mane blowing behind her, wild and messy. Cheeks rosy and ready for a bath, they laughed and joked as they entered their home. Jimmy also watched the bairns.

'You see. There is life back in the old place, David.'

Chisholm nodded. Painful as it was to see another family living where he should have raised his own children, he knew he must end the misery.

Breaking the baguette into two large chunks, he ripped open each piece and placed slices of cheese to fill the void, along with bits of salad to grant his body a morsel of healthy nutrition. They sat in silence, munching and taking in the view overlooking the lochs. The sun set to the west; vivid oranges and reds staining the water. It was a beautiful evening. Both knew more words would come, more tears too.

When David parked the car outside Mackay's house an hour later, he knew he would be walking back to the Bed & Breakfast. In Jimmy's lounge, the past poured out, as did the golden spirit, bottled and labelled Balblair. The whisky would bring them contentment and a bond of friendship they both needed. Eventually, he strolled back to his bed, with a stomach full of chocolate and *"the water of life."* His frozen heart, a glacier formed long ago, flooded with warmth, had begun to thaw.

†††††

This evening, I wish the detective wisdom. May the Goddess Snotra[16] bring him knowledge and perception as he gathers information, revealing my death and my life. His perceptions and instincts will hold fast.

The complex taste of his whisky is built on firm beginnings, from the purest of water from Highland burns. Together with peat and heather, the elements dwell in harmony in every drop of the nectar he tastes. I watch him pour out his soul as he sips Balblair's finest.

His glass is full, rich, and mature. He's a fine man. I find comfort that my story is in his hands. People underestimate him. His brain works quickly, and now that his heart is alive once more, he is no longer numb to emotion. His contentment thrills me. An ice-cold heart begins to thaw, dripping onto Jimmy's carpet, flooding his house, rushing down the street in a torrential storm, and gushes into Loch Dubhglas.

He knows the person I became. The identity meant there was no future for me, but he will find my past. Snotra, guide him to enlightenment.

SNOTRA
Goddess of Wisdom

CHAPTER 10
Day 9 : Wednesday, 1st October

Helen knocked impatiently on David's bedroom door, eager to share the news. He called out to her to wait a few seconds whilst he dressed. As the door opened, Helen was surprised at his appearance. Unshaven, bleary-eyed, and not yet fully awake, his demeanour was unusual. Normally her boss was precise and sharp if anyone was late, but here he stood at his doorway, dishevelled and tardy.

'The chief's been trying to get hold of you. Why did you switch your phone off?'

David dashed to his mobile on the bedside table to check. The battery was flat. Annoyed at himself for not putting it on charge overnight, he quickly connected the lead, and within seconds, ping after ping could be heard as voice messages and texts were rapidly announced.

'Not sure what happened! I never sleep like this normally! What does McLeod want? Did she tell you?'

Helen nodded.

'We are summoned to meet with Sir William Altingham. You know the guy, *"Mr. Keep It Clean, Make It Green,"* the Member of Parliament who started that campaign to green all the towns and cities down south. Apparently, he has travelled up from London to stay with a friend on one of the estates, and as a government minister, he would like an update on the case so he can personally inform the Prime Minister of how our enquiries are proceeding. I didn't realise members of the British government were briefed about murder. Did you know?'

Without pausing for an answer, twirling around, she showed off her outfit.

'Look, I put on some decent clothes for once!'

He nodded but refrained from commenting on her smart apparel: a rather short, purple skirt and black tights that seemed to elongate her legs and a bright pink top, partially covered by her familiar leather jacket.

'What time are we to be there?'

'You need to get a move on; our appointment is for ten o'clock.'

Water trickled through his fingers as Chisholm attempted to liven himself by splashing it onto his face. In minutes, he was ready to leave, immaculate as ever. Meetings with government ministers didn't happen every day, and he didn't want to be late. If anything, it was more out of curiosity that he hurried to get ready. Westminster must have sent the man all the way up to Sutherland to find out about the national security alert, he guessed. Helen thought it was best to get the other news of the day out of the way as soon as possible.

'You also need to see this.'

She passed him several folded newspapers. As he opened the first one, the headline jumped out at him: *"Drugs Linked to Body in Loch."* The second newspaper had a similar heading. He threw them onto the back seat of the car in disgust.

'Gutter snipes! Why do they make up such stupid stories as these?'

†††††

Helen studied her satnav for directions to the estate, but David knew the way. His teenage memories of earning money as a beater, searching out game birds for the estate guests to shoot, were embedded in his mind: the company of his friends, the money, and the free lunches. It also gave the teenagers something to do over the six-week summer vacation, keeping them occupied on days when the novelty of working full-time on the crofts waned.

Without thinking, the detective directed his sergeant down a single-track lane. He remained silent as she drove through the village of Loch Dubhglas, annoyed at himself for the missed calls and oversleeping.

Helen felt it was best not to comment. His mood had been unusual since the day of the discovery of the body. On the shoreline of Loch Spiorad, more than a week before, she sensed something was not as it normally was with Chisholm. He was severe and sharp, but here he sat in her car, disorganised but pleasant. To get up late was unheard of for him. She wished he would say what was going on with the mood swings, but she knew not to ask.

'Do you know this place? It's just that the map said to keep going along the main road out of Loch Dubhglas for another mile.'

'Yes, I know where we need to go. I worked on the estate when I was a teenager for a few weeks each summer.'

'Do you know the area then? Have you stayed up here on holiday or something?'

'My family kept a croft nearby. I went to live in Inverness when I was young but came back for holidays and then to live for a few years when my mother was ill.'

He never spoke of his background. This was strange and another sign of being out of character. The information David gave Helen did not quieten her mind. She was intrigued.

'Do you still have family up here then?'

Chisholm shook his head.

'No. They're all long gone, but coming back here again has certainly been a trip down memory lane. Here we are. Let's go in the main entrance for once!'

A huge black, wrought iron gate hung at each side of the driveway, marking the approach to the estate for the owner, his family, and guests. Being unfamiliar with this route, even David was interested to witness the *"posh entrance."* All employees were expected to use a less impressive gate half a mile further along the lane.

The smooth private road contrasted sharply with the council one, full of potholes they'd left behind. A row of shiny laurel bushes lined each side of the drive, neatly trimmed to shoulder height. The narrow lane twisted and turned until it widened out, the shrubbery ended, and lush green lawns came into view. To the right, in the distance, was a huge pond. The surface was covered in white and pink water lilies, intermingled with shiny green leaves. To the left of the drive, ancient cedar trees reached into the sky, providing shade for picnics on sunny days. Underneath each trunk, the earth was bare except for gnarled, exposed roots that stretched their limbs further and further away from their belonging.

Helen, a lass from a tenement block in Govan, shook her head.

'Don't you think it's wrong that one family has all this wealth when twenty million more have nothing? It's obscene!'

'Sadly, *"The Haves"* have always done well from *"The Have-Nots."* It's wrong but has gone on for centuries.'

'Who owns this place?'

'I believe the estate has changed hands several times since I was a lad. I've lost track of who owns it now. Usually these days, only foreign businessmen, whose wealth comes from oil, can afford these relics. Just a guess.'

'Well, that's interesting! After all, *"Mr. Keep It Clean, Make It Green"* may be staying at a place funded with fossil fuel money.'

The irony wasn't lost on either of the detectives. It was easy to feel insignificant in a place where cash was king. The drive veered away from the cedars and the pond. A high brick wall was now on either side of the lane, a privacy screen for the eighteenth-century castle with round turreted towers that lay ahead. Even Helen, a true socialist at heart, could not help but gasp at the impressive grey stone building in front of her. The influence of French design harked back to a long-lost world when Scotland and France held close ties through their royal dynasties.

Several flashy-looking cars were parked close to the grand entrance. Daniels parked next to a shiny red Ferrari 488 and smiled for the first time that day.

'Blimey! Someone has money to burn!'

Both police officers adjusted their clothes as they climbed six steps towards the impressive-looking entrance. Helen tugged at the hemline of her skirt, wishing she had chosen to wear trousers instead. Chisholm fastened his jacket and checked the zip on his trousers. He pushed an ornate brass doorbell, which could be heard sounding inside. They waited a few seconds until a man in his forties appeared, dressed in a black suit and white shirt, looking formal and serious. On showing their identity cards, he beckoned them into an ornate hallway decorated with a marble floor and high white ceilings. They stood at the bottom of a winding staircase, carpeted in a plush dark blue tartan. A series of large oil paintings covering each wall: subdued Highland scenery and wildlife in each piece of art, all echoing dark, heathery hills and the hunt for game.

The man led them to a study, a few doors away from where they'd entered the building. A library, full of ancient leather-bound books, filled three sides of the room. From the ornate white plastered ceiling down to the polished, wooden floor, the shelves were full of history. He beckoned them to sit on an enormous brown Chesterfield couch. Around the outer edges of the room, a herringbone parquet floor peeped out from a huge grey tartan mat with its beige and wine lines. As they stepped onto the carpet, both felt their shoes sink into the luxurious pile.

'I'll let Sir William know you are here.'

Once alone, they scanned the room and the opulent environment in which they found themselves.

'All we need now is the fire to be lit, a pipe in hand, and a dram or two of the finest whisky.'

For once, it was David who jested. Helen nodded, still taking in all the history of the place. She cast her eye towards the large French windows. A golden retriever scampered across a highly manicured, vivid green lawn, closely followed by a young woman dressed in a pink hoodie and blue jeans. Both disappeared from view.

The wooden door behind them burst open, and in came a distinguished man, tall and smartly dressed in a tweed suit. Secretly googling his name earlier in preparation for the visit, Helen bit her lip in an attempt not to smirk. Wikipedia stated his age was sixty-five, but he looked younger and was very handsome. The stories online stated an age gap of forty years between him and his latest wife. Number three spouse was, like the first and second ones before her, blonde with long legs, plastic breasts, and a fake smile. The detective sergeant sensed he was attracted to a certain type of woman. No doubt he could charm his way out of any sticky situation if headlines were believed. The ladies seemed to love him, no matter how many times he married or how many times he cheated. He was wealthy, and that was all that mattered to some females.

Stretching out his hand, he greeted them. His Oxbridge voice filled the room, as if he were speaking to a large, rowdy crowd in Parliament. Helen sensed he held her hand for a moment too long. She felt uneasy by the way he cast his eye down her body as he approached. He mistook the shudder she gave as a gentle tremble when he touched her skin. Perhaps she was excited at meeting him. Women always were. He smiled, charmingly polite. Repulsed at his manner, she locked eyes with him, staring and refusing to break her frown. She had met his type before, a male who thought he was God's gift to women.

'Thanks for coming. I appreciate you are busy with this investigation. How are things going? I have spoken to your superiors, but I thought I should get a briefing from officers on the ground.'

Chisholm took the lead, trying to ascertain the minister's knowledge of the case.

'I'm not sure how much you know, sir.'

'There's not much I don't know. Unidentified toxin similar to ricin, I hear. Is there any truth to this being drug-related? I've seen the headlines. Any news on who the woman is yet?'

Chisholm shook his head. He wasn't able to confirm the woman was Anna Green until there were any DNA matches, so he chose not to mention the new lead.

'Terrible tragedy for the woman. Is there any truth in it being an Eastern European gangster? Perhaps a sex worker on the run from him because she escaped his clutches, or she double-crossed him in a drug deal. They are the only people to get their hands on old stocks of chemicals such as A4-7 or the like these days.'

'We are getting dribs and drabs of information from the public, but it seems no one knew the woman. Obviously, the substance does make one consider the Baltic states as a starting point. As always, we follow the evidence gathered, rather than guessing. There is no link to drugs, although stories are appearing in the press connecting them. We need to squash that rumour.'

Sir William was satisfied, although they had given him no new information. He rose to his feet to dismiss them.

'Well, thank you for coming once again. I'll give you my number should you get any more leads. I'd really like to keep the P.M. briefed. As I was up here on business and taking several days away from everything, it did seem appropriate that I should speak to you on behalf of His Majesty's government. It's a matter of national security if there are idiots going around poisoning people.'

The minister paused before checking his watch, then offered some obligatory politeness.

'Would you like some refreshments before you go?'

The detectives shook their heads, understanding full well that the invitation was not sincere. Meeting a Member of Parliament was unusual for both of them, and they wanted to escape as soon as possible. Sir William handed Chisholm a business card and reiterated the need for communication as soon as there were any updates on the case.

'If we are finished, I must get on. Flying back to London later after a few days up here. It's been a good trip, but I have pressing engagements back in the capital. Good to meet members of the Northern Constabulary. John will see you out.'

He opened the door, and as if rehearsed thousands of times, the man who had shown them into the study appeared. The servant led them back to the main entrance and out onto the steps without saying a word. The door closed, and the detectives were back in the driveway. As they headed towards the road, away from the opulence and grandeur, Helen and David relaxed.

'Thank heavens that's over. I hope we don't have to contact him again.'

'So do I, but I sense he'll be rather pushy until this is over. Used to getting his own way, no doubt. I'm glad we don't get a murder like this every day. Can you imagine constantly briefing ministers? Let's get back to the real world—a murder in Loch Spiorad! Can you drop me off at the next turn? I left the car last night so I could have a few drams with an old friend.'

Helen could not hold back.

'Blimey, Chisholm! There's a whisky or two in the old fox yet!'

'There's more, Helen. Since I spoke to you last, I went into the local shop, and the shop assistant had some interesting news. I didn't tell Sir William. I want to keep this more hush-hush for now. We are being played.'

†††††

In the late afternoon, as blood sugars lowered and with the team's enthusiasm dwindling whilst they awaited DNA results, spirits were renewed when some female village stalwarts entered, bringing homemade baking treats. All the ladies were not a day younger than seventy. Their silvery grey and white locks sparkled from shafts of light that came into the hall from a high window above the proceedings, making them look like the heavenly host. All wore knee-length cotton raincoats in a rainbow of colours. Each woman, if seen on her own, would have appeared frail and old, but together, in their group of seven or eight, they turned into a force to be reckoned with. No police officer would want to confront them if they began to riot.

The group of ladies was led by an elderly woman, cloaked in purple attire that accentuated the whiteness of her hair. She was neither meek nor mild and certainly wasn't an angel. By the way she spoke, it was clear her first language was not English. A Gaelic speaker, born on the Isle of Lewis, her voice sounded different from the women surrounding her. Despite her diminutive stature, she showed a confidence that none of the other women possessed. As the spokeswoman, without being invited to do so, she addressed the ensemble on behalf of the cooks. The hall fell silent. There was a presence about the woman that made everyone pay attention.

'Good afternoon, officers. My name is Flora MacAskill, the chairlady from the Loch Dubhglas church committee. Our members thought we should welcome you to our village, so we have made some cake, biscuits, and tablet[17] to keep you going.'

A table was quickly cleared for the treats as the elderly ladies dived into their shopping bags and baskets, producing enough food to fill a football stadium.

Little delights wrapped in silver foil were opened. Neatly labelled tops were taken off plastic containers and placed underneath each box of goodies. The smell of warm sausage rolls and quiche wafted throughout the hall. Fairy cakes, iced with various shades of pink, blue, yellow, and green, were covered with hundreds and thousands and other decorating treats. Sultanas, currants, raisins, and candied orange peel had been soaked for hours in whisky, and turned into rich slices of fruit loaf. Gingerbread men and other biscuit treats were unwrapped, as well as gorgeous cubes of tablet that melted in the mouth as soon as they were placed between the lips. The baking was an instant success with the police officers, many of whom had eaten little since breakfast and faced a long journey home. None regretted sampling more than they should.

'We want to help in any way we can.'

The women nodded in unison.

Helen thought she would use her initiative with the small group in front of her. Ladies like these always knew everyone in their village and what went on.

'Do any of you happen to know of someone who drives an old red transit van?'

Flora MacAskill's tone instantly changed from a meek churchgoing woman to a veritable Rottweiler. She snapped the answer, clearly having an opinion about the man.

'Alec Sullivan does, the local mechanic. He's always up to no good!'

Helen continued, ignoring the way the lady answered.

'Anyone else?'

No one had anything else to say on the matter, so Helen changed her questions, directing them towards the identification of the unknown victim.

'Do any of you recognise the description we are circulating about the person found in the Loch Spiorad? A white, slim built lady around twenty-five to thirty-five, with green eyes and auburn hair.'

Once more, the leader of the group took control, answering on behalf of the others.

'One of the reasons for bringing the baking was to say we think she may have been to our church a few times.'

She sniffed heavily, her voice dismissive. Her thoughts about the woman spewed out, leaving no one in any doubt she had any time for the lady.

'Not a regular churchgoer. She only graced the Lord with her presence two or three times, and that was months ago. No one knows her name nor address.'

'Did anyone speak to her?'

They all shook their heads. Helen's shoulders sank as hope disappeared as quickly as it arrived. Then she saw her, a woman at the back of the group, her hand half raised.

'Madam, did you speak to her?'

'No, but my friend Iris did.'

Her head gestured to a woman standing next to her who uttered not a word. All eyes turned to a lady with greying hair, wearing a deep red-coloured raincoat... her face now as crimson as her clothing. She frowned at her companion, uncomfortable at being thrown into the headlights. Composing herself with the briefest of smiles towards Helen, she nodded. The women, not knowing of their timid companion's contact with the mysterious visitor, swung around to glare at her. The sea of pensioners parted, and she stepped forward, nervously biting her lip. Her eyes shot to the ground. Iris Stirling was unused to being the centre of attention. Flora MacAskill tutted her dislike of this news.

'You spoke to her? 'Why on earth did you not tell me?'

Ignoring the questions, Helen continued.

'What can you tell me about her?'

Iris spoke quietly, barely above a whisper. Helen leaned forward to catch the words the woman said.

'Would you prefer to speak privately?

The elderly lady nodded. Mrs. MacAskill scowled, turned sharply, and marched out of the door in disgust. A couple of her followers scurried out of a side door at the back of the hall to escape her wrath. Hell hath no fury like Flora MacAskill. The rest stayed put, wanting to know what Iris had to say.

In a quieter part of the room, away from everyone else, Helen repeated the question. Recovering from the shock of being publicly revealed, the old woman was calmer, and her cheeks were barely pink. This time the woman spoke more confidently with a Scottish twang.

'My friend, Morven, made more of a story than was true. I spoke to the woman just a couple of times. She was a quiet lassie. She seemed reluctant to join in any church activities other than services, but I got the impression she wanted to, as she seemed a lonely lady. I hardly had any conversation with her.'

'Did she tell you her name?'

'No. She was a nervy type, constantly looking over her shoulder. The last time I saw her, about a month ago, she was outside the local shop with another lassie. It was unusual as she was always on her own. I didn't tell the other women as they would have made a fuss, and it would have been the talk of the village. It was rather late when I went out, just before the shop closed. I ran out of milk, and they would all...'

The woman paused. Helen repeated her words in the hope that she would continue her train of thought.

'They would all...?'

Leaning into Helen's personal space, the woman whispered so that no one could eavesdrop.

'Judge me for being out so late when I should have been getting ready for bed. The fuss they would all make if they saw what I saw, and knew the things I know about her but I keep those kind of things to myself.'

'What fuss? I'm not sure what you mean.'

'I felt sorry for the girl as she always came across as so lonely. I was glad she had a friend. Can you imagine the fuss if that lot saw them?'

She nodded towards the small group of women who were still tightly packed in a huddle, gossiping about what their friend could possibly be saying to the police officer.

'Look at them blethering away to each other. What would they say if they saw two women kissing in the shadows behind the shop?'

Helen's demeanour changed. Her tone was sharper. She sensed she knew the answer. It was more of a rhetorical question than one where she expected an answer. Attempting to be less defensive, she tried to soften the question, making it less aggressive.

'What would they have said?'

The old lady cupped her hands, and leaning closer to Helen, whispered,

'They would be the talk of the village. I think they were lovers.'

†††††

After the home baking was demolished and teas and coffees drunk, Chisholm took Helen and Euan to one side and in hushed tones created a plan. For now the shopkeeper's witness statement and the address to where mail was posted by Anna Green were not revealed to anyone but the other two detectives. It seemed letters were always sent to just one place in the West Midlands. David wanted to pursue the lead and requested Euan accompany him.

The young officer was delighted and readily agreed, despite knowing he would be missing a Saturday match at Ross County, his beloved football team, which he and his pals affectionately called *The Staggies*. Weekends usually meant a few beers before and after the match, a curry at his favourite Indian restaurant, followed by Sundays recovering in bed for half the day. A weekend away with the boss and a promised bevy or two sounded less favourable, but he was interested enough in the case to want to see where the jaunt would lead.

At the end of the day, the doors were locked so no public could enter. Each member of the group was asked for updates.

When David shared the scientific evaluations just received from the lab, everyone could sense the gravity in his voice as he informed them of all the data.

'The test results show a DNA match for hair samples found on the woman and in the shower trap. The lady who lived at Dubhness Cottage is the same lady who was found in the loch. Our victim is Anna Green. There are no DNA matches on the database, so we'll widen the search tomorrow to see if the ancestry sites have any potential links. Helen, can you follow that line of inquiry with Shona MacPherson, please?'

Euan reported last but one.

'All leads about a potential wedding or any occurring in the last year are dead. No wedding notices were posted, and all celebrants known to perform ceremonies in the entire area drew blanks. There were no announcements in the *Raggie*[18]. It doesn't look like the woman married anyone in the last few months.'

Next, Chisholm held up the newspapers, revealing the headlines about the links to drugs.

'This is rubbish. We have no scientific evidence whatsoever of this being about substances like cocaine. Where these journalists are getting their stories from is ridiculous! They should be fiction writers.'

He flung them on a table and shook his head.

'I know several of you have been searching for any ladies by the name of Anna Green in the Highlands. All matches were eliminated. Helen, you have spent the afternoon chatting with villagers. Any updates, please?'

Her mouth dried as she began to share the conversation between herself and the lady from the church group. The tips of her ears and her cheeks began to glow. She tried to act her casual self, but the thumping in her head and in her chest made it difficult to breathe.

'From information gathered from a villager today, one evening, about a month ago, a woman matching Anna's description was seen exiting the local shop, and in the shadows behind the building, she was spotted kissing a woman with long dark hair .'

Chisholm homed in on two young male officers poking each other in the ribs, quietly jesting at the possibility that Anna was in a lesbian relationship. His words were sharp and to the point.

'Grow up, the pair of you! I will not tolerate anyone on my team making homophobic jibes or comments. It's juvenile and reportable. Helen, can you get the witness to give a more detailed description of the lady Anna was seen with?'

No reply came. A door closed at the far end of the hall. Casting an eye around the room, he realised that one member of the team was missing.

†††††

Tears streamed down onto her cheeks, blurring her vision so much that she pulled into a lay-by. At least she recognised it was too dangerous to drive in the state she was in. She stopped the vehicle and sat, head in her hands. No number of threats by senior officers would make the hurt go away. There were always fools who couldn't keep their homophobic opinions to themselves.

Prejudice existed in the police force, the army, teaching, and in every walk of life, it seemed. There was even a campaign to stop a Gay Pride march in Inverness a few years before, with plenty of signatures gathered from across the Highlands.

In Glasgow, there was much less attention when two women walked into a bar as they were amongst thousands out clubbing or in a pub each weekend. The looks since she'd moved further north were there on any afternoon, having coffee in a café. The questions on everyone's lips, watching her and her girlfriend holding hands as they talked about their future together, were sometimes vocalised in voices deliberately far louder than a whisper, *"Do you think they are lesbi-friends? Have you seen the gays slobbering all over each other?"*

It was best to avoid some of the pubs where they knew the taunts would be unbearable or where someone punched a lad for looking at him in *"a gay way."* There could be no Catholic wedding that Helen dreamed of since being small. It was not permitted and probably wouldn't be for several centuries to come.

She was getting married in a small, intimate ceremony in a hotel on the banks of Loch Ness. No one from work would be invited because they didn't know of her impending nuptials, not even Chisholm. She felt a pang of guilt every time she thought about the lack of an invitation to him. He was a decent man who held no prejudice, but she did not want to burden him with her private matters. She was furious with herself: the response to comments in the hall, running away, and even the tears.

The secret she kept from her work colleagues lay buried and would not be dragged out of her for fear it would harm her career. She was not ashamed of being gay, but she knew the preconceived ideas of being in a single-sex relationship and what it could bring to a job that was already hard. She had been *"out"* for years, telling her mother when she was fifteen, but the secret at work took its toll on her. The open, jokey manner she offered in the office was a smokescreen, diverting others away from the real Helen.

Finding an old hanky in her jacket, she wiped away her tears and told herself she was being silly. She needed to pack the emotions away in their box. Scrambling down the list of contacts on her phone, she found her fiancée's name. She dialled the number and heard the reassuring voice at the other end.

'I'm heading back. It's been a bit of a day. Can you order Chinese for delivery in about an hour? Love you!'

The voice echoed.

'I love you too. Drive safely.'

By the time she reached home, Helen managed to calm herself. The road was relatively quiet, and the traffic over the Kessock Bridge was not too busy. She filled her mind with wedding plans. Her dress fitting was only days away. The image of her gown lifted her spirits, and the knots in her stomach were replaced with bubbles of nervous excitement. Narrow-minded comments would not break her, nor the joy she felt for the upcoming nuptials.

On reaching home, as she opened the door, she was greeted by an over-enthusiastic black Labrador who leapt up to express delight at seeing his other human. After twenty licks from a moist, pink tongue and numerous sniffs around her pockets to ensure there were no doggy treats to be had, Odin bounded off in search of other, more interesting opportunities to steal food. The Chinese takeaway, delivered five minutes before, smelt delicious. The dog fancied his chances of a successful mission to gain more treats.

'You're back just in time!'

'I have brought gifts. Do you fancy some wine?'

Georgina popped her head around the door at the news. She could see a bottle of Prosecco and a small package of silver tinfoil baking leftovers from the church group shared out amongst the police officers. The contents she'd stuffed into her bag before walking out of the hall were intact, thankfully.

'You sounded weird on the phone. Are you okay?'

'Nothing that can't be put right with the Chinese, a glass or two, and you. Everything is okay. Work just got to me. One of the young coppers made a comment, as it looks like the murder victim at Loch Spiorad might be gay.'

'That's his problem, not yours. Did you report him?'

'No, David jumped on the comment immediately and gave him a warning. I'm sure it will calm down tomorrow, but for some reason, it got to me today. Anyway, let's change the subject. How did you get on with your assignment?'

'Sit down at the table. I'll bring in the food before Odin gets his paws on it!'

Right on cue, the dog appeared as the meal was brought in. They sat eating for a few minutes, his eyes following each forkful entering their mouths. He knew from trying the begging routine every evening he would get scraps despite having wolfed his own meal less than twenty minutes before.

'How did the assessment go on the Norse goddesses?'

'The assignment went well. I got an 'A,' so I'm pleased. It was well worth focusing on three of the goddesses and putting in those extra hours of research.

Studying Hel, Snotra, and Iduna in greater depth got me the better mark, thankfully. The lecturer liked the title of my thesis, *"Norse Goddesses—The Relevance to Feminism in the 21st Century"* so I may still get a first.'

'There is no doubt in my eyes, through the work and effort you are putting in. The thesis will be brilliant, and you'll be a published best selling author after all of this.'

Her partner beamed. Helen concentrated on twirling some noodles around her fork as they chatted.

'How's Chisholm? Is he still odd?'

'He told me today he grew up in the area around Loch Dubhglas. It was a surprise. *"D.I. Iceberg"* is definitely thawing.'

'From what you tell me, he needs a good woman in his life. Shame we are both spoken for. Is he still pretending he is married?'

'He never mentions being divorced from Jane. He would hit the roof if he realised I knew. I've not mentioned a word of it to anyone at work. It's a small world that you know her from your days at the hospital. I want to say something to him because he's clearly affected by the split, but he is such a closed shop about his family. I wish he would open up and stop being so guarded about everything. He's so full of tension, and his mood swings have been fierce since we've been on this case.'

'But Helen, you don't share your story with him, do you? You haven't told anyone on the force about me, yet I talk about you all the time. You can't expect to have a deeper relationship with your boss if you aren't honest either. Have you thought about that?'

She knew Georgina was right. It was a topic discussed at length, but Helen seemed immovable in her belief that news of her sexuality would cause problems at work. There should be no need to talk about being gay or straight. She wasn't ashamed of who she was, what she was, or who she went to bed with, but she still did not have the courage to be more open at work about her future wife. Officers continued to be suspended pending investigations over inappropriate social media comments on a range of topics, including lesbianism.

Chisholm did not talk about his life. Why should she? It was a working relationship; sharing personal details with her boss was unnecessary. An unspoken agreement not to share their lives was long established; each had their reasons.

After today, telling David about Georgina felt more difficult than ever. What would be her fate if he or her colleagues got wind of her marriage? Her mind flooded with panic for the second time in a few hours. She didn't think she had the strength to tackle the homophobia that she knew existed amongst some of the officers in the force. The jokes, the innuendos, the comments about being different in any way were ingrained into the fabric of the uniforms of some. Being gay, a woman or being an officer of colour brought prejudicial views from misogynists and racists who sadly still were employed as police to keep the streets supposedly safe.

'If you speak out, these emotions you are experiencing will lessen. You know it, and I know it.'

'I hear what you are saying, but it doesn't make things any easier. The young officers today joked openly about lesbians. What would they say away from my face?'

'The only way you can change attitudes is to conquer your fears and lead from the front. Be brave, and you can face anything!'

'You mean like the Valkyrie[19]? But aren't they all dead?'

Her girlfriend nodded and hugged her.

'Look at Odin. He will help!'

As Georgina patted his head, the Labrador wagged his tail, hoping for another walk before bedtime. One or both humans would oblige. Helen nodded. She wanted to clear her head. Rather than having a restless night without sleep, she needed to get the endorphins moving to alter her mindset. She knew her lover was right, but finding courage was hard. On these evenings, when her job bore heavily on her mind, Georgina tried to support her. While Helen was out with Odin, she would create her version of heaven for her girlfriend's return: a warm bath infused with lavender, scented candles, a mug of hot chocolate, and a bar of Dairy Milk.

The two detectives do not see what I see. The smell from the last of the summer's roses wafts into the room as the dog bounds through the French doors, into the library ahead of the woman. No one notices there is a tiny red ladybird with black spots landing softly on its petals. I listen as the

woman speaks. She has only one question to ask. It is blurted out before the man has time to pat the golden retriever.

'Well?'

The abruptness annoys him. His curt reply hides nothing. 'They don't yet know her.'

'Christ! It won't take them long. What should we do?'

'We are doing nothing. I have a flight back to London this evening. No one knows you are here, apart from me and John. Make sure it stays that way. You got yourself into this mess, Samantha. As usual, I'm picking up the pieces. Try to stay out of trouble whilst I'm away. My name won't dragged into this; am I clear?'

She shakes as she nods, thinking that everything is all her fault. He storms out of the library; the door slams behind him. He considers instructing John to drive to the middle of nowhere and dump her and the dog, but he has an affection for the mutt. She will stay, for now.

I prepare to take flight. Today the air is still. Apart from the roses, autumn scents abound, full of decaying vegetation and mustiness. Consumed with sadness, I feel the detective's anguish, recognising the pain and hurt that my mortal soul once felt. A prejudice no one can understand unless they walk along the same path and in the same shoes as myself and Helen.

Humans make choices every single day. Some are decisions either made in a rash moment or through considerable contemplation. What to eat, what movie to watch, or what clothes to wear consumes our thoughts, but other decisions are complex. Hesitation leads to unhappiness *and feeling unfulfilled. To move forward and live without lies is hard for those who dwell on the other side of prejudice. We are who we are. There are no choices or decisions. To deny ourselves the truth, we remain, until to the end, rotting away like unpicked summer fruit.*

CHAPTER 11
Day 10 : Thursday, 2nd October

Climbing out of the inspection pit after a busy morning sorting some brakes on a Land Rover, there was nowhere for Alec Sullivan to hide when he spotted David quietly enter the garage. Spying police were paying another visit; frustration and anger rose within him. He wiped oil from his cheek with a rag, then grabbing a large wrench, he attempted to exert his authority with the weapon by tapping it in his left palm. He was more than willing to fight, especially when he felt trapped. The sight of Helen and another police officer in the doorway sent his anxiety into free fall.

Not wanting a confrontation, David spoke quietly to him, attempting to calm the situation.

'Don't do anything foolish. I've only come to ask some questions.'

'Leave me alone. I haven't done anything.'

'If you haven't *"done anything,"* why are you so reluctant to speak to me? By not cooperating, it makes it look like you do have something to hide. As you can see, there are more officers around. I can get a warrant to search these premises if you persist.'

With determination chiselled in his expression, Alec lurched forward, lifting the wrench above his head. His anger exploded. The wrench was his first and last hope. The dilemma paralysed his ability to think clearly. If he fought, he would be back in HMP Inverness. If he fled, he might get away. Instinct crushed rational thought, and cornered like a wild beast, he lashed out. He hesitated for a split second too long and lost his balance as he made one final attempt to rush out of the workshop. With an almighty bump, he landed on the oil-stained concrete floor, launching the wrench into the direction of Chisholm, The missile sent the detective diving for cover. Forcibly pinning Sullivan to the ground, the constable knelt on him whilst Helen placed handcuffs around his wrists. Once he was on his feet, the uniformed officer cautioned him whilst the detective checked on David.

'Are you okay, Boss?'

Chisholm was already standing, slightly worse for wear. He held up his hand to signal to her that he was unhurt. The landing on the garage floor had been uncomfortable, but he counted himself lucky to have no broken bones, just minor grazes on the palms of his hands and on his knees. The lump of metal had missed him by a fraction. The worst damage was a slightly dishevelled look to his once pristine suit; a dive from his old goalkeeping days had saved the detective. He dusted himself down as he gathered his thoughts. Determined not to display any emotion, he addressed the mechanic in a firm, controlled voice.

'You, sir, will be taken to Tain police station, where I'll be joining you shortly for a chat. It's not worth injuring a police officer for whatever it is you're hiding.'

Sullivan scowled. The pleasant, jokey personality he'd displayed when Helen first encountered him had vanished without a trace. He certainly wasn't flirting with her now.

†††††

Tain, the oldest burgh in Scotland, lay miles away south from Loch Dubhglas in the county of Ross-shire. The sheriff's court was an impressive eighteenth-century building in the high street. A bell, dating back to 1630, was housed within the ancient property, rescued from a previous construction that had been severely damaged by storms in 1703. The huge tower with a conical spire dominated the structure, rising high above a number of bartizans[20], projecting out from various angles on the top of a stone parapet. Many of the striking features of the building remained unspoiled from centuries of justice. Slithers of light crept in through the narrow arrow slits on each side of the tower. In all, the building resembled a French chateau rather than a place for Highland justice.

Tucked in one of the back streets away from the beautiful architecture and the busy thoroughfare stood a small, unimpressive, modern building, the only police station for miles. Alec knew it well. Suspects were brought from across the middle and east of Sutherland, as well as villages in that part of Ross-shire, to be interviewed. He was familiar with the Sheriff's Court too. Attacking a police officer with a wrench would attract attention from the procurator fiscal. Charges would be brought against him, but first he had to be questioned about the murder.

Sat with an on-duty solicitor by his side, the mechanic began to realise his latest outburst would bring another court appearance and would ruin the business he had built up. As always, a red mist masked his judgements, this time emanating from panic and guilt.

Daniels sat opposite, alongside her boss. Neither was amused at the outburst at the garage and wanted answers. As she began the formalities and started the recording of the interview, Helen hoped that the man would not start the crap that she often heard, the infamous *"No comment."* There was always some reason for saying that phrase, and often it hid a multitude of sins committed by the criminals in front of her. Rarely were people innocent when they came out with the bullshit.

'Let's start at the beginning. Why did you become angry when D.I. Chisholm entered the garage?'

'No comment.'

The annoyance of the phrase crossed her face. She scowled but attempted to hold her patience.

'Were you busy in the garage? Is that the reason for the frustration?'

'No comment.'

Her buttons pressed and short on patience, she glared at him and snapped.

'Is that all you have to say? No comment?'

Sensing Helen was struggling to be polite, David decided to offer the mechanic some home truths.

'Look! Do you realise how serious this is? A woman was found in Loch Spiorad, a few miles from your garage. A red transit van was seen in the place where the body was dumped. As the owner of such a vehicle, we want to eliminate you from our enquiries, but you need to help yourself and cooperate. You've already committed an offence, an unprovoked attack on a senior officer. Had the wrench hit me, you would be facing even greater charges. Don't you think this has gone far enough? Clearly you need to get something off your chest. By doing so and helping police, your information may help a murder inquiry.'

Sullivan sat in silence. He glanced briefly at his solicitor, then glared at the detective. His piercing blue eyes often started fights in the pub when he wanted to menace or threaten someone. David stared at him, refusing to give way. The battle lasted another thirty seconds or so before the mechanic blinked. Water from a paper cup flew everywhere as the mechanic leapt up. The solicitor told his client to sit down, but he ignored the remark. David thought it best to suspend the interview. A few hours in the cell might calm Alec's rage.

†††††

Lying on a metal bed in a locked cell that smelt of Jeyes Fluid brought back memories of Alec's time in prison.

The grazes on his arms from falling onto the concrete floor in the garage were irritated by the coarse grey blanket wrapped around himself. Perhaps the strong odour of the disinfectant cleared not only his sinuses but also his senses as he decided he would tell the police what he knew. After all, he had only taken away some black bin bags: no questions asked, got the job done, and was paid up front. The instructions were clear enough: pick up some rubbish from a cottage at Dubhness and dispose of it in different dumps across the area. He should have known things were never that simple. All he'd done was to take a piss down by the loch after collecting the trash. The rage shown to the police officers was about embarrassment and stupidity at jeopardising his future for a small amount of cash.

To get himself out of this mess, there were two choices: confess all to the police or find the person who got him into this bother. For the first time in his life, talking to the police seemed the best option. When he got bail, he intended to hunt down the stranger with no identity.

†††††

The beam across Helen's face was enormous as she imparted the news at the briefing that Alec had spun a wondrous tale, freeing himself of all blame. A few hours of discomfort had brought him to his senses, although she had to admit she was surprised at his poor story. Looking at his record, he seemed an institutionalised petty criminal and thug, but not a murderer.

'He says he had a phone call asking him to clean up some rubbish from the cottage and got paid in cash left in an envelope under one of the black bags. He never went into the cottage or had any keys.'

David raised his eyebrows as she gave him the news.

'Really?'

'Oh yes, Boss! There you have it in a nutshell. He says he took some black plastic bags from Dubhness Cottage to various rubbish dumps locally.'

'Why was his vehicle, with a dodgy number plate, seen where the body was dumped?'

'He claims it was coincidence and that he decided to find a place to have a piss before heading back to Loch Dubhglas. He put the false number plates on because he hadn't gotten round to doing the MOT on the van.

'Coincidence! Driving around with the van being checked for mechanical faults is the least of his worries right now! What about the car?'

'He knows nothing about it. Claims he did not touch or dispose of a vehicle. He says there was no car in the garage or on the drive. He looked in the garage in case there was anything he could sell on.'

'Did he admit to knowing Anna?'

'He claims he does not know the woman and has never met her. But if she had a car, there's a likelihood she took it for servicing or for an MOT. It's the only garage for miles.'

It made sense what Helen said, but when he imagined the mechanic carrying out a murder using an unknown chemical agent, it was a non-starter. For David, there were vital gaps of information missing, and from everything he knew about the case, the story didn't add up to make a satisfactory hypothesis.

The corpse and everything about the case were odd. Executed with precision, showed planning with a bizarre modus operandi. This suggested military-style training, not the actions of a rough and ready mechanic who fancied his chances in brawls when his temper or booze got the better of him. His profile didn't point to him being an assassin, but if, like he confessed to being a clean-up guy, he must surely have more information about this particular job. A rotting stench of fish overwhelmed Chisholm's senses.

'Perhaps he's been set up as the fall guy. He might have a temper, but I can't believe he's an assassin, not looking at his criminal records. Let's speak to him again. Get his brief back in. There were fingerprints taken from the cottage on the bathroom cabinet, but no matches were found on the database. He has a police record, so the marks are not his. We also need to know where he dumped the contents from the property. McLeod is not going to like the bill for the forensic team to travel back up to Sutherland.'

David walked into the interview room late that afternoon, unsure of what more the suspect would say. The story needed further investigation, and he wanted to delve into the mysterious phone call tale to see if he could find any evidence to substantiate the mechanic's story. So he began with his opening gambit, praying he would glean more information.

'Thank you for what you volunteered so far, Alec. It's important you give us every possible clue about the phone call you took and the caller's identity. Tell me, what did the person sound like? Anything you noticed about them?

The man across the table had nothing to lose now that the police knew the truth. He wanted a murder charge off his back. He'd never been involved in serious shit like that and was scared the coppers would frame him. No way was he being sent down for something he hadn't done.

'I was in the garage working, and a call came in. When I answered, the caller asked if I could discreetly pick up some bits and pieces from a moonlight flit. They asked me to go up to the place at a certain time in the evening and dispose of all the rubbish at various tips in the area.'

'What did the voice sound like? Man or woman?'

'Well, I thought at first it was a woman, but then as the instructions went on, the voice was deeper, so I guess a man. It was hard to hear. The line was poor.'

'Come on, Alec. If you want me to believe you, do better than this.'

Blood rushed to the mechanic's cheeks. He clenched his fists, fighting the urge to punch the table or the detective.

'Honestly, you have to believe me. I couldn't tell.'

'Were they Scots?'

Frustrated, and desperate for the questions to be over, Alec relented.

'No, a foreign voice, Eastern European.'

'That's good information, Alec.

'I'm not going down for a crime I didnae commit. I admit I'm handy with my fists and drive without an MOT occasionally, but I wouldn't kill a lassie.'

'How did you get paid? Did you meet the caller?'

Sullivan shook his head.

'I told the woman copper; I never met the man. I was told the money would be placed under one of the bags of rubbish, and it was. Three hundred pounds in cash, twenty-pound notes.'

'How did you get inside the cottage?'

'I didn't go inside. There were about five or six bags. I couldn't see them at first as they were placed on the other side of the porch and hidden from the road.'

'So you never met the person who asked you to do the clean-up?'

'For fuck's sake! No! I didnae meet the person and right now, I could kill the bastard if he dared to show his face.'

Chisholm lowered his voice and gestured with his palms to calm down. A tiny droplet of sweat formed on Alec's brow. Instinctively, he wiped it away with the back of his hand. All he wanted to do was lash out at anyone because of his stupidity to get involved with the clear-up.

'Okay. Let's calm down and move on. You never met the caller. Was your van parked at Loch Spiorad on the Monday evening in question?'

Leaning back in his seat, Sullivan arched his back to stretch. The bed in the cell had been uncomfortable, and his back ached. Somehow, he held himself together.

'I was told to arrive at eight o'clock. I picked up the bags and loaded them into the van as fast as I could. I drove like the clappers away from the cottage. To be honest, when I got there, something didn't feel right, and I nearly legged it. I stopped at a pull-in by the loch for a piss and was going to have a fag. The bags stank of bleach. I wound the window down for a second or two to let some air in, but an estate car pulled up just past me. I didnae want to get caught with a van full of stuff, so I took off. Before you ask, I had false number plates on because of the MOT. The officers won't find the made-up ones. I threw them away at the dump because I was angry with myself for being tempted to drive without an MOT and jeopardising the business. I wish I'd never seen those bloody plates or the money.'

'Have no fear, Alec. The search team will find them. They are sifting through junk as we speak. What about the car?'

'What car?'

'There was a car at the property.'

'I've already told you. I didnae see a car, and no vehicle was mentioned in the clean-up. All I did was take some bags. I thought the caller was a nut job. I only agreed to get rid of the fuckin' stuff because he said he would tell the police I'd falsified MOTs. He knew me, he said, and that I had my sticky little fingers in all sorts of dodgy deals. When I told him to prove it, he started threatening he would harm my ex-girlfriend and the kids. He scared the shit out of me, so I agreed.

His head dropped. The bleak future he faced galloped through his mind, and not being there for his children. It would be the end of his business and the attempt at a decent life, all for three hundred pounds.

'Come on, Alec, getting rid of a car would be easy for you. Sell it on. Were you told you could keep the money?'

Exasperated at the questions thrown like grenades into his head, the suspect relented.

'Enough! For fuck's sake, I can't take any more. Okay! Part of the deal was to get rid of the car. A mate gave me a lift to the lane at eight o'clock to collect the rubbish. You can ask him. He knows nothing about any of this and just did me a favour by taking me up to the cottage.

When he drove off, I picked up the keys and the money from under the bags. I'd planned to take the rubbish in the car, but when I opened the garage, I saw how tidy the vehicle was. Stupidly, I decided to return with my old van. It was about forty-five minutes before I went back. I hid the car behind the closed doors at the back of my garage, and then on the morning after, I put it on the back of my recovery lorry with an old tarpaulin over it.

Your sergeant actually saw it when she came looking for fuel. I drove her back to her car with it hidden on my truck, not knowing she was a cop. Then I drove down to Elgin and sold it for three grand. That's the honest truth. I shouldn't have lied about the car.'

Chisholm thought the story sounded plausible and could be checked.

'So let's get this straight. You changed the instructions you'd been given and went back to your garage for the van?'

The mechanic nodded.

'If I'd put the bags in the car, I wouldnae needed to get the transit, nor taken a piss down by the loch. No one wouldnae seen me and wouldnae be linking me to the murder of that lassie.'

'Finally, some honesty at last! What did you do when you finished cleaning up?'

'I dumped the stuff in my garage overnight, went down to The Blue Cat nightclub in Inverness, and picked up a girl.'

Alec gave up the information readily, informing them he met a woman and they had sex in his van. He remembered as much detail as possible, determined to fight for his freedom and business. The only part he missed was buying some weed and smoking it afterwards.

With a final interview over and being charged for assaulting a police officer, Sullivan was released pending further investigations on other potential charges. Given his previous convictions, it was likely he would serve some time but cooperating with the police would be taken into account.

Without speaking, the detectives left the police station and walked towards their cars. It was only as she opened her door that Helen turned to her colleague. The frown on her lips showed she was still unsure of Alec's insistence of innocence.

'Did you believe him, Boss?'

David nodded.

'Aye, I'm inclined to believe he is telling the truth, for once in his life, to save his skin. He is petrified of a murder charge, or he wouldn't be singing like a canary. Clearly, this caller knew him, but how? A local with a toxic substance? It sounds ludicrous!'

A buzzard swoops down on its target, using its force and power as it goes in for the kill. In the winter months, it preys on invertebrates, but for most of the year, it feasts on rabbits and small rodents. Tiny targets are also worth eating. Having excellent vision means the bird can spot earthworms from a distance as it circles the skies, seeking out anything that moves. Nothing is safe when the raptor is out hunting.

The mechanic is an earthworm, oblivious to the consequences of his stupid actions. Bait, in the form of money, entices him; the threat of exposing his dirty secrets overpowers and controls him. Those with knowledge of other people's lives create havoc, whilst worms dangle and squirm as they are consumed.

CHAPTER 12
Day 11 : Friday, 3rd October

The train from Inverness Railway Station left on time at ten fifty on Friday morning. Chisholm was glad of his last-minute decision to drive back down to his flat on Thursday evening to catch up on paperwork and some washing. Helen was under strict orders to be evasive about their location if anyone asked. Not that anyone would question where the two men were. He and Euan would be out of the office, visiting leads, which wasn't entirely a lie. H.Q. was quiet, and McLeod was away in Edinburgh at a conference. She was oblivious to his plans.

There was something about her David could not explain; it was mistrust, even a dislike for his boss. There were always games when she was involved, putting on a show for higher-ranking officers who saw no flaw in her. Perhaps it was because of the bad publicity evoked before her arrival two years before. Everyone knew of her thirst for promotion. Detectives from other areas had wished him and his colleagues luck in dealing with such ambition.

Never had he kept lines of inquiry from a superior until now. He would log everything down officially when they arrived back in Inverness. Besides, he was due a couple of days off work. The case was steadily progressing, and he didn't expect any imminent breakthrough or arrest. Having spent a few hours earlier staring at a computer screen, he was ready to rest his eyes during the journey south.

As the train pulled out of the station on time, he shuffled to get comfortable in his seat, contemplating the weekend away and the plan of action. He turned to say something to Euan but heard a loud snore emanating from the young detective. They hadn't even passed the outskirts of the city.

Chisholm thought he would also close his eyes. It would be a busy couple of days, and he was already tired with all the paperwork from the case. His eyelids closed, the gentle sway of the carriage and the rhythm of the train speeding south would soon put him to sleep. Behind the detectives, a young boy's voice chattered in the background. Wishing he had brought his headphones, David attempted to block out the sound.

'Mummy. Will we see the Loch Ness monster?'

A woman with a southern accent laughed.

'If you close your eyes and listen, you might hear her snoring.'

'But I'm not tired.'

'Well, I am! Play quietly.'

'Listen, Mummy. Nessie's snoring.'

Chisholm opened one eye and glanced at Euan. Children were not his thing. His mind drifted back to a time when he and his ex-wife had considered becoming parents. Grimacing, he silently wriggled to ease away tensions in his shoulders. The sound of the child drifted into the background as he fell asleep. Occasionally, when woken by the snoring monster, he would nudge the creature before falling back into dreams of the Kinness croft.

After changing trains at Edinburgh in the afternoon, their second journey would take them right into the centre of Birmingham. Pulling from his backpack a dog-eared copy of the A to Z of the city, he located the address they were to visit. *"Brum,"* as locals called the city, was a place he'd visited before. Jane originated from there, so it wasn't entirely unfamiliar.

On Saturday morning, the detectives would get a taxi to the address Janice, the shop assistant, had spoken about and time to do any follow-up work necessary before returning to Inverness the following day. The meticulously planned precision of the expedition left little to chance. Two rooms in a budget hotel in the centre of Birmingham were only a few minutes' walk from the railway station.

Euan stirred when the woman conductor rolled the tea trolley towards him. The smell of tea aroused his senses, and kept him awake long enough to drink it and consume a packet of crisps before he began to snore again. It was only when their imminent arrival was announced in Birmingham that he opened his eyes once more. The young detective constable raised himself up, scrunching his head into his shoulders to relieve the discomfort he had from a cricked neck.

'Are we here? That was quick!'

'Just coming into Grand Central Station. Don't forget your rucksack.'

For the first time ever, David felt like the parent of a teenager, except this 'son' was in his mid-twenties and twice as gormless.

†††††

Euan had joined the team barely a year before. From the age of seven, he dreamed of being a police officer and a detective from all the old cop series his family watched on television. He had been delighted to become a detective after four years on the force, and, unbeknownst to anyone, he secretly liked Chisholm. If colleagues found out, they would have ripped the piss out of him in the bar after work.

All the younger officers admired David because he was a meticulous professional, but they only talked amongst themselves about his cold personality.

Chisholm's bark was worse than his bite. He was a conscientious police officer who liked to get the job done properly, without cutting corners. Euan knew he would learn a lot from following his lead.

Their ages and perspectives on life made them seemingly oceans apart, but if anyone paid closer attention, similarities were there in plain sight. His clothes and shoes were a more modern version of his mentor's. The shirts varied in colour, and he wore fashionable square-toed shoes, the type David hated. His slicked brown haircut was full of gel to hold a small quiff in place, whilst David's silver hairline was quietly receding.

Chisholm's personality was much colder. Euan loved hugging people, including his mates, especially after a round or two in the pubs in Inverness or a win for *The Staggies*. Fundamentally, however, both men wanted to bring victims justice for perpetrators' crimes and shared a passion for finding the truth.

The crowds poured out of the train onto a platform as if moving as one enormous millipede, stretching and rising when each pair of feet reached the top of the escalator a few steps away. The two detectives followed.

More people surrounded them as they reached the ticket barrier and passed through the electronic checkpoint. Once in this area, the humans separated, scurrying off in all directions.

Both men found themselves in a concourse at the heart of Grand Central Station, suddenly aware of light for the first time since rising from the dimness of the platform. Glass and chrome surrounded them, and circling above their heads was a mezzanine floor of shops and bars.

Euan gasped. An enormous, mechanical bull stood proudly at the centre of the concourse. Despite being on display for several years since the Commonwealth Games held in Birmingham in 2022, the metal robot was still a tourist attraction, towering above travellers who stopped to pause to take selfies. The pair stared for a few seconds in awe of the sheer size of the model.

The station was full of people from all walks of life and from every nation on the planet. From when people came over from Ireland just after the turn of the 19th century to seek work, Birmingham had been home to many people from across the world. Jane's family had been one of many who moved to the city over a century before.

After the Second World War, the Windrush generation from the Caribbean settled in the suburbs along with folk from the Indian subcontinent. Each community brought a different level of diversity to the area, helping the city to become a truly varied population as communities learnt to live with one another. Curry houses, Balti restaurants, and market stands full of Jamaican fruits and vegetables had recently been joined by shops from Eastern Europe to satisfy settlers from Poland, Lithuania, and Estonia. The people in the railway concourse were a living history of the city's varied and vibrant identity. They made their way through the crowds to the exit.

Expecting to take a good, deep intake of fresh air after being on a long journey, Euan's chest tightened at the stench of cigarettes from smokers taking a crafty fag before heading inside the train station or lighting up at the end of their journey. Everywhere, people milled around like a colony of ants. The frantic pace of life, compared with the city of Inverness, was overwhelming: crowds of people rushing past despite it being after seven o'clock in the evening, buildings towering high above, and the sound of traffic surrounding them.

It wasn't often he felt a viper wrapping its body around his throat. Coughing and wheezing, he was greatly relieved to feel his inhaler in his jacket pocket. With asthma diagnosed at an early age, he thought his police dreams would be over, but his condition was very settled. Rarely did he need his blue medication these days, and for once, his mother's advice to carry it at all times was heeded.

They made their way along the busy streets, through an underpass, and up some steps until they arrived in Centenary Square, the first piece of open land not completely covered with architecture from a variety of eras.

An impressive-looking building stood at one side of the space, which the senior officer informed Euan was Birmingham Library. It rose ten levels into the sky above them. Wrapped like intricate lace around the building, large black circles of metal forming repeating patterns covered the upper and lower storeys. Woven into the delicate design were smaller, white circles of metal. The middle layer of the library was decorated in a bright gold, making the black and white circles stand out even more. The very top section of the building, smaller than the rest and without the floral metal work, David told Euan, were terraced gardens. Neither man knew whether to love or hate the construction. It was certainly striking, and there was nothing to compare it with in Inverness.

Skyscrapers surrounding the open square dwarfed vehicles and people. As they approached the entrance of another huge glass-fronted building, Chisholm explained the covered concourse they were to walk through was the city's International Convention Centre.

Inside, dazzling white walls and bright blue pillars rose high into the air. Both added drama to the venue. To the right, various levels of the building were exposed by glass and chrome, stairs and escalators, making it a magnificent place to hold international business conferences. Mezzanine terraces made the vast, open spaces impressive as they rose up into the air. A café and cloakroom seemed hidden, almost crushed by the levels above. Every now and again, huge, polished double wooden doors broke up the industrial landscape of the space.

One of the doors was open, and they caught sight of the grand Symphony Hall, often hosting orchestras and musicians from around the world. Euan had been to pantomimes in Inverness at the theatre and cinema complex in Eden Court, but this place was enormous in comparison.

Through the walkway to the other end of the building, they went. Once outside, they found themselves near a bridge over a canal. David instantly recognised the location.

'This is Brindley Place. It used to be a run-down, rat-infested area, but it was cleaned up, and the canal's been used as a feature within a complex of hotels and bars.'

Around several more corners they turned, still overshadowed by huge skyscrapers, until they reached their hotel.

'Do you fancy a beer, Boss, after we've checked in?'

Chisholm nodded. He'd told the young policeman he would show him the bars around Birmingham, and he didn't intend to break his promise. He saw it was a chance to get to know the newest recruit to the team. Losing the tie would be a necessity, the suit too. It was a good job he had packed some jeans and a t-shirt. Now all that was left to do was find their rooms.

✝✝✝✝✝

Nightlife in the city was busy and wild, especially on Friday and Saturday evenings. The two men walked along Broad Street, incredulous at all the bars, restaurants, and nightclubs on both sides of the road. This was an area of Birmingham less familiar to David, although it was highly popular with young local people and tourists. He thought Euan would like to experience the place. The younger officer's eyes were on stilts: the choices of venues, the drunks, and the women who caught his eye.

However, mindful of the fact he had his boss in tow, he agreed to visit a nearby pub seen in a brochure in his room where Bill Clinton once drank a pint. Since being old enough to sample alcohol, he had found a thirst for real ale, so the pub suited them both. Exposed brickwork gave the place an industrial feel, yet a mixture of leather and wooden seating brought class and interest. Each lifted their glass to sample the brew. Neither spoke for a couple of minutes as they took in the surroundings and adjusted their eyes to the dim lighting, lost in admiration for the décor. Finally, nodding towards his glass and then licking his lips, Euan acknowledged his boss's presence.

'Not bad, eh?'

Chisholm lifted his pint in agreement.

'Not bad indeed. Let's agree not to talk shop!'

✝✝✝✝✝

I loved the hustle and bustle of living in Birmingham, the place of my birth. Famous, in days gone by, for heavy industry, the motor trade, and chocolate, people recently associate it with the Peaky Blinders television programme. Long before anyone from distant lands came seeking a life and to work in the area, gangsters existed, as they have done in many cities.

Imagine as dusk is falling, two cars, one a white Mercedes, the other a black BMW, with darkened glass and its rear window shot out, race along an ordinary street, not far from the city centre. A gunman hangs half out of the front passenger door of the Mercedes and fires a semi-automatic gun. Although the gangs intend only to kill each other, they pay no attention to the safety of anyone around them, in a car or on a pavement. It was at this moment, as a fourteen-year-old in my father's car, overtaken by the rival gangs, that I knew the job I wanted to do when I grew older. I should have been scared, but something attracted me to living on the edge.

It's not gangs or the city that unsettles me. I want the detectives to find my truth, but in so doing, they will disturb my past. News of my death will upset the one person I loved most in the whole wide world.

CHAPTER 13
Day 12 : Saturday, 4th October

Although it was Saturday morning, both detectives were up early, ready for the day ahead, despite their evening spent visiting pubs. As they emerged from their hotel, they retraced their steps back to the heart of the city, near the railway station. Budget accommodation did not offer the luxury of breakfast, except at an exorbitant price. Both spotted a café and, without uttering a word, crossed the road in unison towards it.

With a meal digested, accompanied by several cups of strong tea, they emerged from the café into the sunshine. Vehicles were everywhere, engines buzzing annoyingly in the background like angry wasps gathered around fruit. Into David's mind came the geologists. He hoped they were gone from the Bed & Breakfast in Loch Dubhglas.

They strolled towards a taxi rank a short distance away. For the first time since arriving in the Midlands, they discussed the task ahead. A black cab was parked at the head of a line of taxis with its front passenger window wound down. After a brief exchange to ask a likely fare to their destination, they got in and set off for a twenty-minute journey, accompanied by a jolly driver, keen to show off his city to the men. His Bengali music blared away in the background as he pointed out several landmarks.

The taxi wove its way through the chaotic streets, double lanes of traffic in all directions, until finally it left the city centre and headed for the suburbs. Turning off main roads and through side streets filled on either side with row upon row of houses, the landscape now looked different. Only occasionally did they catch sight of a block of flats. The driver fell silent; his music offset the noise from the cab's engine.

Homes in varied styles demonstrated some of the different eras of house building. Roads, sometimes lined with trees, began appearing together with older buildings with more character and charm. Gone were the glass and metal skyscrapers in the city centre and the huge towers of concrete.

Without warning, the taxi turned right at a street sign labelled Dark Lane. There was nothing dark about the place. Neither was it a lane anymore but a street full of 1930s red brick semi-detached houses with semi-circular bay windows. Cars and vans filled driveways and lined both sides of the road.

The taxi stopped at number 322. Chisholm paid the driver, and the detectives got out. The cab moved off as the men glanced around at their new surroundings. Parked opposite was a red Peugeot 2008. A woman in her late thirties got out of the vehicle. Her cropped blonde hair complemented her golden-brown skin. Chisholm guessed immediately that this was D.I. Julia Cavanagh, an officer from the West Midlands police force.

'D.I. Chisholm, I presume?'

A smile flashed across her face. From her jacket pocket, she displayed her warrant card to the men. Her hand stretched out to meet Chisholm's. Despite her Caribbean looks, her accent was Brummie—pure and strong.

'Hope you both travelled down well and enjoyed your evening in Birmingham.'

'A pleasure to meet you, D.I. Cavanagh. Yes, the journey was fine, and Birmingham certainly welcomed these two Highlanders last night. Thank you for agreeing to do this on a Saturday. This is my colleague, D.C. Euan Sinclair.'

Both male officers showed their identity cards, more through habit than need. Her smile broadened as she greeted the younger man, relieved her trip across Birmingham had not been a waste of time.

'Nice to meet you guys. You're a long way from home. Thanks for contacting West Midlands Police. I've made checks on the house you want to visit. There is little information in the database about any residents from the property, just an older guy living on his own. One small check I ran came up with a strange message about classified information. Probably an error. You know what it's like, but I thought it was worth mentioning.'

'Thanks for doing that. Yes, probably an error. We get that sometimes ourselves for no apparent reason.'

By now, the three officers were standing at the door. Julia lifted her fingers to the brass knocker and rapped on the dark blue wood. Inside, the sound echoed in the hall, startling the old gentleman boiling a kettle for his second cup of tea of the day. She knocked again before he had a chance to get to the front door. Grasping his walking stick, he tottered into the hall, muttering under his breath.

'Impatient bugger!'

Then, more politely, he raised his voice and shouted to the caller,

'I'm coming.'

When he opened the door, panic rose at the sight of three police officers, all showing their identification. Trying to mask his emotions, he stared at a hanging basket, still full of blooms, across the road. George Rose instantly knew his daughter was dead. A fear of the inevitable, festering away for so long until it had become raw and angry, raced through his bones, his lungs, and into his heart. It finally erupted. He managed to shuffle to his chair in the living room and sank heavily into it before his legs gave way. His stomach lurched. Taking a deep breath, he tried to take in what was being said.

D.I. Cavanagh led the conversation to explain the reason for their visit. Her voice, light-hearted and jolly a few minutes before when introducing herself to David and Euan, became more formal.

'I am a detective inspector from West Midlands Police. These officers are from Police Scotland and work for the Northern Constabulary in the Highlands.'

The old man's head sank into his chest; grey skin pulled tightly against his jaw. Mr. Rose could no longer stop the torrent of tears from flowing, deep pools of water gathering over the years. Covering his eyes with his fingers, hoping these officers would disappear as quickly as they had appeared in his life, he broke down.

'We have come to ask you about a lady who sends you mail from the northern Highlands.'

'It's Freya, isn't it? Is she dead?'

Unsure who the woman was that he mentioned, Julia continued.

'We are here to talk about a lady called Anna. May I ask who Freya is?'

Suddenly, a thunderous pain became sharper and more intense. Agony seared deep within his heart until he sat paralysed with fear. The secret was burdensome; he must not tell. He pressed his lips tightly together. Staring at the detectives, the storm continued to rise. He wanted to run like the wind as he had done in his youth, but useless elderly legs, full of arthritis, prevented him from doing so. He sat in a lightning storm, trying to hold fear at bay. Staring at the detectives did not make them vanish. Then, yet another bolt of seething pain took hold of his whole body.

Parched blue lips gave the first sign that something was wrong. The officers had all noticed he was in shock at their arrival but had expected nothing like this. Rose gasped for air, but none would enter his lungs. Grabbing hold of his jumper, he clasped his chest, knuckles white with tension.

'Are you okay, sir?'

'Freya...'

'Mr. Rose, who is Freya?'

There was no answer. The old man's eyes rolled back and then closed. Something was terribly wrong. The visitors jumped into action. Chisholm grabbed the man's wrist to seek a pulse. Without speaking, both men lifted Rose out of the chair and, as gently as they could be, placed him on his back on the floor. Euan knelt beside him and checked for breathing. By now, the man's skin was moist. A grey pallor washed over him as he made one final gasp for life.

Cavanagh telephoned for paramedics while Euan and Chisholm took turns breathing into the man's mouth, filling his chest capacity with air, then pushing on his chest in the hope he would miraculously come back from the dead. They continued as a tag team until the ambulance arrived exactly eight minutes later. Despite attempting to shock the man into living again, the defibrillator had arrived too late. Precisely ten minutes after arriving at the property, George Rose lay dead on the multicoloured rug in his lounge. The storm raging within him was now gone. The secrets he knew could no longer be told.

†††††

Back at headquarters, Cavanagh envisaged mounds of red tape, forms to fill, and statements taken. Chisholm was numb. His arms and shoulders were still taut and tense from attempts to resuscitate a potential witness who might have identified the woman in the loch in Sutherland. Euan, who normally had a smile for every occasion, sat in silence.

The Scottish detectives were both weary. Their trip to Birmingham had been far more eventful than planned. Thankfully, they had train tickets booked for Sunday morning, so there was still time to find more information about Anna Green and her links to Mr. Rose.

The questions began. Had they put undue pressure on Mr. Rose? Did they think an unannounced visit was the best approach for the case? What state was the man in when they first saw him? Some of the questions were impossible to answer. They had barely spoken to the gentleman. His reaction was unexpected. They hadn't even given him any news about the body of a woman found so far away.

Everything would be fine according to Cavanagh's superiors, just a formality. The man had a history of heart issues, according to his medical records. The cardiac arrest could have happened at any time. There was no next of kin according to any available information.

David's plan to keep the visit low-key seemed like a pipe dream. McLeod would read the riot act in her sarcastic, smug voice. As the two travellers finally emerged from West Midlands Police headquarters, the light was fading. A day that had started full of promise for identifying a murder victim had turned into a complete disaster. Without speaking, they made their way to the nearest bar, and each downed a pint as if it had barely touched the surface.

✝✝✝✝✝

Dad! Dad! I watch as his soul rises from his discarded shell. Within a second, he is gone towards the exquisite light. There will be no place in limbo for him by my side. The presence, which was once his, moves towards the infinite brightness humans are destined to face—unless they are like me, lying here in this void or gone to eternal hell. My father was never destined for anywhere other than the light. Forever with my mother now, it is the only comfort I can grasp.

The sight of his mortal bones shocked me. When I last saw him, he was happy, fit, and healthy. This is what I've done to him. Not only was my life destroyed, but his too. The secrets I asked him to keep were too onerous. They changed him—his frailty, loneliness, and his death—all my fault and too painful to imagine. Hope ends here.

CHAPTER 14
Day 13 : Sunday, 5th October

Early the next morning, David and Euan were more upbeat. Establishing if there was a link between Anna Green and Mr. Rose remained urgent. Their train back to the Highlands was due to leave four hours later. Armed with a warrant, Cavanagh, Chisholm, and Sinclair returned to Dark Lane. The police had secured the house, but luckily Cavanagh had the forethought to get access to a front door key. Curtains twitched next door as the three detectives walked up the path. David made a mental note to speak to the neighbour in case they knew any family history.

The house lay empty and cold. The previous day's drama vanished, replaced only by despair. A sadness lingered in every room for a life snatched away. It made the three detectives long to distance themselves from the place, and to have space to deal with a grief they individually felt for a stranger.

Once the Rose family's pride and joy, the home was cluttered and untidy. A mound of unopened mail and newspapers filled a small wooden telephone table in the hall. Unwashed mugs lay in the sink along with used plates and cutlery. Cobwebs hung from the faded pink lampshade overhead. A lifetime of knickknacks sat on the mantelpiece, covered in dust. An image of George Rose, in his younger days, and a teenage girl with long auburn hair took centre stage. Instantly familiar, the female had an enormous grin, blissfully happy, with no cares in the world. His loving arms were wrapped around her in a bear hug that she clearly adored. They stared into a camera lens, smiling at David. The joy in their faces was painful to observe. He was familiar with their deaths and turned away for a second to compose himself. Needing to focus on the task ahead, he studied the photograph to glean any more information.

There was no longer doubt that this trip to Birmingham was a wild goose chase. Looking back at him was Anna Green, seen only in a lifeless form until this moment. It was the woman from Loch Spiorad. As he stared into the image, his mind could not escape the fact she had been deliberately targeted, assassinated by means of a toxic poison. Finally, she was beginning to give up her secrets.

In the chaos of the previous day's visit and its aftermath, Chisholm had not seen a likeness between the auburn-haired beauty and Mr. Rose until now. Studying the photograph, the same bone structure in the face, the same colouring, the same smile were all now evident. In the image, the pair were younger. His short hair showed traces of an auburn tinge, and he was clean-shaven; not so grey nor unkempt as the man David witnessed dying less than twenty-four hours before. This chap had pride in his appearance. He wore a dark suit, and a white shirt, with a smart, dark tie. Her hair was shorter: shoulder-length and styled with a fringe. They had to be father and daughter, the detective concluded. Then he thought about George Rose's final word, *"Freya."* Who was Freya?

'David! Come and look at this!'

A female Brummie accent broke the silence. Following Julia's voice, he moved through the hallway to a dining room. She stood in the doorway. Her dark eyes sparkling for the first time that day.

She pointed to a photograph on the wall, this time in a silver frame. Much larger than the one on the mantelpiece, this image was startling. As David moved towards it, he shook his head in disbelief. Could he really be looking at Anna Green in a police uniform? Her auburn hair was scraped into a bun. With a cap under her arm, she stood proudly, ready to do her duty, beaming from ear to ear that she was a serving police officer. It was a standard photograph that everyone had taken when they had completed their initial training. He had one somewhere in a box he had never got around to unpacking after the divorce.

'What the hell? How could her name not show up when we ran fingerprint and DNA analysis?'

Information was held on all officers for elimination purposes. It didn't make sense. Euan had been upstairs, rifling through drawers and wardrobes. He held an old school report book in his hand.

'Boss, I think we have finally found Freya!'

Inside the book, on the title page, was a photograph of the green-eyed loch goddess. The two younger detectives chatted about the find, excited to have achieved their goal in establishing an identification of a woman murdered five hundred miles away. Neither Julia nor Euan heard Chisholm whisper as he turned back to the photograph.

'You will come home.'

As he knocked on the shiny red door, the curtain twitched once more as it had done an hour or so before. A vision of brightness greeted the officers when the door was unlocked. Slender and elegant, a woman stood in a shocking pink sari patterned with intricate golden thread, vividly coloured bangles jangling from both wrists. Her smile was as warm as the colours she wore. Guessing who they were, she placed her two palms together and bowed her head as if in prayer and greeted the officers. When she spoke, there was just a hint of an Indian accent; clearly her roots were firmly in Birmingham.

'How can I help you, officers?'

As an employee of the local police force, Julia answered and explained their presence.

'We wondered if you knew anything about the man next door.'

'Come in. I have plenty to tell you.'

She led the three detectives into a bright, beautifully decorated sunroom at the back of the house. Two luxurious couches filled the space. An array of paintings covered the walls, exotic splashes of colour reminding Chisholm of a holiday he'd once experienced in India years before. He surmised she was a similar age to him but showed no signs of greying hair.

The hostess left her guests for a minute or two, then returned with a tray of teacups and a fine china teapot, together with a plate of spicy homemade biscuits. Once her guests were served tea, she sat down on a large red leather footstool opposite them and relaxed.

'My name is Anika Chopra. I have lived in this house for over thirty years, since I was twenty, in fact.'

'How well do you know the Rose family?'

'I used to know them well, but over the years we've grown apart. My children grew up with their daughter, Freya.'

As Anika continued, the two senior officers listened while Euan took notes.

'The couple moved in a month after us, so we were all new neighbours to the area. George and Maggie were older than me and my husband by about twenty years. They took us under their wing because we were still young when we got married.

A couple of years later, Maggie Rose and I fell pregnant around the same time. For her and her husband, it was a miracle. They had been trying for a baby for years. Freya was born a fortnight after Ashok, my son, so they were in the same primary and secondary school year together. When younger, they were thick as thieves, and everyone laughed when they announced one day they would marry, at the grand old age of eight. For a time, our families were very close. But later we seemed to drift apart, although there was never any intention on anyone's part.'

She paused for a moment, smiling at the memories, long-forgotten images playing through her mind. Then the sparkle faded from her eyes as she recalled the next part of the story.

'Tragedy struck when Freya was thirteen and Maggie died of breast cancer. George and the girl were heartbroken. Nothing seemed the same after that. My husband also passed away a couple of years later. Ashok and Freya went their separate ways after sixth form. He went to Warwick University to study chemistry, and she went to university in Nottingham to study early mediaeval history. Afterwards, she joined the police force and went to the Met. in London. She came home on leave regularly. Ashok tried to rekindle their friendship, but Freya wasn't so keen, and besides, she was based down south. Eventually he gave up trying; he is married now, and I have a grandchild on the way.'

Her face lit up as she glanced towards a photograph on the wall of a couple in Indian wedding outfits. David listened intently. Impatient to know about Freya, his question spilled out, more formally than needed.

'When did you last have contact with Mr. Rose's daughter?'

She sighed. Light disappeared from her face once more, and for the first time Mrs. Chopra's voice cracked as she explained her links with the family and their shared history.

'The last time I spoke to Freya was about three years ago. Months later, when there was no sign of her visiting, I asked how she was doing.'

A tear droplet trickled from the corner of her eye onto her cheek. As she wiped it away, she continued,

'George said that she was on a special assignment that went wrong. When he finished speaking to me, he simply turned and went back into the house. I often heard him sobbing after that when I was in the garden, so I never felt it was appropriate to ask more questions.'

'Went wrong?'

Chisholm desperately hoped Mrs. Chopra could clarify what she meant. She lowered her voice so that the outside world couldn't hear. The detectives all leaned forward in unison, trying to catch words that were barely audible.

Her cheeks were now moist as she sobbed.

'Everything went wrong. She went into hiding, and her dad said she wasn't allowed to speak to him or visit anymore. He was heartbroken at losing the only other blood relative he had. She went into...'

There was a pause whilst she gathered her thoughts, trying to remember the phrase she had long buried in her mind. The detective finished her sentence for her.

'Hiding?'

'No! Witness protection!'

At that moment, everything became clear. There were no records for Freya Rose because she had stopped existing three years before. Her fingerprints were removed from the database to obliterate any memory of her. This did not bode well for his investigation. Having identified the body in Loch Spiorad, he needed to know what the hell had driven a serving police officer into such severe circumstances as to be placed in witness protection. The red tape in accessing files of someone deliberately hidden could prove impossible. Clearly, if, like McLeod had mentioned before, MI5 were involved, it was a matter of national security. He kicked himself for not realising the significance of her words.

They needed to be back in the office on Monday morning, but although he wished he didn't have to disclose the weekend's events, he couldn't hide vital information on a murder case.

Freya Rose was a police officer placed in witness protection. Anna Green was an alter ego for a woman who could no longer exist. Taking a new name had not been a security blanket because someone had found her, perhaps because she couldn't cut all ties with her father as she should have done. Sending letters to him from the post office in Loch Dubhglas might have caused her death. Someone could have found her identity.

His other thoughts were about the preservation of evidence. He knew he needed to bag any relevant documents and photographs quickly in case outside interferences took over the case. Ensuring he linked George Rose and his loving daughter Freya to the woman in the loch was vital. His unease at the discovery, compounded by a niggling feeling in his mind, made him realise that unknown forces were at work and they would attempt to bury any evidence of the Rose family.

A statement would be emailed to David once it was written up by Julia and signed by Mrs. Chopra. He would fight anyone who tried to sweep this information under the carpet. From a couple of colleagues whose cases involved MI5 in the past, he understood games were often played, and if it was in the interest of national security, secrets were buried.

Freya had been an unidentified corpse. Now with her real name exposed and a past life emerging, nothing could silence the truth. The desire for Chisholm to conclude the case and to find her murderer was stronger than ever, especially now that he realised the woman in the loch was a police officer given a new identity.

There was a train to catch. Cavanagh managed to navigate the city traffic and got them to Grand Central railway station ten minutes before the train was due to leave. They raced to the ticket barriers and ran down the escalator to the platform. Within two minutes, the guard blew his whistle, and the journey back north began.

Euan felt in his pocket for his trusted inhaler. It had seen more action over the last forty-eight hours than in the previous five years. His older colleague sat quietly pondering the events of the weekend: a second death in the same family and a victim with two names and two very different lives.

Religion never appealed to me until they moved me to Loch Dubhglas. It was the despair of never being myself again that led me to seek answers on how to cope with the

rest of my life without any past friends or my father. Even when I needed God most, in those times of utter despair, I rarely attended church services for fear of being the centre of attention. Only when I could hide in the shadows, perched on a freshly polished pew, did I find a modicum of solace. I prayed to God that I would find peace, but it seems He wasn't listening. Why would He? I ignored Him all my life as Freya. Why should He listen to a woman called Anna? She was a stranger to both of us.

To be exposed, I'm forever free of the burdens of other names given to me. Living with different identities was complicated. The name Anna Green means hopelessness and filled me with dread. It is only a matter of time until they realise who they are dealing with.

A transitional wind from summer to autumn blows across the Midlands, through the Lake District, picking up force as it travels to the Borders, through the Central Belt, and blasts from the Cairngorms towards Inverness. Then it makes haste until it gains full strength in the Dornoch Firth and storms towards Loch Spiorad. If you listen, the wind howls and screams a warning.

'I'm Freya Margaret Rose and I'm coming for you!'

CHAPTER 15
Day 14 : Monday, 6th October

On Monday morning, bright and early, Chisholm was at his desk in his office in Inverness. Everything was neat and orderly, with pens in place just how he'd left them on Friday morning. He sat pondering the next line of inquiry, then began making sure everything to date was logged. He started to write up reports from the week before, tackling the endless forms for the incidents in Birmingham.

Euan appeared fifteen minutes later, looking tired after a weekend away and two long train journeys. David looked up from his computer; the young officer winked through the glass at his superior as he strolled to his desk. He did not intend to compromise the Birmingham adventure and knew to keep his mouth shut. His boss had shown another side of himself on the trip to the Midlands. The detective, who never showed emotion and was always calm, no matter what chaos was going on around him, was good, easy company. Something about this case was making him different. *"The Iceman's"* exterior was melting rapidly.

Helen had not been in touch during the weekend but was eager to hear if there was any news. When she arrived shortly after Euan, she grabbed something from her bag, stuffed it into her pocket, and headed for David's office for an update. He signalled her to enter and shut the door. Quickly filling her in on all the information he and Euan had gathered, she sat down in the only other chair in the tiny room and tried to digest everything the D.I. recounted, overwhelmed by the news. It was a lot to take in: a man deceased from a cardiac arrest, Anna's identity revealed, and Mrs. Chopra's information.

'What about the parcel Janice said was posted on the day Anna, aka Freya, died? Did you find it?'

He shook his head. She was just about to ask more questions when the door opened, and in walked McLeod. His face burnt; the jaunt to Birmingham needed explaining. Perhaps she already knew and had come to discipline him. He could not hide the identity of a murder victim, nor would he impede a criminal investigation. She would take him off the case and perhaps give him a written warning. He would not let Euan take any blame. He wished the lad no harm in his career. How stupid he had been to think he could keep this information to himself! Taking a deep breath, he was about to confess about the weekend and all that had happened when she spoke.

'You need to get back up to Loch Dubhglas immediately. There's been an incident at Dubhness Cottage that needs to be investigated. Take Helen and that young officer, Euan, with you.'

She was about to leave the room when David's guilt got the better of him. The truth would be revealed eventually, so it was best to get everything out in the open, no matter what the consequences.

'Ma'am. There's something you should know. I take full responsibility. It was my idea, and at no time did it cost the police force any money. I took Euan down to Birmingham on Friday afternoon. I wanted to follow up on something a witness disclosed in Loch Dubhglas. There has been some significant new evidence that has come to light. It's more imperative than ever we find who killed Anna Green. She was, in fact, a police officer, working for the Met. and was placed in witness protection by the sound of it, although there are no police records which is bizarre. Her real name was Freya Rose.

We secured evidence from the family home in Birmingham. I have a birth certificate, an old hairbrush from her room, and a number of photographs. DNA will be taken from the father to ensure it is a parental match to his daughter.'

The room spun. He held his breath and waited for her to start as the events were divulged. He knew everything he was guilty of before she could explode at him. For a moment she said nothing, trying to make sense of all the new information, shocked at Mr. Rose's death. When she did speak, Alison's voice lowered to a whisper.

'Keep this information quiet. The fewer people who know, the better. Of course there will be an inquiry into the death of Mr. Rose, but from what you say, his health was already poor, and I don't think there will be any disciplinary action. I would have done the same myself, following up leads.

No wonder people are sniffing around this case who never normally put their fingers in any pie. I've had all manner of calls from not just senior officers but MI5 bosses. Wolves are at the door. I'll keep them away as long as I can. David, stay up in Sutherland, out of the way, get this case cracked, but be careful!'

Glancing at each other, the realisation of the seriousness of the investigation and the turn it was taking hit home. How did a Met. policewoman with a new identity end up dead in Loch Spiorad? Even more worrying was the fact McLeod addressed him by his first name. This was serious. She scurried back to her office, stiletto heels clattering on the tiled floor. The detectives gazed at each other but did not speak. Helen stood up, pushing a small white envelope deeper into her jacket pocket.

†††††

Euan was full of the trip to Birmingham, and he chatted away like background noise as Helen drove north. She shook her head or nodded at the right moments but didn't take in much of what he said. She told him firmly that he must keep his mouth shut about what he and Chisholm knew about Anna. For now, their unidentified woman was Anna Green, not Freya Rose, and he must remember this.

David had planned to return to Sutherland later that afternoon, as there was some unfinished business with the evasive mechanic, and he had a special evening planned with

Jimmy. The command to return immediately took him aback, as had McLeod's response to his visit to Birmingham. What was so urgent at Dubhness Cottage to warrant a visit from three detectives?

When the sign for Loch Dubhglas approached, he was surprised how quickly the journey had taken and aware of how glad he was to be back. His newly packed overnight bag lay in the boot of his car. There was no real need for him to stay longer in Sutherland as the most senior officer on the case, but McLeod was insistent on staying out of the way. It seemed he was destined to rekindle his love affair with the place.

†††††

There was still a small police presence at the community hall. When the detectives arrived unannounced, the officer on duty leapt to attention and tried to look busy. No villager had been near all morning.

Helen offered to drive the short distance to Dubhness Cottage. When they approached, a police vehicle was parked in the shingle driveway. The uniformed officer had been called to the property when Glen, the old crofter, peeped through the windows early that morning. Since the SOCO team left, he had avoided entering the building. Each time he contemplated going inside, he shivered. Having finally plucked up the courage, he looked through a window to find some disgusting messages on the wall. Shards of glass from the front door lay in the porch and in the hallway. The police were called once he'd sat down to catch his breath. He didn't think he could take much more stress.

Helen stepped out of the car and walked back towards the gateway to take in the view, but haar obscured much of the beauty. Draped in an opaque mist, a melancholy blanket covered the fields for as far as she could see. Bracken and ferns dipped in green during the summer months now had faded to a pale earthy hue. Feeling the cooler air grasping at her cheeks and hands, she shivered. It wasn't merely from the chillier, grey day; there was something unsettling. Her thoughts were broken by an anguished voice behind her.

'Helen, come and see this!'

Her stomach lurched; she wasn't ready for drama. The weekend with Georgina had calmed her and lifted her spirits. Life was great, and not everyone was an arse. Fearing the worst, a dead body perhaps, she entered the porch. Stepping over shards of glass, her eyes caught sight of the red globules on the floor before she saw the walls in the hallway. For a moment she questioned if it was blood but guessed it wasn't from the thickness and intensity of colour.

Time stopped. Her head pounded with the sound of her heart beating so quickly. Her instinct was to run, but her feet were like lead as she attempted to lift one foot in front of the other. The ceiling seemed to push her to the ground, crushing her chest with its weight. Grasping in her pocket for support, in the form of the envelope addressed to Chisholm, she squeezed it between her thumb and forefingers. Naive to the cascade of emotions, Euan broke the silence.

'Do you think this is a hate crime? With this level of abuse, perhaps it's a homophobic murder?'

The same thought ran through David's mind; the words and phrases of loathing were daubed on every wall. How could this be anything other than a hate crime? As he read *"Slut"* and *"Lesbian,"* his heart sank. In each room, the messages got worse: *"Dyke," "Whore."* Even across the mirror in the bathroom, the graffiti continued, *"Homo."* In the bedroom, the message was very clear. *"Sinners repent!"* Large red crosses were displayed in every room.

Less than three hours before, the bones of a theory were mapped out to seek a killer who sought out a police officer hidden in witness protection. The modus operandi seemed to fit the bizarre death, maybe a contract killing. Witness protection was costly and never offered lightly. Freya was given a new life to avoid something or someone.

Somehow, these slogans and abhorrent messages turned everything upside down in this theory. Was everything connected? Was this a prejudicial death, nothing to do with Freya being in hiding? Surely her change of identity was linked to her murder. This must be a smokescreen.

'Helen, I want you to lead on this. Check out all local ironmongers. There are a couple in the area who may have stocked red paint.'

Never usually questioning his leadership, Daniel's reply was sharp.

'No. I don't want to. Why does it have to be me? Why can't it be a man?'

Puzzled at her response, the detective spun around to his sergeant. She had never questioned any of his judgements before or his instructions. With bewilderment etched on his face, he looked at her for an explanation.

'I hate to do this, Helen. Give me one good reason not to assign you to this aspect of the case. It's an urgent line of inquiry, which means a more senior officer than Euan. For goodness' sake, what's the problem?'

Trying to hold his temper, the tiredness of a busy weekend, together with the frustrations over the case, got the better of him. The temperature plummeted in the room. Fearing a showdown of ominous proportions, Euan looked at his shoes. Sharper and snappier than his normal calm tone, David added,

'Give me one good reason!'

A low, painful cry, stifled and hidden at first, grew louder. Initially, he did not appreciate where the sound was coming from. A wounded animal, trapped somewhere in the house, was his first thought. Then he realised the source of the distress, was emanating from Helen. Neither man knew how to react. Euan's instinct was to hug her, as was David's, but when his boss signalled with his eyes to leave the room, he obeyed.

Helen's legs had collapsed beneath her. She sat in a heap in the middle of the living room, quietly sobbing. David knew only one way to address the situation. He sank to the floor next to his sergeant and touched her arm.

'Whatever this is, it doesn't matter.'

Consumed by sadness, pools of water created damp patches on her jeans. Bubbles of snot oozed from her nostrils. Ever prepared, David felt in his pocket for an packet of tissues he had carried for the last couple of years, in case anyone became hysterical. Jimmy had been the first to take one, just days before. Helen had not been on his radar as the one to take a second.

Without looking at him or acknowledging his words, she readily accepted his offering and wiped her eyes and nose. Mascara mixed with salty water, left dark, moist, streaky lines on her cheeks. She was not a pretty sight.

The D.I. persisted. He would not and could not leave her like this.

'Sorry!'

'There is nothing to be sorry for. What on earth is this about? Come on. You can tell me anything.'

The sharp, cold exterior that David showed to the world, his invisible jacket for self-protection, completely melted. Shaking her head, Helen slowly raised her eyes to meet his gaze.

'No. It's just this case. It's gotten to me. I'm being silly.'

'You are not being silly. Something's obviously wrong. Tell me.'

From her pocket came a crumpled envelope that had once looked pristine. She had nothing to lose and everything to explain.

'Please don't judge me! I'm more than this!'

Her plea caused David to frown. The wrinkles, not normally dominating his brow, were severe. His lip puckered. He was puzzled, and he stared at his colleague in disbelief. Helen was jolly, the life and soul of every party outside of work. Her smile lit up the office, and she was the one who always raised the spirits amongst the team of detectives when matters got serious or cases were difficult. She was not known to be emotional and was excellent in a crisis.

Taking the envelope from her, he saw his name written with a smart calligraphy style in black ink. Only the lowest point of the envelope seal had been stuck down, so it was easy to open and reveal the contents. Pulling out a thick cream card with *"Wedding Invitation"* written in gold italics, David had the first clue as to why his sergeant had unravelled in an emotional heap.

She stared at him, trying to read his thoughts, scanning his expression for any minute alteration in his mood. Sensing he was being judged, he smiled, trying to distract her with a joke, but he fully understood why she sat on the floor, in a blubbering mess.

'So, it's wedding nerves? Trust me, it gets worse a fortnight before the nuptials! Now stop this greeting.'

Miss Georgina MacDonald and Miss Helen Daniels
wish the company of
David Chisholm and guest
at their wedding on Saturday, 20th December
at Glen Ness Hotel, Inverness at 2 p.m.
A wedding meal will commence at 4 p.m,
followed by an evening disco at 7:30 p.m.
R.S.V.P.

She recognised a bullshitter when she saw one. Rather like a baby elephant taking its first steps, she ungainly pushed herself up from the floor by her hands and feet. Brushing her palms over her clothes to clean herself up, she avoided his gaze for as long as she could. Stronger, exposed, but defiant, she pointed to the canvas of words sprayed in red on the cream walls of the room.

'Now you know why this is personal. This is the hate in my life. All I, and countless other women and men, have done is to find love in a different way. We hurt no one in our choices.'

He smiled and handed her another tissue as the one she held to her eyes was soggy and disintegrating.

'I only know a wonderful, talented detective who cares about victims and has a passion for bringing perpetrators to justice. You are you; a funny, clever lady with a zest for life and a heart of gold. You are not this.'

He waved his arms in the direction of the slurs on the wall.

'Help me find out who did this. It may have nothing to do with the murder, but it may be the killer who is back to spread their filth and hatred.'

She nodded an acceptance to the challenge. By now the tears had dried. Most of the mascara trails had been wiped away, but one or two faint lines remained.

'Wash your face before we leave. Here's some more hankies to dry yourself. By the way, I'll be delighted to attend your wedding. Not sure about the plus one, as I got divorced a while back. How would you feel if I took Euan?'

Both detectives laughed so loudly that the noise brought Euan back into the room. Whatever the reason for Helen's meltdown had been, it was resolved. The young officer was relieved.

'Euan, we need some analysis on the paint used on the walls. Stay put and get someone back up here to take some samples, please. Do a search of the property for any clues about the paint. We also need photographs, as this is criminal damage. Helen, let's go back to the village hall and get some calls made.'

The young officer's morning had been quiet, waiting for the forensics team to arrive to examine the paint. In the meantime, he scouted around the cottage, searching for anything of interest. Naively thrown in a hedge, not far from the bungalow, were three empty cans of red spray paint. Euphoric, Euan laughed at his find. Careful not to contaminate any evidence, he took photographs on his mobile phone but left them in the bushes. When he zoomed in on the images, he could see a sticky label on one of the cans. There, above the price, clearly printed, was the name of the local ironmongers in Loch Dubhglas.

He strolled back along the lane, towards Dubhness Cottage. The uniformed constable would take him back to the village when other officers eventually arrived.

Both Chisholm and Daniels were deep in thought as each drove the few miles back to Loch Dubhglas. Few people were out and about. A cold air spread across the village chilling the bones of the residents and visitors, compelling them indoors. Those who were brave enough to be out near the loch had donned the first outings of hats and scarves of the season. A couple of camper vans were still in the area, but, for the most part, the streets were quiet.

As they drove into the car park, David felt a warmth towards the place. The magic of Loch Dubhglas was about connecting with the past, being proud of his roots, and no longer hiding from them. His conversations with Jimmy and Glen had helped. He sat for a moment, trying to summarise everything in his head, pondering too on the graffiti.

He noticed his sergeant's reluctance to walk into the incident room without him. She hung back, playing with her car keys. Quietness and being subdued were traits never usually associated with Helen. Sensing her mood, he distracted her once more.

'Come on. Let's talk through strategy before you head back to Inverness. I've paperwork to fill in about my adventures in Birmingham.'

Only when you have walked in similar footsteps of someone whose experiences are like yours, can you understand. The woman detective experiences a pain I recognise. The prejudices she faces are the ones I faced; her fears are my fears. It is only now that I am without fear or pain that I can conclude nothing matters but love.

CHAPTER 16
Day 15 : Tuesday, 7th October

The local ironmonger, Sutherland Emporium, was a box of delights. Winter bedding plants, encased in rows of white polystyrene, lay in boxes on the pavement outside the huge glass shopfront. Faded white postcards, now with an aged ochre hue, offering such novelties as *"Cockatiel for sale, with cage,"* *"Bales of hay,"* and *"Wanted—a gardener for mowing and weeding"* concealed a few of the many items crammed into the display on the other side of the glass. Everything imaginable, apart from human food, was sold there, although another sign on the door, *"Rump steak for sale,"* did offer culinary possibilities.

Having never seen such an establishment before, Euan peered into the room as he stepped over the threshold, agog at everything for sale. An old screen, covered in a wallpaper once sold, was placed behind the window display to enclose the shop till away from prying eyes, stopping light from entering the room. An ancient metal lampshade hung from the ceiling, offering a single bulb as the only source of artificial light. Shadows cast darkness on the premises even on bright days. His eyes widened at the treasures inside once he had grown accustomed to the dimness.

On both sides of a narrow gangway leading to a counter were products of every description. Boxes and packages of electrical items, bags of potting compost, a garden incinerator, buckets, troughs, and mops and brushes covered the flooring to the left and right. Taller boxes at the back, smaller items at the front; each with a familiar price sticker placed on the front of the stock.

Half lost under trinkets and ornaments, candles, batteries, and torches was an old cream laminate work surface where a small space had been left empty for the shopkeeper to place items being paid for. Behind, sets of small wooden drawers rose from floor to ceiling, covering all the walls of the shop except the glass frontage. Contents of each container were known only to the shopkeeper and his faithful assistant, who would push a ladder to the selected area of shelving before leaping onto an old wooden rung to reach higher prizes. Sometimes they would scuttle from drawer to drawer until a certain size of nail or screw was located.

Even a young man, with little interest in gardening or DIY, was taken aback at the place. He was transported back in time.

'Can I help you?'

A cheery male voice brought him to present day. The shopkeeper, a small man in his seventies, smiled politely at him, proud of his long established business. Now balding, with more white wisps of hair in his moustache than on his head, he stood ready to pass pleasantries while the young man determined what he wished to buy. He was confident whatever it was, that he would have it in the shop—somewhere.

When Euan introduced himself, the shopkeeper's twinkly eyes did not dull. Instead, he moved along the length of the counter to a small wooden gate previously unnoticed by Euan. Unlatching it, he manoeuvred himself through a tiny gap in the stock to stand next to the police officer.

'I was wondering if you could remember selling any cans of red spray paint in the last month.'

The shopkeeper smiled and, with his index finger, tapped the side of his head.

'We sell many items, but all purchases are logged in my manual computer.'

Not understanding the irony of the joke, Euan asked,

'Can I have access to it, please?'

Turning to his assistant, the man winked before holding out a hand for his ledger to be passed over the counter. From his chest pocket on his dark dungarees, he pulled out a pair of reading glasses, one arm kept in place with a sticking plaster. He put them on and proceeded to check his facts before he spoke. He opened the book to a particular page and, with his finger, slowly traced through the entries. Three-quarters of the way down the page, he stopped.

'Last Saturday, I sold three cans of red spray paint to Mrs. Flora MacAskill of Wester Dubh. She paid in cash.'

He coughed gently and smiled again.

'Well, everyone has to pay in cash, as we don't have a card machine! I told this information to the plain clothes officers earlier today.'

Euan stared at the man. Bemused, he was unsure he had heard the shopkeeper's words correctly. The comment had caught him off guard.

'I beg your pardon. Could you repeat that? I don't quite understand. You have already told some police officers about the cans?'

Without showing any sign of weariness at having to repeat himself, the man nodded. Euan left the shop confused, and puzzled at what the shopkeeper had reported to him.

†††††

She knew they would come. The pensioner sat in her coat waiting for the police car to pull up outside the house. Clutching her Bible close to her bosom, she prayed she would overcome her aggressors. Although her hands trembled, she wanted to protest. Her faith would carry her through if she went to prison. With a husband in his grave, her two grown-up children and grandchildren abroad and none seeking further contact with their pious relative, no one would care what happened. Too often her principles had driven people away. Long hours praying in church or at home brought no comfort. Loneliness might be the cause of her actions, or maybe a bitterness and lack of empathy for anyone who didn't fit her rigid sense of correctness.

Her *"friend"* Iris shared the sighting of two women kissing behind the local shop after being bullied into telling her about the conversation with the police officer. Having gleaned this information, she set herself the task of showing outrage at such an occurrence in Loch Dubhglas. Her protestation against moral sin needed to start somewhere. Every single word of the Holy Book was true, and fornicators in same-sex relationships were left to damnation. With nothing to occupy her mind, the ideas against her beliefs rotted, eating away any common sense she had.

No one knew of the nightmares she was experiencing, visions of her dead relatives calling to her. Her defence lawyer would argue that she showed early signs of dementia and that medical reports considered she might be suffering from a psychotic episode. In truth, she had always held a hatred for anyone who was different.

Her childhood had been strict. No toys on the Sabbath, swings tied up, and best clothes worn to worship God. Nonbelievers were Satan's workers, to be burnt in a glowing heap of sinners. Only when her mild-mannered, and kind husband had encouraged her to move to a less harsh church, had she had an opportunity to meet less fervent worshippers. A brainwashed mind could not be healed.

When one of her grandchildren announced he was gay, visions of him and his boyfriend repulsed her. In her decayed mind, *"gay"* meant happy and always would. She showed no mercy and expected none back for her actions. She should be punished for her criminal act, but she was proud of the stance she was taking. Surely the minister and the parish members would give her character references. After all, she knew many of their secrets.

The doorbell rang. Pushing herself up from her chair, she tried to remain calm and certain of herself as she opened the door. However, the sight of a police officer and a young detective made her shake uncontrollably.

'Flora MacAskill? My name is Detective Constable Euan Sinclair. Can I come in and talk to you, please?'

Nodding, she stepped away from the door, leaving the policeman to close it. Suddenly, she felt an almighty weight on her shoulders, crushing her into submission. At that moment, after years of hatred and prejudice, her sins came crashing down and lay at her feet, ready to repent. There was only one thing to do.

Euan looked at the eighty-six-year-old lady lying prostrate on her faded Persian rug, repeating over and over that she was sorry for her sins. For a few seconds, he didn't know how to react. Then a greater fear engulfed him. How on earth was he going to get her up from the floor, and stop her crying, before arresting her?

†††††

The interview with Flora MacAskill was short and painful. It was clear she wasn't of sound mind. When a social worker arrived with a doctor in tow, the decision was made to take her to New Craigs in Inverness for assessment. A few days in the psychiatric hospital would determine Flora's future.

The unravelling of a woman so publicly shocked both Chisholm and Daniels; the fragility of her mind was evident as they'd questioned her and as the woman's thoughts were unlocked. To the detectives, she looked like an elderly grandmother with a purple rinse, but they had to treat her like a criminal for the break-in, the damage, and the homophobic slogans of hate. Without a doubt, her crimes were terrible, and the female detective felt a loathing of the woman, no matter what her age.

The dilemma spinning around in Helen's mind wouldn't stop. Prejudice and a lack of compassion had brought about the old lady's demise. Were these justifiable excuses to let Flora off lightly, with a rap on the hand, pay for damage, and give her a stern warning? Or should the procurator fiscal weigh in, with an appearance in court and the chance of being locked in a cell? Given her good character previously and her penitence, it would be highly unlikely she would have a custodial sentence.

'Don't you think she is getting off lightly?'

The comment, tossed in the air for debate, had not come from someone affected by the graffiti. Chisholm pondered the question Euan asked. The mere mention of the name *The Craigs* brought waves of sadness to the senior officer.

'No, I think the burden will cost her more dearly than we can ever imagine. She may never go home again, so her independence might be lost forever. From what I gather from a call I took from one of her children who lives in Australia, this breakdown has been long overdue.

Not an excuse, but her God-fearing upbringing was common back then. It hasn't been that long since ferries weren't permitted to run to and from the Outer Hebrides on Sundays. Flora MacAskill was of an ancient stock that still exists in parts of the Highlands and further afield. Even today, there are families with strict Free Church backgrounds who uphold these traditions. It's a harsh, uncomfortable, and unyielding upbringing for many modern eyes.'

'But she's full of hate and venom!'

'Not necessarily, Euan. Aren't we guilty of our own prejudices if we judge others because of their belief systems or ways they want to live their lives?'

Whilst the two detectives continued the debate, Helen remained silent until she could not stop herself any longer.

'I am happy in my own skin. I'm proud to be in a single-sex relationship, and I want to shout it from the rooftops. I'm getting married soon to the love of my life. What I don't understand is the lack of acceptance and tolerance of all humankind.'

Euan, without a thought she was his superior, held out his arms. Helen, shocked at her outburst, accepted the gracious, and much-needed bear hug from a colleague. Shaking from her declaration, his gesture deflected the drama. A clumsy embrace brought redness to their cheeks when they both realised anyone could walk in on them and misinterpret the moment. They parted with a grin, and the young man nodded as Helen jested,

'Now get on writing up that report, you old softy!'

The large knot, made of many intricate fibres, lay in David's chest, crushing him until nothing made sense. Heavier and heavier the knot grew until he realised it was the elephant in the room that would not grant him air;

two locals had been brought in for questioning, but neither was an assassin. The mechanic was just an idiot involved on the fringes of crime. The pensioner had tightened the threads, leaving him restless and struggling to breathe.

Alison McLeod said from the start MI5 would be involved. Where were they? No one had shown up in Loch Dubhglas or made themselves known to him as the SIO. Who were the *"officers"* visiting the ironmonger's shop before he'd even assigned Euan to the task? Then there were the headlines in the newspapers and across the television screens of rumours that persisted, linking the murder to drugs, which were a ridiculous pack of lies. There was no clue as to who was feeding elements of the press these untruths. Having investigated a number of murders over his time as a detective, this case felt different, wrong even. Vital pieces of a jigsaw were missing.

A chemical agent was a serious cause of death. He didn't mind if the case was taken over by MI5, but what he felt uneasy about was not knowing what was really going on and who was in charge. Everything could be ripped from him at any moment. The fear of missing something vital tightened the knot more within his chest.

From now on, team briefings would be sparse in information sharing. The real meetings would be held with only the two other officers he could trust. He always played every crime investigation by the book, but something was amiss. A hunch brewed in his mind, but first, he should look at all the evidence in Inverness. The problem was he'd been told to lie low in Loch Dubhglas.

✝✝✝✝✝

Buildings held secrets, especially when the walls were thin. Helen protested about meeting in the car, halfway down the A9 in the dark.

'What are we doing here?'

'Because I have decided to play things safe, just you and I for once, away from the station.'

'Do you realise how you are sounding?'

Without pausing for an answer, she continued,

'You are turning into a conspiracy theorist. A few days ago, you mentioned MI5 because of the chemical element to the murder. I've been wondering about when they will get involved. The chief talked about three suspects with the capability of supplying such a toxic substance. We have heard nothing more about any of this. Why?'

'Exactly, Helen, I've been thinking the same. We've only been given half a story. For now, we'll do what we can to investigate this murder. Let's look at the footage you got about Alec in The Blue Cat nightclub, and see if he's telling the truth.'

As she pushed the memory stick into her laptop, they gazed through the video replay for the evening concerned, and found the relevant footage.

A group of rowdy drinkers sat in a corner, a mixture of men and women. In view, in the middle of the group was the woman who had attended the charity ball and had been named as a person of interest by McLeod when she'd visited Loch Dubhglas. She was laughing and joking.

'Isn't that Natasha Boskova?'

'Yes!'

'What the hell is she doing there?'

David shrugged his shoulders, wary of anything he'd witnessed in the days since Freya's body was found. Everything was complex, and nothing made sense.

The familiar mechanic strolled into the bar and sat on a stool as he had described in his interview. After ordering a drink, he sat sipping from his glass for a few minutes. With a pint almost drunk, one of the females left the group and stood behind him. It wasn't the supermodel, but when Alec cast one eye over his shoulder, he smiled at the dark-haired lady wearing a pink t-shirt, black jeans, and high heels.

The statement he had given was accurate. Around thirty minutes after moving to another table and buying several rounds of booze, the couple left. No shot or angle of the camera caught the woman's face.

By scanning through more footage, Sullivan and the woman were next seen outside the nightclub. They pushed their way through a small group of men who were smoking.

No one seemed to pay attention to the pair as everyone seemed past the point of being merry, given the way most were staggering. A short way from the venue, footage from cameras in the multi-storey car park had been obtained. Normally they would have been overwritten, but a technical fault meant the cameras had not recording since the murder.

Again, the woman and Alec came into view. Lights flashed on the vehicle as they walked towards it. The mechanic opened the back door, and the female threw her heels into the van and manoeuvred herself inside. Sullivan jumped in behind her and slammed the door shut. The rocking of the transit began a few minutes later. In all, the session was quick. The woman backed out of the van doors, high heels intact, exactly twelve minutes and fifty-four seconds later. From a handbag, she produced a cap. Lowering the peak so most of her face was obscured, she placed it on her head and walked away. Alec did not emerge from the vehicle until the next morning. He opened the back door, jumped out, and stretched his shoulders and arms, then lit a cigarette.

'It looks like he's telling the truth, but that's a massive coincidence. Boskova was in the same nightclub.'

'He can't be very bright, and he is easily flattered, given the speed of the whole dalliance. Tech' can't find any information on the phone call he received. It's a dead end. What do you think about searching for DNA samples in case we need to find this woman? She might be on the database.'

He shook his head, but the cogs in his brain gathered speed. The thought of the mechanic being able to carry out a targeted assassination felt wrong.

'Sullivan is a petty criminal. After all, he is only singing because he is keen not to go down for murder. Let's look into his bank records and that garage. He may not know the woman in the bar or even her name, but someone clearly knows him and wanted a fall guy.'

My tears rain down across the Highlands, filling all the lochs and lochans. Burns and rivers overflow. Puddles form

on the pavements in Loch Dubhglas and create watercourses where roads should be. Rainwater gushes into the old drainage system under the villagers' feet as they dash into their houses from walking their dogs or race from cars to their front doors, glad to be home and dry from the deluge outside. Children dawdle as they walk home from school, water dripping from their foreheads and onto their noses. Sticking out their tongues to taste the weather, they enjoy the sensation of being drenched before running home to be chastised for being soaked.

It's no surprise there is so much water in Scotland. Rain is constant at various times of the year. Once, when I fancied a day away from my prison at Dubhness Cottage, I drove to the other side of Inverness and stopped the car to view the famous Loch Ness. It is not the largest or the deepest loch in the country, but it is the most famous. Years ago, even as a child growing up in Birmingham, I'd heard of the humped-back monster who lives in the deep waters surrounding Urquhart Castle. I dreamed one day I would meet Nessie, and she would bring me luck. It's safe to say I never met the creature or spied any tell-tale signs of her in the water. Perhaps that is why I never had any luck in life.

Had I had any good fortune, I would not be lingering in this hinterland. I need to come to terms with the fact I may dwell in the place for all eternity. I'll never be anything other than another lost soul in a dark chasm full of emptiness. I used to think monsters lived in such locations; they did in fairy stories. After working in the Met. I know the earthly world is full of monsters. and wolves.

CHAPTER 17
Day 16 : Wednesday, 8th October

Alison put down the phone. She was pleased with the progress. There was a positive amount of information gleaned, even if most was from a persistent offender like the mechanic. As for the detention of a local stalwart of the community in the psychiatric hospital in Inverness, she wondered if there would be repercussions. A pensioner taking it upon herself to daub the walls of Dubhness Cottage with homophobic slogans had to be held to account for her crime. McLeod held no sympathy for either.

The minister, Sir William Altingham, whom David and Helen had met, wanted an update. She'd spoken to him several times on the telephone, but his business interests had now brought him back to the Highlands, and he wanted a meeting. Keeping a minister informed might lead to some good contacts. She agreed to the appointment without looking at her schedule; it was imperative to fit him in at any cost. Aware of the tabloid headlines, she knew he had an eye for the women.

Making a mental note to slip into the short black dress and high heels that always got her noticed, she crossed off her list several jobs she should have completed before the lunchtime meeting with him.

She was desperate for the next big promotion, which would be surfacing shortly, so she needed a good bunch of quick results. Any other tasks could be dealt with later, but for now her mind was awash with meeting a minister. Connections were everything. This was a priority.

Walking into the hotel with five minutes to spare before her appointment, Alison's heels sank deep into the blue woollen carpet. This was clearly where people with money hung out. Even for someone who fancied her chances of promotion to the higher ranks of Police Scotland or further afield, the place was posh.

A tall maître d'hôtel, impeccably dressed in a black suit, approached her, and offered to take her red jacket. Then he clicked his fingers and a young male waiter appeared. She followed the man to a table by the window, overlooking River Ness. She nodded her approval as he offered her a jug of water and glasses.

Rarely showing nerves, she felt apprehension at meeting the minister. Rumblings that Sir William might stand for party leadership would mean he could be the next Prime Minister. Contacts told her that he stood a chance. Making his acquaintance would be beneficial.

When he arrived, he wasn't alone. A plain clothed bodyguard accompanied him into the room and sat discreetly a few yards away.

'So sorry I'm late. Alison, isn't it? Call me Will. Your face is familiar. Have we met before?'

He shook hands with her, and they both sat ready for the briefing. She was about to dismiss the suggestion, his way of breaking the ice, when she froze. A moment in time she would rather forget, flashed through her mind as she attempted to regain her composure. Her head shook, more in denial than to answer his question. Words disappeared from her lips, and she could only manage a banal reply.

'Do you visit the Highlands often?'

'Yes. I visit Inverness regularly, as I am involved in several green energy projects here. I am thinking of buying an estate in Sutherland. I met your two officers there a few days ago. A business partner currently owns it but says he will sell it to me at the right price. Anyway, down to the briefing. What's the news?'

A deafening noise inside her head drowned out the ambient music playing in the background. The sound roaring through her mind changed gear and she could no longer ignore the memory it triggered. Meeting this man in person had unleashed a deep, dark secret from the past, one she wished to forget. His voice exploded in her eardrums. Her cheeks reddened.

Something was familiar about the man in front of her that she had not realised until now. She tried to calm down her breathing, but her heart beat so loudly that surely someone would hear. It couldn't be, could it? A stranger from the late nineties she had tried to forget; a nightmare brought back to the present as Altingham demanded, more sharply with a second time of asking.

'What is the news?'

The pressure of the memory was so intense, like an invisible scarf around her neck, tightening as twenty-five year old recollections marched into the room and held her throat hostage. She attempted to gather her thoughts and answer.

'As you know... errr... we... we have a man in custody who is the driver of a red transit van.'

The minister glared at her, not impressed by the gibbering wreck in front of him. He had heard good things about the officer but was frustrated by her lack of communication skills.

'Is that it? Hardly worth a briefing. I expected more.'

Trying to compose herself, and to ignore the noise from her chest and the minister's disparaging comments, she attempted to take a couple of shallow breaths. The sounds from her ears and chest were overpowering. The pounding of her heart distracted her thoughts and threw her off guard. When words trickled from her lips, even she could make no sense of them.

'He's not... err... said much at present, but my officers are err... experienced. If they can't get him... to talk, perhaps err... MI5 representatives will, if err... they ever arrive. I can't believe the delay in deploying them.'

A passing waitress shot a glance towards the minister as his head tilted back, and a huge roar of laughter leapt from his mouth, reverberating around the walls of the restaurant and drowning out the background music. He lowered his voice for the first time since arriving.

'My dear Ms. McLeod, they have been in Loch Dubhglas since it became clear the murder was by chemical attack. Did no one inform you of their presence? You're rather slack in keeping up to date with the proceedings. I was expecting to come here for a comprehensive briefing and it appears that I know more about the case than you do!'

Embarrassment, coated in deep crimson, spread across her cheeks. She felt stupid, shaking her head in denial.

'No, no, I would have been informed.'

Another roar of laughter. This time, people in the restaurant looked around and stared. They whispered to each other about the famous dining guest, whom they all recognised.

'Detective Inspector Chisholm doesn't seem to be making progress on the case. It's a good job MI5 is involved and on the ground in Sutherland. We can't leave something like this to the local plod to do the spade work. This is a matter of national security. I hear his reputation is good, but I'm told since his divorce, his brain's gone to mush. I suggest you take him off the case, if need be. He is beyond his depth in this investigation, as you seem to be too. You don't want your force to look weak, not in these days of cuts and reorganisation of policing in Scotland. There are some rising officers to take your place. I personally know some of them, the sons or grandsons of friends of mine. All these youngsters are coming up through the ranks, snapping at the heels of old-timers like you. Shall we order? I'm starving.'

Her appetite had vanished. Instead, she chewed over the minister's words, barely touching the steak she ordered. For the first time in years, Alison McLeod felt small and naive, insignificant, in fact. She had no knowledge of agents being in the village, nor had she known of David Chisholm's divorce. Sitting in the swanky restaurant with Altingham, she felt stupid. He, on the other hand, used to the sound of his own voice, made small talk about how he was leading initiatives to turn all cities in the United Kingdom into car-free zones. When he offered to pay the bill, she didn't argue. Even her hospitality allowance didn't run to this place.

She willed the floor to swallow her so that she could rid herself of this man. He had not recognised her, or if he had, he chose to ignore the fact he had raped her twenty-five years before. The mask of confidence she had hidden behind since joining the police force vanished, and she struggled to breathe as the flashbacks returned.

There she was, once more the naive teenager, choosing to be smuggled into a Perth nightclub by her older friends. Heels and makeup had hidden her tender age. Her short black skirt and pretty, cropped top acted like nectar as the bees circled, drawing ever closer.

One man, old enough to be her father, had snatched away her innocence in a dark alleyway behind the club that night. His name remained a mystery, and she would never see him again—until now. His upper-class English accent seduced her as he plied her with champagne and charmed her with his witty jokes and stories. Always shallow and stupid, she had been smitten by the way he flashed his cash; his wealth was appealing to a girl who had nothing. How could she not have recognised him before? His face was constantly splashed across the newspapers and television.

Trembling, she struggled to speak, leaving Altingham to chat, not particularly to her but to the room. In public he always put on a show, playing a performance, pretending to be decent and likeable.

When they parted on the bottom step of the hotel entrance, his handshake lingered as his eyes met hers, and his grip tightened, making her fear that he recognised her.

Determined to remain strong, she pulled her hand away from his grasp. A photographer appeared from nowhere, and without permission, began clicking away with his camera, recording their meeting for the world to see. Normally she smiled for publicity shots, another opportunity to promote herself, but for some inextricable reason, she blamed the cold wind running along the Ness when her eyes filled with tears. Standing close to him, in a body-hugging dress, she felt as exposed and vulnerable as the seventeen-year-old standing dishevelled and lost in a Perth alleyway. She wanted nothing to do with this man. Long ago he had taken her innocence, and she had lived to regret the incident every single day of her life since.

†††††

Back in the office and still trembling after her encounter with Altingham, Alison's first instinct was to report off duty and go home. Instead, she sat upright at her desk, staring at the photograph of herself on that proud first day in uniform, recalling the emotions she'd felt way back then. It was the first time after her encounter with the man in the alleyway that she felt almost human; that maybe life was still worth living, after months of imagining the rancid taste of alcohol as his drunken lips met hers.

Normally, she would telephone Chisholm and offer him a piece of her mind: give him a dressing down over the slowness of his investigation, the need for rapid results, and instruct him to change focus. Something stopped her. Silence seemed a better option for once.

From her conversation with the minister, it had become clear she and David were pawns in a bigger game than she imagined. She had been one of Sir William's game pieces before, and she wanted no part of him. Twenty-five years of nightmares and guilt needed exorcising. No more locking the memories in a dark place in her mind, keeping up her barriers against the world. For the second time in her life, he had belittled her. She made the decision to leave the office and drive north. She would not let him ruin her again. She was stronger, older, and much wiser.

Despite being a career police officer, ambitious to rise through the ranks quickly, in her day as a detective, she had been good at her job. Within all the trash pouring out of Sir William's mouth at that luncheon meeting, certain truths nagged away at her as she wondered how she'd been oblivious to the presence of MI5 operating in

Loch Dubhglas as soon as chemicals were found to be involved in the woman's murder. She'd been told by her boss what she could and couldn't say to Chisholm when she'd driven up to the incident room and handed out information about the three oligarchs.

Glad that she refused to drink alcohol at lunch, she was fine to drive. It would clear her head and give her space to think. Nothing had prepared her for this encounter with her past. To examine her beginnings was painful and exhausting. Only when she joined the police did she find salvation. Tears dripped steadily at first, blurring her vision as she wiped them away. Soon her cheeks were stained. Then, as if someone finally turned on a water hydrant, they gushed until she could no longer see to drive safely. She pulled into a lay-by. Her eyes were swollen and sore.

All she could picture in her head was a dark alleyway. She didn't know where she was and kept stumbling in the stupid heels she was wearing. Her head was fuzzy with the concoction of different booze she had drunk. This man was delightful, worth a bob or two, and polite. A kiss and a cuddle wouldn't do any harm. Her mother's words of being careful, not staying out too late, and watching who she mixed with, were drowned out by a wish for excitement.

Instead, a man old enough to be her father took her virginity against a crumbling red brick wall and a row of black plastic dustbins. She begged him not to, but he stifled her cries with his hand pushed firmly across her lips when she protested. Several empty bottles of lager lay smashed on the floor beneath her feet as he pushed harder and harder into her naive little frame. Rats, not two metres away, heard her gasp. The stink of piss filled her nostrils as vomit flew from her mouth five minutes later. Even drunk, she felt filthy and used. The guy, so charming and generous before the alleyway incident, took his hand from her mouth, zipped up his trousers, and walked away into the night, leaving another little tart to spew her guts.

The disgust on her parents' faces was never forgotten, nor the disappointment or lack of joy of making them grandparents in their late thirties. She remembered the questions, the accusations, and the arguments. It was never mentioned again after the adoption papers were signed and the baby was taken away. It could not be seen, so it didn't exist. She had gone along with the plan, stupidly never raising an objection. There was nothing to be done. She didn't know the man's name.

Her parents wanted no police involvement to embarrass the family, as she had willingly accepted his advances despite being so young. They repeatedly chastised her for drinking, for being loose in morals, and for being so stupid. Sometimes she wondered if she had dreamed the events, but the strange nightmare that recurred every few months, and always around the month of June, made her remember the reality of her decisions that night.

She closed her eyes and recalled her parents' faces. They were never quite the same after the shenanigans of her teenage years. Both had died in their late forties, neither recovering from the shock of that day. There were no more tears. There was no point. They lived and died with the shame she brought on the family and never forgave her or mentioned the pregnancy again. From then on, no matter what she did, nothing was ever good enough to put things right.

When calmer, she drove on, an emotional wreck, hiding behind the stoic face of the chief inspector. As if sensing her mood, rain lashed down on the windscreen as she arrived in the village. The storm clouds followed all the way up the A9, the first droplets of water falling just after the Cromarty Bridge. By the time she saw the sign for Sutherland, the temperature was several degrees less. The chill wind she had felt in Inverness turned icy as she stepped out of the car in Loch Dubhglas.

By now the light was fading fast. Making her way to a local bar with accommodation advertised in the window, she booked a room for the evening. She showered, just as like twenty-five years before after her first encounter with Altingham. Feeling grubby and soiled, she scrubbed her body until her skin was raw in places. Although it stung, she gained pleasure from the pain the water gave her.

Later she dressed and went to seek Chisholm in the incident room. Lights were still on as she crossed the road and made her way to the village hall. At first, he did not identify her: no make-up, high heels, or dresses; just red, puffy eyes that told him she had been crying. The woman walked into the room in a black padded jacket, zipped up as far as it would go to keep warm. Blue jeans and white trainers made her unrecognisable. Her dark brown hair was partially covered by a blue beanie hat emblazoned with *"USA,"* a memento from a trip less than a year before. It was only when she spoke that he knew the visitor.

'David, we need to talk.'

Shocked at the revelation that this was Alison McLeod, his first response was garbled.

'I'm sorry—is that you, Chief?'

He faltered. He never called her *"Chief."* His cheeks reddened with embarrassment.

'Yes. I apologise for not warning you of my visit. I have something I want to discuss with you and felt it best not to speak over the phone.'

Taken aback at her apology, words failed.

'Is there somewhere we can talk in private, away from everyone?'

'Yes, of course. I was about to leave, just clearing up a few loose ends. I have a plan for where we can go.'

Within a few minutes, the pair took off in Chisholm's BMW with a simple offering of Orkney cheese, bread, and crisps. Two bottles of spring water completed the purchase from the village shop, where just two weeks before, Anna Green, aka Freya Rose, stood waiting to be served.

A quietness fell between them as the car travelled further north to Loch Spiorad. He was still in shock, and she was lost in thought. Headlights pierced the darkness that fell. Remnants of police incident tape, still wrapped around a tree trunk, signalled the arrival at the place where the investigation began. With the engine turned off, both looked at each other and began to talk at the same time.

'I want to say…'

'We got off on the wrong…'

David gave way to his superior.

'I want to say sorry. I know I can be difficult sometimes and demanding. I expect the best from my officers. The thing is, David, I think we need to start again for the good of this investigation.'

The detective inspector nodded. McLeod continued, sharing her concerns.

'I had the misfortune of speaking to Sir William today. He asked to have an update over lunch. He's not a nice character, rather manipulative and brutal, if I'm honest, and not complimentary about how the case is progressing. He was highly critical of us both. I suppose this is how these people advance themselves.'

David wanted to use an old phrase his grandmother had said time after time, *"Pot calling the kettle black!"* but he bit his tongue. He felt a truce was necessary.

Something was troubling his boss. He noticed how tightly she crossed her arms against her chest, as if protecting herself. Her face was pale, almost ghost like, and she kept checking over her shoulder in case another vehicle approached. McLeod was clearly spooked by something but he didn't have the kind of relationship with her where he could ask if everything was okay. He wondered why she'd been crying but it was futile to ask. So he simply commented on the M.P.

'Perhaps it's normal for a minister to be involved when the cause of death is by chemical attack.'

It was almost as though Alison hadn't heard his comment. She didn't reply to what David had said. Instead, she continued with her own trail of thought.

'Altingham insisted MI5 officers are already in Loch Dubhglas. Do you have any inkling if he might be bluffing? He seemed very well informed.'

As she began to speak more tactically about the case, her shoulders dropped and some of the tension she'd been harbouring eased. For once, she listened to David's theories on the mystery agents. The next few minutes were spent hatching a plan to encourage MI5 to work with the police officers, and not in hot competition with them.

David insisted on spending the night at the Bed & Breakfast. Even though Rachael and Jimmy protested at his decision, he was adamant, promising to return when he could. He needed an evening to complete some paperwork and would be late to leave the incident room. He wanted a clear head for the next day, which he knew would become muddied by several tots of the amber nectar if he had stayed with his father's old pal.

There was something about connecting with the couple that gave him comfort. Increasingly, he found great joy in spending time with them, getting to know them and reconnecting with his past. Why had he not gone back to the village before? He concluded that it hadn't been the right time, until now.

When he finally attempted to settle down in bed, he thought his mind was too active to fall asleep, but he drifted off quickly and dreamed of the Milky Way and millions of stars.

†††††

How incredulous is the night sky? I would look up at the stars and find pleasure in knowing they were constants in a world that is forever changing. Even when there were clouds hiding them, the certainty that the constellations were still in position brought great comfort. For humans, the wheels of life and death weave in and out of time; babies are born, people pass. As the planet spins around the sun and the seasons come and go, the rhythm of life continues as it has for thousands of years. Summer has departed, autumn will fade into winter, then spring will approach bringing new life and hope once more.

In Norse mythology, Iduna [21] *was the goddess of many things including immortality, and also known as the rejuvenator. Like the springtime she represents, buds are forming in the detective's mind. I will help him to nurture them. May they blossom and grow the fruits of truth and justice. Only then, will the circle of my story be complete.*

SHE WHO WAS

I am oceans,
Vast and deep.
Home to creatures
From when life began.

I am the wind,
Calm and still.
Powerful and chaotic,
When I rage.

I am fire,
Roaring fiercely,
Leaping and dancing
To no one's tune.

I am the earth
Where humans die
Dust to dust,
Ashes to ashes.

Four elements of life,
The roots of mankind.
Yet aether forgotten...
What about the stars?

IDUNA
Goddess of Immortality

CHAPTER 18
Day 17 : Thursday, 9th October

With breakfast underway at the Bed & Breakfast, David ignored the two geologists. Seemingly, it was their final day before travelling south according to their endless chatter and attempts to engage him in tireless conversation about a pile of rocks they were studying at the table. The detective sat stony-faced, preparing for his day ahead, hoping for more revelations. McLeod's visit had provided enlightenment. For once she seemed human, fragile even. Sir William Altingham was certainly under her skin.

A noise in the hall signalled a visitor. The two geologists looked up from their discussion on Torridon sandstone as the owner led Alison McLeod into the room. Back in her high heels and a navy blue, figure-hugging dress, she scanned the room before walking directly to the detective inspector's table. The owner was about to leave when the chief addressed the three strangers.

'If I can have your attention, please, I'd be grateful. I am sure you know my colleague, David Chisholm. He's the SIO who's been working on the murder inquiry for the past fortnight. It is time, we feel, to work together.'

If David had misread the situation, she would have egg on her face. Instead, the owner shut the dining room door and pulled up a chair to sit with the geologists.

'Great work, McLeod. How did you find out?'

'Oh, I take no credit whatsoever for this piece of detective work. That is entirely down to David. May we ask your names, or is that not allowed?'

'Let's use first names. I'm John, lead on the investigation in the murder inquiry, and my colleagues, Simon and Janine. Congratulations, David. I'm impressed! How did you guess? I'm curious!'

Chisholm began to laugh at the ridiculousness of his answer as he explained.

'I surmised for a while that something was amiss. When one of the detectives went to the ironmongers and found two "police officers" had already been asking questions about spray paint, unbeknownst to anyone, I went back to the hardware shop and asked about the detectives. It was perfectly clear who the agents were.

However, having local knowledge of visitors proved most beneficial; there was something about being overenthusiastic about rocks whenever I entered the breakfast room. And you, John, you might be MI5, but my friend Jimmy told me the owners of this place went away for four weeks on a surprise cruise they mysteriously afforded. Bob & Barbara, the true owners, are known for being penny pinchers and certainly do not spend their money on cruises. It's the talk of the village.'

The laughter rang around the room. Loch Dubhglas gossip had solved the puzzle of MI5. When they'd all had time to take in the news, John began the briefing.

'It was only yesterday it was confirmed that Freya Rose was the murder victim. She was a serving undercover police officer who was placed in witness protection. We tried to gain access to her records, but it seems they were sealed at the highest levels of security. We've made some progress but it's all very strange and highly unusual.

It also seems more than a coincidence that three known, and highly influential oligarchs, were in Inverness on the night when Freya died. All have fabulous alibis as they were in the presence of some of the top police officers in northern Scotland.

However, we are now excluding one person. Natasha Boskova has no known connection to the Highlands. She was invited to the event that you both attended because of some charity links she has and remained in Inverness overnight, visiting a club called The Blue Cat which I'm sure you are both familiar with. Currently, we are not pursuing her for this murder. For operational reasons that I can't go into, we have deleted her name from our list of people of interest.'

McLeod and Chisholm looked at each other for answers. David interjected.

'We have a local suspect, Alec Sullivan, who claims he doesn't know who killed Freya and was merely paid to take rubbish and a car from Dubhness Cottage. He was in the same nightclub as Boskova afterwards.'

John continued, determined to let Boskova be dropped from the investigation.

'Having slipped away from the charity do, Natasha met up with her entourage who travel with her. Only one woman remains unidentified. She did not stay long with the group and apparently went off with a guy she met in the bar.'

'Yes, the mechanic, Sullivan.'

Trying to take in all of the information, David sat tensely, wondering what else the agents would divulge. Alec had disappeared with a woman from Boskova's group. He wanted to ask more questions, but Janine explained the information gathered about another of the three millionaires.

'Dima Chenko has links to various investments across Scotland and, of late, particular interest around Aberdeen. Business has no borders to him, as his concerns reach every corner of the globe. He recently bought a distillery in the region, which has meant him travelling to Inverness for publicity.

He is under investigation for money laundering and is good at evading the cyber traces we run, but we have extracted some information. We are slowly finding evidence to show his involvement in various avenues of corruption. He has offshore accounts where he stashes cash, and is very capable of supplying items containing chemical agents. We can't find links to anything Freya may have been investigating. He remains a person of interest, but we suspect at the moment untangling any links between Freya's death and him will be complicated, lengthy, and unlikely.'

McLeod considered the remaining suspect who hadn't yet been mentioned by the agents.

'And what about Roberto Marino? What have you found out about him?'

Simon spoke for the first time.

'Marino owns land and property in Sutherland and nearby Ross-shire, which came as a surprise to us as he purchased it under a company name we didn't realise was linked to him. He spends time at his Highland home infrequently. He flew back to London after the event in a private jet, then on to New York. As a *"legitimate"* entrepreneur, his contacts are everywhere. He has friends in high places who seem to stay on his estate more than he does.'

Puzzled by the remark, David and Alison looked at each other for an answer. Their jaws agape, the penny dropped and, in unison, they uttered the same name.

'Sir William Altingham!'

The next part of the discussion revolved around the minister. The agents asked if the officers knew anything about him. In a monotone voice, and without emotion, McLeod quietly advised she had recently meet with him for a briefing on the case but remained silent for most of the conversation. No one particularly noticed that her skin paled and her hands were moist. David related the visit to the estate near Loch Dubhglas before asking the burning question in his mind.

'You don't suggest Altingham has anything to do with the murder, do you?'

He searched for reactions but concluded little from the nonchalant expression each member of MI5 wore. Simon continued.

'We have reason to believe he knew Freya Rose from her previous life.'

An involuntary whistle slipped through David's lips after hearing this piece of shocking news. McLeod's tone was sharp as she snapped.

'Why were we not told of a connection? That is a vital piece of information withheld. David, we don't know of a link to Freya, do we?'

Chisholm shook his head. The cogs in his brain whirled into action at this news.

'How did he know her?'

'It wasn't until late yesterday that we established a link when we finally accessed some of her records. She was a nanny to his young daughter.'

'But I thought she was a policewoman!'

'You gathered she was undercover?'

David nodded as Janine continued.

'Freya Rose was a talented police officer. Her potential to work within our department was spotted at training college, and after a brief spell of working in Birmingham and for the Met., she was recruited, working undercover on a number of cases. It turns out that her final assignment was as a nanny in the home of Sir William Altingham. Certain lines of investigation meant MI5 and MI6 wanted information about his business associates.

After going undercover and being in position for a few months, we gathered she suddenly requested to be out from the surveillance as she feared her cover was about to be exposed. Her handler removed her quickly, and she disappeared. All safe houses were recorded as per procedure but evidence gained from Freya's surveillance was never logged.

Her move to the current address near Loch Dubhglas was never filed because less than twenty-four hours after the move, the handler was involved in a motorcycle crash and was killed along with the driver of the other car. It seemed a genuine accident, and the coroner brought in a verdict of accidental death. We shall now do a full investigation into the incident. The usual task of assigning another handler mysteriously never happened, which is completely against protocol. Coincidences in this game don't exist.'

'So, you're saying no one knows what Freya and her handler knew or where she was hiding when she moved here to Sutherland?'

'Correct.'

For a second time, Chisholm couldn't hold back on his reaction to the news.

'Bloody hell! That's a major cock-up! This case has just taken a sinister twist!'

All three agents nodded, but only John spoke.

'We suspect *"Mr. Keep It Clean, Make It Green"* may not be as wonderful as he makes everyone believe. Freya Rose was placed in his house to find information about his involvement in an arms deal we suspect is linked to the Kremlin. Intelligence in our possession shows Roberto Marino supplied a substantial amount of weapons for the current conflict in the Black Sea region. If Altingham is involved, his green credentials are, let's politely say, compromised. The scandal of a high-profile minister of His Majesty's government being involved will have huge, and significant consequences around the world. The Baltic states are already edgy, from all this news in Washington of peace talks with the Russians.'

The room fell silent as everyone pondered war beginning in other areas of the former eastern bloc and the pressures on leaders to create a European army given the crises in recent peace talks.

'Naturally, this is all confidential and highly classified information. You are only being told this as senior officers who need to be in the picture of how crucial this investigation is, and how delicately we must proceed. Sir William must not know we have him in our sights; hence why Police Scotland and MI5 have made a hash of the case in his mind. If he contacts either of you for more information, tell him bits to keep him sweet but not this aspect of the case. He's not a stupid man, far from it. In fact, he excels at covering his tracks.

He knows we are in the village and is briefed with information we feed him. He has no knowledge that we are here to investigate him and his connection to Marino as well as the murder. We don't recommend announcing the release of Freya's real name or that she was a police officer, but key detectives should be aware. As for Altingham, no one should approach him as he remains a person of significant interest for other matters. Organise a press conference to say you are doing a reconstruction of Freya and hoping the mystery woman she was seen with comes forward. Generate a bit of publicity to see what happens.

†††††

McLeod hid her discomfort until she got back to her hotel room. Deeply annoyed and frustrated with herself for not speaking of her awful history with the minister, she sat on the bed and burst into tears. It was personal, too close to home to share, murder or not. She'd suggested the incident room remained open for a few more days following the reconstruction, and then all investigative work would take place in headquarters in Inverness.

Helen was surprised to see McLeod and Chisholm casually strolling into the hall, deep in conversation. The sergeant knew her boss's feelings towards the chief, and whilst he would never openly criticise her, or anyone else for that matter, usually his mood was different when the chief was in the same room. There was a tone to his voice, and a bristling of actions that always spoke volumes of his dislike for her.

Today was different, and Daniels sensed something was afoot. Chisholm stood closer than usual to McLeod;

his ear bent near her lips as the chief said something inaudible to anyone else.

David asked only for the detectives to be present and for a row of chairs to be arranged in a semicircle, facing the stage. He moved to the front of the hall as three strangers slipped into the back of the room. His words were chosen carefully, and the mood changed as he gave an update.

'This morning, Chief Inspector McLeod and I attended a briefing session to share information pertaining to the murder of Anna Green. I can now confirm Miss Green was, in fact, a police officer from the Met. She was put into witness protection for reasons that are currently classified and relocated to Sutherland when an operation she was working on went wrong. Her real name was Freya Rose. Most information about Miss Rose will remain only with police at this moment, but to the public, she will be known as Anna Green for a little while longer.

We thank officers from MI5, who are also working alongside Police Scotland, for an insight into the officer's background before she went into hiding. A reconstruction will be set up, using a lookalike, to see if anyone else will come forward with more information.

As you know, she was spotted by a witness one evening with a woman a couple of weeks before her death. Our priority must be to identify this unknown person, who we believe may have been in a relationship with the police officer. This lady is of major interest to us.'

Voices buzzed within the hall, breaking the silence. David hushed everyone. His calm, authoritative voice took control of the proceedings, as he would at a press conference hurriedly arranged in Inverness for the next day. Unseen to anyone but Chisholm and McLeod, the three strangers slipped out, satisfied the announcements would flush some rats from under the floorboards. The only problem was that no one knew from which direction they would scurry.

†††††

Vermin will surface eventually after hiding in plain sight. A trap set on the day of my death will catch them unawares when they least expect it. They will smell danger only at that moment when they have tasted the treat, enticed by the sweetest of smells, mouths watering at the pleasure that lies in wait. With the swiftest of motions, the trap will snap, the steel pin crushing their bodies or skulls with a bolt of thunder. I will look on and laugh at their demise. For they will be punished, in one way or another.

CHAPTER 19
Day 18 : Friday, 10th October

The press conference, chaired by Alison McLeod, went well. She made sure she wore something that turned heads when she walked into the room. With a final glance in the mirror to ensure her makeup was perfect, she adopted a wry smile to mask any emotions she wanted to bury.

Flashes and the sounds of cameras clicking reassured her she was in the spotlight. Her confidence, knocked by Altingham, returned, especially now she knew he was of the worst, viperous kind of crook as well as a rapist.

He'd threatened her cherished career and reputation, making her feel like trash, but she would have the last laugh. Men like him needed to be extinguished from public life, and she was going to entrap him if it was the last thing she ever did. This case would catapult her to the higher echelons of policing. Too much was at stake to let him get under her skin again. A performance worthy of an Oscar was required. Nothing less would do.

As she read from a statement, she clenched her hands together under the table, leaving her knuckles white. David sat by her side, playing his part when necessary. Suddenly, she'd seen his real worth in Loch Dubhglas. Regretting her attitude toward him in the past, he was a steady captain to be trusted in steering the way through the turbulent waters of this case.

The information released to the public did not include the news that the murdered woman was a police officer. Neither did she mention Freya's undercover assignment was to root out Sir William Altingham's dirty deals in financing weapons destined to kill innocent citizens. For now, these golden nuggets would remain known only to a handful of key detectives and MI5 agents who stayed in the shadows. To the world, Anna Green was the victim and a request was made for the lady seen with her to come forward to be eliminated from their enquiries. When a reconstruction was announced, question after question rained down on the detectives, but together, McLeod and Chisholm held a steady ship to weather the media storm they encountered.

†††††

The plan for headlines worked. Some journalists coined the phrase *"The Lady of the Loch."* Far less emphasis was placed on the case being drug-related. The search for the mystery woman seen in the village was a priority, with a re-enactment planned within twenty-four hours.

With publicity for the case, experts came out of the woodwork to be interviewed about supplies of A4-7 and other chemical weapons. One professor theorised an old stock was used as it was believed quantities of similar material went missing at the end of the Cold War. He could not corroborate his beliefs to journalists, but there was enough information to warrant MI5 and MI6 quietly taking a look into his work and speaking to him, away from the razzmatazz of social media and television.

In the midst of numerous calls, David received a message to contact the shop worker in Loch Dubhglas. The madness of the last couple of days was taking its toll on him. Needing relaxation and peace, he decided to switch off for twenty-four hours and head back to Jimmy's.

He would speak to the lady who had given him the information about the address in Birmingham the next day. He also needed to clarify a couple of points from the old lady who had seen Freya kissing the unidentified woman behind the shop. There would be no option to switch off until these tasks were completed.

He would stay with Jimmy as he needed a break from everyone and everything, plus the Bed & Breakfast was no longer an option. The fisherman and his wife were delighted the detective was taking up their offer of accommodation whilst he worked in the area.

The journey to Sutherland seemed to pass quickly, and he felt himself longing to reach the sanctuary of the place. Several weeks before, he'd dreaded even hearing the name of Loch Dubhglas; now, returning within twenty-four hours didn't feel odd.

October wrapped an autumn cloak around the village. A dazzling display of oranges, reds, yellows, and browns reflected on the loch. The cold air meant villagers bundled themselves in well-insulated jackets, woolly hats, gloves, and scarves.

A few miles before the sign announcing the arrival in Loch Dubhglas, Ben Meagaidh came into sight, showing its first peppering of snow on the slopes and summit. David was glad his bag was packed with warmer clothes. Forever a Sutherland lad, the coolness of the weather at this time of year would never be forgotten.

Jimmy opened the door with a wide grin from ear to ear. Cupping his hands around David's outstretched palm, he vigorously shook it to welcome the detective into his house.

'Is this your new weekend place, Loch Dubhglas?'

'It's a great habit that I never thought I would adopt.'

'Come in, laddie, come in! You're most welcome. Rachael's waiting. The oven's hot. She's been busy cooking!'

†††††

After placing his travel bag in the bedroom, David went downstairs. The smell of food replaced the fragrance of potpourri, which normally lingered throughout the house. By the time he reached the dining room, his mouth was watering.

Rachael greeted him, offering a seat at the head of the table. A series of crock dishes covered the wooden surface, each displaying an array of colourful vegetables. Silver serving spoons were placed in each container.

Three plates were piled high with a hearty portion of Cockburn's champion haggis from Dingwall.

'Wow! It's my favourite. How did you know? There was no need to put the red carpet out for me. This looks a feast for kings.'

'It is our absolute pleasure. We're both delighted you've returned into our lives. You don't know how much this means to Jimmy and me. You've mentioned that haggis a few times, so we thought we would get one to celebrate your return to Sutherland. Now fill your plate, but leave room for pudding!'

Several hours later, with the food eaten and the fragrance of whisky replacing the smell of the meal, David, Jimmy, and Rachael moved to the lounge, where the heat from a wood-burning stove soon warmed their cheeks.

They began to look at a pile of old photographs in a box brought down from the loft that afternoon. The images were all new to Chisholm. The memories poured out from things Granda and his grandmother told him. There was his father laughing and joking, captured on a boozy night out in the local pub. Others were taken on sunny days on the croft or proudly standing with a prize sheep at the annual sale in the auction yard.

In all the photographs, his father wore a huge grin. His long, dark sideburns almost matched the length of his hair, a typical look of the early 1970s, along with flared jeans and a cheesecloth shirt. David lifted one image for closer inspection. This one, like all the others, showed the huge resemblance he bore to his father. There were so many similarities between them, unnoticed over the years. He was more than double Donald's age when he'd died. His dad would be forever young as time slipped away for those left behind.

Lifting another picture to catch a better light, he spotted her straight away; his mother, who months later had tried to kill herself because of the heartbreak of her soulmate's death. A searing pain brought David back to reality. The warm, idyllic life he could have experienced with his mother and father vanished, and the cold emptiness felt for so long returned. Sensing the change in his guest's mood, Jimmy picked up an image on top of the pile of photographs.

'She was a bonny lass, your mother. She couldn't help what she did. Her heart was too broken to mend, but I can tell you one thing, David. She loved you. There was no question of that. She left you with your grandmother and grandfather because she knew you would be well cared for. She couldn't have imagined your journey into adulthood would be so difficult, losing all four people early in your life.

Don't blame her. She too lost both of her parents when she was young. Grief is a strange thing. Back then, there was no counselling or help. In places like The Craigs, electric shock treatment was supposed to cure all, but it wasn't the answer for some lost souls. She was a casualty of everything that happened in her life before the Chisholm family and what happened when you were born.'

'I hear what you're saying, Jimmy. I've tried to come to terms with everything. At times, I felt abandoned; I use that word because that was how I felt growing up. She abandoned me when I needed her most. As I grow older, and I try to see through other people's eyes, I know she was incredibly fragile because of grief.'

Rachael spoke for the first time.

'David, you can't change the past, but you can change your future.'

He stared into the fire. Never had better advice been offered to him.

†††††

There are clues to how long some of these people have dwelt here in melancholy, lost between Heaven and Earth. Their clothes offer hints in terms of decades or even centuries, the human time since they passed into darkness. None of us know the final chapter of our story; that is the only true puzzle humans cannot solve. The date and time each of us will die remains a mystery, even for those terminally ill patients who see their life slipping away. Those who attempt to cut their lives short don't know if they will be successful.

We have no concept of whether there is an afterlife nor where our fate will take us. For many faiths, worshippers seek reassurance that their destiny after death is a place called Heaven or Paradise. Others call it Moksha, Nirvana, or Asgard. Fallen warriors would be sent to Valhalla. The names for Hell are endless, as are the names given by different religions to the underworld. I never considered that I committed such a sin that would result in me being sent to any of these dark places.

Having never killed anyone, stolen anything, or committed adultery, the worst crime I could hold my hands up for was to tell lies: a web of deceit told for worthy reasons to keep others or myself safe. The reality that my soul could remain without passing to light torments me; I never asked for, or wanted, this limbo. Why must I be punished for being murdered? Did I not suffer enough?

The weather in Loch Dubhglas is cool. The inhabitants of the village do not linger in the streets any more. Their hope for the return of warmer days has vanished. The detectives slowly unpeel another layer of my history. Explaining who I really was and who I became will take time for the police to digest.

CHAPTER 20
Day 19 : Saturday, 11th October

The smell wafting from the kitchen reminded him of long-forgotten breakfasts. Steaming hot porridge lay bubbling in a pan ready for serving. Three large spoonfuls were transferred by a steady, experienced hand to a blue breakfast bowl ready to be enjoyed by the visitor. Taking a small silver spoon, he dunked it into a pot of yellow honey before lifting and twizzling the substance and drizzling it over his porridge reminding, him of days gone by. The creamy stickiness slipped from his cutlery to his throat, warming his mouth with joy and ecstasy. All he could taste was his grandmother's food.

Afterwards, David ventured down into the village for two appointments he'd made to go over a witness statement, and to sign another. First he visited the home of the woman who had witnessed Freya kissing a lady, hoping to get more information.

Iris Stirling had discovered newfound confidence since the leader of her church group had been arrested for the vandalism at Dubhness Cottage. All her life, she was seen as a wallflower, hiding in plain sight, never taking centre stage, and keeping herself to herself. Whilst she wouldn't want to take on the role of leader, now that Flora MacAskill was gone for good, it seemed she basked in her moment of glory being important in a murder investigation.

When the bell rang, she jumped up from her chair, ready to answer questions. She was prepared for the detective inspector's visit. Looking at her work, she hoped he was as pleased as she was.

Welcoming Chisholm into her lounge, she offered him a green corduroy sofa to sit on. Once her visitor was settled, she insisted on bringing in drinks and home baking cooked the evening before after taking the call about his visit. When she finally sat down, David was able to begin his questions.

'Mrs. Stirling, I've come to discuss your last sighting of the lady we now know was murdered and placed in Loch Spiorad. I want to take you back to that evening. Tell me what and who you saw as you went into the shop.'

'That's easy. As I entered the shop, someone held the door open for me as she left. I am certain the lady was the one I saw outside a few minutes later. When I went in, I saw Janice, the shop assistant, with the red-haired woman. She was buying some bits and pieces. There was no one else about. She turned around and smiled as I came up to the counter behind her. We didn't speak, although I'd seen her a couple of times at church.

When I'd tried to engage her in conversation in the past, she'd been very shy. She reminded me of one of the battered women I used to support when I worked for a charity linked to domestic abuse. She seemed fragile, and very vulnerable at the time.'

'So can you describe who and what you saw when you left the shop?'

Iris smiled.

'I can do better than that.'

Intrigued, Chisholm watched as she pulled something from a large plastic case placed against the side of the couch. She laid the container on the coffee table, and lifted out a piece of paper about A3 in size. Turning it over, she revealed a pencil sketch of a scene: two women kissing, locked in an embrace. The details of the drawing brought the image to life.

'In my younger days, I loved art. I haven't drawn in years, but I thought this might help. Here are two more artist impressions.'

From the case came a couple more drawings, all in pencil: one with a full-length sketch of the woman who had left the shop before Freya and another of the woman's face in detail. Staring back at David was a slim, beautiful woman with long, dark hair.

'The image from the back of the shop was in shadow, but this is the woman I spotted. Her clothes were distinctive, as you can see. When she held the door for me to enter the shop, the light was reasonable so I got a good look at her.'

'These are superb. Thank you so much. And you are certain about the symbol on the top?'

'Oh yes. The gold motif caught my eye on her hoodie. I know it from somewhere, but I just can't recall where I have seen it before. Perhaps you will have better luck than me in placing it.'

He studied the logo.

'It's like a capital S, do you think?'

'No, the lines of the shape were straight. I wondered if it was a bolt of lightning.'

He turned the images around to see if he could make sense of the shape. Perhaps Helen or Euan might have more luck in identifying it. Probably a brand logo he didn't know. With all three drawings rolled up and fastened with a rubber band, the detective thanked Mrs. Stirling and left.

Having phoned ahead to the shop, another member of staff informed him Janice was not working that day and to make his way to her house near the school. She'd been evasive in signing a formal witness statement,. He needed her to confirm everything that she'd mentioned when he'd first met her, including the address in Birmingham.

She stood in the window, and lit another cigarette as he walked up the garden path and rang the bell. Once inside, the shop assistant showed him into a hazy lounge. On the coffee table, an ashtray was overflowing with nub ends, most from fags smoked that morning.

'You'll have to forgive me. I'm a bag of nerves with all this business.'

'There's no need to worry. No one knows about your evidence. I've come to finalise your statement.'

'Are you sure? I've had journalists asking me questions, even a camera crew.'

'I gather they've been asking all the shopkeepers and many of the locals about the woman discovered in the loch. So, it's not just you they're hassling.'

Janice inhaled the cigarette deep into her lung before answering.

'I've told them nothing.'

'Good. I think that's wise, and I strongly advise you to keep it that way. This is a murder inquiry, and we don't yet know the full extent of who's involved.'

A plume of smoke rose above Janice, spiralling and spinning into faint wisps. Chisholm tried his best not to cough as he read out a statement. He'd captured all the details about the victim posting parcels, and he wanted to clarify the evening she had been seen with someone else.

'Did you ever see anyone else with the woman? Think hard. I know it's not easy, but she came in at night mainly, didn't she?'

'I just don't recall anyone with her. I only saw her speak briefly to someone once in all the times she visited the shop. It was a young woman who entered just before she did one evening. They might have known one another, but whatever was said, it was very short and not a conversation. The other woman came to the counter and paid for some wine, I think. That night, the usual lady didn't post anything.'

'That's good, Janice. Now think, what did she look like? Can you recall anything specific or unusual? Tall? Short? Old or young?'

'Youngish, tall, twenties, no older than early thirties.'

Finally feeling he was getting somewhere before he died of smoke inhalation, he continued to pull answers from the shop assistant. She stubbed out the cigarette and lit another instantly.

'How about hairstyle? Long? Short?'

'Long, dark hair. I can't remember the colour of her eyes, but I do recall her hair. She was a rather beautiful lady, with lots of gold jewellery and rings. Oh, and a necklace with the letter 'S' in gold.'

'How did she speak? Was she Scottish?'

'I can't remember. She may have had a Scottish accent.'

'Finally, can you take a look at these images? Another witness has drawn them. Do you think this is the woman you saw with the victim?'

Janice stared at the pictures. She considered them for a second and shook her head.

'No. That wasn't her.'

Chisholm was disappointed. He'd hoped to release the drawings to the public to appeal for the woman to come forward.

'You're doing well, Janice. I've written up the rest of the statement as we've spoken, so no one else needs to visit. Are you happy to go over it and sign?'

He read out what she had said, the description of a possible associate of the murder victim and the details she remembered of the one encounter. She stubbed out the cigarette. Clutching the pen between her nicotine-stained fingers and thumb, she scribbled a signature.

He stood up, pleased to be leaving the house. Only after walking down the path did he cough to try to rid his lungs of the nicotine breathed in for the last twenty minutes.

Janice watched him go as she lit another fag. Her nerves were shot to pieces because she had lied to a policeman. Perhaps lied was too strong a word. She had not been entirely truthful. She had seen the woman in the drawings and, worse still, knew her name. Both were secrets she wanted to keep hidden.

†††††

With both interviews completed, Chisholm went back to Jimmy's house for lunch. Rachael liked to keep her guests fed well. Always one to over-cater, the three plates on the dining room table were overflowing with a mound of vegetables, potatoes of two kinds, and slices of thinly cut beef. Yorkshire pudding and lashings of gravy completed the meal. David's mouth watered. Since returning to Sutherland, his appetite, which had vanished a couple of years ago, was back. They fell silent for a few moments as each savoured their food.

When the three plates were half empty, they chatted away, relaxed in each other's company. Without any thought for the case, the detective expressed his surprise at the wind farms that had popped up in the area. A nonchalant shrug of the shoulders suggested Jimmy's thoughts on the developments.

'Aye, lad. There's little the locals can do. They aren't pretty things—unsightly, if I'm honest, but they've been going up for a few years now. Some folk say they are good for the communities and that jobs are given to locals. It's all tosh. The companies employ contractors from other places. I dinnae ken one local lad or lassie who got work from them.'

Rachael interjected, fearful her husband would continue his sermon.

'There's a huge wind farm planned on one of the local estates that's causing a bit of a stir. The owner's a billionaire. What's his name, Jimmy? That cook from the telly.'

'Oooft—you got me thinking. Wait. It's coming to me...Roberto Marino!'

David's interest in the conversation was suddenly aroused. His ears pricked, but he tried to stay calm.

'You know the estate he owns, David. The one you said you worked on as a teenager, Knocbrannan.'

His ears now fully alert, the detective within him jumped to attention.

'He knows lots of people, that Italian mannie. My friend Kathy's daughter works up there as an assistant of some kind. Kathy says they have some famous guests, some off the television. A few days ago that minister who keeps on about green energy was visiting again. He is always there. Supposedly interested in buying the place!'

He wanted to rush off straight away to find Kathy's daughter, and ask about the visitors Marino had staying, but instead he remained silent. Excusing himself to visit the bathroom, he called McLeod to inform her of the news. Perhaps somewhere in this mess were wind farms.

†††††

Jimmy stared at David, trying to gauge his mood, surprised at the question. Chisholm repeated himself.

'What say we take a run out to Clachan?'

It was Saturday afternoon, and the detective was up to date with his work. Helen and Euan were in Inverness, and there wasn't much he could do until Monday morning when the filming of reconstruction at the shop was planned. Sunday would be spent with Jimmy and Rachael, and he should be relaxing, but he felt the need to do something for the case. He hated the idea of sitting doing nothing, and the journey would serve two purposes.

'If you're sure, I'll tag along. It's been ages since I was up that way.'

The younger man wasn't entirely sure why he'd suggested the idea or why he'd asked Jimmy to go along, but something niggling in his head told him that he needed to face the final barriers in his mind. Perhaps, he would then be able to move on with living instead of stagnating. Maybe, further down the line, there might be space for someone else in his life. He wasn't even sure if that concept was viable; all he did know was he wanted to change. The visit would also clarify a few thoughts about the case rushing around in his mind.

Clachan was twelve miles from Loch Dubhglas on the road west towards Ullapool. After leaving the village behind, the men travelled through an area of grazing land for cattle and sheep. Standing away from the rest of the Highland cows in one such field, a handsome woolly ginger beast rubbed its cheek and neck on a post beside a galvanised metal gate. He stared at the humans passing by, unperturbed at their brief presence, and stood his ground, informing them this was his land.

They continued until the grassland gave way to pine forests on both sides of the single-track road. The banter between the two men subsided, and they grew silent, each in reverence, preparing themselves for the journey of remembrance. This was the area where David's mother was born and grew up, where generations of Sutherlands lived and died. Many folk in the county shared its name.

High on a hill, an old croft house came into view, abandoned and forgotten, like the land on which it stood. The dilapidated state of the two-storey building was clearer once David had parked the car, and the men set off up to the higher ground. Several of the windows no longer had glass, and the curtains, that had blown in the winds for many years, were just rags. There was no longer any paint on the front door, and the window frames and sills looked rotten. The gutters spilled over with vegetation, and black streaks of overflowing water were evident in several places where there were still signs of grey harling.

The biggest shock was that the charred remains of the roof rafters were still visible. Where once a fire raged, a black carcass replaced the soul of the place, leaving the house interior exposed to the elements. Time had stood still for decades. David was coming to terms with his past in Sutherland, but this place was desolate and he would never count it as home.

It wasn't safe to go too close to the structure, not that he had the desire to do so. The windows had once been covered in soot. Then, over time, the rain, snow, and whatever had been carried on the wind obscured the glass, making it dull and grey. In the next few decades, nothing would be left of his Sutherland family home other than crumbling stones and broken slates. Somewhere in the cemetery in Loch Dubhglas, Chisholm's unknown grandparents lay in a double grave without their only child. He made a mental note to find their resting place. It upset him to remember her wish not to be placed with them but to be alone miles away in Inverness. He regretted not breaking his promise and returning her to them.

His throat dried, and it wasn't a chill wind that moistened his eyes. He didn't know what he'd expected. Seeing the house where his mother and her family had lived brought a sadness he'd not anticipated. Swallowing deeply, he tried to suppress his feelings but this final piece of his Sutherland history needed addressing. He had no recollection of his maternal grandparents. They'd died before he was born in a terrible fire when his mother had been staying at her cousin's house in Kinlochbervie. At the tender age of sixteen, she lost her parents, her home and her sanity as the flames engulfed everything she'd loved. How could someone ever try to rebuild their life after that?

For the first time ever, he could understand why his mother had seemed absent for so many years of his early life: the breakdowns, the endless tablets she took, the therapy she tried, the suicide attempts, and the times in The Craigs. With the tragedy of her parents dying, and then her husband's death a few years later, just after David was born, it was no wonder she was screwed up. He felt her loss deeply as he stood outside what was once her home. Jimmy placed a reassuring hand on the detective's shoulder, as if reading his mind. He didn't speak; this wasn't the time.

†††††

Later, when they'd given each other space to remember, and for David to begin grieving for another part of his past, they moved on to the other reason for visiting the area. To the west of the Sutherland property, the edge of the Knocbrannan estate was visible. The land lay barren, cleared of any traces of the ancient hardwood and pine forests that had once formed a natural boundary to the outer reaches of the estate.

The decision to stop the managed forestation of the area was fairly recent. Whilst wood production had brought a good source of income in the past, the changed use of the land would yield a higher amount of cash. The scoping plans, written by men and women thousands of miles away, working for electricity production profit, would destroy the countryside. Marino was set on renting out acres and acres of his estate for the wind farm and battery storage facility. If the project got planning consent from the Scottish Government, the Highland Council had no power to refuse, meaning the entire deal with Altingham would be worth far more. The siting of the turbines and pylons would, of course, be hidden from the cosseted world of luxury found in the estate house, leaving any wealthy owner oblivious to the monsters knocking on the doors of everyone else living in the region.

David could see what was at stake. The locals who worked for the celebrity cook talked about how frequently Altingham visited the place, and why he wanted to purchase it so badly. The minister's view of any wind farm project, especially one in his backyard, would look good for his green credentials. The hills were covered in hundreds of thousands of fifty-pound notes. All the detective could see was a motive for silencing anyone who might threaten his proposed acquisition.

David is vulnerable. If it means truths are uncovered, I think those driven by greed are capable of anything. As he steps into the past, I understand his fear of returning home, and his grief for the life he lost. Emotionally and mentally weary of the baggage he carries, he may not see, just like I did not see, how vulnerability causes gaps in the heart into which evil can seep. Attempting to communicate with the detective is all that I can do. Seeking comfort in the fact he is wise brings hope. Somehow, I must warn him. The wolves are circling in all directions. Smokescreens and mirrors deceive everyone.

CHAPTER 21
Day 20 : Sunday, 12th October

The end of the freshwater fishing season had passed several days before. They didn't even take rods. All that Mackay and Chisholm intended to do was to sit in a rowing boat in the middle of Loch Spiorad to exorcise ghosts. There were few words spoken on the drive there and less on the shoreline at dusk, both men lost in thought at the significance of the occasion. It was only when they were out in the centre of the loch that Jimmy mumbled a few words.

'I do appreciate this, David. I've not had the nerve to come out here since...'

His words faded. Still haunted by the image engraved on his memory from his last session in the water, he shuddered. The sunny smile that usually spread across his face disappeared. Placing a hand on his arm, Chisholm patted him, protective of his father's best friend now that they were becoming closer.

'I said I would never do this again, after what happened.'

'Old habits die hard.'

David's reply was not intended to cause the fisherman upset nor to become philosophical. It shot out of his mouth before there was time to think. Jimmy nodded.

'I think something else died that night, laddie.'

They sat for a few more minutes, reflecting on the loch goddess. Both had seen her dead body: Jimmy finding her lifeless in the water, and Chisholm witnessing her intimate postmortem. It was the most private of moments two humans could share with a stranger. David wanted to move the conversation on, not wanting to dwell on Freya's death, but there were no words, and each man fell silent once more.

No sound could be heard apart from the creaking of the boat as it rocked gently in the breeze. Behind them, a few metres in the distance nearer the landing, a fish jumped. The soft splash it made in the water caused David to jump.

'What did you do that for?'

The D.I. laughed.

'Sorry, Jimmy, the fish surprised me!'

'What fish?'

'It was just a fish jumping over there.'

'I didnae hear it. I should wear my hearing aids.'

The admission made Chisholm stop jesting. If the fisherman had not heard the noise, might he have missed sounds in the dark on the night he discovered the body? He said no more, not wanting to alarm Jimmy to the possibility.

For the next few hours, they spend time talking over old memories. Jimmy was full of stories about the past. Tales of David's mother and father, never heard before, brought them to life as he listened to the fisherman.

Chisholm also shared memories, recalled angling the waters with his beloved Granda and laughed at his grandfather's yarns: the biggest fish, the catches he had made, and the creatures who'd escaped. When the sad stories came, neither man hid the tears spilling down onto their cheeks. With all the talking done, and they'd eaten some of Rachael's cheese and pickle sandwiches, they sat mesmerised by the ripples on the water slowly spreading in the cool breeze.

It was time to head home to bed; no midnight expedition for either that evening. Their spirits were restored with Jimmy's return to Loch Spiorad and David's return to his family. Each hoped it wouldn't be the last time they were out in a boat together. Next season they vowed to attempt some fishing.

The sky was black as they rowed back to shore. They were packing their waders into the boot of Jimmy's old Astra when David thought he heard a noise a few metres away.

Suspicious of anyone near the loch, he walked towards a vehicle that had parked nearby. The driver remained in the car but he watched as a dark figure get out of the front passenger seat, opened the back door to retrieve what looked like a tripod and camera bag, and started to stroll down to the shore. He felt in an inner pocket for his police badge. As he got closer he realised the stranger was a woman.

'Hi there, I'm Detective Inspector David Chisholm. The police are investigating the death of a lady whose body was disposed of in this loch almost three weeks ago. I'm just curious as to why you are at Loch Spiorad.'

'I am here to photograph the aurora. There's a chance of a good display this evening. It's a brilliant place to capture a photograph or two. My name's Katie Harrison.'

Delving into her bag, she found a crumpled business card and handed it to him. He pondered her northern English accent, wondering if she was a tourist but said nothing.

'Have you got time to see the Merry Dancers in all their glory?'

He nodded, never having seen a display of the Northern Lights despite living his entire life in the Highlands. Jimmy, curious about the conversation, joined the pair. He caught the end of what they were saying and was keen to share his experiences of seeing the many nighttime displays that he'd witnessed over the years when out fishing.

'There was a brilliant display the night I found the body in the loch.'

David spun around, surprised at the news his friend had shared.

'You never said that in your statement.'

'I forgot. It wasn't relevant, was it?'

The stranger mentally reviewed the recent displays she had photographed, and the locations visited.

'What night are you talking about? I was out here a few days ago for a brilliant display.'

'Monday, 22nd September.'

'That date rings a bell. Let me check!'

Chisholm heard the click of her camera being switched on. A light emanated from the back screen as Katie searched through images stored on a memory card. Pausing to look at the date on some of the photographs, she confirmed she had been at the loch on the evening of the murder. After getting her bearings, she pointed to a section of the shoreline a few hundred yards away.'

'I set up the tripod on the most southerly section of the loch, over there.'

'What time was this? Did you see anyone when you were here?'

'It was about quarter past eight. When my husband approaches a site where we shoot, he always turns off his headlights in case it ruins a shot for any other photographer who has beaten us to a location. You can ask him if he saw anything. I was too busy photographing to notice. I don't remember anything except there was a boat in the middle of the loch a while after we had set up. I got some shots. Look.'

A male voice called out into the darkness.

'Is everything okay, Katie?'

'I was talking to your wife, sir. I'm a police officer investigating the murder of a woman whose body was dumped in this loch. It seems your wife took photos on the night in question, Monday 22nd September. Can I have your name, sir? Did you see anyone?'

The man got out of the car and briskly walked towards them with a camera bag on his shoulder and a tripod in his hand. As he came nearer, he could see the two strangers more clearly and answered the police officer's question.

'Hi! I'm Jake Harrison. We were out here on that Monday evening. I can be certain as we went on holiday the next day. We got back yesterday and haven't been out with the cameras for more aurora shots until now. I do remember several strange things about the night in question. Within about twenty minutes, there were lots of comings and goings with three vehicles parked at separate times, making it highly unusual as we rarely see anyone unless it's another photographer. I set up my camera over here. It was hard to see what was going on in the dark, as it was a new moon but someone emerged from the water just after we arrived. It looked like they'd gone for an evening swim. It was a warm night, so it would have been a peaceful thing to do.'

He pointed towards part of the shoreline, close to the reed bed where Jimmy had been trapped.

'They came out of the water and went back to their vehicle. The car moved away just a few seconds later. I heard the engine, but they didn't put their headlights on when they drove off. About ten minutes later, another vehicle pulled up; it was a van if I recall. It was only when a third car came into view that the van drove off. I saw someone pushing out a rowing boat on the loch a few minutes afterwards. We left about half an hour later. Normally we see no one when we come here, so all this activity was odd.'

'Do you mind if I take the memory cards in your cameras so that we can look at the images that night more carefully?'

The couple looked at each other and nodded in unison. Katie ejected the card and reached into her camera bag for another so she could continue the search for the Aurora Borealis. After a few seconds, there on screen was a green arc, much brighter than could be seen by the naked eye. All four gazed in wonder at the sight before them; a vivid green semicircle with a series of red flares shooting into the night sky.

Stumbling across two people who had been at the loch on the same night Freya had been dumped confirmed the information Jimmy and Sullivan had mentioned. The sighting of another vehicle arriving before the van was significant. Jimmy would have failed to see the photographers. They'd parked away from the usual pull-in; their car was dark, with the lights turned off as they drove away, and most importantly, their electric vehicle was practically silent. He thanked the couple and asked if they would give statements as soon as possible.

†††††

Faint whispers of a delicate grey grow into a roar of passion and vibrance as the night sky is filled with greens, reds and pinks. The Mirrie Dancers "mirr", as they say in Shetland, meaning shimmer. In Orkney the tradition is that they are a gathering of spirits, benevolent and mischievous, who come out to play in the night sky. In Moray, the lights are often called "heavenly dancers." May they guide the detective to the truth as they dance and enchant him with their magic.

Exotic dancers,
Pirouette for me.
Move and captivate with your charms.
Entice and tempt with your glowing figures.
Arcs of green and rays of pink.
I watch you rise,
I watch you shimmer,
Enchanted by your magical tricks.
In the darkness, wooing stars,
Only moonlight keeps you at bay.
Lure me, seduce me as I observe your curves,
Casting your spell upon the Earth.
Flickering and twinkling to the beat
Of Nature's mysterious rhythmic show.
Perform for man until the end of time,
Sending hope to all who see.
Guide me, beguiling light of light,
Embrace me with your wonderful caress.

CHAPTER 22
Day 21 : Monday, 13th October

The filming of a model wearing a long, wavy auburn wig walking into the shop made for eerie and uncomfortable viewing, as re-enactments always did. A woman with long dark hair was also filmed entering. Against Janice's witness statement, David had located a hoodie similar to what Mrs. Stirling had suggested. It took several takes before the director of the video was satisfied he had the appropriate amount of footage for screening on television, and still images for press releases.

For a few hours after the media replayed the scenes, villagers returned to the hall to offer possible suggestions for the woman seen with Anna. Freya's real identity was kept hidden, as was the information about the two ladies kissing, for fear it would bring more homophobic attacks on Dubhness Cottage. David instructed that a constable be placed at the bungalow for a couple more days in case anything else occurred.

When there was a chance to sit down for a much-needed coffee break with Euan and a few other colleagues,

Helen saw the drawings made by Iris Stirling. Astonished at the detail the old lady had managed to capture, she studied the symbol on the hoodie, recognising the marking instantly. She lived with Norse runes plastered all over her house, in books, on walls, and in her memory. Georgina had taught her the meaning of them and how to read the marks. Without thinking, she was confident of the image, and what it represented.

'That is the rune *"Sowilo,"* which is a symbol for transformation. It's the union of energy and movement.'

'How do you know that?'

'My fiancée, Georgina, is just completing her degree in Viking studies. I see the symbol every day!'

She sat back, feeling pleased with herself on two counts: for recognising the rune and for mentioning her girlfriend for the first time at work. Whilst her cheeks flushed at her name, it was from the stuffy air in the room rather than through embarrassment of *"outing"* herself at work. No one commented. The conversation continued, and the world kept on turning.

Later, when she passed two junior colleagues in the corridor, the man and woman fell silent and stopped their conversation abruptly as she walked by. This time, however, she didn't crumble or rush to her car for sanctuary. She held her head high as she glanced back at them, before snapping,

'Haven't you two got work to do? We're in the middle of a murder case here.'

The pair of detectives made a hasty retreat; one into the hall, and the other left the building to continue with a few house-to-house calls. As she walked away, she defiantly held back any tears. This was only the first day. The journey to acceptance would not be embraced by everyone immediately, but silence was no longer an option. It never should have been.

†††††

Later that afternoon, when work was over for the day, Chisholm took a stroll to the chippie just as the fryer had been turned on. He reflected on the last few weeks. With the smell of fried fish filling the air and tempting his taste buds, he vowed that the following day he would tackle some burning issues that needed addressing about the case.

He wanted an update from Euan, but the young detective was still up to his neck in rotting vegetables and goodness knows what else at the local dump, as he scoured for the missing rubbish bags and items from Dubhness Cottage. It was a thankless task, dealing with the filth and the stench. Even the thought of sifting through the waste made David retch.

When he reached the bottom of the high street, he crossed the road and stopped to take in the serene view of the loch and the land beyond. Why had he delayed visiting Sutherland for so long? It was in his blood, part of who he was, and yet he had denied himself the place. The last few weeks had seen him visit the county more than he'd ever imagined possible. Suddenly, David realised he didn't want to leave. Unlocking the truth was exhilarating and shocking in equal measure.

As if to announce this startling piece of news to the world, a rumbling sound from his stomach informed it was time for food. At the thought of the fish supper he'd promised to pick up for Jimmy, Rachael, and himself, he quickened his steps.

Back at Mackay's, they settled down to eat. Once more, the haddock flesh melted in his mouth, devoured within minutes. Caught on the west coast earlier that morning, the meal he'd continued to drool over for the past few days surpassed any image in his head. When David revealed a yearning to move back to the county of his birth, Jimmy jumped to his feet and shook his hand. Rachael burst into tears and hugged him.

†††††

For so long, I questioned my past. Why me? Why was I chosen? Of course, I already knew, deep down, the choice of some man in an office who glanced at my photograph for a couple of seconds and decided my fate. He did not know me; it wasn't personal.

The reasoning behind the decision to alter my destiny, ultimately costing me my life, seems too pathetic and vain to mention. I had a "pretty face." A sprat to catch a mackerel, except the small fish to be caught turned into an enormous great white shark. Its attack was deadly once it sank its teeth into me.

Myself and the detective share more blood than he realises. I inherited my looks from my mother's side of the family, all born with red hair and green eyes. Originally from the Highlands, my mother's family left over two centuries ago, moving south and away from the Clearances. I wonder if some of those grey shadows I see are distant relatives who found no serenity or justice, and roam the hinterland, trapped forever.

Like them, I had no say in where I lived because I was baggage, herded from place to place. First Wales, then Milton Keynes, followed by Bristol. After Manchester offered no protection, a short time in Glasgow was next on the list followed by minimal notice to move on, yet again.

"No time to explain. You're compromised. Ten minutes to pack."

Stupidly, I asked no questions. The urge to break free from the invisible prison bars that kept me hidden became strong, but I knew it was pointless to escape. There was no turning back.

Although she was born in Birmingham, and several generations before her too, Mum talked often of her heritage and the place she longed to visit, but never did. Neither of us realised her dream of Sutherland would be my final home, the place where I would die.

I wouldn't have chosen the area but I understand why the detective has fallen back in love with the land and the people. In other circumstances, I might have learned to love the county, but it never felt right. It was too isolated. Too far away. Nothing like home.

As justice creeps closer, may it guide me to the exquisite light. It's almost within my grasp.

CHAPTER 23
Day 22 : Tuesday, 14th October

Whilst some of the uniformed police officers manned the village hall, Chisholm decided he and Helen would pay one last visit to Janice. Her request not to be in the video was easily accommodated because another shop assistant was on duty when the reconstruction filming took place.

David wanted to question her further about the woman Iris Stirling had drawn, keen for her to look at the images again. He felt she'd dismissed them too easily, and that concerned him. When he'd first met Janice she had been chatty and cheerful, but during his previous visit she was edgy, and her behaviour had troubled him. For some reason, he had the distinct impression Janice was lying.

Half expecting her to be watching through the window, chain-smoking on her twentieth fag of the day, he noted instead that the curtains were closed as they walked up the path. As he went to knock on the front door, he saw it was ajar. Pushing it a little further, he called out. No response. He called again, louder this time.

'Janice. It's D.I Chisholm and D.S. Daniels. Can we have a word?'

He pushed the door until it was fully open and stepped inside the hallway.

'Janice. It's the police.'

Swinging around to face Helen, he said,

'Do you smell what I smell?'

Neither officer could avoid it. His stomach tightened. Distinct and obvious to those who knew, the stench was stronger as they moved further into the house, away from the front door. Although he suspected it was pointless, he called out to the woman several times more, but he was met with a resounding silence. Once experienced, the pungent odour was obvious, and never escaped the senses. They stepped towards the lounge where, days before, Chisholm had been overwhelmed by the blue haze of nicotine. This time, the air was full of the unforgettable stench of death, which suppressed the smell of cigarettes.

Janice was sitting in an armchair, her head resting back as if she had fallen asleep. An unlit cigarette lay between the index and middle fingers of her right hand. A pile of nub ends was stacked high in an ashtray on a side table next to her chair. Her eyes were open, but all life was extinguished from them. Blue, downturned lips made her appear miserable. Any sign of life was gone.

Drawers had been pulled out from cupboards; bits and pieces of Janice's life lay strewn across the floor. Every room had been ransacked.

The detectives moved back to the front path. There was no need for a pathologist to announce the type of murder weapon used, but it was important to preserve a crime scene. A knife plunged deep into Janice's chest made it clear how she met her end.

††††††

With all the formalities completed and the body removed to the mortuary in Inverness, Daniels and Chisholm sat in the village hall reeling at the day's events. It had been an unexpected few hours, full of forensics and paperwork. Links to Freya's death were urgently sought.

'A working hypothesis is that the killer felt Janice knew who the mystery woman was and silenced her before she could speak to us. When I interviewed her on Saturday morning, she was nervous and chain smoking non-stop. I got the strong impression she was holding something back. By going public with a re-enactment and appealing to the public for information, this could have panicked the killer.

The shop assistant must have had something they were looking for as the place is trashed. There's a link to be found. It's too big a coincidence for a key witness to end up dead.'

Helen nodded in agreement. For the first time ever, she heard panic in the senior officer's voice as he continued.

'It also means the killer is still in the area. The drawings Mrs. Stirling made are going to be released in the next few days, and although her name won't be mentioned, it might be prudent to put a police car outside her house just in case the killer knows that she also saw the woman at the shop. There's already been three people dead who are linked to this case if we include Mr. Rose's untimely death. We don't want a fourth!'

†††††

When David walked into the Inverness mortuary, Tim Shore noted less tension in the detective's face than the last time he had seen him. Knowing that the observer would not enjoy the joke, he made light of the event.

'We really must stop meeting like this.'

Normally, Chisholm would ignore the quips, but his response surprised his colleague, as did his smile.

'Thanks for making this post-mortem such a priority. Nothing happens in Loch Dubhglas for hundreds of years, then like waiting for a bus, two murders occur in just a few days. It must be something in the air around there!'

Taken aback by the joke, Tim grinned, preferring this newer, warmer version of the detective. He and Jarvis got down to work. The postmortem was straightforward, the cause of death being a single stab wound to the left side of the chest in the mid-axillary line. Tim sounded like a medical textbook as he recorded his findings.

'Fourth intercostal space. A pericardial tamponade was lethal in this case as the victim was undiscovered. The killer knew what they were doing. It was precise and exactly where a stab would be fatal. No need for overkill or multiple lacerations. Forensics will confirm, but my guess is not a great deal of blood spray. However, the killer would have had some blood on their clothes and skin from such a large knife.'

He turned towards Chisholm and stopped recording for a moment.

'She would have lost consciousness quickly as, in layman's terms, the pericardium, which encloses the heart, filled with blood. The heart rapidly compressed, constricting its function.'

'So would she have died immediately?'

'I would say within minutes. Also, by the look of her lungs, she had done significant damage to them by smoking. I'll stick my neck out and say there are signs this woman was in the early stages of lung cancer. The blood and toxicology will confirm this, but there's a tumour in her right lung and a buildup of fluid.'

He returned to making his voice notes as David thanked him and slipped out of the room.

†††††

With her eyes sore from a computer screen, Helen took a walk down the corridor to the canteen to get a drink. When she returned to her desk, three new emails had arrived. All contained news she'd been waiting for. Picking up the phone, she rang David to inform him.

'Boss, news is back. Forensics picked up prints from the knife recovered from Janice's chest, but they turned out to be her own. Still no clear news on the bathroom cabinet print. They're running enhanced tests to check if anything can be gleaned from the information already obtained, but there's still no matching prints on the national database. And finally, the enhanced images taken by the photographers on the night Freya's body was dumped haven't shown anything of interest so far.'

'That's disappointing. So, no link between Freya's murder and Janice's, but my working hypothesis remains that the shop assistant was murdered because she knew something. Despite not appreciating the connection, this new turn of events must take us a step closer to finding a killer. I'm heading into the office first thing in the morning to brief McLeod. I'll meet you there.'

In Loch Dubhglas, the wind blasts through the hills. The day is dull, and people complain they cannot get warm. Yet, it isn't the weather that makes them shiver. A killer has taken one of their own. They close their windows and lock their doors, something they never normally do.

No one can be trusted; everyone is a suspect. People they have known all of their lives are scrutinised, their characters stripped apart to offer a suggestion of who could possibly be a murderer. Although they have no evidence, and only a fraction of the detective's knowledge, they think two deaths so close together in time and location are linked.

The gossips accuse; truths spill out, as do lies, filling the loch with conspiracy theories and tales, so unrealistic that friendships and good neighbours are abandoned. They race to conclusions that someone amongst them is guilty. No one knows who, and panic festers.

I am sorry that my death has caused such bile, and more bloodshed, but I tell myself nothing is my fault.

CHAPTER 24
Day 23 : Wednesday, 15th October

Vision was difficult through the mask and breathing apparatus. Sweat from the heat of his hazmat suit trickled from his brow onto his nose, and his skin was tinged with dampness, but Euan Sinclair was determined to continue the mission to a satisfactory conclusion.

Trash from the final skip lay on white ground sheets in an incident tent a short distance away from the large metal container. Every black bag had been emptied onto the cloths and sieved through for clues. Much of the search had proved pointless to him and the small team of young police constables tasked with the wretched job. One man was even taken off the site because of his constant and uncontrollable retching. Euan held the operation and the group of officers together, ploughing through the onerous responsibility by visualising the end of the search.

Nothing stood out to anyone. All other skips and sites mentioned by the mechanic had been sorted meticulously; just a few final bags to search. The hunt for clues appeared fruitless, but a tiny nugget of hope remained. As Euan strolled towards the remaining ground sheet, something caught his eye. At first, he blinked, trying to eliminate any false truths from his mind, but an object glistened near the edge of the top left-hand corner of the sheet. As he bent down to examine whatever it was, he gasped. A small, glossy black box lay upside down, contents strewn onto the matting. Something sparkled. His instinct was to move the wooden container to get a better glimpse of what lay half-obscured, but experience, and the fact Chisholm would read him the riot act, made him call for the photographer. His boss's words rang in his ears.

"At all times wear full safety gear. Look from a distance. Do not touch anything. It could well be toxic and kill you!"

An hour afterwards, patience now wearing thinner and excitement mounting, he watched as an officer dressed in full chemical protection gear retrieved the precious find with help from a mechanical device. The item, a silver bracelet with a bird charm, was placed in a canister, secured with a lid, and put into an evidence bag to be speedily transported by police escort to Glasgow for testing. Somehow, after observing rubbish for days, Euan's persistence had been rewarded.

†††††

They sat in McLeod's office ready to share updates. First, David gave news about the search at the local dump. As he relayed the news to his boss and Helen, all three officers felt relief at the find. No one knew if the bracelet was the murder weapon. Only time would tell once tests were carried out.

'Any news of Freya's mystery companion?'

Chisholm shook his head.

'No one seems to know her. We've wondered if she just happened to be in the shop at the same time as Freya, and that Mrs. Stirling was wrong in her statement. It wouldn't be the first time we have an unreliable witness. Janice was adamant the drawings were not accurate, but I'm sure she was lying. We didn't put them out to the public. Maybe we should chance our arm and use them.'

'We have nothing to lose. Yes, David, put the image of the unknown girl out, but not the picture of them kissing. That will only bring homophobic comments, and we can do without that distraction.'

Helen didn't flinch or make a comment. Several weeks before, she would have run to the toilets, frightened that she would be exposed, but now she had a newfound confidence. Instead, she outlined her findings about the Italian suspect, Roberto Marino. The senior officers had quietly agreed to research him and Sir William, despite what the agents had shared with them. If the M.P. was involved in Freya Rose's death, the detectives wanted no cover-ups to protect a government minister's reputation. Learning Freya was assigned a case to investigate Altingham meant they needed more information than the three MI5 agents would share.

'The links between Marino and the minister are strong. When we spoke to Sir William, he was at the billionaire's house. According to local gossip from those who work on Marino's estate, the minister is a frequent guest despite his host rarely joining him. Marino's visit for the charity ball was unusual. He tends to travel between his London base, New York, and Rome. There's much talk Sir William is buying the place and that surveyors have been checking it out within the last week or so.

From various accounts, it seems by renting out the land to wind farm companies, usually from overseas, each turbine brings in funding of tens of thousands of pounds per year purely because of their location. It's a tidy profit for allowing, say, twenty turbines on the estate, away from the big house, of course. Freedom of information requests are very vague on the exact figures, but it could be in the region of six or even seven figures for landowners. *"Mr. Keep It Clean, Make It Green"* is all over the headlines about improving the infrastructure around the National Grid. He naturally never mentions he has his own business interests when pushing through planning reforms for such ventures.'

David interjected.

'I'm frustrated that we've been prevented from investigating Altingham. He's wasted police time by requesting updates in his ministerial capacity when all along he has personal interests he's not divulged. He had a motive to kill Freya because of something she found out about him whilst she went undercover in his London home. He has connections to people who can supply weapons of all kinds, and the money to pay for someone to do the job for him. I wonder if Alec, the mechanic, has had dealings with the estate or Sir William.'

When McLeod heard the minister's name, the thought of being in the same room as the man sickened her. She was cautious and nervous. Her palms and forehead were damp, and the foundation she wore couldn't completely hide her flushed cheeks.

'Altingham's like Teflon. Nothing sticks! We can't go against MI5 advice. He'll employ the top briefs in the country who will create smokescreens to avoid cases ever getting to court. To cap it all, we might put a stop to something agents are investigating about his links to Marino, which takes priority for national security reasons. It's frustrating, Chisholm, but our hands are tied.'

Neither Helen nor David particularly noticed as she picked at the quick around her nails, but both sensed a tension in her voice at this watershed moment in the case.

✝✝✝✝✝

What can I say about Altingham? There are no words. He is the reason I left behind my family, friends, and any semblance of normality. The rotten stench of corruption follows him wherever he goes. He hides behind a background of privilege, power, and money.

Do I hate him? Yes, I detest the monster. His evils will come to light, and he will pay for his crimes. He stole my life, but he isn't my killer.

CHAPTER 25
Day 24 : Thursday, 16th October

A day later, David sat at his computer, brows furrowed, as he processed the information gathered so far. The most frantic of knocks on the office door, followed by a young uniformed police officer bursting into the room, interrupted his train of thinking and alerted him that something was amiss. Breathing heavily, the young constable gasped as he imparted the news.

'Sorry sir, but you'll never guess who's turned up asking to speak to the person in charge of the Loch Spiorad case!'

'Surprise me.'

Whilst clearly the young officer was excited, Chisholm remained calm.

'Natasha Boskova! Can you believe it? She's here with two guys. Looks like they're bodyguards from the size of them!'

The detective leapt to his feet and followed the officer down two flights of stairs and through a rabbit warren of corridors until he reached the public area in the police station. What the hell was the millionairess doing here? He and McLeod had been warned by MI5 to cease investigating her further as she was *"not a person of interest."*

David's search for information on the supermodel had lingered in his mind. He never read the tabloid newspapers or glossy lifestyle magazines, but Helen knew who she was, as did Euan. Controversy seemed to surround her, usually around her behaviour in public and her clothing, or lack of either. The tabloids stated she frequented rehab clinics often for drug or drink abuse or sensationalised her romantic liaisons, which played out in the public eye.

She was famous for her outrageous costumes, with fashion houses competing to engage her for their shows. Of late, she seemed destined for politics since she had cleaned up her act after joining a right-wing Christian group.

There at the front desk, just as the young constable had said, was a tall, wafer thin woman, with long dark hair, accompanied by two tall and extremely muscular men dressed in smart suits. On this occasion, she wore an oversized cream jumper that ended at her thighs. Her long, pencil-thin legs were covered by black leggings. David decided this must be her casual attire, as she was wearing expensive-looking cream trainers. A chunky golden chain hung around her neck with a couple of matching bracelets around her wrists.

Perhaps it was an age thing, but the performance she was putting on did nothing to enamour her character or looks to him. There was no doubt she had a pretty face, but it was masked by an incredibly ugly scowl. Her husky voice only offered a hint of her Eastern European origins; a strong American twang was now more prevalent.

'Are you the officer in charge? I need to speak with you.'

'Yes, I am but before we can talk, I need to call my sergeant to come and join us.'

'No!'

Her reply took him by surprise as her voice was sharp and insistent.

'Just you!'

Acknowledging her with a nod, he replied,

'Okay, but I'm afraid the bodyguards will have to wait here. I can arrange a cup of tea for them while you speak to me. You are perfectly safe in this station. No one will harm you.'

She hesitated longer than was necessary, clearly uncomfortable with David's statement, but dismissed the two gorilla pets, telling them to wait in the entrance. David led the way to an interview room. She sat on a plastic seat opposite, staring intensely at him with her piercing blue eyes whilst he introduced himself and stated that he would like to record the conversation.

'Do you have any objections? For advice, if you wish, you could have a solicitor present.'

Natasha's scowl grew as contempt crossed her face, but she nodded, giving him the go-ahead to start the interview. Pressing the recording button, he gave the formalities of the date, time, and those present; then he began.

'For the tape, could you confirm your name, date of birth, and address, please?'

'My name is Natasha Boskova, born 28th December 1994. I don't give out my address to anyone. I own six apartments around the world. My agent will provide contact details later to satisfy your purposes.'

With neither warmth or sincerity in her tone, she began to disclose what she wanted to say. No one dictated to Natasha Boskova, supermodel.

'I hear whispers you think I'm involved in the murder in Sutherland. That's ridiculous. I understand people are asking questions of my contacts in the Highlands. I come for one thing only, the whisky. You can't beat Scotch.'

'Why do you think we would be interested in you? You're a model, aren't you? Not a killer.'

'I'm not the bitch everyone thinks I am. This is the image I portray for work.'

'I'm delighted to hear that. Can we get to the point of why you want to speak to me? You haven't come all this way just to tell me to back off.'

He couldn't help but be irritated by her performance. The façade annoyed him. She was as fake as the long, dark eyelashes that fluttered at him and the make-up she used as a mask against the world. Her eyes narrowed as she frowned at the detective. Not used to people who snapped back at her, she gazed at him, looking for a chink in his armour. He refused to flinch, which made him interesting to her.

'You are looking for a woman I met in The Blue Cat nightclub in Inverness. I don't know much about her.

She tried tagging along with the group, hoping for smack and free drinks, I guess. These days most of my friends are clean, so none of us get tempted. Don't believe all the media hype. I haven't done drugs for three years, but it's good for publicity, believe it or not, to have a junkie model. Cocaine's not something I'm proud to admit I used, but it's part of my history.'

'Had you met her before?'

'Several times over the last couple of years I've seen her in clubs or bars when I'm in London. I knew straight away she was a junkie. Thin as a rake, shaking, begging for a fix. She looks better now, but I am wary of ex-junkies. She's a good-time girl, clinging like a limpet to the hope of being granted access to the inner circles like mine and other celebrities.'

'Do you have a name for her?'

'People call her Sammie.'

Chisholm sat back in his chair. The intensity with which she stared at him was tiring. He realised she was analysing him for responses, and he was determined to show no emotion. He wasn't sure if she was telling him anything that was true, but he needed to listen as there was a point to her being there.

'Why was she in Inverness?'

'I have no clue. To find her here in the Highlands was a big shock for me.'

'How do you know we want to speak to her?'

She rolled her eyes.

'You think I'm linked to the woman dumped in the loch because of my background and contacts. Get this straight, I don't know the woman or anything about her.

I was in Inverness. I spotted you at the charity ball, sitting in a corner, out of the light, sipping a beer, avoiding the champagne. Your bow tie was untidier than it should have been because it felt like a noose around your neck.'

Ignoring her perceptive observations of him, he persisted with his questioning.

'Tell me about the woman.'

'After the event, some of my associates met at the nightclub. Apparently, Sammie heard we were in town and came in about half an hour after we arrived. She had not been invited; smack heads rarely are. I'm never sure what her game plan is, but for once, she didn't want drugs or drinks, which makes a change.

She kept looking around towards the bar, desperate to catch anyone's attention. A guy came in who I didn't recognise, and she made a beeline for him. After a couple of drinks they left. In the past she's been known to prostitute herself to anyone who will give her money, drink, drugs, or connections even. I guess he had something to offer her as she didn't return.'

David had nothing to lose. The woman irritated him with her teasing of information, but she'd given very little away.

'You have contacts with some powerful people.'

An explosion of laughter shattered the tension. For once, the tough femme fatale act dissipated, and the young model relaxed.

'That's ridiculous. Whoever told you this information is lying. I used to take and deal drugs. Hands up! That was my life, but I'm clean and have been for three years. I have a business to run and I've never killed anyone.'

'That you know of! Drugs kill people every day.'

He pondered the game she was playing. Why was she here in Inverness police headquarters? Perhaps Sammie was a junkie or a dealer who was threatening to blab or had crossed her in some way. She stood up and held out her hand. He noted the nails that were long, shiny, and fluorescent pink.

'I am done, turn off the tape. This conversation ends now. There is nothing more to say.'

He stared at her, and then she smiled and winked. The shock made him obey despite his reservations about the woman in front of him. He finished the formal interview, stated the time that the interview was concluded, and stopped the recording. Suddenly, she leaned close to him and, in a hushed, unexpected tone, spoke in whispers with a softer American accent.

'Sorry. I have seconds to tell you what you need to know. Don't ask questions. Just listen. Do not react in any way or blow my cover. Three years ago, the real Natasha Boskova died of a drug overdose, alone in an hotel room, after escaping her bodyguards for a few days. I was ready to move into place within hours of her death. My bosses in the FBI had monitored her every move for months and knew her habits. They say everyone on the planet has a doppelgänger. Mine was Natasha Boskova.

John sent me in person because he knew you would delve into my background and wouldn't stop investigating me. We don't want you to blow my cover. He told me to tell you he was sorry about burning your breakfast.'

David's eyes grew wider, and his jaw dropped. How did she know this? A huge stick of dynamite exploded somewhere in his head, interrupting his thoughts and floored him with her sudden change of persona. It threw him off balance, leaving him speechless and vulnerable.

'Your colleagues must not know about this conversation. You have the taped conversation for anyone who asks. Wait for Sammie to emerge from the address I will give you and follow her out of Loch Dubhglas. Arrest her for speeding, do a drug test, and then ask questions before the expensive lawyer turns up to represent her, and trust me, they will turn up to sweep everything under the carpet.

In those few minutes she'll be frightened, and you will start to have answers, maybe. No more questions. Otherwise, you will wreck the last three years of my undercover work. I'm gathering evidence about the biggest drug ring operating across countless international borders.

I don't know who killed the woman in the loch, but Sammie is linked to your case. You're dealing with people who would not hesitate to kill me or you to protect themselves and the corrupt circles they move in. It will cause a ripple effect when police question Sammie, bringing fish to the surface of the water. By catching a sprat, together we can catch a mackerel.'

As she whispered an address, David felt his legs shake. What the hell was this case about? Questions erupted from his mind. How had *"they"* replaced Natasha? Had *"they"* killed her? How did this woman before him convince everyone she was a world-famous supermodel? How long had she prepared for this role? There was no point in asking even the basic puzzles, so he didn't even try to extract answers. The world of spies was an alien concept to him.

Natasha's voice instantly changed as she returned to full supermodel mode. Her own character sank back into the darkest of shadows. The whispering stopped, and her booming voice reappeared.

'We are done.'

Startled at the transformation, he felt in his pocket for his car keys. For once, he was lost for words. There was no time to consider what the hell had just happened or how a dead body in a remote Highland loch was linked to secret agents. It was beyond comprehension.

Chisholm rushed out of the building alerting no one of his intentions. He had to trust what Natasha told him; the reference to John convinced him. Why else would she risk the case? Three years undercover. He wondered if she knew reality anymore; always pretending to be someone else must take a toll on her soul. There were no breaks or holidays. She was always in the role. Where did Natasha end and a secret agent begin?

This was the undercover life Freya had led, pretending to be someone else in the complex circles investigated by MI5. What secrets had she uncovered that made her handler pull her out from an operation so quickly, without any warning and without more senior agents knowing?

He started the engine, ready to travel north. After navigating the traffic island at the entrance to headquarters, he followed the signs for the A9. He knew the route and his destination. The journey gave him time to reflect on the fake interview. When he arrived in Loch Dubhglas an hour later, he drove past the address and found a lay-by a few hundred yards away.

This whole case was built on coincidences. Natasha had told him the arrest must look natural. He was putting his whole faith in a woman who wasn't who she said she was, and relying on her version of truth. He grimaced. Could this be a millionairess's little joke, teasing and distracting the officer in charge of a murder inquiry, with the opportunity to arrest a suspect? What if *she* was the killer?

Natasha's statement contained both lies and truths. He wasn't sure what was fact or fiction, but he was prepared to wait. An hour later, as he was giving up hope and wondering if he was being tricked, a red sports car emerged from the driveway onto the lane. He gasped when he spotted the driver, a young woman with long dark hair.

As soon as she was out of sight, he tried to make a call using the buttons on his steering wheel. No signal. In frustration he picked up the offending mobile phone that lay on the passenger seat. Connected to the Wi-Fi in the car, he moved it about in a vain attempt to get even one bar. In disgust, throwing it back onto the seat, he needed to keep up with the driver or he would lose her. Single-track lanes would hopefully slow the woman down.

To reach the main road, the lane twisted and turned several times. The car in front did not speed off initially. It was only at the junction, a few miles further along the lane, that it veered right and immediately gathered speed on the A road south, away from the village. David followed; he must be ready and time any intervention just right. There were few opportunities to overtake and stop a speeding vehicle in this location. It must not look suspicious or like a trap.

The road began to rise. With clear vision, he could not see any cars travelling in the opposite direction. All he needed was for the vehicle in front to speed off, and then he must catch and overtake it. As predicted, the car in front began to shift away. The speedometer moved around the dial, fifty, sixty, and then raced towards seventy. Seventy-one, seventy-three, seventy-five.

His target looked in her rearview mirror as lights flashed behind her. Would she chance going faster? The brow of the hill neared. This was his time to catch her, or she would escape. He knew the road ahead led to twists and bends with no opportunities to make the manoeuvre safely. There would be all hell to pay if he caused an accident or she crashed into another vehicle because he'd made her panic. There was no room for error.

With his foot pressed firmly down, he sped past the sports car, flashing his hazard lights. Remembering he should breathe, a gush of air left his lungs and mouth in relief as he began to ease his foot off the pedal and drove in the middle of the road. There was no place for her to under or overtake him. She slowed down and followed the signal he had given with his hand and arm when winding down his window. He had her. Jumping out of his car, he felt for his warrant card and flashed it at her startled face.

'Despite my lack of a uniform, I'm an on-duty police officer. Do you realise the speed you were travelling at, Miss? I have video evidence of you driving at over seventy-five miles per hour. Please pull into the lay-by ahead. Then turn off the engine and step outside of the vehicle.'

The woman nodded in contrition as she complied with his demands. Her small, pale face and slender frame made her look younger than her twenty-five-year-old body.

When they were safely off the road, he and the woman got out of their vehicles. He noticed she was wearing a navy hoodie with a gold Sowilo logo. There was a vulnerability in her voice as she spoke, trying to choke back the tears.

'I'm sorry. I won't speed again. Can I go now?'

'I need to take some details from you. You were driving over the speed limit and in a dangerous manner. It's all captured on video. A uniformed police officer will arrive shortly with a breathalyser.'

Just as he spoke, a police car approached and turned right across the road to pull into the lay-by. Thank heavens he'd persisted with his radio and managed to get a signal. He'd also spoken to Helen who was driving back to Sutherland but had diverted to meet him in Tain. As he arrested the driver for speeding and informed her of her rights, he hoped this was the woman who could unlock more information.

She shook, not only from fear, but her body screamed for something to ease her discomfort. Damp lines beneath her eyes suggested she had been crying for hours when David and Helen entered the interview room at Tain Police Station. In reality, it was only five minutes since she sat down on the grey, plastic chair. The sobbing began as soon as she was sick in the lay-by and had continued for the last half an hour as she was transported by police car to Tain. Keen to speak to her before any lawyer turned up, Helen began.

'My name is Detective Sergeant Helen Daniels. This is my colleague Detective Inspector David Chisholm, whom you have already briefly met. We would like to question you about a number of things, including dangerous driving. Thank you for taking a breathalyser test, which was negative, and for further taking a blood test when you were brought to Tain Police Station. We await test results. You have the right to legal assistance if you wish. Do you want to take up the offer of an on-duty solicitor?'

'I want no lawyer, but one will come.'

'Did you call one?'

Shaking her head, the two police officers looked at each other, then at the tangled mess in front of them. The bones in her face seemed so close to the surface of her white skin that they might pierce it if her facial expression changed.

She sat in a white disposable boiler suit because her clothes were covered in vomit. Both noticed the uncontrollable trembling.

'For the tape, what is your name?'

'Sammie.'

'Sammie what?'

'Sammie Stewart.'

'Is that your full name?'

'Samantha Altingham-Stewart.'

An involuntary gasp shot from Helen's lips.

'I knew I'd seen you somewhere before—a few weeks ago in the gardens of a large estate in Sutherland, you were playing ball with a dog.'

'Charlie.'

A huge sob followed, with the thought of losing her dog now firmly in her mind.

'Why were you at the estate?'

'I was visiting Sir William Altingham.'

'Are you a friend of his?

Sammie shook her head.

'He's sadly my only living relative. My adoptive mother was his sister. She was the black sheep of the family, just like me.'

'You use the word *"was."* Where is she now?'

'Dead from a car crash, hence why my uncle feels a small iota of responsibility to me, even though I am a huge disappointment and am *"in the same mould"* as my mother even though we shared no blood. My adoptive father also died in the crash. I have no *"family"* apart from that arsehole Altingham. I'm a loose end he doesn't need in his wonderful and perfect life.'

'Why are you a disappointment?'

'I have been drunk many times and had a drug habit, but not anymore. He will think I am back on something.'

'I take it he doesn't approve of the drug taking and the drinking?'

'Absolutely not! Will I go to prison? I can't bear the thought of no longer seeing Charlie.'

'It depends if there are drugs in your system, the speed at which you were travelling, and of course, you may have previous convictions. Do you have any penalty points or anything else you feel you should tell me?'

'No. I haven't used drugs for six months since...'

'Since when?'

The detectives both sat up in unison, eager to hear what Sammie said next.'

'Since I became engaged.'

She sobbed uncontrollably, her body rocking backwards and forwards as if trying to soothe herself. The lost, childlike woman in front of them was a sad sight to behold.

'Do you need a break?'

'No. No more secrets. I need to tell the truth.'

David held his breath. What was she about to confess? Was she the murderer?

'I want to start at the beginning. It's a story of lost loves. I met the love of my life, got off drugs and drink because I wanted to prove how much I cared and wanted to give up my old life to settle down. But it wasn't to be. Interference came from my uncle when he found out I was cleaning up my act. I think he didn't like the fact I was changing, and I was no longer going to be under his control.'

Staring at the floor, she paused for a moment to gather her thoughts, wondering how quickly her uncle would find out about her arrest, already knowing his reaction. He would roll his eyes and grimace with disgust at being let down by his niece yet again. Then he could play the role of saviour, as he had time after time before when she was in trouble. She hated his guts for always smothering the flames ignited within her when she tried to be independent and make her own life choices. It was as if he kept her in a gilded cage and enjoyed the agony she felt when he clipped her wings. She had no money of her own, poncing off him whenever she needed cash. The vicious circle never ended. He fed her bad habits, loved her to fail, played the hero in saving her, and spent money for therapy and rehab. Then she would repeat her behaviour over and over again.

'When I finally plucked up the courage to tell my future spouse that my uncle was Sir William Altingham, she went ballistic two days before a special day we had planned. She swore at me for keeping such a secret and told me our engagement was off.

As usual, I messed everything up. I didn't take the split well and did a terrible thing in Inverness. I met a man in a bar, got drunk, and had sex with him in a van. It was stupid; the biggest mistake of my life. I'm an idiot.

I drove back up to speak to my uncle the next day, after I sobered up. He'd known nothing of my plans to move out and live with my girlfriend. He wasn't even aware that I had someone special before then. I cried and told him she was the love of my life and that she had changed me forever. When I showed him her photograph, his mood instantly altered. He was livid. It was as if they'd already met and knew one another, but as far as I am concerned, they were strangers. He suddenly lost his usual, false charming act and showed his true colours. He wanted to get rid of me for causing trouble. Of course, when on television, he shows a theatrical side to him that everyone recognises instantly.'

'Did they know each other?'

'God, yes, I think they did, but neither would confirm anything. It was only when I mentioned my uncle's name that she went apeshit. A couple of days later…'

Her voice faltered. Her head dropped, and tears fell.

'Do you need a break?

She shook her head, wiped a tear, and looked straight at him.

'A couple of days later, I heard that a woman with long red hair was found dead in a loch near where my girlfriend rented a property. I knew it was her and thought that she killed herself. Then I later found out she was murdered. Uncle said to keep quiet as the police would think I had something to do with it. This is all my fault, a punishment on me because I had sex with a random stranger in a bar after arguing with my fiancée, like it was an act of revenge.'

'For the record, what was your fiancée's name?'

He already knew the answer.

'Her name was Anna, the woman in the loch. I swear I never saw her after we had a massive row about my uncle. We were to hold a special ceremony to commemorate me moving in with her, nothing official. We planned to get married next year, on the anniversary of when we first met. I would never kill her; I loved her.'

Suddenly, the gibbering wreck in front of them changed. She wiped away tears that were falling onto her pale cheeks.

'Finally, I found a purpose to care about myself, to make changes to my life choices. My uncle will want me to return to my drug days so he can control me. I'm going to prove I can stand on my own two feet. He's deliberately stalled every move I've made to gain my inheritance by getting his solicitor friends to tie everything up in red tape, but he's in for a shock.'

'How did you meet Anna?'

'I stopped my car near Loch Spiorad one day and got out to stretch my legs. She appeared from nowhere, like it was meant to be; destiny we both called it as we were both in need of friendship and love. Fate brought us together.'

'Why did you drive from Loch Dubhglas so fast?'

'I thought Uncle William had sent his henchmen to do the same to me as they did to Anna.'

'So, you believe Sir William had your fiancée killed?'

'Who else could it be? There was something between them. As soon as Anna heard his name, she flipped out; the atmosphere changed, and our relationship was off. It was like walking on eggshells. My uncle clearly knew Anna when he saw her photograph for the first time. Obvious there was history between them that neither of them would speak about. I'm glad you arrested me. I want to know how Anna ended up dead, and if Uncle William murdered her.'

Tears fell like a waterfall in full spate, and she sobbed uncontrollably. Her crying sounded like a wounded animal trapped in a gin trap. David muttered something about taking a break, but Helen could only hear a distracting white noise, which grew louder in her ears. She looked at the surface of the desk that separated her from Sammie, unable to make eye contact for fear she would burst into tears. With the formalities over, the sergeant rose to her feet, muttered her thanks, and rushed out of the room, leaving an incredulous detective inspector and a bewildered suspect to stare at each other.

David was convinced by Sammie's story. She had been open with him, and her story made sense. He didn't think she was a flight risk, although she had tried to run when he'd driven after her. Given what she'd said, it was highly plausible her uncle's overwhelming coercive control was the reason she was trying to escape. He weighed up the possibility of her being Freya's killer. The grief of her lover's death was raw and honest. Her blood test results were negative so the story of her departure from drugs was true, and she had no alcohol in her system.

The links to Altingham couldn't be denied, but currently, Chisholm was under strict orders not to approach the minister. He was frustrated that *"Mr. Keep It Clean, Make It Green"* was on the point of being arrested for all kinds of misdemeanours but couldn't be questioned about Freya's murder.

†††††

Sir William Altingham sank into the leather, wing-backed chair and smiled. It was a rare day, with nothing planned. His life always seemed organised with meeting after meeting, lunch dates, followed by drinks and meals, all in the name of government. If it wasn't his ministerial duties, it was his business interests. When he was up in the northern Highlands, life was generally simpler. He planned time out walking the estate lands, away from conference calls and schedules.

It was days away from the state opening of Parliament, and he wouldn't be able to return until probably Christmas. He knew he would have a battle on his hands if wife number three had any say in the matter. She would want to spend the festive season in Chelsea, so would his young daughter. They both complained the Scottish air was too cold, even in the summer months, but he was set on buying Marino's estate, especially if the land was profitable.

He stood up ready to make a move for an afternoon walk, not wanting to waste a moment of his precious downtime when the butler politely tapped on the door and, without waiting, hurriedly entered the room.

'It's your niece, Sir William. She's been arrested, and is being questioned by Police Scotland at Tain Police Station.'

'Oh, for goodness' sake! That girl is just like her bloody mother, always in some kind of trouble. If the press gets hold of this, they'll have a field day. Get my lawyer on the phone, NOW! Then fetch my boots and walking stick. I fancy an amble around the estate.'

The expensive solicitor from Inverness arrived at Tain Police Station, and was surprised that his client had vanished. There was no reason for Chisholm to hold her. She had given the detective the address of an ex-school friend she would stay with in Perth and begged him not to disclose her location. Apart from driving over the speed limit, there were no charges against her. She would pay her fine, have points deducted, but she wasn't an assassin.

When Sir William returned from a walk along one of the trails on the estate. Charlie didn't greet him. The dog had disappeared, along with all of Sammie's belongings. Her habit of absconding was legendary. By stopping her bank cards, she would return. Little did he realise, she had finally decided to fight for her inheritance, and he no longer held her in shackles now she was free of her addictions.

†††††

My beautiful Sammie, why did it have to be like this? We were content together like two lost beings who finally found the missing part of each other. Happiness lay in our future, but it was never meant to be. My fate was misery.

How could I possibly have a "happy ever after" life because of all that has gone on in the past?

Altingham was always going to haunt me. Why did you have to be related to him? You never mentioned his name in all our conversations. Now I understand why you are as you are, a delicate butterfly ruined by him. I wonder if you know Altingham like I know him. Please God, let his dirty, corrupt secrets be hidden from you. I pray when the lid of Pandora's Box is lifted, the lies, deceit and the real truth will spill out.

Run away and do not look back, Sammie. He stole my freedom three years ago. Please do not let him destroy you anymore than he already has. Wear the hoodie with the Sowilo symbol that I bought you with pride. Live life to the full; grow from these experiences and find hope.

A blanket of warmth wraps around me,
Caressing my heart with a wonderful light.
The love we share sets me free.
A blanket of warmth wraps around me.
The magic of friendship is the key.
With a sweet embrace, you hold me tight.
A blanket of warmth wraps around me,
Caressing my heart with a wonderful light.

CHAPTER 26
Day 25 : Friday, 17th October

After a morning and most of the afternoon tackling a mound of paperwork and chasing up the photography lab, he decided to speak to Helen about Sammie and Altingham when an unexpected phone call came through. The voice on the other end was familiar but one that David needed to search for in the recesses of his mind. It was a woman's voice, with a hint of a distant land she'd once called home. It was hard to make out at first as her words were spoken in a hurried whisper.

'Detective Inspector Chisholm. Is that you?'

'Hi, who am I speaking to?'

'This is Anika Chopra. You came to my house a few days ago, in Birmingham.'

'Yes, Mrs Chopra, I remember. How can I help?'

He was reassured to put a name to the voice, which satisfied his memory. As she spoke, more of her Birmingham accent was prevalent.

'Is there any chance you can return to Birmingham? Something has arrived in the post, which you need to see. It's urgent.'

'May I ask what it is?'

The whispered response surprised David. Her voice was less confident than he had remembered, and edgy as she emphasised the final word.

'It's best not to discuss it on the phone, but I implore you, it *is* important!'

'I'll get down as soon as I can.'

The call ended before he could add any more information about a potential time of arrival. Logistically, he could catch a flight down to Luton, Gatwick, or Bristol the next day, but from the voice at the other end of the phone, there had been nervousness, and given all the events of the last few weeks, he didn't want to take any chances. Without a word to anyone, he picked up his car keys and left the building.

†††††

The drive to Birmingham allowed Chisholm time to gather his thoughts on everything that had happened over the last month. Some things made no sense as to how Freya had died.

For once, the A9 was fairly quiet with little traffic. When vehicles approached from behind, he checked in the mirror in case anyone was following him. Cars passed him passed when they could. No one stayed behind at a distance to track his movements, but he remained alert. There were few hold-ups except for roadworks for dualling parts of the A9, the main arterial route south. The temperature dropped suddenly as he reached Drumochter Pass. From there, he continued towards Perth, driving at the speed limit, in an attempt to reach Birmingham by nighttime.

He stopped only once for a break at Annandale Services. Darkness fell quickly, and his eyes were tired. He attempted forty winks, but adrenaline was his enemy. The fear in Mrs. Chopra's voice was concerning. All Chisholm could do was plough on until he could drive no more. He stopped to refill: for him, a strong coffee and a blueberry muffin; for the car, a tank of petrol. Mundane tasks such as eating and speaking to late-night workers at the petrol station took his mind off murder for a few moments.

The sugar rush and caffeine worked quickly, and before he knew it, he had crossed the border into England. As the M74 became the M6, the miles closer to Birmingham meant he would be there before breakfast. Andrea Bocelli looped over and over as he drew nearer to signs for the city. Nine hours after he had begun the journey, he turned into Dark Lane and found a parking space as close as he could. David decided to sleep in the car until it was a polite time to wake up the Chopra household. His eyes closed. Sleep came quickly and deeply. When his mobile phone bleeped to awaken him, he was ready to face whatever the day would bring.

†††††

As he sleeps and gains strength, he dreams of an owl out hunting in the moonlight. Loch Spiorad is bathed in a silvery hue. Its calm beauty enchants and captivates all who see it so late in the evening.

From the safety of an old barn where she sleeps by day, the female ventures out to seek food. With the moon so full and bright, her prey cannot hide. The stars of Orion, his belt and bow, twinkle and shine in honour of the huntress, determined in her task. The gentle breeze aids her flight as she soars over the shiny waters, seeking her treasure. She lands on a high branch of an old ash tree and observes movement in the grey shadows. Decisive and precise in her timing, she swoops low, by an old stone wall, to claim a tiny vole as her first catch of the night. She will hunt with her mate until they are both full. They hoot and screech, telling each other of their finds. Their young have gone, dispersed to other areas, so it is only the two that need sustenance.

Winter is coming when food may be sparse. She hears the sounds of nighttime, when most humans sleep. She stays alert until the stars disappear and she returns to the comfort of her barn.

Soon, everyone will know who killed Freya. I gain comfort that it is nearly over. Light will return, guiding me to those who love me. My destiny will be fulfilled, and finally, my soul will rest in eternal peace.

CHAPTER 27
Day 26 : Saturday, 18th October

She had been waiting. There had been little sleep for Anika. Had David realised, he could have knocked on her door in the middle of the night. No light had been visible from the street, so there had been no clues to the occupant's insomnia.

The mirror told no lies; a face haggard, exhausted, and nervous stared back at her. Despite splashing water to make herself look refreshed and applying makeup to be presentable, the worry marks did not vanish. She tried praying, but only small comfort was gained. Chisholm must come soon, she hoped.

Hearing the sound of the post flap, she dreaded what the postman would bring this morning. Yesterday's bombshell had been unpredicted and unwanted. A second tap of the flap alerted her that it wasn't the mail. She raced down stairs but stopped short of opening the front door. She needed to be careful and would not open it until she knew who stood outside.

'Who is it?'

'It's me, Detective Inspector David Chisholm, Mrs. Chopra. I came as quickly as I could.'

Clutching the latch tightly, she closed her eyes for a split second, thankful that her prayers had been answered after all. He was here. He would know what to do. Tiredness slipped from her face as a smile replaced her exhaustion.

'Thank goodness you are here. Thank you for coming so quickly, Detective!'

He followed her into the conservatory and sat at her request. On the wooden coffee table in front of him lay a large white padded envelope. Beckoning David to take it, he first inspected the writing with Mrs. Chopra's name and address: an unsteady and rushed hand, with partially formed letters on occasions. Immediately he noticed something odd; the postmark was Inverness as expected, but dated five days after Freya's death. From out of his pocket, he brought out a pair of disposable blue gloves to wear.

Together, his brain and fingers, both adept at guessing objects before seeing them, identified the package contained a book of some kind. The weight indicated something substantial, not flimsy or capable of being easily bent.

As his eyes caught sight of the object, he glanced at Mrs. Chopra. Neither spoke, but the look that passed between them indicated a gravity to the moment There, emblazoned in gold on a brown leather A5 book, was a single word, JOURNAL.

'Look at the postmark. This was mailed three weeks ago, but because there have been all those postal strikes, as you are probably aware, there must have been a delay in delivering it. I hope it has answers. I only read the letter and telephoned you immediately.'

Mrs. Chopra handed him a folded piece of white paper. Hurriedly, he opened it and read.

"Dear Mrs. Chopra,
Please forgive me for not contacting you for a while. Circumstances meant I moved away from my job in London. I need to ask a big favour and hope you will agree. Keep this journal safe and give it to the police. I don't want to worry Dad any more than I have already. You've kept an eye on him since Mum died. You are the only person I can trust.
Love,
Freya x"

Wiping away more tears, Anika looked at the policeman. She needed hope that he would use this precious last gift to find Freya's murderer. No words passed between the two adults for a moment or two.

His hand trembled as he opened it and flicked through the pages, trying to comprehend what was in front of him. His eyes widened as he saw the handwriting. It was noticeably different from the lack of precision on the envelope and Mrs. Chopra's letter; the style was neater, the formation of letters was far better defined, and it was less scrawly. On the inside front cover, she had written, "This is the story of Freya Margaret Rose."

He turned to the first entry, a letter outlining her history, running for the first few pages of the journal. Flicking through the leaves, he saw an explanation of how she came to be placed in witness protection and then multiple entries, in the style of a diary, outlining in detail what had happened since, and what being given a new identity meant.

As he read, he could hear Freya's words bouncing around the walls of Mrs. Chopra's sunroom. Her voice was everywhere; her whole life lay before him, the secrets she kept for so long, released. Why she had gone into hiding. The truth poured out. He felt Freya's desperation and loneliness as he read each entry about the new life she had tried to create for herself. Page upon page of sadness for a life she had lost, and some brief moments of joy when she felt her new identity seemed to be working. Sammie had told the truth about their relationship.

Ever the police officer, her death were systematically recorded in this much-needed journal, and he honed in on this fact, pleased her truth would be told. Freya Margaret Rose had risen from the dead, and finally revealed her secrets. There was no silencing her from this moment onwards.

Chisholm put down the journal for a moment or two to digest what he was reading. He had grown to know the woman over the course of almost four weeks. She was feisty and brave. As he turned the pages to read the final few entries, a feeling of anxiety and doom rose in his heart.

He had not expected her death to affect him so acutely, and his eyes became misty.

Her last entry was dated Monday, 22nd September, the same day as her murder. Her death, like the final few years of her life, was meticulously detailed. Incredulous at the contents, his body shook. Maybe it was through tiredness at the long journey or maybe through the rage spewing from a deep pit in his stomach, the tremors continued to rise through each sinew, each blood vessel, into the cavity of his chest, through his lungs, into his heart. Anger consumed him. Suppressing his feelings was of little use. Each part of him shook uncontrollably with fury. Mrs. Chopra gripped his arm to calm him.

'You will get the murderer, won't you?'

'Have no doubt, Mrs. Chopra. This is gold dust. Freya was an incredible police officer. She named her murderer.'

Somehow, Freya had realised it was the end and managed to post the journal. Everything dropped into place. One person had known a parcel was sent by the murder victim on the day she died—Janice! Suddenly it struck him; the brown tape that sealed the package seemed out of place, untidy even. When he looked more carefully at at everything for a second time, he could see the seal on it had been cut and then re-secured. The postmark was five days after Freya was supposed to have sent the parcel in Loch Dubhglas. Maybe Janice knew who the killer was, even before the young detective was dead.

Questions and various scenarios galloped through his mind. Why was the parcel not stamped on 22nd

September? The postal strikes happened after 27th September, which explained why it was delayed in being delivered to Mrs. Chopra. Janice told him Freya was waiting in the car park for the shop to open so she could post a parcel.

Fingerprints and perhaps DNA would prove or disprove his theory, but it made sense. Had Janice opened the parcel, read the journal, and blackmailed Freya's killer, and in so doing, got herself killed?

†††††

When he awoke in Anika's spare bedroom several hours later, Chisholm felt rested. The pounding in his head, and the twisted knots in his stomach, constants since he had first travelled to Loch Spiorad, had ceased. Hearing music downstairs, he sat up. Arching his back to stretch his body for the long drive north, he was ready to begin the journey to justice. He stepped into his shoes, and as he was tying his shoelaces, a knock came on the door.

'Detective Chisholm. You said to call you at ten.'

There on the landing was Anika, now looking more at ease, just as she had been the first time he had met her. There was a radiance about her that brought hope. Colour had returned to her cheeks, and her bright turquoise top enhanced her fine features, making her eyes sparkle. This was the first time he had seen her in western clothes. There was something about her beauty, no matter if she wore a sari or jeans.

'Come downstairs and have some breakfast. You must eat before driving back.'

On the kitchen table lay a breakfast full of fruit and goodness. Yoghurt and muesli, porridge oats. A selection of healthiness that David rarely chose these days. His first meal each day, from Moira's café, was through convenience and habit. He knew his cholesterol would be affected by his dietary choices, but his spark for life was lost, and he couldn't be bothered to eat a balanced meal.

'I sense you don't look after yourself. I see it in your eyes. You eat rarely, but when you do, it's unhealthy. Am I right?'

'How on earth can you tell? I've eaten better for the last few weeks.'

'There are many tell-tale signs. Let's not go into them now. Eat so you are ready for eight or nine hours in the car.'

'Next time, you can explain.'

'Next time? I do hope you mean that.'

Both glanced at each other and smiled before coyly casting an eye to the floor. There had been an instant attraction when he'd first met the lady but she was assisting with information about the Rose family. Work and play were never linked in his world. It could complicate matters but, as she stared at him with her stunning brown eyes, he somehow knew the feelings he was experiencing were reciprocated.

Full of health and vitality from the better food choices, Chisholm left Anika, the package safely deposited in his overnight bag on the passenger seat beside him. He telephoned Helen to explain his absence, not giving much away as to the contents of the journal. He did not want to put anyone in danger. He told her to cover for him if any questions were asked. Saying he was out on signal somewhere north would suffice for the day. Instructing her to meet him at eight o'clock the next morning, along with Euan, captured her interest. When she told him the results of the enhanced photographic images taken by the Harrisons didn't make sense, he told her he would explain everything in the morning; it was complex and too important to relate in a telephone call. The call ended and he immediately rang McLeod to brief her, telling every detail about the contents of the journal so she could prepare for the next day.

So he drove north, leaving England and the Central Belt behind, heading towards Inverness, Loch Dubhglas, and to Jimmy's. He stopped only a couple of times to drink coffee, and to stretch his legs. He smiled as he bought several bottles of water and a pot of salad. The force of Anika's magnetic personality would soon pull him back to Birmingham, he felt. There was an attraction between them. He knew he hadn't imagined it when she smiled.

There is a phrase used by Scots, "Where do you stay?" There is a lack of permanency to an incomer's ears, but for people from the north, it means the place where they live. I think it suited my predicament, for I never "lived" once since moving to Sutherland; I barely existed. Yet, I will be forever linked to this land where I was killed.

Tomorrow the truth will be known, my killer exposed, and maybe my soul will be freed from limbus.

CHAPTER 28
Day 27 : Sunday, 19th October

The air from her breath lingered as Helen stepped from her car. Euan had snored gently in the passenger seat for a good hour or more on the journey to Sutherland. She had drowned out the noise by playing music, but he'd not stirred after passing signs on the A9 for the Black Isle. Chisholm had asked to meet at Loch Spiorad, which had surprised and intrigued her.

Three other cars were already at the location. Daniels and Sinclair were greeted by an unexpected sight. David was deep in conversation with four people. Both young detectives were surprised. Chisholm looked up and immediately introduced the visitors.

'John, Simon, Janine, this is Detective Sergeant Helen Daniels and Detective Constable Euan Sinclair. The chief, you already know. Neither is aware of developments.'

The formality of shaking hands over, the pair stood and listened.

'For some time, I knew MI5 would be involved in the investigation into the death of Anna Green aka Freya

Rose. I was told that they would take over the case at some point, and that is happening after we move into the final phase of the operation.'

Rapidly trying to recall faces, Helen quizzed,

'You came into the incident room, didn't you?'

John answered.

'Yes. Our brief was to merge in as tourists. No one pays much attention to them, especially geologists with a passion for lichen.'

Janine continued,

'We didn't want to expose our identities, as it's useful, in cases like this, to stay in the shadows. As soon as a nerve agent was known as the murder weapon, it was inevitable MI5 would be involved.'

As a lightbulb was switched on within Euan's brain, he smiled.

'So two of you were officers asking questions at the ironmongers? Now, I understand.'

John nodded.

'Absolutely. We stalked Flora MacAskill. She is guilty of homophobia, graffiti, and inciting hatred, but not murder. Sadly, we didn't pay enough attention to Janice. Perhaps she would still be alive if we had.'

Alison McLeod had stayed silent until now.

'David's about to fill us in on all the developments. This is his shout, and it's been decided he will make the arrest.'

They all listened as Chisholm explained where he had been, and the details in the journal. What was discovered was incredible. Freya had been a key witness in her own death, outlining the whole story for them. As each police officer and MI5 agent absorbed the news, their eyes latched onto the loch, drinking in its beauty for a few moments. Then came the formalities: the next steps and the part each would play.

†††††

Helen's stomach lurched as the house came into view. This was it, the culmination of hours of detective work which had finally led to the moment of arrest. Chisholm rang the bell and waited. Both felt emotional and exhausted, but they had a task to do and needed to be calm. There was no need for introductions this time. Both detectives nodded as the door was opened. Calm and calculated, the greeting was warm.

'Morning officers. You're up bright and early. Would you like a drink? And I've been baking again.'

Helen tried hard not to smile at the irony of the offer from the elderly woman wearing an apron. The involuntary movement of her bottom lip and cheek betrayed her thoughts of taking a refreshment from the person in front of her. Chisholm took control of the situation, as always, calm at a moment of crisis.

'No thanks. I'll get straight to the point. Did you ever go to Dubhness Cottage where Anna lived?'

'Yes.'

'Why didn't you tell police officers?'

'Because none of you have ever asked me!'

'We have a witness that saw you at Anna's house on the day before she died. You were in the garden.'

'What witness? I've only ever been to Anna's house once. I can't remember when it was. I told you, I didn't know her well.'

David was intent on bluffing. The old crofter, Glen Mackenzie, had only seen a glimpse of someone entering the cottage on the day before Freya died. Glen hadn't given any indication if it was a man or a woman. Probably her lawyer would contest such a sighting, but he persisted; his patience was waning. The questioning would continue at the police station in Tain.

'Iris Stirling, I'm arresting you on suspicion of the murder of Anna Green, also known as Freya Rose. I am also arresting you on suspicion of the murder of Janice Milton. You do not have to say anything, but anything you do say will be noted and may be used in evidence. Do you understand?'

Her voice picked up a notch or two as she began to protest her innocence.

'No. I don't understand! When I came to the village hall with the church ladies, I never planned to talk about the woman I saw at the shop, as I keep myself to myself. One of the other women thrust me into the spotlight. She knew I'd spoken to Anna a few times when she came to church. Surely talking to a woman a mere handful of times is not an excuse to murder her!'

Once more, David attempted to ask if she comprehended what he was saying but Iris interrupted. No longer mild and inoffensive, the woman in front of the two detectives became stronger and bolder as she raged,

'Arresting me? Why would you arrest me? What evidence have you got to question me for two murders? They said on the television Anna was poisoned! This is ridiculous. It's that girl she was with at the shop who killed her. I even gave you drawings to help identify her. She's the one you should be arresting.'

Although he felt the familiar knot of anxiety return to his stomach, Chisholm attempted to retain his composure, and held his nerve. He started to repeat the police caution but Iris screamed,

'She is the murderer! Why aren't you arresting her?'

Trapped like a bird in a cage fighting for its freedom, her anger grew. She scowled as she battled, her temper no longer hidden as her florid cheeks blazed. She defiantly shouted,

'I'm innocent! Do you hear me?'

'Mrs. Stirling, it's no good protesting. We have evidence to suggest you are the murderer which we'll discuss at the station.'

'Well, if you're so clever, you tell me now!'

'We have Freya's journal, the one you were looking for at Janice's house.'

Suddenly, her rage dissipated and her calmer, genteel personality returned. She picked up her mug of tea and pulled a small dispenser of sweeteners from her apron pocket. Dropping a couple into her drink, she swirled them around to dissolve the saccharine substance. Lifting the liquid to her lips, she smiled, muttered something unintelligible, and allowed the tea to slip down her throat. David stared at her for the briefest of seconds, then jumped to his feet, knocking the cup from her hands. She laughed.

'Too late. I've drunk most of it.'

'Oh, for pity's sake, Iris! Why did you have to do that?'

He screamed for Helen to summon a doctor, and felt compelled to shake the woman, to make her vomit, but stopped himself. Quietly, he sat back down in his chair, his head in his hands. The paperwork would be endless. It was a scramble for checkmate in a deadly game of chess but Helen was oblivious to what was happening. She frantically scanned both Iris's face, and David's, for answers.

'If I'm not mistaken, Iris has just slipped something lethal in her tea.'

The sergeant's eyes grew wider, incredulous at the news. Her mouth dropped open. The old lady laughed at her expression of horror. Immediately, her Scottish accent disappeared, and she was no longer playing the role of a sweet old lady. Stunned, Chisholm and Helen watched her as clear Slavic sounds poured from her lips.

'Have no fear. I shall give my confession so you can get your neat answers and conclude the case. Record it on your mobile before the doctor gets here.'

Fingers trembling, David found the app and pressed record, hoping her words would not become too slurry.

'Iris Stirling is a pseudonym I was given in the 1950s. My birth name was Irina Volkova, born in St. Petersburg after the Second World War.

I confess to the murder of Anna Green, also known as Freya Rose. Before retiring, I worked for many years as an undercover agent for Her Majesty's government but also for my motherland; you would call me a double agent, I suppose.

I was lifted from a mundane existence as a secretary in the U.S.S.R. to a life in the shadows because of my excellent language skills. I am fluent in seven languages, meaning I could fit into so many places across the world unnoticed, working in offices with fake references, listening in on telephone conversations, and typing letters for men who thought me too dumb to understand the gravity and secrets they were spilling.

I travelled the world, and at some point in the early 1960's, I was recruited into the British Secret Service. As you can gather, I have no conscience about my actions. I've killed more people than you can ever imagine, sold my body for the most sordid of secrets, stolen, lied and cheated all of my life because a mission must be completed, no matter what the cost. When I retired five years ago, I chose to settle in the Scottish Highlands in the hope of a quieter life.'

She sniggered at the irony.

'So why did you kill Freya, and in such a barbaric way? Was it Altingham?'

Now that she was exposed, Confidence replied,

'Victorious, one last time, Freya was a loose end to be dealt with, one last favour for those who remain anonymous. Who gave the order? I will go to the grave with that knowledge, but it wasn't anyone on your radar, not anyone associated with my birth country. Nor was it Altingham who will eventually be exposed for his crimes. That piece of shit's been under surveillance for years; a loose cannon various prime ministers and senior officials were concerned about. He's always known the right people to speak to, and who could influence his career. He's a slimy little bastard, and dangerous with women, but had nothing to do with this killing.

Freya died due to a nerve agent injected into her skin courtesy of a charm bracelet I gave her as a present for her sham wedding.'

With a failing voice, she sniggered again and continued, 'All that rubbish of *"Something old."* Your faces!'

She became more serious, her words more intense.

'In 1967, the UK government secretly sent several agents, including myself, to support the US government in disposing of chemical weapons in Operation CHASE[22]. I was asked to steal several vials of the substances for future reference, but kept one for myself, in case I ever needed it. Amongst my many talents and skills as an agent, I was taught to braze and solder metals. So you see, this was not the first time I've been involved in creating exquisite weapons.'

David wanted to record every detail before it was too late.

'You made the bird charm?'

'Not just any bird! It had to be a raven. To some they are creatures who feed off the dead and are unclean, Leviticus 11, 15. To others, like myself, they're the bridge between the living and the dead.'

Neither of the detectives could believe what they were hearing. Concerned with the change in her pallor and her irregular breathing pattern, David pressed on with questions.

'Why did you kill her, Iris?'

She ignored his question and began another bible quote.

'Yea, though I walk through the valley of the shadow of death, I will fear no evil.'

'What about Janice? Did you kill her?'

Now her breathing was more laboured. The sentences were broken but her words still full of bitterness.

'Janice... greedy, foolish bitch! Stabbed her with a kitchen knife. Tried to grab her mobile. Blackmailing me, saying Freya kept a journal. Refused to tell me where it was. Searched everywhere. A loose end normally not left. Janice asked for money to stay silent. Stupid woman!

'Who ordered Freya's death? Who helped you put her in the loch? Surely you aren't strong enough to carry a dead body from a car?'

Poison coursed through Stirling's body, grabbing hold of any remaining strength and casting it aside. The two detectives glanced at each other dumbfounded as Iris Stirling slumped back. Her head spun, and as she gripped the armchair, her thoughts slipping away to a Caribbean beach at sunset, the sea trickling through her toes as she walked along the water's edge. Her lover, last seen in 1982, was standing, holding out his arms to greet her. No longer wanting to be without him for another second, she began running on the warm sand to be at his side.

Hesitance whispered.

'I'm weaker now officers. Let me go gently into that dark, silent night.'

David pushed for the ultimate answer before it was too late. His voice was urgent. There was little time left. Barely managing a whisper, she stretched out her hand to touch something invisible.

'I'm coming, Gustav.'

'Iris, who gave you orders? 'Who helped you?'

Confidence reared her head in one last act of defiance.

'I am the puppet master who silenced the weak.'

The old woman slumped backward in her armchair. She just wanted to dream.

'Iris, who was it?'

A gentle purr from her snoring filled the room momentarily, then silence descended as her body relaxed and fell still. She who was a professional assassin was dead. Her goal, to kill for one last time after retirement, had been achieved in double measure.

†††††

Everyone needed some time away to process the events of the day. After a specialist search of her house and all formalities were completed, they awaited the arrival of an independent investigation team to establish the facts behind Iris Stirling's death, and if it could have been prevented.

Images analysed from the photographers' memory cards showed a woman in a black wetsuit emerging from the water. Was she capable of carrying a dead body into a loch? Common sense would say not, but Iris was a remarkable woman, and the team realised what an accomplished assassin they'd been dealing with. It was highly likely to have been her. The height and build of the person in the photographs matched Stirling without any doubt.

One crucial set of results proved evasive and the detectives' impatience heightened as they waited to learn whose fingerprints lay on the bathroom cabinet. No match had previously been found. Iris was now the prime contender. It wasn't an error on her part; leaving a print was a final calling card as she knew no database contained her details.

The two police officers turned left out of the police station in Tain and headed to the high street, hoping the coffee shop was still open so late on a Sunday afternoon. Lights twinkled from the café as they approached. A woman sweeping the wooden floor smiled as the bell rang on the back of the door, announcing their arrival.

'Are we too late for something to drink?'

'No, you both look like you could do with a pick-me-up. The urn's still on, and there are empire biscuits left in the cake stand. What will it be?'

Chisholm asked for two mugs of tea and a couple of the sweet treats. As they stood waiting for the order to be completed, they both spied somewhere comfortable to sit near the window. As their weary bodies finally sank into the brown leather sofa, they sat collecting their thoughts, munching biscuits, and staring into their drinks. Helen broke the silence first.

'How did you know that the sweetener was poison?'

Chisholm shook his head.

'I didn't. Something felt wrong when she smiled. Suddenly I realised. I can't believe I was stupid to fall for her trick. How idiotic was that? Four deaths, Helen! This is a nightmare. I'll be put back in uniform for sure now.'

As the café woman counted the cash in her till, he gave Helen a sideways glance. His voice descended into a whisper.

'You do realise, because of all of this, I'm finished.'

'What? David, you've been incredible throughout this investigation. I actually think this case has had a positive effect on you. You seem much happier, and if I dare say, far more cheery.'

'Do you think so? It's a long story, too complicated to go through this afternoon. Suffice to say, Loch Dubhglas was where I grew up and went to primary school for a few years when I lived with my grandparents on their croft. It's been tough to revisit the village because of some bittersweet memories, but I am feeling better for spending time up there. I should have put my demons to rest years ago, but I didn't. Perhaps this is my penance: a complex murder inquiry in Sutherland. In the last few weeks, there have been four deaths: one through a heart attack, two murders carried out by a professional assassin, and a suicide.'

'Who gave the orders? Who was Stirling's accomplice?'

'I haven't got a clue. It wasn't Alec Sullivan; he would have easily given up her name to save his skin. Did you hear the changes in her voice as she was dying? She would have been capable of faking a telephone voice if she had paid for the rubbish to be cleared. I think she used him just so she could get rid of the car easily. She could have cleared everything herself but chose not to.'

Helen nodded and added her own thoughts.

'Yes, we got the impression someone blackmailed Alec, and let's face it, as a local, Iris would have known about him and his dodgy dealings. She used him.'

David fell silent for a moment. Something was still troubling him as he replayed the events in his mind.

'Almost at the end, she said that she was the puppet master who silenced the weak. We assumed someone else was pulling the strings, but what if she just went rogue at the end?'

'You mean she made the decision to kill Freya because she told Iris about being in witness protection?'

'Someone who has spent their life in the shadows, killing to order, perhaps decided to silence a woman she saw as weak for blowing her cover as an operative.'

'Freya was at her wits' end. Sammie had been lying, and the worst possible person, the one she was running from, was the fiancée's uncle. She was frightened and vulnerable. Those who were supposed to protect her had ceased to do their job. It was no wonder she confided in a seemingly harmless older woman she'd met a few times in the local church. Sadly, in a moment of utter despair, she chose to unburden herself to the wrong person.'

Outside, the light was fading. Chisholm focused on folk passing by the shop wondering if anyone glancing through the window at himself and Helen would be able to work out the strain they'd both been under for the past few weeks. He focused on Helen once more as he continued, again lowering his voice.

'At the beginning of this case, we thought Freya's assassin might be untraceable. At least we solved that part of the story. As to who ordered her execution, she hinted it was for national security. British? Russian? She might have decided to just kill purely because she still could. Iris Stirling was a remarkable woman. Although she was well into her seventies, after what she revealed today, I think she was capable of operating on her own. She was a highly-trained expert and, above all, a lone wolf.'

Helen despised loose ends and, with her desire to have the case completed and wrapped up with a smart bow, she turned her thoughts to the minister.

'What do you reckon will happen to Altingham? And what about Sammie? I guess she won't have any happy endings.'

'The noose is tightening on Sir William. I'm sure our friends at MI5 will bring him down. As for Sammie, let's hope she can start a new life, keeps clean, and stays away from her uncle. Apparently, he had solicitors stalling over her inheritance so she had no control of the money left to her from when her parents died.'

David rubbed his eyes and sighed. He was exhausted but felt the urge to philosophise.

'Recently, I read an article on Albert Einstein, who once said, *"Coincidence is God's way of remaining anonymous."*

After this case, I'm still not sure about coincidence. Perhaps fate might be a more fitting word. It was fate that brought Freya into contact with Altingham. Fate she relocated to a hiding place where Iris Stirling, an old spy, was living a blissful and quiet retirement. Was it fate that played a part in her meeting Sammie, a woman with an association to the same man Freya abhorred? If you consider every aspect of this case, it's all been guided by fate, or coincidence.'

Stepping back from his conversation with Helen, he fell silent. He mulled over the personal coincidences that had brought him back to a happier existence: a body found near to Kinness, reconnecting with Jimmy, the man who discovered Freya, then meeting Glen, who talked about crofting in the old days, and visiting Mrs. Chopra. When he thought of Anika, warm feelings were ignited. That she had been the person Freya entrusted with the precious journal meant something. It was almost as if Freya had brought two lonely souls together because of her death. Everything was fate.

†††††

In Norse mythology, three weavers create destiny by using the threads of the past, present, and future. The three women Norns who control fate, Urd, Verdandi, and Skuld, sit at the base of the world tree, Yggdrasil, and draw water from the Well of Urd to decide the fates of the gods, goddesses, and mere mortals. The water holds the memories of everyone.

As I leave the horrors and injustices behind in the darkness, my passage towards the light begins. David and Helen will move on with their lives and their work, but I shall always be part of them. Both have changed because of my death. These detectives were assigned to my case through fate. Threads from the Web of Wyrd created by the Norns bind me to them forever. May they find peace and happiness always.

CHAPTER 29
Day 28 : Monday, 20th October

David's eyes were rooted to his computer. He stomach lurched. The hand of fate, or coincidence, had struck for a final time. To convince himself that the screen displayed the truth, he needed to ask some uncomfortable questions. Not wishing to prolong the agony and potential embarrassment, he decided to act immediately. When he knocked on her door, he paused for a second after hearing the familiar voice.

'Come in.'

He stepped into her office and noted how pristine she looked in her uniform, ready for a function later that afternoon. She glanced up from her laptop, glasses perched on the end of her nose, a recent addition that still troubled her, but a necessity as middle age closed in around her.

'Good morning, Ma'am. Could I have a word, if you've got a few minutes to talk? I have a puzzle of a delicate nature I need to share with you before anyone else is aware. As you know, we questioned Samantha Stewart about the death of Freya Rose.'

Peering over her glasses, the chief gave him the nod to continue, not realising why he had come to speak to her.

'It's delicate, Ma'am, an awkward matter, and I'm not sure how to say it without causing any distress or embarrassment to you.'

'What is it, David? Spit it out!'

'Well, it's like this: Sammie's DNA shows a very close match to your details on the national database.'

Trying to be as diplomatic, and as delicate as he could be, he began. Words he'd never expected to say to his chief inspector.

'You are Samantha Stewart's mother according to DNA. I'm not sure how that can be possible. It must be a mistake, or someone has made a stupid error. Unless, of course, you can shed any light on the subject.'

Her head dropped. Her eyes could not meet his. How could she explain the impossible. Gulping to moisten her mouth, she tried to compose herself for something she should have spoken about twenty-five years before. Her voice was quiet and subdued, no longer the confident Perth accent she used to give out her orders across her division.

'I think the results are true. I swear I knew nothing about the woman's identity. The reason that Samantha Stewart shares my DNA is because I believe she could be my daughter.'

Remaining poker-faced, he stared straight at the floor, unsure if he should make eye contact with his superior as she continued her explanation of past events.

'One night back in 1999, I managed to get into a nightclub in Perth as an underaged teenager. I was seventeen, and loved booze, and life after dark. I drank heavily, but in my defence, I never took any drugs, none that I know of, anyway. I had gotten admission to the club by lying about my age. There were no I.D. cards needed back then. I wore my high heels, a skirt that barely covered my bottom, and a tight little top that left not much to the imagination. Bear in mind this was long before I thought of a career in the force. I was just a kid, rebelling against parents who saw my future at university.

It was early April. I should have been home revising, but once again, I slipped out of the back door when my mother and father weren't looking. One of my friends, who had passed their driving test, drove me and a couple of other girls into Perth.

Once in the club, I began to get drunk. Men would come up to me as my clothes were, no doubt, provocative. I paid no heed to the fact it was dangerous to be knocking about with older guys. One man from down south was up on business. Well, that's what he told me. I didn't catch his name. He bought my drinks and plied me with champagne, showing off his cash. I was barely seventeen, but I looked older. I was flattered and my head was swimming after about three glasses.'

David nodded, trying not to cast a judging eye on his boss. 'Did he rape you?'

'Yes, David, He did. I was naive. He asked me to go outside to have a cigarette, and stupidly I followed him around the back of the club, up a dark alley. I tried to scream, but he put his hand over my mouth so no one heard my cries. I never saw him again, or so I thought.

It was only when I met him a few days ago in Inverness that I recognised him. He had changed; he was older, but the charm factor was there, well, at least at first.'

'And your daughter?'

'I was just finishing school, from a strict Free Church background, and suddenly found myself pregnant. It was, of course, a shock. I stopped having periods, but because I was young, I convinced myself that many girls were irregular. By the time I discovered I was having a baby, it was too late to do much other than have her adopted. My parents sent me to stay with my Aunty Hilda in Dundee. There, the baby, a girl, was born a few months later. I handed her over on the day she was born; all I know was she was adopted. I could not keep her, so I felt it was best to disassociate myself from her and the whole ordeal. It was the only way I coped with the trauma.

I have no idea what happened to her after, except I was told she was to be adopted by a family with some considerable wealth. I swear I did not know she would be sent to Altingham's sister. From what I've read of the family over the last few weeks, they hail from Perth.

I was ashamed of myself and so were my family. My dad was a sergeant in the police, and my mother was a school teacher. Both had strict views, even then, on sex before marriage. So, in summary, it seems this woman, who was born to me, is the product of a sordid ten-minute rape in a back alley in Perth. No wonder she has turned out to be fucked up!'

With her speech over, her eyes brimmed with tears. Horrified at what had become of her daughter, she immediately knew she would resign. She could not be a senior officer, in command of police across Highland or elsewhere, with a daughter who needed help. Her head dropped at the consequences of a stupid seventeen-year-old lass who should have known better.

'Who was the man? You say you recognised him recently in Inverness.'

The thought of Sir William repulsed her, and her memories felt all the more shameful because her rapist was him.

'David, I won't ever name him publicly, but I will tell you that his world will collapse one day without me telling his dirty little secret. You will deduce who I am speaking about but I will not say his name. The irony that her father has had a relationship of any kind with her breaks my heart. All I want is the opportunity to attempt a relationship with my daughter if she wants to know me. This is the only time I will ask two favours of you. It contravenes data protection and all kinds of regulations, but please permit me to access Sammie's contact details.'

'You can do that without asking my permission.'

Fighting back the tears, she nodded.

'I know, but I want your blessing.'
'What's the other favour?'
'Your discretion.'
'Naturally, Ma'am.'

Realising that her hands were trembling and her eyes were full of tears, David felt it was best to leave her to absorb the information. Without asking permission, he left work, got in his car and drove north. He needed peace and space to gather his thoughts. The conversation played over and over in his mind.

When she confided in him, her words had struck him like bolts of thunder. From her frank description of her teenage self, it was clear she was no angel. Maybe her memory of the guy who had abused her years before was incorrect, but he sensed she was probably right; it was Altingham. She didn't want to air her dirty linen in public. In the cold light of day, he wasn't surprised. She was adamant she wouldn't report the rape; there was no evidence apart from a twenty-five-year-old lassie turning up as her daughter. It might have been consensual; her word against a man who had committed a crime a quarter of a century before. Not even DNA could prove a rape took place in Perth that night. Chisholm wasn't happy a rapist was walking the streets, but the chief was determined to say no more.

†††††

The crisp white envelope was propped against a fancy pen holder purchased when she gained a promotion to the Highlands. Made of boxwood, it had been polished at the end of its construction to make it an exemplary piece of expensive bric-a-brac on her desk. It lay, alongside other examples of her false lifestyle.

The handwritten letter and envelope showed no signs of the torrent of emotions that had racked though her as she composed what she needed to say. With her two-hundred-pound fountain pen, she had addressed her superior to inform him that she intended to step down from her duties with immediate effect. She had not explained why, and he would not care about the reasons Alison Macleod was tendering her resignation. He would want no scandal or any negative news reaching the press. This way, without spelling out her past, everything would be kept quiet.

Her decision was made without hesitation. For the first time in her life, she was a mother. Her flesh and blood needed her now. Her daughter had always needed her, but she ignored her pangs of guilt and, long ago, any maternal feelings had been buried deep inside in order to survive.

Her new role was quickly evolving and would take all of her strength. With Chisholm acting as an intermediary by telephoning Sammie's mobile, she was confident for the first real time in her life she was making a positive life choice. She wanted a second chance at motherhood, even if it was thrown back in her face. Samantha needed her. Keeping her away from a drug habit would be hard, but Alison was stronger than ever now. She would concentrate on the job she should have taken on twenty-five years before. If her daughter allowed her into her life, she would fulfill her role as a mother until her dying day.

She stood up, adjusted her uniform, and then picked up her cap and briefcase before leaving the room. There was no turning back, she knew. She who was a chief inspector, full of ambition and drive, no longer existed.

I see two damaged women who need each other, but it will take time to learn and understand the roles of mother and daughter. Sammie needs to grieve for her lost childhood, the world and the people she thought she knew, and my death. Only when she has accepted the past can she try to mend her broken heart. May she rise like the sun and bring warmth to herself and all those who love her.

EPILOGUE

He cast his eyes over the journal one last time before he placed it in the case box destined for storage. It was time to move on. Freya's words still haunted him, and he struggled to imagine what she experienced in those hours before her death. Where she had found the fortitude and strength to share her life and her death with him, he had no idea. Without her testimony, Iris Stirling would have carried on with her mundane existence in retirement, and her neighbours in Loch Dubhglas would never have known they had a double agent and murderer in their midst.

He began with re-reading the short letter that accompanied Freya's story.

"To Whom It May Concern,
If you are reading this letter, I must be dead. When I first went into hiding, I felt I should make notes on everything that happened. I fear I have been poisoned. Mrs. Chopra has been sent my letter and my journal for safekeeping and will pass everything to the police.
Freya"

The first time he'd read the journal in Birmingham, the words blurred as he gripped it to try and control the trembling of his hands. Now, the words were familiar, but he still found them astonishing, even though he knew their ending.

"You will find attached a witness statement about a telephone conversation I heard back in late March 2022 at the home of Sir William Altingham. Please find and use these documents as evidence in Operation Owl and against my killer, if I am dead.

Firstly, I ask that if I am dead, my ashes are taken to my father in Birmingham so that they can be scattered near where my mother lies. I had hoped, like in the circle of life, I would die after my father, but if I have been taken sooner, I pray he will come to terms with what happened and that my death causes him less pain knowing I did this for him and all good people like him. He was a police officer, and despite many arguments in my youth when I fought against him, becoming a member of the force was something I wanted to do to bring some good to the world.

I was never meant to lead an ordinary life, nor be a heroine. I'm actually a coward, as I'm sure I never faced my demons and definitely avoided telling the truth about myself. I think I was in denial for many years about certain aspects of my life. For a former police officer, an admission I've told lies is shocking. It has only been since Operation Owl began that necessary lies were used to protect me.

I pray my truth is told and that everyone knows what happened to me. I began keeping a journal years ago, but this one details every event since I was asked to work undercover. It's always been what I shall call an insurance policy, hidden away for my eyes only, in every place I am moved to, until now.

If a police officer is reading these words, my death has surely passed and the wolves have finally caught up with me. You know the end, so let me tell you the beginning.

For your benefit, as an unknown reader, I was born on 16th December 1993 and named Freya Margaret Rose. I lived in a happy home, content with my life and family, until Mum passed away. I was barely a teenager but Dad and I continued to live at 322 Dark Lane, Bournville, Birmingham after her death.

Life changed for Dad and me after that. We developed a tight bond, and that is why I could not abandon him completely when Operation Owl went wrong and I was pulled off the job. At that point, I should have ceased all communications with my past world, but occasionally, I send a letter or a little parcel at Christmas or for his birthday. He does not know where I am, but he knows I am alive. I pray it will be someone kind who informs him I am dead.

I joined the West Midlands Police Force, and after a couple of years on the beat in Birmingham, was recommended for a transfer to the Met. Initially, I hesitated about leaving my home city and Dad, but he gave me his blessing and wanted me to take this fabulous opportunity. Life in London was crazy and hectic, but I loved the buzz and vibrancy of the city and my work too. When I finally became a detective, it was the job of my dreams.

One morning, a superior of mine approached me and asked if I would undertake a special assignment, going deep undercover to get information about a politician. It was at this point I became someone else. The politician, Sir William Altingham, was a member of parliament and had risen through the ranks to become Minister for Energy. My brief was to enter his house as his youngest child's nanny and protector. He was told I was an ex-police officer with excellent credentials. What he didn't know was my real name and that my role, while under his roof, was to spy on him.

I adored Isabella, his young daughter, keeping her safe morning, noon, and night. She was a sweet seven-year-old kid, and looking after her was easy. It made me think about what my own children would be like. My chosen career would be the prologue for one day being a mother. I held her in my arms when she was ill and felt sorry for the child as no one cared for her. She had the most expensive clothes and toys, attended an exclusive day school for the children of the super-rich, and had horses in stables on several estates owned by her father. All she wanted was a hug, encouragement, and time to talk. I sat with her for hour upon hour, playing with her, reading stories, or just talking to her as her father lay in other apartments with his mistresses. His wife lay in her own bed, lonely and hazy, hung over again from bottles of champagne and three lines of coke. Enjoying my job was a perk of the operation.

My surveillance began, observing the visitors, listening to his bugged phone calls, and rummaging through his paperwork when I had the opportunity. I gathered intelligence and dutifully reported back to my handler: a pleasant chap named Phillip, who praised my work and encouraged me to take greater risks. I started to gain a clearer picture of the minister's involvements with an Italian guy by the name of Roberto Marino. He would visit Sir William's London home every few weeks, and they would dine on food Marino cooked in Altingham's kitchen. Then they would retire to the study and talk behind closed doors. Of course, I recognised the visitor's face; he was constantly on the television. In public, they talked about food and good wine, Marino's homes in Italy, and the poor British weather. Behind those study doors, there were often raised voices, angry at times, then whispers when they remembered people might hear them.

One day I overheard a conversation, a telephone call on loudspeaker, when his study door had been left ajar. His impatience at some deal that was going wrong made him careless for once. Blurted from his lips were dirty secrets and lies, words contorted and twisted to suit his greedy agenda. His anger and venomous remarks were shocking as he tried to blackmail Marino.

In truth, the man who had employed me to take care of his child wore two masks. One was of a thoroughbred English gentleman with impeccable manners, Oxbridge educated, a Member of Parliament, and a government minister who cared about the environment. The other facade was one of a person who lived in shadows, in a world of hatred and destruction, driven by profit and greed, with a cruel temper, and capable of anything he could get away with. Emblazoned on his old-boy ties were insignia of Eton, Cambridge, and the Army, all together in bed with Evil. Under a ruse of green credentials, his fame and fortune seemed linked to saving the planet when, in reality, he was supporting the Earth's demise.

"I'm sick of waiting, Roberto. It's been a month since the invasion, and I, for one, want to see a return on my investment in the *"Old Bear."* The money from my offshore account was transferred over weeks ago, way before everything kicked off on 24th February. The cash spent on supplying tanks and armoury to ease the invasion should have meant the fall of our mutual friend's enemy days ago. You told me we would recoup our money tenfold as soon as those sunflower oil factories and lithium mines fell into red hands, but now you're saying more money is needed! What is in this for *me?* I'm sending nothing until I get some return. We agreed and shook hands on a deal."

His lack of conscience in funding arms to a foreign dictator, aiding the invasion of another country, was shocking. All he was interested in was making a profit for himself while millions of people suffered. War brings the minute hand on the Doomsday clock closer to midnight, but he didn't care. How could *"Mr. Keep It Clean, Make It Green"* be involved in potential genocide, dispersing people from their native land and stealing their assets?

Marino's determination was crystal clear as he bit back at Altingham. He argued the terms of the agreement, but it was at this point the conversation turned sour; both threatened to blackmail each other. The stakes were high for each man, it seemed. The Italian taunted him.

"You knew exactly who you've got involved with. Don't lie. Life could suddenly become very difficult for you!"

The minister lost his temper.

"You don't scare me. If this goes wrong, we both have plenty to lose! And I'm warning you, if the shit hits the fan, I'll take you into the gutter with me!"

He slammed the phone down but must have heard my footsteps as I attempted to tiptoe away from his doorway. I was the child's nanny and bodyguard who had stupidly dropped some books on the floor in the hall. In the seconds it took to pick them up, my fate was decided. I had only one foot on the stairs when he saw me. He closed his study door, and I continued up the steps, hoping I had bluffed my way out of a tricky situation, but he knew.

His next move was to find what I had heard. An hour later, he approached me in the laundry room as I ironed his daughter's blouses for school. Like a military operation, his plan was carried out with perfection.

"As your employer, it is my duty to ensure your health and well-being and to get to know the woman who protects and takes care of my daughter. I like to take all new employees out for a meal. Put on that little black dress I'm sure you have in your wardrobe for such occasions."

His invitation took me by surprise. It was obvious what motive he had, but his form of attack less so. We were within a hair's breadth of nailing Altingham. Phillip was desperate for my cover not to be blown and reassured me I should go. Stupidly, I declined to wear a recording device. It felt best to calm the situation down and not to tempt fate; a decision I bitterly regret.

A charming evening, with a charming gentleman, in a charming restaurant, ended with him attempting to rape me in the kitchen. Every other evening this was the room where his daughter would chatter away to me as I heated milk and poured it into her favourite mug before bedtime. Rebuffing his advances sealed my fate.

"What's the matter? I thought we could have a cosy chat and get to know one another a little better. My wife doesn't mind my dalliances; we have an open marriage. No one will know."

I pulled away from his clumsy grasp, but he came again, pulling me closer and tighter this time. Frantically unzipping his trousers with one free hand, he then grabbed the hem of my dress and reached for my knickers. I feared he would enter me if I did not escape. It took all of my strength to push him away, yelling a long-held secret I wanted immediately to retract. At a moment of rape, I had *"come out."*

"I am a lesbian. Don't touch me, or I'll use this!"

Clasping the largest kitchen knife from the block on the marble worktop, my hand shook as I held out the implement, jabbing the air as a warning to keep away from me. He roared with laughter.

"So that is your problem. I thought you were a tight little bitch. I'm sure I can persuade you to prefer men when you experience me."

Courage was draining from me. I had one last ploy to rid myself of him. Still gripping the knife, I blurted out a deal.

"That phone call you made today, about the arms deal, would make big headlines should it ever get out. Here's what's going to happen. Zip those trousers. I pack my bags and forget everything I heard. I'll disappear. You'll never see or hear from me again!"

The offer I made stopped him in his tracks. All thoughts of Operation Owl disappeared as I protected myself from the vulture. My bargaining chips were poor, but I hoped it would be enough to get him away from me.

He had the information he wanted. I knew his secret; he knew mine. I was naive in thinking I could stop a man of this kind by blackmail. After all, he was a master of that game. His demeanour changed instantly. Adjusting his clothing, he sneered and nodded.

"Agreed. Don't cross me again, you frigid little bitch, or I will find and destroy you. I know people who could snuff you out, just like as simple as that!"

He clicked his fingers and laughed.

"Pack your bags. Get out of my sight before I change my mind. No wages, no references."

Pushing clothes into the confines of my suitcase, I frantically packed. Travelling light was a good thing. I left ten minutes later, closing the door, with no trace of me left in my room or the house. At the end of the street, I stopped to take stock. Handbag on my shoulder, a suitcase on wheels, and a puffer jacket to keep me warm; my dignity was intact, but my assignment had failed.

It was late. I booked myself into a hotel. A voice in my head told me to report in straight away, but instead I tossed and turned all night, pondering what would happen next. As dawn broke, trembling with fear, I pressed the keys on my mobile. I still didn't know what to say. I hadn't been raped, but I'd compromised the surveillance. Worse still, I had no evidence of Altingham's dirty arms deals; it was my word against his as to what I'd heard.

The phone rang. Phillip listened, and as I burst into tears, his familiar voice told me everything would be alright. Then the gravity of my situation became apparent. Altingham had no inkling I was working for Her Majesty's government to find out about his deals with the *"Old Bear,"* as he'd called the Russian regime. My bosses were closing in on him, but one silly mistake of dropping books and being heard cost the operation dearly.

The eavesdropping information was not enough. It hadn't been recorded. It was feared Altingham wouldn't trust me not to blab to the police or reporters. He would want me dead before I could tell his secrets. Phillip felt I was in danger, and it was decided I needed to be hidden until they had enough proof to use my testimony in court.

The minister had many dangerous secrets. Paper trails of proof were needed to prosecute him. It could take months to trace the money and account he'd mentioned using. Finding breadcrumbs to begin the task of locating hidden transactions would prove difficult, or even impossible. People like Altingham knew how to hide money. They were masters of deception.

Phillip felt it was imperative and urgent to hide me until the truth could finally come out about the minister. There was a fear I might be silenced before any case came to trial because of his connections. Gathering more substantial evidence could take several more years. Witness protection would be the only way to protect me until such time as I could give a testimony in court. Until then, it would be a new identity, a fresh start.

I was an informer, a witness, and a police officer, but Altingham would find me. He had so many contacts. Phillip and I were convinced someone in authority would give me up for a bribe. Witness protection should have been my safety blanket whilst police investigated his seedy life. From searching his contacts, *"the old boy network,"* no doubt, his many connections knew someone who knew someone. It would be simple to find a weakness in a corrupt police officer, too easy to blackmail them into giving him my new name and location. His murderous fingers were in every pie.

Becoming Anna Green never felt safe. I think about that time a great deal, when the person I had always been was obliterated overnight. The reality of my situation hit home; I would never see my family or friends again. The truth cut deep into my soul. I felt my former life had been erased completely and, to be honest, I never stopped grieving the loss of myself. The pseudonym was not my choice, but it was used to delete any history of being Freya or the girl I pretended to be in Altingham's house.

Storms were coming, swirling around the minister's door, and he knew it. Wolves waited in the shadows, ready to attack. I wanted a new, quiet life away from London. I was moved from place to place because they feared he had someone on the inside telling him where to find me.

Finally, after months of fear and uncertainty in Swansea, then Milton Keynes, Bristol, and Glasgow, Phillip had found me peace of some kind. Even though I was in such a remote area with only a kindly old crofter called Glen as a neighbour, I panicked at the slightest sound, the briefest of shadows, until I could no longer function as a human being.

I realised, about a week after moving to Sutherland, that Phillip hadn't been in touch. He disappeared off the radar, not returning my calls, and I began to think he didn't care or the establishment had finally abandoned me. I was left to my own devices. Each month, money appeared in Anna Green's bank account for living expenses. I guess this was instead of a police pension later in life.

Days turned into weeks, the weeks into months, and here I am, a year in Sutherland has gone quickly. I'm still scared to lay down roots or to run so no one in the world knows my whereabouts."

David flicked through the diary section, saddened by the moves, the fears, and the anxiety running through Freya's comprehensive journal. The account of her final years was painful to read; the toxic stress poisoned her long before any chemical agent was added. It was clear she was paranoid about being found and truly thought the minister would send people to kill her. She'd given up any hope of returning to her old life and her father.

It was only latterly, following her forced relocation to Sutherland, that she'd found a kind of peace when love entered her world, wrapping itself around her like a cloak of warm sunshine. He turned to the page when she'd met Sammie, and sensed the brief joy she felt.

From meeting the woman, and interviewing her, it was clear that her girlfriend had also needed stability. For a brief time, each experienced the other's love. Forming a relationship with Sammie might not have worked but she was finally trying to build a new life.

"Friday, 7th March
Meeting Sammie
I have news! Today, when I felt at peace for once, and with my guard down, I went out with my camera up into the hills. As I walked along the road to the cottage, I noticed a car parked a few yards ahead, near the loch. Racing back, determined to reach the sanctuary of home; a voice broke my silence.

"Excuse me. Do you have a map?"

I swung around, frightened to speak, wanting to run, but a young dark-haired woman with the most beautiful of faces was smiling at me. Her golden retriever barked in the front passenger seat, and she spoke lovingly to it as I was about to walk away.

"Don't you just love them? They understand your soul, you know."

I've pined for my old dog for so long, and seeing another fluffy friend made me forget myself. Her name is Samantha, a bright, bubbly girl who wears her heart on her sleeve. She's very honest about being on the other side of a long drug habit and wants to keep clean. She's open about her bisexuality, and what she's gotten up to in the past. She's thinking life in the Highlands will offer her a new start. We chatted for ages about our similar tastes in music, films, and a love of dogs. Sammie has ignited a spark in me not felt for years."

"Monday, 5th May
Sammie rarely talks about her family. As a baby, she was adopted by a wealthy couple in Perthshire who couldn't have children. Although they hadn't been bad parents, Sammie went off the rails, unsure of her own identity and rebellious at the constraints of her life. She mentioned today about the car crash that killed her parents a year ago. I think the incident brought her to her senses about drugs and her lifestyle. She regrets what she put them through, growing up with abandonment issues, and an identity crisis. She has an urge to contact her birth family. I think it is a good idea and will support her."

"Saturday, 21st June
The feelings between us have grown more intense. Today, after a drive to the north coast, we professed our love for each other, and at Loch Spiorad, she stopped the

car, wrapped her arms around me, and asked me to marry her. I can't believe how lucky I am! We've only known each other for a few months. What a wonderful end to the summer solstice. The proposal was a complete shock; the whole caboodle of bending down on one knee and offering me a Haribo ring as a joke. We plan to make our vows to each other at the loch. Our ceremony won't be official, just a spiritual connection between ourselves. We'll make it legal after a year or so. Sammie will move in with me; I will take her surname and free myself of the burden of being Anna Green. Phillip's lack of contact means I am free. We can disappear to anywhere in the world, me, her and the dog."

David re-read her final entries, wishing that the events could have been changed. When her handler died, she had nowhere to turn. Mistakes had been made. How could no one have been in touch with her? The establishment had certainly failed, or been compromised.

"Friday, 19th September
10:00 a.m.
I timed my route down the hill, along the road to Loch Spiorad and back. My personal best for that circuit! I returned a little slower as the steep climb up the track always makes my heart race faster and my chest tighten. Training helps. After a running session, my mood lightens, and positivity seeps through me.

Keeping secrets scares me. How can I marry someone when they don't know the real me? Forgiveness is what I pray will happen when I tell my story. Where shall I start?

How can I be honest with Sammie? I only know I must explain my life to her. I can't go on lying about myself and my background if she's going to move in with me. We have a simple picnic planned for tomorrow, by the shores of Loch Spiorad, our special place. It's the location where my life changed forever. I will tell her there."

"Saturday, 20th September
11:59 p.m.
I stayed quiet. I'm too scared to spoil what we have together. I must tell her, but not now. I've found someone who cherishes me. Sammie is the only person I can see myself having children with. It's possible now for single-sex couples, and it's what she wants too. She is someone with whom I want to grow old. The demons from my past and the nightmares must stop.

We are making commitments to each other on Monday. It will be a huge first step, but the idea of being with someone else forever, and no longer being on my own, brings hope that there can be a future for me. A happy-ever-after is all I ever wanted. A simple life is all I ask for.

The thought of wearing a special dress makes the impending commitment feel suddenly real. A circle of flowers, created from blooms in the garden, sits on the kitchen table. The headdress will be my surprise. Pink roses and greenery will help bring colour to my cheeks. One good secret I have kept. It smells intoxicating, and brings our red-letter day ever closer."

"Sunday, 21st September

11:00 a.m.

BETRAYAL! This morning Sammie dropped HIS name into a conversation. Has she been the bait, the worm on the end of his fishing rod, reeling me in by using the one thing he knows about me? It seems she has secrets of her own, dreadful ones that all stem back to HIM!

"Uncle Will has agreed to meet you while he is staying in Scotland. I thought we could go and see him tomorrow, get his blessing. He's loaded, and might even give us some money for a holiday. If you agree, I need to warn you about who he is. Don't get put off by his grandiose title or name. If I mentioned the name Altingham, would it mean anything to you?"

I gulped, disbelieving she had said HIS name. Somehow, she had released a trigger. The bullet hit my skull, smashing my brain into a million pieces. I was found, betrayed, and in danger. I AM CAUGHT! A scream couldn't be suppressed. It came from the pit of my stomach, rose through my lungs, and rushed through my lips, piercing the silence I've had in my mind for years. When it stopped, I found myself on the floor, crying like a baby, helpless and lost. Adrenaline raced through my exhausted body, building and building, until I exploded in anger.

"You fucking callous bitch! I genuinely thought I meant something to you! All along, you've been in his pay, seeking me out so he can have me killed. You know this means my death! Well, let him have me!"

She stared at me speechless, startled at my words of abuse.

"What are you talking about? How do you know my uncle? It doesn't make sense! He's a king-sized prick who I only keep in contact with as he's the closest thing I have to family, thanks to his sister, my adoptive mother and father, dying. And he still has control of my inheritance. Calm down Anna. Whatever history you two share, I swear I know nothing about it. Look, if it upsets you so much, we won't meet him."

Sammie tried to put her hand on my shoulder to soothe me. Unsure of my sudden mood change, she genuinely seemed puzzled why I'd sworn at her. She protested as I pushed her away, begging me to tell her what is wrong.

It's too late; even if by a tiny percentage she's telling the truth, she won't understand. Tomorrow is off. I will run away from this persona, Anna Green, and start again, without anyone knowing where I am or who I was. I have to find the strength. He will not win. My head's still reeling. I need time to think. She left, promising, begging me to be at the loch at noon on Monday.

The worlds we've both hidden have come crashing down in our charade of happiness."

"1:00 p.m.
I've broken the habit of a lifetime, been to the supermarket in Tain, and bought two big tubs of bleach, black bin liners, and some cleaning cloths. I should run, with just one bag, but think this place needs deep cleaning. I've always been trained to leave no trace.

I won't tell Glen, the landlord, but I will send him a month's rent once I've found somewhere else to stay so he doesn't think too badly of me.

I'm going to drive as far away from Sutherland as I possibly can. I have no passport but with a fake birth certificate and other papers, I'll apply for one so I can escape this country altogether. The world will be my oyster. Perhaps no longer being in the UK will make the past disappear for good. I'll get a job so I'm not reliant on any witness protection money. They won't trace me."

"2:00 p.m.
I was putting some black bin bags outside when I heard a car come up the lane. I ran in and shut the door. Where could I hide? It was then I realised I would surrender. I can't cope. It's exhausting, and I have nothing left. I'm done.

There was a knock on the porch door. I decided to confront whoever was there, let them kill me, and be done with everything. As I burst into the porch, almost yanking the inner door off its hinges, I'm not sure who was more surprised.

It was Iris, a woman I've seen from time to time, standing in the porch, wanting to talk to me. I'd met her when I first arrived in Loch Dubhglas, lost, alone, and seeking something. For once, I tried religion. She's been friendly when most other worshippers were wary and hostile to a new face.

"Hi Anna, Can I come in? I've met your friend at the local petrol station, and she was crying. She was in such a dreadful state. I begged her to tell me what was wrong and, through her tears, she muttered something about a wedding and her uncle. I thought you might need a friendly face, so I asked her where you stayed. Let's talk this through."

There's something about the woman. Here she was trying to mend the unmendable. She has charisma and a knack for being a good listener. Out came my story, well, most parts of it at least. I said far too much. There's nothing to fear. She's a member of the local church group, and I'll soon be gone from Loch Dubhglas, never to see her again. I'm sick of secrets. Afterwards, she sat for a few moments before she spoke.

"If you intend to run away, where will you go?"

"I have no idea."

"Let this be the start of another chapter in your story. How about I rustle up some lunch at home and come back at 3 p.m.?

It's nothing fancy, just some leftover curry I made last night. If this is your last meal before you depart, promise not to disappear before I return. I insist on making this a day of destiny for you. A meal will be my parting gift."

I nodded, unsure if I would keep my promise, but something made me stay. She returned in less than the sixty minutes she'd suggested. My plan was to leave as soon as she was gone.

She greeted me with a small, glossy, black box, which she pushed into my hand. As I lifted the lid, I exposed an exquisite silver bracelet with a delicate bird charm. I asked what kind of bird it was.

"It's a raven. Put it on. You'll have to excuse me helping you. My fingers are too arthritic to help. It's just a little leaving present to wish you good luck."

The bracelet was beautiful. I wrapped it around my wrist and managed to do up the clasp with ease. The house stank of bleach. I avoided any talk of when I would be leaving and took her onto the patio to eat. She'd even brought plates, glasses, and cutlery. The vegetable curry was delicious, and the rice was freshly cooked.

The weather's still good, and thank goodness the midges have all but disappeared. How can such tiny little creatures cause so much pain? Those pesky insects swarm in a heaving black cloud as soon as the temperature rises. There are still a few around. One bit me on my wrist as I ate the food. The creature must have been nosy, wanting to see my new bracelet. It serves me right for daring to still wear short sleeves in September. I must make a tasty lunch, as there are two small bite marks to prove it feasted on me!

For a few minutes I relaxed, enjoying the final views that had been home for the last twenty months. There's a pang of sadness in leaving, and I found a kind of peace here, especially in the last six months. The meal and company were enjoyable, and I lost track of time.

"Can Sammie be telling the truth? How can I trust her?"

"My dear, if you turn up for the wedding at the loch tomorrow, you will know if she is there. It's plain that she loves you."

"Do you believe in coincidence, Iris?"

"I believe in fate, my dear. It was fate I saw your Sammie today, and fate I came to visit you."

I don't remember much more of the conversation after I drank a couple of glasses of the orange juice. It must have been Iris who cleared up and left because the next thing I remember is waking up on the settee. The house is empty. All I have to do is strip the sheets and duvet cover off the bed and place everything in a black bin bag, but my head feels strange, so I'll lie a while until I feel better. I am too tired to leave today."

"10:00 p.m.
My head's spinning with everything, and my stomach's full of anxiety. I've lain here, writing what has happened today, and finally made a decision. I'll go to Loch Spiorad tomorrow and speak to Sammie. I'll even put on my special dress. If it's a trap, and he is there, so be it. This won't be finished until I face him. I am going to see what she has to say about her uncle and me knowing each other. Was it all deceit? In all the time we've been together, I realise I never saw her home. She said she was staying with a relative, and there was no privacy at her place. Tomorrow will decide my fate."

"Monday, 22nd September
5:00 a.m.
The most important day of my life has not started well! Sweat is oozing out of every pore! Strange, I don't recall Iris's curry being too spicy. Stomach cramps kept me wake for hours, and butterflies fluttering in my tummy are making me nauseous. Perhaps it's my nerves and the decision I've

made. I can't keep running; I have zero energy. The headache is far worse. I don't remember drinking any booze, but I'm dizzy. All I need today is reassurance and strength. I gasped at my reflection in the bathroom mirror, so deathly pale and ghost-like!

"6:30 a.m.
I'm trying to document everything. Nothing can be left in my stomach, yet I keep retching. My body's on fire. Scratching brings no relief. My arms are raw from my attempts to stop the incessant irritation. Hel is here. I smell her. It's my decision not to call an ambulance. Too late anyway; I've been caught. The curry or the orange juice was my downfall. Whatever I've been given is slowly killing me. Whenever I close my eyes, I know the end is near.

    I must find strength to post this journal to Auntie Anika so the truth is told. She will know what to do. I don't want to burden my father. Tell him I love him very much, and I'm so sorry I couldn't make it home safely. No one can truly be protected from wolves for they will hunt until satisfied they have their prey. I know my betrayer, a wolf in sheep's clothing. How stupid have I been?
Freya"

He couldn't resist travelling a few miles north, beyond Loch Dubhglas, to stop and take one last look at the place. Ripples on the surface of the water blew towards the shore. The colourful blanket wrapped around the land was disappearing. Icy winds had begun to steal the leaves from the trees, frittering them away to lie as a vibrant carpet across the road. One of the autumn equinox gales would take them, leaving only the strongest twigs clinging to the boughs over winter.

The watery grave where Freya had been placed seemed bare and cold. A girl with such courage, and so much love to give, would have hated to be alone there. She should have been allowed to make her peace with her lover and start a new life, but her future was destroyed by someone with evil in their soul.

He was glad she was to be reunited with her father and mother in Birmingham. On the first day he'd travelled north, annoyed and lost at having to return to the area, he had made a promise to an unknown woman lying dead in an incident tent. There was no real justice for her death, but her truth had been revealed. Her wish, and his promise, would be fulfilled. Freya Margaret Rose would return home.

A double funeral for her and her father was to be organised by Anika Chopra and her son. Both sets of ashes would be buried within Mrs. Rose's grave at a later date once all the safety procedures and special precautions at the crematorium were carried out because of the chemicals involved in Freya's death. Rather than representing Police Scotland at the service, he had requested several weeks' leave, so he could attend as a private individual. Not only was he exhausted, he needed time away from work to process everything.

As he turned on the engine to pull away, the news came onto the radio. The reporter's excited voice broke his concentration.

'News is just breaking that the Minister for Energy, Sir William Altingham, has been arrested at his home in Chelsea on suspicion of financing weapons of mass destruction being used in Russia's conflict with Ukraine. Unconfirmed reports coming through are that the minister, known by his nickname *"Mr. Keep It Clean, Make It Green,"* is also being linked to a massive drug ring that was busted in New York and Rome during the night.

In other news, reports from Reuters suggest the celebrity cook, Roberto Marino, has been arrested at his home in New York. Police have yet to divulge the charges he might face.'

Thoughts of Freya and the woman playing the part of Natasha Boskova came into his head: two women who put their lives on the line for national and international security. Iris had played many parts too as a spy, but her mind had become twisted, perhaps by the pressures of being someone she wasn't for so long. Taking on different identities must be mentally draining. To live on the edge, as someone else would take its toll. He hoped Natasha, whoever she was, would return to being herself and see her family one day, but he had his doubts. How could she ever learn to be herself again?

He headed south, leaving Loch Spiorad behind him. Passing through Loch Dubhglas, the familiar sight of villagers going about their business, made the end of the case seem real. He would have no need to return, rarely retracing his steps in murder investigation sites. A few short weeks had passed since Helen's call telling him to get up to Sutherland for a dead body in a remote loch. The thought of revisiting his roots had repulsed him, sending his head into a spin, but everything had changed. He could not wait to return, to visit Jimmy, to fish the waters in those parts, and to spend time in his beloved Sutherland.

For the first time in three years, or longer if he was truthful, he saw glimpses of a brighter future for himself. When he spoke to Glen about purchasing Dubhness Cottage, the old crofter had shaken his hand, there and then, to seal the deal. He was going home to Sutherland. It was only an hour or so away from Inverness, and he could easily commute until he retired. The fact Freya had been murdered in the bungalow didn't unsettle him; in fact, he felt her presence was a guiding light. The significance of her death would never fade. Jimmy's words rang in David's ears as he drove.

'Whit's fur ye'll no go by ye. Speak to this lassie in Birmingham, for pity's sake, before you lose her .'

I watched as a stranger rowed back to shore, knowing he had found my body. There I was, floating below the surface of my watery grave, sinking into the darkest chasm. An assassin left me to rot, fish nibbling at my skin, bacteria sinking into my flesh second by second, minute by minute. This was my destiny until a miracle happened. The fisherman saved me from an eternity in

hell at the bottom of a loch with no plaque or gravestone to mark that I had once lived.

My death went like clockwork with military precision. My dignity and future were ripped from me as poison seeped deeper into my body, oozing into every cell, destroying my life. Every microscopic millimetre of me collapsed; my kidneys, liver, and heart all ceased because of a thirst for a final kill.

Shown no pity, I took my last breaths in agony from a tiny speck of metal encapsulated with a nameless poison, created in a distant regime as a calling card. The prick on my wrist had seemed accidental; a beautiful bracelet with tiny shards of metal. I was stupid in neglecting to spot the significance of the raven charm. The bird is always linked to death in Norse mythology. Never worn, my special gown was dumped in the loch to rot with me, along with a homemade circle of flowers. No longer a headdress to symbolise a future; instead, it was a wreath for my death.

Forgiveness is futile for a woman with such hate. The devil invaded her long ago, and stole her soul. To everyone, her earthly appearance was that of a gentle elderly lady, praying in church for her soul but never for forgiveness, pretending to be kind when she was still hunting prey until the end. She lived up to her Russian name, Volkova. It is, after all, the female version of Volkov, meaning "Wolf."

In life, everything was stripped from me, including my name. Against all the odds, I proved strong in battle like my namesake, Freya, the goddess of war, for she is also the divine being of love, beauty, and magic. How fitting it was that I died in Suðrland[23]. As I move from darkness into the light, my revenge is sweet. Death is only the beginning. As I transcend into other realms, I realise the powers I have gained.

One of summer's remaining butterflies' floats with the gentle breeze, landing on the petals of a dying rose. I flutter my wings in an attempt to dry out the stickiness that lingers from my emergence from a cocoon into the world. The coloured symmetry of my beauty moves gently as I grow stronger. I am free. That's all that matters now.

SHE WHO WAS

Inspiration

THE STORY BEHIND THE BOOK

People often ask authors where they get the inspiration for creating a piece of fiction. In the case of She Who Was, it came from a regular bus ride home from work one late summer afternoon around nine or ten years ago.

I didn't make a habit of getting into conversation with people on buses where I was born. Travellers barely looked at one another for fear of encouraging attention. In my early twenties, on a bus back from Birmingham one afternoon, a man stinking of alcohol sidled beside me and became over familiar to the point of making me feel uncomfortable. I got off the bus a few stops early, praying he hadn't followed me. From that moment on, I learnt it was best to keep my head down, look out of the window, and provoke no comments.

It was hard to break that mentality when I moved to the north of Scotland. There were fewer irate drivers beeping their horns, no traffic jams to cause the double-decker to take what felt like hours to travel half a mile, and no weirdos with inappropriate behaviours. I was riding a practically empty single-decker bus twice per day along a road with some of the most scenic views in the whole of the United Kingdom. Tower blocks, endless chip shops, and litter were replaced with rivers, mountains, and pine forests. My lungs struggled to take in the fresh air after years of breathing in pollution.

Now I was expected to "blether." It wasn't so much of a chat, as often the older folk who used the bus needed a listener. I was not used to speaking to strangers, but seeing the same faces week in and week out meant I came to recognise them even if I still didn't know their real names at first. In my head I gave them nicknames. So my fellow passengers were *Smiler, Baldy Locks,* and *Old Mother Hubbard,* to name but a few.

One such woman, nicknamed *Cat Lady*, regularly got on at the stop after me. She was extremely well-dressed compared with other travellers, including me in my workwear. Her complexion was immaculate, with just a tiny hint of rouge and a pink lipstick to brighten her pale face. In a certain light, there were wisps of silvery white underneath her light blonde shoulder-length hair, giving a hint of what true colour lay beneath the dye.

In winter, she wrapped a red woolly scarf around her neck, which contrasted sharply with her long cream mackintosh that almost touched her ankles. Black leather gloves neatly finished her attire, along with a pair of black boots almost reaching her knees. Often, I felt she could have played a femme fatale in her younger days. Despite her youthful appearance, my estimate of her age was mid-seventies. If you looked carefully, there were more wrinkles on her forehead than she wanted to admit, and her hands, when un-gloved, were flecked with age spots.

One afternoon, a year after I had travelled on the bus daily, she spoke to me for the first time properly. Normally she would sit three rows in front of me, but on this auspicious occasion, she sat just a row ahead, and sitting sideways, facing into the bus, she turned her head and began a conversation that lasted for the rest of the twenty-minute journey.

She asked if I had any pets and was ecstatic when I replied that I had two indoor house cats. What followed was a speech about how she kept her five cats safe and how I should do the same.

Then she told me of the life she'd lived in London with her late husband. Each time their jobs, before retirement, were mentioned, she would tap the side of her nose and lowered her voice to a whisper, ensuring no one else could hear.

'Secret government business.'

After that, she would always sit in the row in front, and chat about her cats and her memories. The last time I ever spoke to her was a couple of years later. As usual, she began the conversation as always.

'Have you still got your pussies? You won't let them out, will you? Keep them safe!'

I tried not to laugh; the smutty jokes from the nineteen seventies were out of date. The pleasantries over, she quickly changed the topic as she was bursting to ask a question.

'Have you heard the news? Terrible business!"

Without waiting for a reply, she continued,

'That killer was put into hiding up here. New start, new job, new name, but the same wicked face. They thought they could hide him, but he got drunk and started spilling out the truth when his tongue was too loose. The authorities moved him out quickly.'

When she lowered her voice and whispered his name, the words made me shiver. Everyone knew of the notorious case, and had seen the headlines. It was hard to comprehend why such a murderer would be let out on licence and placed in a location where strangers stick out like a sore thumb.

My routine for catching the bus changed. I never saw her again, although I gather she lived for several more years. Rumours spread that she had dementia, which didn't surprise me. After a while, she went into a care home, and died just a few months later.

To this day, I do not know if anything she told me about herself or the killer was true. Her story was not She Who Was, but a tiny spark ignited my imagination. What would happen if someone, either a murderer or a witness, was moved to a quiet, rural location, where everyone knows something, and someone knows everything?

Endnotes

[1] Hel-The Norse goddess of death and ruler of the underworld who was thrown into the dark, frozen lands called Niflheim. She was responsible for judging the souls of the dead.

[2] Muspell-From Norse mythology, the land of fire giants.

[3] Mors dulcis!-Death is sweet!

[4] Limbus-Originally from Latin, the word means edge or boundary, was used in late Middle English to mean a waiting place for souls. In Catholic theology, it relates to a term for the edge of Hell, an afterlife for those who die in original sin, unassigned to the underworld. The more modern form of the word is limbo. Nowadays, limbus is used to describe the junction of the cornea and sclera in the eye.

[5] MITs-Major Investigation Team

[6] Gie it laldy-to do something with energy and enthusiasm.

[7] Dreich-Originally from the Old Norse drjúgr, meaning enduring or lasting, nowadays the word is usually used to describe dull, gloomy weather.

[8] Scáthach- Pronounced Scar har, Gaelic for "The Shadowy One," a legendary Scottish warrior from an island purported to be the Isle of Skye.

[9] Sergei Skripal, originally in the Russian military but also working for British intelligence agencies, and his daughter were poisoned in Salisbury, England, by a nerve agent, A-234. Both survived, as did a police officer. Weeks later, a couple came across what looked like a perfume bottle unknowingly containing the nerve agent discarded in a litter bin, which resulted in the death of a woman who sprayed it on her wrist.

[10] The Moine Thrust Belt is a tectonic feature of around one hundred and twenty miles in length from the north coast of the Highlands to the southwest of Skye, which helped to form the landscape of this area. It's estimated to have been created three thousand million years ago; Knockan Crag, within the North West Highland Geopark, holds information boards and spectacular views of the surrounding geology.

[11] Strath- From the Gaelic word srath, is a large valley, usually with a river which is wide and shallow.

[12] Spiorad-Gaelic for spirit

[13] Blethering- An Old Scots word for chatter.

[14] A hospital in Inverness offering support for mental health, with secure facilities available when needed. Originally known locally as The Craigs, the hospital that replaced it is called New Craigs.

[15] Sealladh-Gaelic for view or viewpoint, pronounced 'she alt.'

[16] Snotra-Norse goddess of wisdom, knowledge, self-control and prudence.

[17] Tablet-A delicious Scottish sweet made from sugar, condensed milk, and butter. The texture is less smooth than fudge and less soft.

[18] Raggie-An affectionate local name for The Northern Times weekly newspaper, primarily written about Sutherland.

[19] Valkyrie-A group of women who drove the worthy souls of the dead to Valhalla, Odin's creation of a heavenly hall or palace for slain warriors.

[20] Bartizan-An overhanging, wall-mounted turret, popular in Scottish baronial architecture.

[21] Iduna-Norse goddess of spring and rejuvenation who guards the golden apples which allow the gods immortality. She is also called Idun or Iðunn

[22] Operation CHASE took place from 1964 to the early 1970s, disposing of ageing munitions aboard old ships deliberately sunk at sea between the Florida and Bahamas coasts. CHASE stands for "Cut Holes And Sink 'Em". From 1967 to 1968 chemical weapons were sunk into deep water during the ongoing operation.

[23] Suðrland-The Norse name for Sutherland—means "southern land," which refers to the stronghold of the Norse earldom of Orkney and Caithness.